DOCTOR WHO
DECALOG

DOCTOR WHO

DECALOG

TEN STORIES
SEVEN DOCTORS
ONE ENIGMA

Edited by
Mark Stammers
&
Stephen James Walker

DOCTOR WHO

First published in Great Britain in 1994 by
Doctor Who Books
an imprint of Virgin Publishing Ltd
332 Ladbroke Grove
London W10 5AH

ISBN 0 426 20411 5

Cover illustration by Mark Salwowski

Typeset by Mark Stammers Design, London

Printed and bound in Great Britain by Cox & Wyman Ltd,
Reading, Berks

Editors' Note

Doctor Who short fiction has a long and distinguished history. The earliest examples saw print in the first *Dr Who Annual*, way back in 1964, although the Daleks pipped the good Doctor to the post in 1964's *The Dalek Book*, and stories have continued to appear in a variety of different publications ever since that time.

Perhaps the chief exponents of the form have been the fans of the series who, over the years, have put the good Doctor and his companions through countless original adventures of their own devising. Their work has formed a staple ingredient of a whole host of different fanzines – including some, such as the *Doctor Who* Appreciation Society's *Cosmic Masque*, devoted entirely to fan fiction – and a number have since gone on to write professionally.

This book is, however, something of a milestone in *Doctor Who*'s literary history, in that it is the first *bona fide* short-story anthology ever to be published. And rather than presenting a straightforward collection, we have tried to make it even more special by placing the stories within the overall framework of a linking plot – an idea which might be familiar to some from old horror anthology movies like *Dead of Night*. This means that while it is possible to dip into *Decalog* and enjoy the individual stories in isolation, readers who work through the book from the first page to the last will hopefully gain something extra from it.

We would like to offer our heartfelt thanks to all the writers who have contributed to this project – including those whose submissions we sadly weren't able to use – and also to Peter Darvill-Evans and Rebecca Levene at Virgin for their support and enthusiasm.

Read on, and enjoy!

For Gordon Roxburgh (the best man) – MS

For Mum & Dad – SJW

CONTENTS

PLAYBACK (introduction)   1

FALLEN ANGEL Andy Lane   13

THE DUKE OF DOMINOES Marc Platt   47

THE STRAW THAT BROKE THE CAMEL'S BACK
Vanessa Bishop   91

SCARAB OF DEATH Mark Stammers   121

THE BOOK OF SHADOWS Jim Mortimore   155

FASCINATION David J. Howe   197

THE GOLDEN DOOR David Auger   227

PRISONERS OF THE SUN Tim Robins   267

LACKADAY EXPRESS Paul Cornell   297

PLAYBACK (conclusion)   320

Playback

Stephen James Walker

A cool afternoon, a few days short of Christmas 1947. I was
sat in my office in downtown LA with my hat over the
telephone and my legs slung over the end of the desk, practis-
ing my foot-dangling. The air was heavy with tobacco smoke,
so I rested my cigarette in the ashtray and leaned back to push
open the window – the one with the words 'Bart Addison –
Private Investigator' painted on it in big black letters. The
·scent of greasy food wafted up from Frank's Diner four floors
below. It didn't clear the air, but at least it added a touch of
variety.

A few moments later, the open window also admitted a
large purple butterfly, which perched tentatively on the sill
before setting out on an exploration of the room. I watched as
it fluttered past the peeling lemon wallpaper, the out-of-date
pin-up calendar and the three battered green filing cabinets,
two of them as empty as my stomach, before finally coming
to rest on the floor, just inside the door.

Suddenly the door was flung wide open and a man staggered in, inadvertently trampling the butterfly into the threadbare carpet, where it made an unwelcome addition to the
pattern. Following my gaze, he looked down and saw what he
had done, but made no comment. I thought I had better break
the silence.

'Come in, Mr . . . ?'

He left the question unanswered, but came in anyway and
collapsed breathless into the clients' chair on the opposite
side of the desk. I regarded him cautiously. The first thing to
catch my eye was his pullover, a brightly coloured affair with
a question-mark pattern, not quite as tasteless as a Holly-

wood party. Then there were his trousers, light brown with
a large check, just the thing for an afternoon on a hicksville
golf-course. His jacket was a shapeless, dark brown item
which might once have belonged to Chaplin, or maybe
Chaplin's grandfather. The whole ensemble was topped off
with a battered panama hat and a large umbrella with a red
question-mark handle.

I decided to say something else. 'What can I do for you,
Mr . . . ?'

Again he ignored the question, holding up a hand, palm
forward, while he struggled to catch his breath. Eventually
he spoke.

'I'm sorry, Mr Addison. I seem to have been through
rather a trying ordeal.'

He had an unusual accent, which I couldn't quite place.

'You're not from around these parts, are you, Mr . . . ?'

'No.' He gave a strange sort of smile. 'You could say I'm
on alien territory.'

'Yeah, well, I was raised in England myself.' Finally I
decided to get unsubtle. 'So, do you have a name then, or
what?'

Again the stranger smiled. 'Ah, that's just the point,' he
said. 'I do have a name, I'm sure, but right now . . . I can't
quite seem to remember it.'

'I get it. You want to stay anonymous. What is it, a divorce
case?'

'No, no, no. That's not it at all!' He frowned. 'At least, I
don't think so. The thing is . . . I've lost my memory.' He
frowned again. 'Or perhaps it's been stolen.'

I grinned at that. 'Ah. I think you've made a small mistake,
bud. The psychiatrist's office is down the hall, to the left and
along –'

He shook his head, emphatically. 'No.'

'No? You mean you're not looking for the doctor?'

'The doctor . . . ' He paused, as if considering, then shook his head again. 'No. It's a private detective I want. I looked in the city directory. Yours was the first name on the list.'

'Yeah, I get most of my business like that. But, look, I don't see what I can do for you. If you've got amnesia, you need a doctor.'

'No. Something's happened to me in this city. I've been brainwashed or hypnotised or . . . something. Anyway, my memory's gone, and I want you to help me find it. You can retrace my steps since I arrived here. Find out where I've been, who I've seen, what I've done.'

I leaned back in my chair, retrieved my cigarette from the ashtray and inhaled deeply. The stranger watched me intently, and I knew how an insect must feel when placed on a microscope slide. I half wondered if he was playing some kind of a crazy practical joke on me, but he seemed too serious for that, too intense.

'Okay,' I said. 'I'll see what I can do for you.' Well, what the hell? I hadn't had a case all week, so it was either that or sit there staring at the wall. 'My rate's forty a day plus expenses,' I added quickly.

'Ah, money.' A worried look came over the stranger's face, and over mine too. 'I'm not sure if I've got any of that.'

'Well,' I said reasonably, 'why don't you turn out your pockets and have a look? Who knows, you might even have some ID in your wallet and we can wrap this business up straight away.'

Judging from his reaction, this simple idea hadn't actually occurred to him: his face lit up as if I had just given him the next week's racing results. Maybe he'd lost his marbles as well as his memory.

The stranger stood up and began to turn out his pockets, depositing the contents in an untidy pile on my desk. I'd thought he might have maybe four or five items on him, but after a couple of minutes it began to seem that he must have more like four or five *dozen*. It reminded me of a cheap nightclub act I'd once seen, where a magician had opened up a suitcase and dragged out an impossible number of large and unwieldy objects – which in actual fact he'd been pulling up through a concealed hole in the top of his table. Only this time I couldn't see how the trick was done.

At length, the stranger finished his performance and sat down again. 'What, no aspidistra?' I asked. He scratched his head in puzzlement, and for a moment I thought he was going to start patting his pockets, just to make sure. 'Private joke,' I added quickly.

'Private joke?' He frowned. 'But I thought you were a private *detective*.' Now it was my turn to scratch my head. Yes, it really was going to be one of those days.

I leaned forward and started to examine the motley collection of effects now spread across my desktop. A few things I could identify. There was a kid's catapult; a telescope with polished brass fittings; a pair of wire-rimmed specs; an egg-timer; a crumpled bag of jelly-beans; and a rolled up copy of a local newspaper with a headline about the latest UFO scare. Most, though, left me completely in the dark. A disc-shaped mirror with a hole in the middle; a glass phial with a silver clasp at either end and a few drops of mercury inside; a little black cube covered in strange hieroglyphs; a brown, card-shaped piece of plastic patterned with a tracery of metallic solder; and many other articles the purpose and origin of which I could only guess at. Just about the only thing he didn't have there was a wallet, or anything else which might give some clue as to his identity. No business card, no bank book, no library ticket, no driver's licence, no dry cleaning receipt, nothing. There was a draw-string purse containing a few assorted coins of various shapes and sizes, but they weren't like any that I had ever seen before. Whatever they were, they certainly weren't US currency.

'It looks like you're right out of ready cash,' I said at length.

'Oh. Er, does that mean you won't help me?'

I shuffled his possessions around on the pitted wooden surface of the desk, making a pretence of considering the matter. In truth, I was so intrigued by this strange little guy and his crazy story that I think I would have paid *him* to let me take the case.

'Don't worry about it,' I told him. 'When we've found out who you are and where you come from you can settle up in arrears.'

He grinned broadly. 'Good. Well, now that's cleared up, how do you suggest we proceed?'

I got out of my chair and gave him the old pacing-up-and-down act, rubbing the usual thumb under the usual chin. After a couple of minutes of this I looked back at the strange pile of junk on my desk and smiled, an idea coming to me.

'Pick all that stuff up again,' I said, stubbing my cigarette out in the ash tray, placing my hat on my head and reaching for my raincoat. 'We're going for a little ride.'

It was dusk by the time we got where we were going. The road stretched ahead of us like a thin white ribbon curving up into the mountains, the lights of the city forming a splash of oily colour way below us to our left and a steep, heavily wooded ridge creating a dark canopy over to our right. My client had been curiously silent during the journey, not even bothering to ask where we were going or why. He had just sat there staring out of the window, totally absorbed. The way only a stranger would react. Or an amnesiac. I put my foot on the brake and swung the car off the road to the right, bringing it to a stop just by a rickety wooden gate leading to a narrow dirt track. We both got out.

The gate was padlocked, as I'd guessed it would be, so I scrambled up it and hauled myself over the top, almost losing my footing as I came down heavily on the other side. I turned to give the little guy a helping hand, and my jaw dropped as

I saw that he had somehow managed to get over on his own, silently and without visible effort. He was obviously more agile than he looked. I made a mental note to check if there were any circuses in town.

We set off up the ridge, picking our way over the uneven ground and through the tangle of branches which overhung the track from either side. The evening was really closing in now and the bare, windswept trees stood as grotesque silhouettes against the rapidly darkening sky. I pulled my raincoat collar tight around my neck, trying to keep out the chill winter air. My client, though, seemed not to feel the cold. Lost in thought, he pushed ahead with a sense of increasing anticipation. I had to quicken my stride just to keep up with him, and collected a few knocks as I stumbled over loose stones and collided with the occasional tree trunk.

After about five minutes of this, the trail opened out into a small clearing and there, just as I'd remembered it, sat a squat, Spanish-style residence, shrouded in shadow and clinging to the side of the ridge like a lizard to a rock. The stranger's eyes lit up at the sight of it. 'Ah! So this is where I was, you think, when I lost my memory?'

I smiled and shook my head. 'I'm a good detective, bud, but not *that* good.'

'Oh.' His crestfallen expression was almost comical. 'I thought perhaps you'd made a deduction . . .'

'What, like Sherlock Holmes you mean?'

'Er . . . is he another private detective?'

I looked at him through narrowed eyes, again wondering if he was just shooting me a line. 'No, he's the DA's chief assistant!'

'Oh.' Apparently he hadn't caught the tone of sarcasm in my voice. 'Well, what do you suggest we do now? Visitors don't seem very welcome here.' He pointed to a weather-beaten signboard nailed to a post: 'PRIVATE PROPERTY. KEEP OUT. YOU HAVE BEEN WARNED.'

'Oh, don't worry about that,' I told him. 'The owner's a bit of a recluse, that's all. He's helped me out before, in return for a favour I once did him on a blackmail case, and I think he might just have the answer to your little problem.' Despite my optimistic tone, I felt a growing sense of unease at the thought of revisiting that creepy house and its even creepier occupant. 'I guess you'd better wait here,' I suggested, 'while I see who's about.'

Whistling quietly to myself, I crossed the clearing and skipped up the short flight of steps to the front door. I had just raised my hand to work the bell when suddenly a man not quite as large as an office block loomed out of the shadows of an adjoining archway and, coming at me from behind, threw his arm around my neck in a vice-like grip. I reacted instinctively, twisting this way and that in an effort to shake him off, but somehow nothing I did seemed to make any difference. The more I struggled, the tighter his grip became. I began to choke, and decided that drastic action was called for. Stretching back, I clasped my fingers together behind his head. Then, taking all my weight on my arms, I lifted my feet off the ground, placed my soles firmly against the solid wooden panels of the door and kicked as hard as I could.

Still locked together, we tumbled backwards and fell headlong down the flight of steps on to the hard, stony ground below. The force of the impact threw us apart, and at last I found that I could breathe freely again. I rolled away and came to rest against a stack of timber at the edge of the clearing. Looking back, I saw that my assailant – a swarthy, muscle-bound Mexican wearing a native leather jacket and loose-fitting khaki pants tied with a piece of string around the waist – was lying at the foot of the steps, clutching the side of his head. I watched open-mouthed as, without saying a word, my strange new client walked over, picked up a large, jagged rock and lifted it high into the air, obviously intending to bring it crashing down on the Mexican's skull.

'Hey!' I shouted. 'What the hell are you doing? Put that thing down.' I scrambled up, ran over and wrenched the rock from his hands, dropping it back on to the ground.

The little guy could hardly believe it. 'But he attacked you!'

'Yeah, well, he was just doing his job. He's paid to keep guard around here.' I turned to the Mexican. 'Isn't that right, Ramon?'

Rising painfully to his feet, Ramon grasped my hand in his and pumped it so hard that I was worried he might dislocate my shoulder. 'A thousand pardons, Mr Addison,' he said, his face a picture of horrified remorse. 'I didn't recognize you at first. It's been some time since your last visit, and in the shadows by the door . . . How can I ever earn your forgiveness?'

'Don't mention it,' I said lightly, as if this was the sort of thing that happened to me every day of the week. Come to think of it, this *was* the sort of thing that happened to me every day of the week. 'My friend and I have come for a little consultation with the boss,' I added, nodding towards my bemused companion. 'If he's at home, that is.'

Ramon gave a broad grin, exposing a row of crooked and blackened teeth. 'Oh yes sir, he's at home. No doubt he's been expecting you.'

Ramon led us through the musty, candle-lit passageways of the house until we came to an imposing double door upon which had been carved an intricate pattern of weird occult symbols. A stuffed moose head gazed balefully down at us from the wall above. The Mexican knocked on the door and, after a moment's hesitation, pushed it open to reveal the room beyond. It was a large study with bookcase-lined walls, a gently glowing fire set within a sandstone fireplace, a low circular table with three armchairs grouped around it and, in an alcove at the back, a slab-like mahogany writing desk behind which sat the gaunt, timeworn figure of Silverman the Psychic.

Shrouded in semi-darkness, Silverman looked like a corpse. His charcoal-grey suit, though finely tailored, hung loosely on his skeletal frame, and the flickering candlelight cast deep shadows over his sunken features. When he spoke, it was like the sound of leaves rustling in the breeze. 'Come in, Mr Addison, come in.' He showed no sign of surprise at our arrival, giving the distinct impression that he had indeed been expecting us. Rising from the desk, he propelled himself towards us, contorting his face into a kind of macabre grimace which I guess was the closest he could ever get to a smile. We shook hands, and it felt like I was holding a bunch of dry twigs in my fingers. I tried not to grip too hard.

'Er, sorry to bother you, Silverman, particularly at this time of the evening.' To my annoyance, I found myself shuffling nervously from foot to foot, like a naughty school-boy summoned to the principal's office.

'Not at all, Mr Addison. I am, as you know, forever in your debt. You must never hesitate to call on me if you feel my particular gifts can be of service to you.' He turned his steely gaze on my companion. 'Now, won't you introduce us?'

'Well, I'd like to,' I replied, 'but I guess you've really put your finger on our problem. The fact is, I don't know who he is myself – and neither does he. You see, he's –'

'Lost his memory! Ah, I understand, I understand.'

'Yeah, well, he's come to me for help and I was hoping maybe you could find out something about him. I mean, I once saw you do this thing where you looked at a guy's watch and –'

'Was able to discern where he'd bought it, and what fate had since befallen him?'

'Yeah, that's it.'

'Psychometry!' It had been so long since my client had last spoken that his sudden exclamation took me by surprise.

'You're talking about psychometry, aren't you? Yes, that could well prove effective here.' He shook Silverman's hand with rather more enthusiasm than I had done and fixed him with a look of compelling intensity. 'It's absolutely vital that I discover what's happened to me since I arrived in this city. You must help me to remember!'

Silverman gave another of his ghastly, cadaverous smiles. 'Well, I shall certainly do my best, sir.' Disengaging his hand from the stranger's grip, he ushered us over to the little table that I had noticed earlier. At a gesture from his master, Ramon took my hat and coat and hurried from the room, as if anxious not to witness what was about to happen. We then sat down in the three leather-upholstered armchairs – which, now that I thought about it, looked for all the world as if they had been set out in anticipation of our arrival – and Silverman turned again to my mysterious companion.

'Now, sir, perhaps you have one or two articles of personal significance or sentimental value which I might examine?'

I had to stifle a grin as the stranger got up and gave a repeat performance of the stunt he'd pulled in my office, delving into his pockets and bringing out a whole cartload of paraphernalia – including a number of items I could swear I hadn't seen the last time. He dumped everything on the table in front of us and sat down again, an expression of eager anticipation on his face. Silverman didn't even raise an eyebrow. Casting a cursory glance over the motley collection of objects, he reached down and picked up a small but finely detailed model of a bird.

'Yes, I think we'll start with this one,' he announced.

'Well, OK,' I agreed. 'Just as long as it wasn't made in Malta.'

'What?'

'Sorry. Private joke.'

Silverman held the model in the cupped palms of his hands and fixed it with a penetrating stare, looking not so much at it as *through* it. Nothing happened for a moment or two, but then all the candles in the room suddenly flickered and went out. The only source of natural illumination was now the fire in the grate, which guttered violently as if caught in a miniature whirlwind, but the area around our table was bathed in a pool of ethereal light which appeared to emanate directly from Silverman's hands, throwing his skeletal features into sharp relief.

'I see a man,' intoned the psychic, his voice seeming to come from a long way off. 'Tall and elegantly dressed. Carrying a large, rectangular parcel under one arm. And singing. Singing at the top of his voice . . . '

Fallen Angel

Andy Lane

In Memoriam Leslie Charteris, 1907–1993

'Benjamin Bunny's got a fly upon his nose . . . '

The baritone voice rang out clearly through the misty night air, echoing back and forth between the Mayfair houses until it sounded as if a choir were letting down their hair and having a late night revel.

'Benjamin Bunny's got a fly upon his nose . . . '

Constable Sharpless speeded up as he approached the corner, half-hoping to catch a glimpse of the late-night lullaby-merchant, half-hoping that the man would be too far away to bother with. 1933 had been a bad year for arrests as far as Sharpless was concerned, and a decent 'disturbing the peace' would certainly make Sergeant Amies sit up and take notice. On the other hand, it *was* three o'clock in the morning, and the top two items on Sharpless's 'most wanted' list were a cup of tea and a thick layer of ointment on his bunions. Solitary serenaders didn't even make the top ten.

'Benjamin Bunny's got a fly upon his nose . . . '

The voice was getting louder, as if Sharpless and the invisible vocalist were on a collision course. Thoughts of resting his feet on a desk beside a steaming cuppa were eclipsed by the glory of an arrest. A fabled arrest! Somewhere in the suburbs of his mind, a tiny voice began to rehearse the words *I was proceeding in a southerly direction along Park Lane when . . .*

'So he flicked it off and then it flew away, yes it did!'

Bowling around the corner as fast as his ambition would carry him, Sharpless ran straight into a tall figure with a package under one arm. Normally his stout frame came out ahead in collisions of this sort, but the package was hard and rectangular, and one of its corners caught Sharpless a nasty crack in a painful place. He bent double, wheezing.

'Oh, I do beg your pardon, constable!'

A kindly hand supported his elbow until he could straighten up. He found himself staring into a pair of bright green eyes, framed by the kind of face that he had seen on statues in people's gardens: statues of Roman gods for the most part, although the man's expression had something of the youth and devilment of the faun about it.

'Can I ask you what you think you're doing, sir?'

'Of course you may, constable. Ask away.'

This one's going to be trouble, Sharpless thought. 'And what *are* you doing, sir?'

'I'm walking home.'

Sharpless found himself momentarily entranced by the cut of the man's suit. *Suits don't hang like that. They go all baggy and wrinkled after a few hours. At least, mine do.*

'You are aware, sir,' he said, drawing himself up to his full height, which still left him looking upwards into the man's faintly mocking eyes, 'that singing in a built-up area during the hours of darkness is an offence?'

'It *is*?'

A faint doubt crossed his mind. He squashed it. 'Yes sir, it is.'

'Oh.' The man smiled. 'It always amazes me how many ways one can find to give offence to upright citizens without even trying.'

Somehow the keenly anticipated pleasure of an arrest had petered out. There was something about the man that suggested lots of paperwork, accompanied by an unremitting flow of sarcasm and the prospect of a case being thrown out of court. That cup of tea was looking better and better. One last try, perhaps.

'May I ask what . . . ' He checked himself. 'What's in the parcel, sir?'

The man handed the parcel over. It was about half Sharpless's height. Gingerly, the policeman unwrapped it.

'It's a painting!' he exclaimed. 'At least, I think it's a painting.'

'Well done, constable. We'll make an art critic of you yet.'

Sharpless cast a critical eye over the canvas. It was mainly bright yellow, with occasional black squiggles fighting with red dots.

'What's it meant to be, then?'

'It's a portrait of a Madonna with Child, by Reubens,' said the man.

'Ah.' Sharpless inwardly digested this. 'Well, I don't know much about art . . .'

'Enough said, constable,' the man murmured, deftly rewrapping the painting. 'I can see that you are a man of keen and discerning tastes.'

There was some sort of commotion going on in the distance. Shouts and police whistles pierced the mist. Sharpless turned his attention away from the man and towards the sound of running footsteps somewhere along the road.

'I'll let you off with a warning this time,' he announced. 'But remember, there are people trying to sleep. If you're going to sing, sing in the bath.'

'Thank you, constable. I'll remember that. Good night to you.'

'Good night, sir.'

The man sauntered off, carrying the package as if it weighed nothing at all. Within a few seconds, the mist had swallowed him up.

By the time Sharpless turned back, a portly uniformed figure had appeared, breathing heavily, in front of him.

'Sergeant Amies!' Sharpless exclaimed.

'Sharpless, there's been a robbery. Sir Wallace Beary's latest acquisition has been stolen! A painting: modern art if you please. The thief didn't even cut it out of the frame, he just walked off with it, calm as anything. And he left this in its place.'

He handed Sharpless a small card. On it was a drawing of a man whose feathered wings and white robes proclaimed him to be an angel: an impression offset by a devilish smirk and a forked tail.

Vengeance has been visited upon you by the Fallen Angel, it said in tiny gothic lettering beneath.

Sharpless looked at it briefly, and handed it back.

'Another one,' he sighed. 'That's the twentieth this year. What does it all *mean*?'

'You've been on duty all night,' Amies growled. 'Have you seen anything out of the ordinary?'

A thought struck Sharpless with some force, leaving him with the distinct sensation that he was in a lift and had left his stomach back in the basement.

'What was it a painting of?' he asked carefully.

'It was called "Venus in Furs",' the sergeant said. 'Sir Wallace described it as being a dadaist representation of phallic envy, whatever that means. Why do you ask?'

'Well,' Sharpless replied, with evident relief, 'I *did* see a gentleman carrying a painting, but it was a Madonna with Child, by Reubens. I would have spotted a – what was it? – Berber rage at Gallic envy.'

Amies stared suspiciously at Sharpless. The constable stared back. Somewhere, in the distance, a voice was raised in song.

'Clever, clever Benjamin Bunny . . . '

Lucas Seyton let his voice trail away into a chuckle. The gullibility of the common-or-garden policeman never failed to amaze him. Carefully fenced in Amsterdam, the painting could net him upwards of four thousand guineas, but it wasn't the money that brought a gleam to his eye and a lightness to his heart. Lucas Seyton didn't need money.

A sudden scuffle attracted his attention as he was passing the mouth of an alley. He glanced around. Nobody was in sight. The noise was repeated: metal grating against stone. Heavy too, by the sound of it: too heavy to be a gun, which had been his first thought. There were a number of people within striking distance of

London who would have been glad to see him dead. His country house was still being renovated after the last firebomb attack.

Quickly he stashed the painting beneath a car. It had not been moved for some weeks, judging by the leaves piled up around the tyres, so his booty should be safe. Not for an instant did it occur to him that he could ignore the noise. Lucas Seyton – scion of one of the most aristocratic and wealthy families in England but better known to police, journalists and criminals alike as the Fallen Angel – had two character flaws. The more innocent one was an insatiable curiosity.

He moved silently down the alley, not bothering to crouch or scurry, yet still taking advantage of every scrap of shadow. Rotting vegetables squashed beneath the expensively tooled leather of his shoes. Rats scuttled amongst dustbins and over loose cobbles. A length of chain with a noose at the end – a rough child's swing, perhaps – swayed in a macabre manner from a thin sapling that had confounded the relentless urbanisation of England by growing in such a blighted area. The faint light of the moon coated the crumbling brickwork with a thin patina of silver.

He paused as the end of the alley hove into view through the tendrils of mist. Four figures were frozen in a tableau. Three of them gleamed as if they were wearing armour. Their arms were raised and pointing at the fourth, who was pressed against a locked metal door – the rear entrance of a restaurant, perhaps – as if he had been cornered.

'Oh dearie me,' he cried plaintively, wrapping the tails of his long jacket around him for protection. 'Oh dearie, dearie me!'

Although no guns were visible, their presence was implicit. It looked like a simple case of robbery. He didn't even consider slipping quietly away. He didn't approve of theft – not from those who didn't deserve it, at least – and the little fellow looked like the prototypical victim to him.

The Fallen Angel stepped forward.

'Excuse me,' he said, 'but is this the Agoraphobics Anonymous outing?'

The three figures turned towards him with a soft hiss. Their faces were blank metal. Like flower stems, the stalks of their necks were thin and flexible. Their backs were covered with what appeared to be bunched cloth with a silken sheen to it, and their hands and feet weren't hands or feet at all, but vicious bronze claws.

This wasn't just an ordinary attack on a passing pedestrian.

'If I'd known it was fancy dress, I'd have come as Napoleon,' said the Fallen Angel.

One of the three armoured figures took a step forward. Small puffs of steam issued from its joints as it moved. Its blank head tracked the Fallen Angel as he stepped sideways.

A gun appeared in the Fallen Angel's hand as if by magic.

'To quote a line I've heard all too often in my short but not uneventful life,' he said quietly, 'what's going on 'ere then?'

'Watch out for them!' the small man cried. He ran a hand through his tousled black hair. 'They can fly!'

'So can Wilbur and Orville Wright,' said the Fallen Angel, 'but they don't need a tin-opener to put on their pyjamas.'

'No, you don't understand. They're dangerous!'

'Who, Wilbur and Orville?'

'No!' the man wailed, 'the robots!'

The Fallen Angel smiled grimly. 'That's a coincidence,' he whispered. 'So am I.'

The lead creature straightened its arm in a curious pointing gesture. A gout of flame leaped from its fingertips and blasted a chunk of masonry from the wall beside the Fallen Angel. He flung himself to the side, converting the fall into a graceful roll which brought him up against the other wall. He fired once, twice, and watched as sparks flew from the creature's head, as the bullets rebounded and went *spang*ing down the alley.

Another blast sent a spray of brick splinters stinging across the Fallen Angel's cheek. He dropped to a crouch and scooped up a mouldering lettuce, which he bowled underarm towards the creature. The vegetable burst across the creature's metal mask and slid downwards across its chest, depositing a number of soggy leaves across the place its eyes would have been, had it been human. Silently, and with great deliberation, it began to scrape the refuse from its head.

And behind it, the other two creatures began to rise into the air, borne aloft by huge and diaphanous wings that they had kept furled upon their backs. The violent flapping sent scraps of paper and rancid food spiralling through the air, and the fingers of their outstretched hands tracked the little man as he scurried over to join the Fallen Angel.

'I told you they were dangerous,' he said. He had the odd habit of rushing though a sentence as if worried that he might forget how it ended, and then drawing out the last word to make up for the hurry. 'You shouldn't have involved yourself.'

The Fallen Angel looked up. Two of the creatures were circling above the alley like metal wasps, and the one that had attacked him was rising to join its comrades, wings blurred and humming.

'I can't help myself,' he replied. 'Every time I see someone being attacked by flying metal men, I just have to interfere.'

'Well, don't think I'm not grateful.'

'I'm Lucas Seyton, by the way: champion of the fallen, reviver of sunken spirits, recoverer of lost boodle and scourge of spurious morality.'

'And I'm the Doctor . . .' The Doctor's face crumpled into an exaggeratedly worried expression. '. . . But for how much longer, I don't know.'

The first explosion sent dustbin lids spinning like deadly discuses through the night. The second sent the Doctor and the Fallen Angel flying.

Two of the creatures swooped towards them as they lay stunned, whilst the third cut off their escape at the end of the alley. Even as he knocked away the metallic talons flailing at his face, the Fallen Angel's mind was racing around the problem, trying to come up with a means of escape.

A whistle blast at the mouth of the alley cut through the deep hum of the creatures' wings and the sibilant hiss of their limbs. The flailing of claws abated somewhat, and the Fallen Angel's heart turned to ice as he saw, silhouetted in the mist, two policemen.

'Get out, you fools!' he yelled. He didn't have much love for the constabulary, but there were limits.

'Now what's all this then?' said the smaller and more portly figure. The Fallen Angel recognized his voice. It was the policeman who had stopped him in the street. 'Do you know what time it is?'

His words were cut off by a massive explosion. When the smoke cleared, the Fallen Angel could make out two broken bodies sprawled in the road.

'That's it,' he murmured to himself. 'The kid gloves are definitely off.'

He gestured to the Doctor, who was currently sheltering inside an overturned dustbin, to stay out of sight. The Doctor waved a bright turquoise handkerchief in reply, and then mopped at his brow.

The Fallen Angel pried a loose cobblestone from the ground. Hefting it in his hand, he rose. The three metal creatures hovering overhead turned their attention back to him again.

'Hi, fellows,' he cried merrily, 'who's for a game of coconut shies?'

The closest creature swooped towards him. He took three steps backwards and hurled the cobblestone. It caught the automaton full on its smooth face with a distinct *bong!* that reverberated through the night like the chimes of Big Ben. Veering off course, it shook its head as if trying to dislodge an annoying insect.

'Benjamin Bunny's got a fly upon his nose!' sang the Fallen Angel. The Doctor gazed over at him as if he were mad.

Taking another few steps backwards down the alley, the Fallen Angel picked up a second cobblestone. The other creatures were trying to outflank him: moving apart so as to present two moving targets. He tracked them as they flew parallel to the top of the alley walls towards him. His hand moved too fast to see. A stone flashed through the darkness: a satisfying *clang* reached his ears as one of the automata veered away.

The third one was diving feet first at him, claws eagerly outstretched. He took a few more hurried steps backwards, and felt behind him for what he knew had to be there. For a moment his hands clutched at empty air, then the cold chain of the children's swing scoured the palms of his hands.

He ducked, and the automaton's claws scythed through the space which his head had occupied only moments beforehand. With a grasp of spatial geometry more instinctive than planned, he closed the noose over the automaton's ankle and rolled away before it could catch him. The automaton soared away into the sky, trailing the chain behind it in a tightening loop that linked it to the sapling.

Without pausing for thought or breath, the Fallen Angel sprang to his feet and pounded back down the alley towards the Doctor. The automaton, not to be cheated of its prey, turned in mid-air and dived after him.

Explosions punctuated the night as the automaton, tired perhaps of close-range work, fired repeatedly at him. He dodged the brief orchids of flame, and then, at a carefully calculated moment, skidded to a halt and turned to face it. As its featureless metal face and gleaming talons grew in his sight, blocking out the sky, the stars and the alley and reflecting only the fading orange glow of the explosions, he smiled.

'You are aware, sir,' he said in a mock-pompous voice, 'that flying an automaton without a leash is against the law?'

The chain pulled taut in a cacophony of metallic creaks. The sapling bent and creaked alarmingly. Flailing claws cut the air scant inches in front of his face for what seemed like eternity.

And then the elasticity in the sapling won out over the frantic buzzing of the automaton's wings. It sprang back into shape, pulling the metallic creature backwards at increasing speed until the wall intervened.

The ground shook, and flame spilled across the wall of the alley. Twisted metal limbs, cogwheels and pistons rained down upon the cobbles.

The Fallen Angel looked up to see two bright moths with wings of filigree silver flying rapidly eastwards towards the distant crimson stain of sunrise.

'That was very impressive,' said a voice. He turned to find the Doctor looking up at him.

'Cowardice would appear to have been the better part of valour,' he replied. 'I think I hear breakfast calling.'

'You're a cool customer, I must say.'

'Cool as a cucumber but not as green, as my old mother would have said, had she been given to fatuous sayings. Which she wasn't, being too concerned with increasing the family fortune on the stock market. Bacon and eggs, I think, closely followed by more bacon and eggs and a gallon or twain of coffee. And then some more bacon and eggs, just for a change.'

He turned towards the mouth of the alley, but stopped when he saw the human remnants scattered across the pavement and the road. The Doctor cannoned into his back.

'But first . . . ' he murmured, and crossed over to where one of the creatures' bronze claws sat, palm up, on the cobbles. Taking a small card from his pocket, he gazed at it for a moment, then placed it in the palm and walked away.

The Doctor scurried over and picked the card up. He glanced over the sketch of the devil-angel, and read the writing beneath. His mobile, rather rubbery face folded itself into a grimace. Looking after the Fallen Angel, he murmured: 'Hmm, I wonder . . . ' beneath his breath, then followed his rescuer out of the alley.

He didn't have far to go. The Fallen Angel was on his hands and knees retrieving a package from beneath a parked car.

'Now that,' said Lucas Seyton, leaning back and gazing with fondness over the crumb-strewn, marmalade-stained tablecloth, 'was a blow-out and a half.'

The Doctor nodded his head in agreement. He couldn't remember breakfasting so well since that time with Nero. Larks' tongues were small, but an entire flock of them wasn't a paltry amount. He had to admit, however, that there was a lot to be said for bacon and eggs. And marmalade.

He glanced over at his unlikely rescuer. Whilst a silent manservant – an ex-boxer, by the look of him – had cooked breakfast, Seyton had changed out of his refuse-stained suit and into a yellow silk dressing gown. He looked debonair and relaxed, as if he had spent the night doing nothing more strenuous than sleeping. The Doctor, by contrast, felt as if he had been dragged through a hedge backwards. Twice.

It wouldn't have been so bad if he had been in less opulent surroundings. Seyton's Kensington house was furnished in a style reminiscent of its owner – tasteful, expensive and with more than a dash of unconventionality.

'More tea, Archibald?' Seyton asked.

'Yes, please. And my name isn't Archibald.'

'Then what is it?'

'Just call me Doctor.'

Seyton smiled. 'I've never liked doctors,' he said. 'The last time I said "good morning" to my quack he charged me fifteen guineas for the privilege of an answer. Same with lawyers: parasites on the body of humanity. What was it that old Will said? "The first thing we do, let's kill all the lawyers." Add doctors to the list as well. And tax inspectors.' He suddenly seemed to remember the conversation. 'No, I'll just call you Archibald. That way I won't remember you're a doctor.'

'You said your name was Seyton, didn't you? Quite an old family, I believe.'

A shadow seemed to pass over Seyton's face. His voice, when he finally spoke, had lost its usual lightness. 'The Seytons have been around since Harold got it in the eye at Hastings. The family mansion even gets a special write-up in the Doomsday Book as a place well worth razing to the ground. Not a nice bunch of people, what with the *droit de seigneur*, the pillage and the hunting.'

'I thought hunting was a fine old English pastime.'

'Not when the quarry includes women and children.'

Seyton busied himself for a moment pouring a cup of tea for the Doctor and more coffee for himself.

'William Seyton,' the Doctor mused. 'King John's right-hand man. Revived impaling as a method of execution.'

'You've heard of him?' Seyton was intrigued.

The corners of the Doctor's mouth twisted downwards in disapproval.

'I've met . . . people who have.'

'Somewhere along the line the outraged peasantry started calling the family "Satan" rather than Seyton. I'm the last of the line, and I intend to end my days that way.'

'If you go on the way you did earlier,' admonished the Doctor, 'that may occur sooner than you think, mayn't it?'

Seyton took a sip of coffee and smiled. 'Yes, about last night . . . ' he began, and raised an inquiring eyebrow.

'Ah . . . ' The Doctor squirmed in his chair. 'It's going to be a bit difficult to explain . . . '

'You called those things "robots".'

'Robots, yes. From the Czechoslovakian for "worker".'

'They looked more like metal men to me. Metal men with wings.'

The Doctor gazed up at Seyton, startled at his level tone. 'Doesn't the thought bother you?'

Seyton uncoiled himself from the chair and headed for a wooden cabinet. Unlocking the door, he removed an ornate model duck and brought it back to the table.

'Look at this,' he said.

The Doctor looked. Whoever had made the model had been a fine craftsman. The feathers were made of metal, enamelled with a fine blue-green coating that shone from a distance and yet was so finely detailed that the individual tines could be distinguished. He prodded the duck's breast. The metal plumage yielded slightly beneath his fingers.

'Built just under two hundred years ago by Jacques de Vaucanson,' said Seyton quietly. 'One of five in existence.'

He pressed something just beneath the duck's tail. With a slight shudder, the model bird sprang to life, looking around with an intelligent gleam in its glassy eye. Twisting its head, it began to mimic preening its plumage.

'Very impressive,' said the Doctor.

'Clockwork,' said Seyton. 'Over five thousand separate mechanisms.'

Tiring of its ablutions, the duck stretched its neck and spread its wings out wide.

'The wings alone contain four hundred separate parts,' Seyton added.

'Interesting though this is,' the Doctor said as the duck waddled over and began to sip from his cup of tea, 'I fail to see the relevance.'

'If an automatic duck can be built, then so can an automatic man. Even one with wings. It's just a matter of scale. No, the creatures that were attacking you last night don't particularly surprise me. What I want to know is: why?'

The Doctor moved the cup out of the way, and watched disapprovingly as the duck pecked away at empty air.

'The problem with robots is that they can only follow orders, you see?' he said eventually. 'When circumstances change, they don't necessarily have the capability to change along with them.'

'What are you getting at?

The Doctor bent closer to the metal bird.

'Quack!' he said loudly, and again, 'quack!' The duck did not respond.

Seyton just smiled indulgently. 'Whenever you're ready, old crayfish.'

'Those flying creatures were programmed to guard the inhabitants of a particular house, return any escapees and kill anybody that got in by accident,' the Doctor said eventually, having failed to distract Seyton from the question. 'I and my companions . . . appeared . . . in the house. The guards found us, but I managed to escape from them into the open.' He scowled. 'I hid in the first place I came to: the back of a lorry full of cabbages. Of all the silly things to do! I must have run out of the grounds of the house and into a neighbouring farm. The next thing I knew, I was heading for Covent Garden market! I didn't dare alert the driver, because I could see the robots following the truck. If we'd stopped, they would have caught up and killed us both. I hopped out in Kensington, but they weren't far behind.' His face fell. 'I don't know what's happened to my companions, but I have to go back and find them.'

Lucas Seyton leaned back in his chair.

'And what was so important about the inhabitants of this house?' he asked.

The Doctor watched as the duck waggled its tail, looked around, quacked and subsided into quiescence. 'I take it that this object is a family heirloom,' he said, apropos of nothing.

'Yes, but not my family,' said Lucas Seyton. 'I stole it.'

The Doctor glanced up at him out of shadowed eyes. 'Stole it?'

'I steal things.'

'Why?'

'Why not?'

'This is silly!' The Doctor stamped his foot as best he could from a seated position, considering the fact that his feet didn't quite reach the floor. He scowled at Seyton. 'Stealing things is wrong.'

The easy smile dropped from Seyton's features. 'Worse than torture?' he said with quiet emphasis.

'No, of course not.'

'Worse than murder?'

'I don't see . . .'

'Worse than blackmail?'

'No, but . . . '

'My ancestors blackened the family name and destroyed the family honour. I am rich because of the misfortune of others. I vowed years ago to try and do something to atone for that.' He gestured to a garish painting propped up against one wall. 'I stole that last night. I stole it from the house of a man who poisoned three previous wives, having married them for their fortunes. Any money I receive for it will be distributed anonymously amongst the poor. The duck I took from a pornographer and drug-dealer who has lured countless innocent girls into a life of degradation.'

'I see.' The Doctor's voice was quiet. 'You think of yourself as a latter-day Robin Hood, or something like that chap in the stories, what was his name? The Saint? Why not just give away your family fortune?'

Lucas Seyton met the Doctor's gaze unflinchingly.

'Robin Hood was poor and lived in a forest. I like my creature comforts too much. When I die, any money left in the Seyton estate will go towards setting up a trust for those less fortunate than myself. Which includes virtually everyone, as I consider myself the most fortunate of men.'

'And what of the people you steal from? How does stealing one or two of their possessions punish them?'

Seyton strode over to the window and stared out into the street. 'There isn't usually enough evidence to get a conviction,' he said after a while, 'and I won't act as executioner. Taking away their fortune, or their happiness, is about as far as I can go. I know which side I'm on. I sleep at night. Can you say the same?'

'Oh yes,' said the Doctor. 'At least, when I do sleep, I sleep happily.' He sighed. 'In our own way, we're both on the side of the angels.'

Seyton laughed bitterly. 'That's what I call myself,' he said. 'The Fallen Angel. I thought it had a certain ring to it.'

He turned back to the Doctor, and his mask of flippancy was firmly back in place. 'So, Archibald,' he said, 'where do we go to rescue these friends of yours?'

The Doctor gazed up into the open, smiling face of Lucas Seyton, and felt his heart lift. Love them or hate them, you had to admit that humanity was unpredictable.

Personally, he loved them.

'It's a manor house in Sussex,' he said. 'Or, at least, that's what it looks like at the moment. It's got a certain chameleon-like quality about it. I can find the way. I think.'

'And what can we expect when we get there?'

'Danger, of course.' The Doctor scowled. 'No, I can't possibly expect you to help me. It's far too risky.'

'You silly old bear,' said Seyton, 'I've always wanted to go on an Expotition.'

'An expotition?' said the Doctor suspiciously.

'Indeed. And it is because I am a very illegal animal that I will be Useful in the adventure before us.'

Somewhere in the back of his mind, the Doctor smiled, but he made sure that his face stayed worried. Usually it was he who quoted *Winnie the Pooh*. It threw him a bit to be beaten to the punch.

'Are we going for a journey with the goat's new compass?' he asked innocently.

'Indeed we are, old bear. Let's hope we don't reach the end of our brick.'

The wind whipped the Doctor's hair back behind him like the tail of a very short comet. He clutched at the dashboard of Lucas Seyton's open-top Lagonda as it hurtled fast and low around another corner.

'Do we have to go quite so fast?' he yelled above the roar of the engine.

'No, of course not,' smiled Seyton, pressing the accelerator to the floor. The Lagonda leaped forward like a cheetah that had suddenly remembered an appointment.

'What's the customary procedure in these cases?' the Doctor

shouted.

'The crustimony proseedcake?'

A deep sigh was snatched from the Doctor's lips by the slipstream. This incessant flippancy was beginning to get on his nerves. He wondered briefly if he had the same effect on other people.

'What are we going to do when we get there?'

'Oh, I never make plans: I find them so stultifyingly boring. No, my old avocado, improvization is the name of the game. Are you going to tell me who's in the house?'

'You won't believe me.'

'In that case I'll just waltz up to the door and ask if I can come in.'

'You can't do that!'

'Watch me, Archibald.'

The Doctor mopped at his face with his handkerchief. 'Oh very well,' he sulked. 'I'm going to tell you a story about a war, and about the people who started it. They thought they ruled the universe, do you see? They really believed that it was their divine right to order everybody else around, and they were willing to kill everybody to prove it. The problem was, a lot of people were taken in by their claims, and fought for them.' As he spoke, the habitual tone of innocent uncertainty seeped from the Doctor's voice, leaving it cold and hard.

'More people died than you or I could count in a million years. People like you and me, and people not much like us at all. Suns were blown up: worlds were turned inside out. In the end they lost, as tyrants always do, but at such a cost!'

He hesitated, his eyes still seeing the horrors of the past.

'And what did you do with them?' asked Lucas Seyton softly.

The Doctor didn't spot the sudden shift from general to particular.

'What could we do? They were just overgrown children. We couldn't kill them: it would have made us just as bad as they were. So we put them in a prison of the mind.'

The Lagonda slowed slightly, and suddenly veered through a gateway into a field. Ahead of them, a large hangar seemed to be fighting a losing battle against rust.

'We carefully expunged every trace of their defeat from their minds, and we brought them here. We gave them a house and told them that it was a top-secret fortress; we gave them guards and told them that they were servants. They send orders out over the radio, and false reports are sent back to them. They have setbacks, they have glorious victories, but none of it is real. They are happy, and so is everybody else. The house blends in with the surroundings, so nobody thinks it strange.'

The Lagonda screeched to a halt. Light gleamed on an irregular shape in the hangar.

'And when did all this happen?'

'Oh, a long time ago,' said the Doctor, running a hand through his hair and leaving it untidier than it had been. 'A *very* long time ago. Is that your aircraft?'

'Do you like it?'

The Doctor's face lit up. Scurrying after Seyton into the hangar, he gazed in fascination at the large but somehow fragile shape of the twin seater Bristol F.2B biplane.

'It's an interesting story,' Seyton continued as he checked over the aircraft with a professionalism that belied his usual attitude. 'And you just turned up in this house by accident?'

'I turn up everywhere by accident.'

Something caught the Doctor's attention up above the cockpit, on top of the wing, and he stared at it rather dubiously. It looked rather like a walking frame with a set of straps attached.

'What's that thing?' he asked, pointing.

'Oh, nothing,' said Seyton with elaborate casualness.

The Doctor clambered up the side and into the cockpit.

'And how *are* they doing?' Seyton added.

'Who?'

'These mythical rulers of the universe who aren't actually ruling anything.'

'I never got the chance to see them. The guards caught us as we left the TAR . . . ' The Doctor suddenly bit his tongue. 'Dear me, is that a machine gun?' He pointed to a large perforated double cylinder set forward of the cockpit.

'It is indeed, old bear,' Seyton replied, but the Doctor had lost interest. His foot had found a pedal and was vigorously pumping it, causing the wing flaps to jerk up and down and the rudder to fishtail.

'Somehow I never got around to removing it,' a voice said from the shadows. 'Call me an old romantic if you like.'

The Doctor jumped, startled, as a man in tattered flying kit walked towards them, wiping oily hands on a piece of rag. His face was confident and weatherbeaten; his eyes gleamed like chips of blue ice.

'Ketters!' exclaimed Lucas Seyton. 'How the devil are you?'

'Luke! I got your call. The old girl's tanked up and ready to go.'

'Good-oh.' Seyton beckoned the Doctor out of the cockpit. 'Archibald, this is my good friend and fellow reprobate, Paul Kettering, formally known as Squadron Leader Kettering, known now to all and sundry except his landlady as Ketters of Ketters's Flying Circus fame. There is no better flier without feathers, and few with. We were together during the war.' He waved a hand in the Doctor's direction. 'Ketters, this amiable lunatic named Archibald has fallen on hard times. His friends have been kidnapped, he himself is exceedingly bewildered and he is in dire need of a decent tailor. Can we help him?'

'Count me in,' said Ketters.

'Er . . . ' the Doctor ventured, 'might I ask why we need an aircraft? I mean, it's all very nice and everything, but I don't quite see the . . . er . . . '

'It struck me,' Seyton said, 'that the best way to deal with flying machines is in a flying machine.'

'Are we expecting a scrap, then?' Ketters asked, retrieving a battered leather flying helmet from a bench.

'I'll explain on the way,' said Seyton.

'There are only two seats,' the Doctor protested. 'How are we all going to fit in?'

Seyton and Ketters glanced significantly at each other, then up at the biplane. The Doctor's gaze slowly followed theirs to the construction of tubes and straps above the upper wing.

'Oh crumbs,' he cried.

The deep *thrumm* of the wind in the wires prevailed against the growl of the engine and the screams of the Doctor, strapped to the wing-walker's cradle high above. As Lucas Seyton watched the fields and forests of England flow past beneath, he was content. It was only here, high above the hustle and bustle of honest, upright citizens with their tight bowlers and furled umbrellas, that he truly felt at peace.

'What's he burbling about?' Ketters yelled from the pilot's cockpit behind.

'Something about his giddy aunt,' Seyton shouted back.

'Is she noted for her nausea?'

'No idea. Did I ever tell you about the day my Aunt Ada parachuted down from Ben Nevis?'

There was a pause before Ketters replied: 'It'll have to wait, old chap. Bandits at ten o'clock.'

Seyton scanned the skies until he saw what Ketters had already noticed: three small shapes that glinted in the English sunlight as they laboured upwards towards the aircraft.

'They're early,' he shouted. 'We're still half a mile away from the house that Archibald marked on the map.'

'Perhaps they can sniff him out.'

'There's a thought. Maybe I could train one as a truffle-hound.'

The quality of the Doctor's wails changed. He appeared to have noticed the approaching attackers as well.

'Hang on to your seat!' Seyton yelled up to him, 'it's going to be a bumpy ride!'

The metal fliers had adopted a V-formation. Ketters threw the Bristol into a steep climb, trying to put a bit more height between them. In the front cockpit, Seyton fired a few test bursts from the machine gun. Glowing lines of tracer turned the sky into an expanse of blue material seamed with fire.

'Let's smite the ungodly,' murmured the Fallen Angel, and somehow, despite the noise of the engine and the howl of the wind in the wires, Ketters could hear every word.

The first sign of an attack was a series of fiery blooms which opened up in a line towards them. Ketters flung the joystick hard over, and the biplane responded, slipping sideways and dropping a few hundred feet until Ketters started to level it out. The Fallen Angel watched with hawk-like gaze until a silhouette passed across his crosshairs. Detecting the shift in direction as Ketters pulled the joystick back again, he took up first pressure on the trigger. The Bristol was almost straight and level now, and the robot was climbing some three hundred feet ahead of them. He squeezed slightly, and a line of bright flashes connected the gun to the robot. It jerked as a rash of holes opened up across its filmy wings. It tried to slew sideways to get out of the withering blast of fire, but Ketters anticipated and banked with it. The wings were more air than metal now, and as the Fallen Angel watched they ripped apart into silver rags which fluttered behind the robot as it began the long fall to oblivion.

'Oh crumbs . . . ' came a cry from above their heads, 'look out behind you!'

The Fallen Angel jerked around to find two robots on their tail: blank masks reflecting the garish colours of the aircraft and the pale pink face and little round mouth of the Doctor. Ketters, acting on instinct, put the aircraft into a steep dive and kept pushing the stick until they were flying upside down. The robots, taken by surprise, reacted late, by which time Ketters had flipped the plane over and pulled up on the stick to bring it into another loop. By the time he straightened it out, the robots, unfamiliar with the principles of an Immelmann turn, were three hundred feet below and heading in the wrong direction. Ketters pulled the biplane round and dived towards them. The Fallen Angel raked the left-hand one with a long burst, and watched with pleasure as its body disintegrated into limbs, gears and sticky black liquid.

The right-hand one twisted neatly in mid-air and began to climb. Through instinct or intelligence, it managed to put itself directly into the blind spot beneath the biplane.

Ketters pulled the stick over and banked the aircraft, whilst the Fallen Angel unstrapped his webbing and leaned over the side. The bottom wing cut off a lot of the sky, but he couldn't see any sign of the creature.

Until a large metal hand snaked around from beneath the wing, took hold of his flying jacket and pulled him out of the cockpit.

The fields below spun sickeningly as he dropped. Pulling his automatic from his jacket, he attempted to spin around and fire at the creature which was clinging to the undercarriage, but the aircraft was too far above him, and receding with every second that passed. He pulled the ripcord of his parachute, hoping that the drag would slow him down enough to snap a shot off, but the jolt as the chute mushroomed out above him snatched the gun from his hand. He watched in mortification as it fell away. Never one to mope, he turned back to the action, and was just in time to see the robot reach out and shove its arm into the propeller blade. Fragments of wood sprayed into the air, and the healthy rumble of the engine was transformed into an overheated whine. Ketters was fighting to keep the aircraft straight, but the Bristol was noted for having all the gliding characteristics of a loaf of bread. The plane began to fall: gracefully, but uncontrollably.

'Get out!' the Fallen Angel yelled impotently. He thought he could see the Doctor's diminutive figure struggling with his straps, but Ketters was fighting the aircraft every foot of the way.

A gust of wind twisted the Fallen Angel away from the action. He was falling towards a manor house, set in extensive grounds. The ground was approaching as rapidly and unavoidably as the chicane at Brand's Hatch. He jerked at the harness to bring him around again. The Bristol was dropping fast alongside him now, trailing a greasy black plume of smoke. A lone figure hung from a parachute above it: he could not tell whether it was Ketters or the Doctor.

The biplane hit the ground and disintegrated in a fireball. Even as the Fallen Angel was bidding farewell to whoever had remained in the aircraft, the ground turned from an interesting abstraction into a solid reality and consciousness spun away from him like a glittering child's toy thrown into a well.

The Fallen Angel awoke to find the Doctor gazing solemnly down at him.

'You're too ugly to be an angel and I firmly expect to avoid the other place,' he said, 'so I must still be alive.'

'You're a lucky man,' the Doctor replied.

'Unbounded be my joy. Ketters?'

The Doctor grimaced.

'I'm afraid . . .'

'Bought the farm, did he? It was the way he would have wanted it.'

He stood and gazed around at the perfect garden around him, which was marred slightly by the twin shrouds of the parachutes and the seared wreckage of the biplane in the distance.

'And when I die, think only this of me: there is some corner of an English field that is forever Ketters.' He sighed, and turned to the Doctor. 'Well, why aren't we dead?'

'The guards flew over us a couple of times, but I'd covered us with the parachutes, and they assumed we were dead. As I said, their programming isn't very flexible. Is that it, then?'

'Is what it?'

'The eulogy for Mr Kettering. Doesn't it bother you that he's dead?'

'Allow me to explain something, Alphonse . . .'

'I thought I was Archibald?'

'You look more like an Alphonse at the moment. Ketters lived life like I do: on the edge. He didn't worry about dying. When he and I meet up again in the Halls of the Happy Buccaneers, we'll raise a few glasses and laugh about what happened today. I don't intend grieving for him, because I don't think of him as gone, just temporarily mislaid.'

The Doctor looked up into the Fallen Angel's eyes, which said so much more than his words. 'Doesn't anything frighten you?' he asked quietly.

'Only the possibility of a world without fun. Now let's go get your friends.'

They crept up to the manor house through the shrubbery. The building was an impressive Tudor monstrosity, and a quick check over the windows confirmed the Doctor's story that it was designed to keep people in, rather than out. The devices clamped around the frames were not of a design which the Fallen Angel recognized, but their function was obvious, and it seemed to him that there was no way around them.

Unless . . .

'The robots have to get in and out of the house somehow, don't they?' he asked the Doctor. 'Probably though a hatch in the roof.'

'I suppose so, but . . . '

'So they must have something which enables them to get past all the security systems, mustn't they? Something that says, "Hi there, I'm a nasty robot thing, and you don't want to raise the alarm, do you?" or words to that effect.'

'We'll . . . '

'So let's go and have a rummage through the wreckage.'

The body of the robot that had destroyed the aircraft had been thrown clear during the crash, and was buried head-first in a thicket. The Doctor crawled into the bush, and emerged ten minutes later – after many cries of 'Oh bother!' and 'Oh my word!' – with a small piece of technical trickery which was, he assured the Fallen Angel, just the thing they needed. The Fallen Angel slipped it into a pocket and they headed back to the house.

'Climb on my shoulders,' said the Fallen Angel.

'But . . . ?'

'This gizmo may just cover one of us.'

'Oh, very well,' the Doctor sulked, and did as he was told.

And so, not for the first time, the Fallen Angel entered a heavily guarded house through the front door. It had taken him less than a minute to pick the lock, even with the Doctor perched upon his back.

'I'm sure I should have heard about this place,' the Fallen Angel said as he stepped inside the darkened hallway. It didn't look much like a manor house from the inside. The corridors appeared to be made from some white, marble-like material. 'How have you kept it so secret?'

'There's a sort of blind spot which we've cast around the area. Even if people do stumble across it, they forget about it within a few hours.'

'Very clever.'

'Yes, we thought so.'

The corridor widened out into a hall-like area, and the Doctor gave a little cry of recognition. Moving closer, the Fallen Angel could see a blue police box sitting incongruously in the middle of the floor.

'The TARDIS!' said the Doctor. 'It's still here!'

'Well, that's a relief. What's a TARDIS?'

'It's my . . . er, never mind.'

The Fallen Angel would have pressed further, but at that moment the door to the box creaked open, and a girl peeked out. She was wearing a silvery jumpsuit that showed off her admirable body to its best extent, and her cute, rounded face was alive with excitement.

A second face emerged above hers: a fresh-faced young man with a rather belligerent expression.

'Doctor!'

'Jamie, Zoe! Oh thank heavens you're still alive!'

'No thanks to yon metal beasties,' said the young man in a thick Scottish brogue. 'They've been chasing us upstairs and downstairs and . . . '

' . . . And in my lady's chamber, I'll be bound,' the Doctor finished. He was beaming and rubbing his hands together, much to the discomfort of the Fallen Angel, whose shoulders he was still sitting on.

'Aye, that's right! It was lucky for us that we made it back to the TARDIS before they caught us! They can't seem to see us if we don't step outside.'

'Who is this man?' Zoe asked suspiciously.

The Fallen Angel smiled his most disarming smile. 'A mere strolling player, whose only aim in life is the thwarting of villainy and the frustration of sober citizenry.'

'Is he serious?' she asked the Doctor.

'Not that I've noticed,' he said candidly, hopping off the Fallen Angel's shoulders.

'For the love of dear old Aunt Ada!' the Fallen Angel cried, but he was too late. The Doctor had inadvertently moved out of the protective influence of the device they had pillaged from the robot.

The Doctor clapped a hand to his forehead.

'Doctor,' said the Fallen Angel kindly, 'you haven't any brain.'

'I know,' said the Doctor humbly.

It started as a faint disturbance in the distance, and then it grew to a rustling like a forest at night, and then it was upon them. Huge metallic spiders were running across the ceilings and the walls, and emerging from every corridor that joined the hall.

'Get back in the TARDIS!' the Doctor yelled to Zoe and Jamie, but they had already done so.

'The house guards,' he added, turning to the Fallen Angel. 'When I say "run", run like a rabbit.'

'What was the word again?' the Fallen Angel asked as the multi-legged robots scuttled towards them, metallic fangs at the ready.

'Run!' said the Doctor.

And they did.

Access to the front door was cut off by a particularly vicious metal arachnid, so they pounded down a side corridor. Bursting into a room filled with period furniture, the Fallen Angel and the Doctor threw the door shut behind them and started piling up anything that came to hand against it. Tables, chairs, sideboards and bookcases went into the pile. The door vibrated under the pressure of the guards. Plaster began to crack around the frame. The Fallen Angel cast around for anything else that he could use.

'Oh my sainted aunt!' exclaimed the Doctor.

The Fallen Angel turned. Whilst part of his mind registered the fact that the Doctor's aunt was both giddy *and* sainted, and wondered whether to make a comment about vertigo being next to godliness, the rest of it was goggling at the three corpses locked together in the centre of the room. The light from the picture window gleamed off their crab-like, spiny shells, which had been smashed open to reveal strands of bluish meat and the dried remnants of some watery green fluid. Whatever else they were, they were not robots.

'It looks as if they killed each other,' the Doctor said, poking at the nearest corpse with a beautiful Louis XIV chair and then skipping back out of the way. 'The guards were never pro-grammed to deal with this.'

'How do you know?'

'Because I programmed them.'

The door shifted, knocking a sideboard over.

'The window!' they said simultaneously.

They smashed through the leaded glass as one. Alarms burst into life, but they were beyond caring now. The Fallen Angel rolled, sprang to his feet and was ten feet away before he realized that the Doctor had nose-dived into a beautifully kept herbaceous border. He sprinted back, just managing to snatch the Doctor from the multiple arms of one of the guards as it clambered through the window amid a tinkle of glass. A quick glance told him that the room was crawling with the metal creatures.

Half way across the lawn he could hear claws ripping up the ground behind them. Sharp talons clutched at his jacket, but he pulled free and kept on running. For a small man, the Doctor moved fast. His tails flapped behind him in the wind and he was bringing his knees up so high that they kept hitting his chest.

A spiked metal pincer caught the Fallen Angel's shoulder and pulled him back towards a gaping maw in which he could see serrated teeth rotating against one another. He bid farewell to life and love and merriment.

A deep staccato noise drowned out the gnashing of teeth, and the metal spider's legs started to fly off at unusual angles. The Fallen Angel rolled free and watched in delighted disbelief as the pursuing hordes seemed to disintegrate in a hail of hot metal. The covering fire was coming from a section of shrubbery, and he and the Doctor crawled towards it on their bellies to avoid the same fate as had befallen the guards.

'What ho, old man,' yelled Ketters as they entered the bush. He was sitting cross-legged on the ground with the Lewis gun from the Bristol in front of him, its mounting stuck into the ground. The roar was deafening.

'What ho, old gooseberry,' rejoined the Fallen Angel, reclining lazily beside him. The Doctor, meanwhile, was panting and puffing and generally looking done in.

'You look like you're in trouble,' Ketters shouted, still firing in short bursts. The ammunition belt rattling through the gun was more than half empty.

'A gnat's eyebrow, that's all. I see you didn't go down with your ship after all.'

'Damn parachute strap got caught on a bit of metal in the cockpit.'

Out on the lawn, there was mayhem. Waves and waves of spidery guards were rushing onwards to destruction.

'By the time I'd got it free,' Ketters continued, 'I didn't have enough time to open it properly. I dived out as the old girl hit the trees, and managed to land in some ornamental lake they've got back there. By the time I'd climbed out, you'd gone, so I rescued old Doris here and sat waiting for you.' He swivelled the gun to aim upwards and began shooting down the few humanoid guards who remained to get airborne. 'And what sort of day have you had?'

'Passable, old chap,' said the Fallen Angel, and took a deep breath. There were close shaves, and there were close shaves.

The firing stopped. The Fallen Angel could feel the heat radiating from the metal of the gun. Smoke drifted across the lawn, and the pile of assorted body parts upon it.

'Well,' he said, 'mark one up to the Angels.'

Sauntering across the churned up ground and stepping amid limbs and claws which still feebly grasped at nothing, he took a small slip of card from his pocket and dropped it gently on the head of one of the spiders.

'They're a long-lived species, Crustacoids,' said the Doctor, wringing his hands, 'and we didn't expect them to kill each other in some petty feud.'

He was standing in the centre of Lucas Seyton's dining room, explaining what little he could to Seyton himself, Paul Kettering, Jamie and Zoe.

'Happens in the best-run governments,' Seyton drawled from his position lounging across the sofa. 'Maybe they didn't actually rule anything, but they thought they did. They probably fell out over the price of bananas on Venus, or something equally important. Have another glass of bubbly.'

'Oh, I don't think . . . Well, perhaps just one more.'

'So what happened about the guards?' Ketters asked.

'A fault in their programming,' the Doctor replied. 'They were never told that the people they were guarding had to be alive. They were just as happy to guard corpses as living creatures. My fault, I suppose, but I can't be expected to think of everything, now can I?'

'And how many other houses full of war criminals of that ilk can we expect to find scattered across this sceptred isle?' Seyton said as he refilled the Doctor's glass.

The Doctor avoided his gaze.

'None,' he admitted. 'There's a little asteroid somewhere for them nowadays, or so I'm told.'

'So what happens to yon big house, then?' Jamie asked.

'Oh well, it will be cleared up, don't worry. Now, what do you say to . . .'

'Cleared up by who?' Zoe asked pointedly.

'Oh, by the people who put it there, I expect,' the Doctor said, his eyes warning her not to take the subject any further. He drained the glass in one. 'Now I really think that it's time we should be going.'

'Oh, but Doctor . . .'

'It really is.'

And that, more or less, was where it ended. Seyton and Ketters affably bid farewell to the people with whom they had but recently shared something of an adventure. They all knew that they would never see each other again, but nothing was made of it. Light banter was the order of the day.

'Oh, Doctor,' said Seyton as the little man made for the door, 'there's something I'd like you to have.' He went across to the sideboard and removed the mechanical duck. 'Just to remind you of our adventure.'

'Oh, I couldn't possibly . . .' the Doctor protested. 'It's stolen! And besides, didn't you say there were only five ever made? No, I really couldn't!'

'It's all right,' said Seyton, 'I stole the other four as well.'

He smiled easily as he watched the three of them leave. One of them – the little man with the long black coat – was making little quacking noises as he clutched the metal duck to his chest. Already Seyton had forgotten his name. Words were circling lazily around his mind – *There's a sort of blind spot which we've cast around the area. Even if people do stumble across it, they forget about it within a few hours* – but he was sure that it wasn't important. After all, what was?

He turned to Ketters, who was frowning as if he had mislaid some mental luggage.

'What were we talking about, old beetroot?' he asked.

Silverman gave a shuddering sigh, as if waking from a long and impenetrable sleep, and replaced the metal bird on the table in front of us. The strange glow which had surrounded his hands quickly faded, leaving the room in almost total darkness. We sat for a while in complete silence, then I got up and relit the candles with a match from my pocket.

Propping myself against the mantelpiece, drawing as much comfort as I could from the meagre warmth of the fire, I turned to face the psychic. 'You know, Silverman, I think you've been reading too many comic books. I mean, what was all that about?'

Silverman stared down at his skeletal hands, his expression unreadable. 'I assure you, Mr Addison, that I can recount only the images my mind divines from the objects with which I am presented. My own thoughts and experiences have no bearing on the matter.'

My client was rocking gently backwards and forwards in his chair. 'Well,' he said, 'at least we know who I am now. The Doctor.'

I raised an eyebrow. 'Oh? How come?'

He was taken aback by my question. 'Er . . . isn't it obvious? I mean, it was the Doctor who got the clockwork bird. And you heard how Silverman described him: a short man with dark, tousled hair.' He pointed to the curly locks protruding from beneath the brim of his hat.

Silverman shook his head. 'I'm sorry, my friend, but you are mistaken. The Doctor's appearance was similar to yours in some respects, but not the same. Besides, the events I described occurred some twenty-five years ago, and he was older than you are now, not younger. I fear we must continue our efforts if we are to discover your true identity.'

The psychic looked up at me and, nodding in reluctant agreement, I returned to my seat.

Having briefly perused the objects on the table, Silverman reached down and picked up the glass phial I had noticed earlier. It was mounted on silver clasps with a thin silver chain running between them, and inside it were a few drops of mercury.

Hunching forward in his chair, Silverman held the phial in his cupped hands. 'Please, both of you concentrate on the object,' he instructed, 'and we shall see what it has to tell us.'

As before, a miniature whirlwind seemed to erupt, swirling about the room and snuffing out the candles that I had only just relit. The glow returned to Silverman's hands, bathing us in a pool of unearthly light. 'Again, I see a man,' hissed the psychic. 'Dressed in black and bearing a dark, malicious countenance.' He drew a sharp intake of breath. 'A man of immeasurable evil!'

The Duke of Dominoes

Marc Platt

The slanting rain reminded him of prison bars.

From the back of the car, the Master watched the cigarette butt that hung from the corner of Sam Kulisa's mouth. The stub had gone out, perhaps long ago, but Sam still chewed determinedly at it. The white-walled tyres squealed as he swung the black Buick out of the side street and away from the museum. Not worth lighting the stub, reckoned the Master. Not with this interminable rain.

The Master's pinstriped suit was damp. He straightened his display handkerchief and eased up the brim of his brown homburg. 'I trust that Esterhazy has been dealt with,' he said coldly.

He could hear the smirk in Sam Kulisa's answer. 'We gave him the slug like you said, Dook . . . er, boss. Put him out like a light. Then his car went off the end of the dock. Too bad. He won't be no more trouble.'

'You filled the car with concrete, no doubt. I could have wished for something more subtle.' The Master smoothed out his greying beard with a gloved hand. 'Well, at least Joe Clementi may think twice before sending another hitman after me. What else?'

'Margie put a bottle in the back for you. It's the latest batch from the garage.'

The Master clunked open a compartment in the door. Inside, next to the Colt .45, was a bottle of amber liquor. He sniffed at the contents and choked. 'What's that idiot Hamilton doing? I gave him precise instructions. He's been using rotten potatoes again.'

'I thought that's what hooch was, boss.'

'Then something's wrong with the fermentation. No one'll buy this stuff, let alone drink it. As usual I have to do everything myself!'

'It was a whole lot better when you was bootlegging it from the other garage, boss.'

The Master scowled. The whereabouts of the other *garage* was a sore point. 'Until that situation is rectified, Kulisa, we are forced to produce whisky in Hamilton's rusty still. Even if a stew of vegetable starch compares miserably with what a nutrient synthesizer can manufacture.'

'Yes, boss. But Margie says supplies are getting low. And the clients could be trouble.'

'The clients can wait.'

So they drove the sodden morning streets in silence.

The Master's eyes bored at the back of Sam Kulisa's squat human neck. Just another rough-cut ingredient simmering in the immigrant melting-pot of the USA. Clumsy in body and mind. Give a hundred years or so, and the plastic cards from the Webster-Sayuki Credit Houses on New Nippon would be smarter.

'Something's up,' muttered Sam after ten minutes, the stub jiggling impossibly up and down on his thin lips.

The Master leaned forward. 'And what brings you to that conclusion?'

'No cops, boss,' Sam said. 'Not in their usual hang-outs. Officer Haggerty – he's always on the corner of Racine, four blocks away. Never changes, any morning. And where's O'Connor? Every day he eats at Mason's Drugstore. Has his own seat in the window. And if Mason's out playing poker all night with the boys, his wife gives O'Connor more than breakfast . . . They play "poker" too.' He sniggered and nearly lost his stub.

The Master said, 'I take it that this Mason was at home today.'

'Saw him in the window, boss. But no O'Connor.'

'And thus we deduce that the police force in this miserable city has business elsewhere.'

'Sure, boss. Something's up.'

'So you said.' The Master glanced at the instrument on his wrist that passed for a watch. 'Put your foot down, Kulisa. It's nearly seven o'clock and I'm expecting an important call.'

He sank back on the cracked leather seat and endured the barrage of jolts that went with riding in a thirties limousine – little more than a box on wheels. The rain had stopped at last. Prohibition Chicago, grey buildings cut of solid wet smoke, juddered heartlessly past outside. Another weary dawn dragged itself into existence. Shabby figures trudged the streets in search of work or food or just another drink.

He watched the gloomy edifice of a Mission Hall slide past, the foolish light of hope and goodness streaming from its open doors. He sneered, almost laughed. His own circumstances had become intolerable. Nothing went right any more. It was this miserable planet. He longed for the smooth luxury of a skim-speeder, shooting him away from the reeking city up into the open sky and beyond. Impossible now.

Yet everything had gone perfectly at first. This plan he had conceived, a magnificent scheme, was worthy of his fertile mind alone. Every detail had been meticulously prepared – every strand sliding neatly into place. And this time no one was going to interfere – especially not one person in particular, who made a habit of putting his metaphorical oar in.

Already the Master had spun a web of strategies across the gulf of time and space, garnering fragments of information from charts and scrolls in the Great Library at Alexandria and from hieroglyphs in the Domdaniel caverns on Strava. Doom-laden prophecies and future legends foretelling the rise of the self-styled Ministers of Grace and their suicidal complicity in the death of the Universe.

From a dozen far-flung cosmic moments, the Master had recovered the shards, long-lost fragments of eternal power. And in a distant place he had dared assemble them, binding their influence to his obeisance, uncertain of what he was creating. And then realizing, as the power grew, that he was assembling God. Nothing simpler. But God would answer to him – the Master, the power behind the Throne.

And at last, the whole outrageous, thrilling conceit pivoted on one final detail. Insert one final key, a handle to make the absurd barrel-organ of the Universe turn to his tune. It had all gone perfectly. Until . . . until his TARDIS had been stolen.

Half a block from the Imperial, the Buick slid to a halt. There were police cars clustered at the front of the hotel and two officers stationed at the lobby doors.

'We're obviously expected,' the Master said. 'Take the car round to our private entrance.'

The staff of the Imperial never noticed him using the laundry elevator by the kitchens – he had *persuaded* them not to notice. Standing amid the stacks of fresh towels, the Master brushed the smuts from his dark suit and was ferried directly up to the hotel's penthouse suite.

From the service landing, he could hear Margie's voice raised in the suite's main lounge.

'How many times d'you want it spelt out? The Dook ain't here. He didn't say when he'd be in. And I don't know nothing about this guy Esplanady.'

Margie del Monsalvat, born Margery Stokes, the leggy show-girl he'd first encountered in the illicit depths of the Rhinestone Club. Then at a baseball game. Then at the Civic Opera. After that, in a dark alley, just at the moment he caught Toni Ciro, another hood from Joe Clementi's mob, sneaking hooch from the garage. She hadn't batted a painted eyelid when he'd compressed Toni. She'd just hidden the shrunken body in her valise and thrown it in Lake Michigan, where all the evidence of every crime in Illinois seemed to be deposited.

'God, you've got cold eyes,' she'd said. 'I like that. It's sort of cute.' So he'd taken her under his wing, made her a few promises, and soon knew all the joints and contacts in Chicago's rotten underbelly.

'Esterhazy!' snarled a man's voice from the lounge. 'Maximillian Esterhazy. A dead Kraut in a car in the lake.'

'Maybe there was nowhere else to park,' suggested Margie. 'I told you, we never heard of him here.'

'He was just a small-time crook, but I reckon he'd set his sights on bigger things. Why else would he have newspaper cuttings of your friend Dook Domini in his wallet?'

The Master cursed to himself and accessed the astro-synchrometer on his watch. In grey Chicago it was nearly seven in the morning, and on Blue Profundis in the Sappho System, on the Polar coast of the Isle of Mists, it was almost suns-down. By Galactic Relative Time, his call was due any minute.

'So maybe the schmuck has a hero-worship fetish,' said Margie's voice.

'*Had*,' corrected the interrogator. 'He drowned in cement before the water got to him. There's a lot of crazy people out there, Miss del Monsalvat. So what's your obsession? After all, Dook Domini's no Gary Cooper.'

'Perhaps not.' The Master was framed in the gilt doorway. 'But I'm very particular about the company I keep.'

'No kidding.' A heavy man in a heavy coat swung to face the Master. A uniformed policeman blocked the other door.

Margie, her hair caught in frozen yellow waves like Jean Harlow's, sat tightly in a leather chair. A line of smoke curled up from the Lucky Strike dangling between her fingers. 'Dook, this is Chief Mulligan. He's been waiting for you since early.'

Police Chief Mulligan had the weary look of someone who had given up the ghost without giving up hope as well. His tiny eyes had sunk into his crumpled face like two blueberries dropped into an hour-old strawberry ice. 'You keep strange hours, Dook. I don't recall that you've been in Chicago more than a couple of months, but I get reports from all over about you.'

'I must apologize for keeping you waiting, Chief,' smiled the Master. 'I'm a very busy man, but I'm always at the service of those who enforce the law.'

'That's what I thought. Every evening you're at the boxing or the opera or some fancy civic reception. Out all night too, so I hear. And you spend most days at the Wainwright Museum. Don't you ever sleep?'

The Master's smile intensified. 'Just taking in the sights, Chief.'

'So you won't be staying long.'

The Master glanced at Margie. She was engrossed in a cigarette burn in the carpet. 'Who knows? I've been made so welcome in your city.'

'You must try the baseball too, before you go back to Mexico or Rio or Europe. Pardon me, but where did you say you came from?'

'Once my business is concluded, I shall depart.'

Mulligan nodded. 'Profitable business, of course. Whatever it might be?'

'Private business,' the Master said, glancing at his watch again. 'Thank you for your courtesy call, Chief. But if there's nothing else . . .'

The crumples in the Chief's face congealed into an uneasy frown. He shifted from one flat foot to the other and back. 'You see, Mr Domini . . . Dook, you see that could be a problem. There's some very . . . some big fish in this city and they don't take too kindly to someone, an outsider they don't know, trying to . . . so to speak . . .'

'Spit it out, Chief,' laughed the Master. 'Or leave the threats to the experts. Who sent you on this errand? Was it Joe Clementi? He runs the police on this precinct, doesn't he? Or does *he* answer to someone too? Someone like Al Capone?'

The policeman took a step in from the door, but Mulligan raised a weary hand. 'Okay, Frank, you can wait in the lobby.' Meeting the Master's cold stare head on, he waited until the door closed before intoning, 'Let's say that Clementi makes a substantial donation to the police benevolent fund each year.'

'But if someone else were perhaps to make an even more generous contribution, he might sway police activity in his favour.'

You had to listen to that voice – cultured, potent, undeniable.

Yet it had softened, almost into a lullaby . . . or a caress. Mulligan swayed a little. His hand went to his collar. That stare could have burned him in his boots, but it felt like smooth bourbon seeping directly into his head. 'Yeah, that's exactly what I meant,' he heard himself say.

And the burning eyes replied, 'But you don't want money, Chief Mulligan. You want to help me. And I *do* need your help, Chief. In fact I demand it of you. Your unquestioning service.'

'Unquestioning,' Mulligan mumbled.

'That's right. You must obey me. I am . . . I am your Boss.'

'Obey. Yes.' Mulligan stood in guileless acceptance, content to ponder his new situation at the expense of all else.

'Looks a real dummy, don't he?' observed Margie.

The Master smiled and filched a wallet from inside Mulligan's coat. 'And not a moment too soon,' he said, extracting thirty dollars for himself. He showed the family photo to Margie, who cooed at the bonneted baby, then slotted the wallet back into its owner's coat. 'Thank you for your donation, Chief Mulligan. No doubt, I'll be in touch.'

Mulligan sleepwalked out.

'And you must go too, my dear,' added the Master, pointedly.

'That call you were expecting,' crooned Margie. 'It came through about an hour ago.'

'What!'

'So I put it on hold for you.'

The Master hurriedly tugged open the drawer of a walnut desk. A small mirrored box sat inside with a flickering green display on its lid. 'How did you know about this?'

She sidled towards him and draped an arm over his shoulder. 'I always wanted to be a secretary. It was my mother who pushed me into show business.'

'What have you seen?'

'Oh, don't be cross, Dook. They got tricks like that in the movies. It's all done with something like mirrors.'

'You've seen nothing,' he insisted. 'Nothing at all.' But her eyes had a way of avoiding his stare. Before he could stop her, she leaned forward and touched the side panel on the box.

She gave a little scream. An envelope of light surged up out of the box and parcelled them. The Master's hand clamped on to her arm like a vice. 'Don't move!'

The penthouse suite of the Imperial Hotel was eclipsed by a flickering glow. Smoke drifted through a platoon of tall columns, like the front of the Wainwright Museum a dozen times over, only several of them were thrown down in the general rubble. A fire burned close by, just where the bathroom door had been. It burned silently. There was no sound at all.

The Master released his grip and Margie slumped petulantly to the ground. 'Neat trick,' she complained. 'But the talkies have arrived.'

'Be quiet!'

Not a sound. The smoke didn't smell and the blaze was as cold as a film fire. Beyond the paved area, the land fell away to the dark green seas that circled the ancient Isle of Mists. The twin suns of the Sappho system had already sunk beneath the bowed horizon. Overhead, clouds ripened like bloom on the skin of the plum dark sky. The Master felt the night chill in the pit of his stomach. He'd had a palace here, built in his name, glorifying him for the new age of splendour he had brought to Blue Profundis. That was three weeks ago relative time. Plenty had changed since he'd left.

Something that he had taken for a rock struggled up out of the ruin. It faced him, beaded eyes glinting in the firelight. Its robe was torn and dust clung to the ornate encrustations on its blue, byzantine lizardhead. In its tendrilled hand, it clutched a mirror box like the Master's.

Margie tried to squeal, but her throat had thankfully dried. The creature's head was weaving back and forth on its extended neck. The broad lipless mouth moved silently. The brute faltered, shook the box, and splinters of sound crackled through to them.

'My Master. You return to mock us.' A trident tongue flickered between its jaws.

'Havuri-sss-Cazcim. What's happened to my palace?'

The creature was shuffling closer. 'You have brought destruction on your servants, my Master. Why do you do this? You promised us great power and salvation. Why do snatch away everything you gave us?'

'I have done nothing to harm you, Havuri-sss-Cazcim.'

'Not so, my Master. By your will, a sudden storm burst from the Temples of Eternity. A thousand dust demons and whirlwinds. A great eye of lightning which has destroyed the land.'

Rooted to the spot, the Master could only observe the local image thrown up by the reality transmitter. It was enough. His sudden rage exploded out. 'Who's tampered with the surge buffers? You imbecile, may your eggs be barren, I entrusted you with their safe-keeping. I made you my Grand Vizier, guardian to all my plans. But you've let someone else near them. Who was it?'

'No one save you, my Master. I kept your faith.'

'Rubbish! You've let someone combine the power of the icons I gave you. Years of my work has been destroyed! And the power unleashed will be uncontrollable. Tell me who it was!'

The serpentine creature was almost snout to nose with the Master. 'You came as a prophet and still seek to deceive us. We are your victims. We know the ship in which you travel.'

The Master froze. 'What ship?' The flood of his rage shivered to an icy trickle. 'A ship like mine?'

'It was your ship, my Master. I saw it myself.'

'Describe it. Was it blue? Shaped like a tall casket with a lamp on its roof?' He physically braced himself for the answer.

'No, my Master. It was *your* ship, as it always was – with the shape of a carved sarcophagus.'

The Master's temper scarcely wavered. 'Then it's someone else. Someone who's after the power I've gathered. They've already stolen my ship and now I'm being framed.'

'You tempted us with your gifts of power, Master.'

'And *you* snatched them up with unmitigated greed!' He

smirked. 'No matter. Do you think I care for your people now? You've failed me totally, Havuri-sss-Cazcim. All I want is my power!'

He stopped. A new star was rising above the horizon. It was rising fast. Spears of light shot down from it as it approached across the sea.

'Our world is nothing now,' the Vizier retorted. 'Ten thousand ages of Blue Profundis wither like a cankered vine. We pay the price for our unholy avarice.' His tendrilled hand snaked out to grasp his tormentor, but found only a substanceless phantom. 'You, my Master, you are accursed too. May your skin never shed and your hearts burn in your body. We should have known you. You are the very Devil incarnate.'

'Then go to Hell,' said the Master.

They heard the crack of the lightning spears as the star drew closer. Then, as if it had finally found the quarry it was hunting, the star plunged like a comet directly at them.

The Master slammed the side panel on the box. For a moment, they were at the heart of a cold explosion. The blazing shape of Havuri-sss-Cazcim disintegrated inches from the Master's face. Then the penthouse suite of the Imperial Hotel was back and he stood in a cold sweat, with Margie clinging to his leg. In his hand, the smoking transmitter box shattered like glass.

The Master fell into the safety of a chair. 'Who's doing this to me?' he muttered. 'I'm a sitting duck in this place. I want my TARDIS back.'

He looked down and saw Margie staring up at him. She knew too much now and his use for her must be finished.

'Jeez,' she said. 'I was wrong. You don't get scenes like that at the movies. And in colour too.'

On the other hand, if she was that stupid . . . He stood up and poured himself a large whisky. Not Hamilton's latest brew, but a supply he'd had sent up from Kentucky.

He put down his glass and picked up his hat. 'I'm going back to the museum,' he said. He scrutinized his features in the gilt rococo wall mirror. The tread marks of Time were taking their toll. Blue veins showed like tendrils under the pale skin of his temples. He snorted at his body's frailty and straightened his tie.

'You look real washed out, Dook,' she observed. 'I'll drive.'

He thought for a moment, then nodded.

They went out the back way, passing Kulisa asleep in the chef's office amid a scattered deck of cards. In the car, the Master activated his watch's distress call and listened for any response to the hyperspace sonic flare. It was the last piece of useful technology he had. The rest, including his tissue-compression eliminator, had gone when his TARDIS had been stolen.

As usual, the first transmissions he picked up came from a local American radio station. A sickeningly cheery variety programme was playing. He cursed and boosted the reception. Out of the air came a distinguished, but sepulchral voice enunciating: 'This is the British Broadcasting Company. And now a talk by Miss Florence Thorpe-Dickson on "Shopping and Cooking".' He spread the receptor net wider. Against the fizz of celestial artron, he heard signals from spaceships that pass in the cosmic night – a merchant trader advertising its wares, the greeting whoops of two Gug-trucker freighters overtaking each other on the nearby salt route from Proxima Centauri. No response from his own TARDIS. From maybe 500 light years distant came the distress call of a beleaguered ship as a pirate fleet of Grakinese Corsairs circled in for the kill. No one would bother to listen to its puny cry for help. Nor to his own, for that matter.

Margie drove Michigan Avenue as if all the legions of Hell were in pursuit. The Master decided not to look back, just in case. The sooner he reached the museum, the better. Whatever it was that had pitted itself against him, it must be seeking the final key too. So he must reach the object first, whatever the cost. Even if, from the apparently flimsy protection of its glass display case, the key had defied his every attempt to reach it for the past 94 days. Once he had it, he would start again. At least, he consoled himself, he could rely on the girl.

Her voice startled him. 'Are you gonna break your promises to me too, Dook?'

'What are you saying?' he snapped.

'Don't push me now,' she said. 'I'm doing nearly forty.'

'My dear Margie, don't you trust me?'

'Is it worth it? You tell me, Dookie. I don't wanna land up fried like that reptile friend of yours.' She spun the wheel, taking a slippery corner with a screech of hot tyres. 'You realize we're being followed,' she added.

The Master glanced back. There was a box-shaped black Portsmouth on their tail. More specimens from Clementi's mob, no doubt.

She put her foot down and shot a traffic signal, narrowly cutting the path of an oncoming truck. Its horn blared. The Master clung helplessly to his seat. He was in her hands.

'You've forgotten your promises already,' she added, swinging the Buick blind into another side street. 'What about the big Spanish house in Hollywood? One with red roof tiles and palm trees. And when are you going to introduce me to your movie friends?'

'You seem to see me as some sort of Svengali,' he protested.

He heard a sharp rataplan of gunfire from behind and ducked as the rear window exploded in. Margie leaned in over the wheel, pushing hard on the gas.

Another Portsmouth had pulled out of a side-turning behind them. The hood in the passenger seat was half out of the window, wielding a machine-gun.

The Master snatched the Colt .45 from the door compartment and tried to aim at the car. He risked a couple of shots, but couldn't target the driver – Margie was zig-zagging too much. Another spray of bullets punctured the back of the Buick and took the Master's hat off. He felt a burning sting on his forehead.

Ahead of them, a battered Model T Ford was chugging up the centre of the narrow street. It loomed in the windscreen. The

Master lunged forward for the steering-wheel and was slapped back. With a yard to spare, Margie spun the wheel and mounted the sidewalk, clipping the Ford's rear. She reached the end of the street and swerved sharp right, still half on the kerb, half in the gutter.

The Portsmouth tried the same, but the Ford's startled owner was careering out of control all over the street. He hit the Portsmouth side on, sending it into an abrupt head-to-head encounter with a fire hydrant. The local street kids acquired a new and unexpected fountain.

'You know Svengali?' said Margie, once it was clear their pursuers were incapacitated.

'What?'

'The little Ruskie who keeps the bookshop on 23rd. Or is that Svodoba?'

The Master was using his display handkerchief to mop the blood from his right temple. The bullet had only grazed him and the wound would heal in a couple of hours. Meantime, he did not want to listen to Margie's prattling. His scowl was taking root. Companions, for all their uses, got too close and demanded too much. So why bother? They didn't trust him and he certainly never trusted them. The insufferable Doctor was welcome to them all. Even so, he had to admit that he needed Margie just for the moment. Clementi was getting too persistent in his attacks.

'Of course I haven't forgotten my promises,' he assured her. 'It's all a matter of time.' He tried once more to catch her eyes in the rear-view mirror. For a moment, he thought they returned his burning stare with interest. Then she put her foot down and the jerk pinned him to the back seat.

When they reached the Wainwright Museum, it was closed. The air had turned humid, threatening a storm. Margie stood awkwardly on the wide front steps, holding the Master's gun, while he forced the primitive lock. A huge statue of Abe Lincoln carrying a child scrutinized the intruders. The inscription on the plinth read:

> 'With Malice towards none;
> With Charity for all;
> With Firmness in the Right,
> As God gives us to see the Right.'

Margie giggled. 'He has a beard like you,' she said.

'Just another sitting target, like all presidents,' the Master answered. 'It goes with the job.'

'Are you still going to stand for Mayor?'

The bolt clicked and he pushed the heavy door ajar. 'It entirely depends on how long I'm forced to stay.'

Mayor of Chicago was a little parochial. He fancied he'd settle only for Emperor of the Universe.

The entrance hall of the museum was cold and cavernous. Margie's heels clattered on the stone flagging. They had almost climbed the central staircase when a shout interrupted their progress. A tubby and irate custodian, obviously rudely awakened, was hurrying towards them. The Master started down to meet him as he blustered up the steps. The little man met the intruder's burning stare and faltered, his mouth dropping open like a drowned fish. The Master stepped closer, bird-of-prey eyes intent on their victim.

A gunshot echoed round the hall like a thunderclap.

The custodian, his shirt suddenly wet crimson, somersaulted backwards over the bannisters with a look of astonishment.

'What do you think you're doing!' the Master exploded. His Colt .45 was sitting in Margie's hand, steady as a constant mudstick.

'I thought it would save you time,' she said.

'You know, my dear, it is possible to be too resourceful for your own good.' He was polite because he was still looking along the gun's barrel. 'Now just leave the close encounters to me. Mm?'

He stretched out his empty palm. She held his look for a long moment, then handed over the gun. 'So which way do we go?'

He led her through the exhibits to the Hall of Geology. Margie eyed the displays of mineral samples and declared, 'Not my sort of rocks.' The Master stopped in front of a small and dusty glass cabinet. He walked reverently up to it as if approaching an altar.

The cabinet contained a lump of brown rock, the size of an elephant's dropping. A card called it *The Flagstaff Tektite. Found on Mount San Francisco, Arizona, 1871.*

'Touch the glass,' the Master said.

Margie ran her finger across the top of the cabinet. The film of dust was undisturbed. She shrugged. 'It feels kind of weird. Like it isn't there.'

'Exactly!' The Master crouched to the level of the object.

'So what is it?' she said.

'To all appearances, it's a common or garden meteorite. A shooting star. A chunk of space debris.' He unstrapped his watch and held it against the glass. 'At least that's what we're supposed to think.'

The watch face was etched with a set of windows, each glinting with glowing numbers. 'You see? Nothing.' But he didn't bother to show her. 'And do you know why that is?'

'Search me. Is this what you come to look at every day? Something that isn't there? Jeez, I need some breakfast.'

'Of course it's there. But there's a high-tension Time Brace around it. At any given moment, the tektite is five seconds ahead of us in Real Time. Therefore the image we see is of the tektite five seconds ago. And I cannot reach it. I've tried a thousand ways, believe me.'

'You want to steal that?' She was incredulous. 'Dook, there's a hundred paintings in the city gallery that would look better in our penthouse, or wherever it is we're gonna live.'

The Master looked a little shifty. 'Perhaps. But not all the diamonds or gold or bootleg liquor on this miserable planet would give me a billionth of the power held in this single chunk of rock! Even I cannot conceive of its magnitude! I must have it!'

She studied him, fingering her bag nervously. At last she said, 'Okay Dook . . . sweetie, so what do we do?'

'We work day and night to find a way to release it. This is the key to unimaginable forces, but someone else is after it too. You saw what happened on Blue Profundis.' He turned and saw that she was backing away. 'What's the matter? I promised you a share in this, Margie, but I need your help. Especially if time is running out.'

'Oh, my,' intoned a voice with a deep Southern lilt, 'and time is such a precious thing.' Moving out of the shadows was a tall dowager of uncertain age – the more the Master looked, the more uncertain he grew. Her silver hair was combed back and she was wrapped in a fringed shawl embroidered with Indian patterns over a black, full-skirted dress. Around her sleeve glinted an engraved armilla of dull silver. On her hands, she wore gloves like black lace spider's webs. She looked as if she'd just come in from a temperance meeting – a meeting held about a hundred years before.

She sighed. 'You do realize that the Thought Core is quite safe from your interference. I assume it was you who woke me. There's no one else in the building . . . apart from my dead guard.'

'The Thought Core?' said the Master. 'Is that what it's called? Then who exactly are you?'

The woman smiled grimly. 'Wainwright . . . for the time being. This is my museum. Wainwright's just a name – the latest of quite a few . . . Mr Domini.'

The Master smiled back. 'Mrs Wainwright, I can see there's no need to mince words with you.'

'Just Wainwright. And I know your reasons for coming. You're not the first and you won't be the last.'

'We'll see,' nodded the Master. 'Tell me, how long have you been here?'

Wainwright subsided on to a bench. 'In the Windy City? Well now, about sixty years I guess. Ever since a gold prospector picked up the Thought Core down in Arizona and brought it back here. It took some getting back, I can tell you.'

'That was very careless,' said the Master. 'So since then you've increased your vigilance.'

'The people in the big city imagine themselves to be so much more sophisticated. I lived among the Apache for close on seven hundred years. The called me Cloud Buffalo then. And there was no trouble until the white settlers arrived. Progress. I've seen where it leads.' She sighed again. 'I'm sorry, Mr Domini, it's a wearisome task watching over the Core. I would offer you coffee, but you are an intruder.'

'Please, please, I understand. We *are* enemies, after all.'

'And the Core *is* quite beyond your reach,' she reminded him, but she was clearly charmed by his manners. 'You do understand why it must never be released?'

'I know that its appearance is nothing to do with its content. If ever it was reunited with its other components, its power would be immeasurable.'

'Reunited? My dear Mr Domini, now let me tell you that it was never united in the first place. The other components are long-lost. We saw to that.'

He took the liberty of sitting next to her. 'I see. My researches never yielded that information.' He pondered for a moment and then added, 'I take it I have the honour of addressing one of the Ministers of Grace.'

She nodded slowly. 'It's a mighty long time since anyone called me by that title.'

'It's an exceptionally long time before you will even be born,' smiled the Master. 'Perhaps you could enlighten me as to why you and the Core are here.'

She glanced with some curiosity at Margie, who had withdrawn to the far end of the room. 'Don't mind her,' said the Master. 'This is beyond her.'

Wainwright drew her shawl tighter. Her voice went cold. Her bony fingers clutched at the silver armilla. 'It's what *will* happen. In the last dark age of our Universe, after all Creation stops expanding, when it all collapses back again into nothing. In that one terrible, crushed moment of oblivion, the slate will be wiped clean and a new Universe will be born. They call that moment by many names. The Mighty Crunch or the Big Bang or the Final and First Event. But we named it the Great Purge.'

'Well, hallelujah to that,' said the Master.

'Quite right,' she nodded. 'The age from which I come was a terrible, shrinking, bloody time. It was ruled by the Order of Alchemaitres – a cruel tyranny given over to much wickedness and lax morality. And don't imagine that the threat of impending extinction could drive them to repent their ways. No, not for one moment. Instead, the Alchemaitres sought to perpetuate their evil line. They instilled the essence of their Order's revolting power into a vessel designed to survive the Great Purge.'

'Cheating God?' added the Master with relish. 'So in the next Universe, they'd play God themselves.'

There was no stopping her now. Her outrage was in full flood. *'They would sow their poisoned seeds into the untainted land of the next Creation.* The Book of Auguries. Article 31, Verse 12.'

The Master placed a consoling hand on hers. 'But I'm sure you made every attempt to stop them.'

She snatched her hand away – probably the hand used for tambourine waving. 'Please, Mr Domini. No familiarity. We, the Ministers of Grace, are pledged to make our stand against such innate corruption.'

'Of course.'

'And we succeeded. The vessel of the Alchemaitres' evil, the Godhead as they dared to call it, was shattered. We disguised the broken shards and cast them back into the dark fog of time.'

'Because you couldn't destroy them totally yourselves, could you?' smirked the Master.

'No, sir. That's true. Even in pieces, the Godhead itself resisted. So each separate shard was hurled at random back into the past. With time ending, there was nowhere else for us to hide them.'

'And you got the short straw, Wainwright,' he observed. 'You had to come back in time to guard the Core.'

She rose from her seat and moved towards the high window. A squall of rain was dashing against the glass. The rippled light marbled her stony face with tears that her old eyes were too dry to weep. 'Only one volunteer was needed. The other Ministers were doomed to stay and face oblivion. It was a small price to pay for the safety of all Creation. All the other fragments are irretrievable, thank heavens. So you're wasting your time here, Mr Domini. It's time you left Chicago . . . and this planet.'

'Laudable,' exclaimed the Master. 'How reassuring to know that our morals are so entirely safe in your hands. Of course, there is one flaw in your arguments, my dear.' He was already at her shoulder, whispering his taunts like a lover whispers forbidden desires. 'Do you know why I've come? I think perhaps you do. You should be terrified – because I, the Master, have committed the utmost crime. Something you'd never have dared.' He fingered the braiding on the back of her dress. 'I've gathered your forbidden, *irretrievable* fragments and they're mine to do with as I will.'

She remained still, only inclining her head with the slightest movement towards him. Her voice came deep with suggestion. 'Is that what you want? The dominion of your will over everything . . . to the extinction of all else? Only *your* creations? Could you bear to be so alone?'

'I've been alone forever,' he murmured. 'Yes, I could bear it. It's what I've always wanted!' He let his gloved hand slide slowly up towards her throat. 'Isn't that what anyone wants? Isn't that why you stole my ship from me?'

'What?' She shuddered and pulled away. 'You are pitifully deluded, sir. Mercy on it, we're all deluded!' She turned accusingly on the display cabinet and its innocuous occupant. 'This is some trick of the Core. It's still powerful, for all the strictures on its form, but it has no morality. It gets up to all sorts of tricks.'

'Wainwright, I warn you, everything I tell you is true.'

She had gone as pale as a cave-eel. Again she touched the silver armilla. 'No. It's inconceivable. The act of uniting the shards – that would be a heinous, monstrous crime, unmatched in all history.'

The Master's breast swelled with pride. 'Why, thank you, Minister.'

'You would place the whole of Creation in unimaginable danger.'

'It's already done. It's under my control. Nothing will happen until I wish it.' His voice lowered. 'Or you advise me.'

To his intense annoyance, she ignored him. Instead, she walked towards Margie, who was skulking by the door. 'And what have you seen, my dear?' she said.

'She knows nothing,' interrupted the Master.

'Thank you, Mr Domini,' snapped Wainwright. 'The girl can speak for herself. You'd be surprised what humans pick up on.'

'Margie,' the Master instructed, 'you know nothing.' But he saw to his disgust that Margie was gazing blankly into the old harridan's eyes, in a way that she'd never done for him.

'What did I see?' she said. 'I'll tell you what I saw. It was all crazy, like some movie, only real. Jeez, there was this big kind of ancient ruin, you know? Did you ever see *Intolerance*? Well like that, but all burned out. And some guy, real ugly like a big blue skink in a bath-robe . . .'

The Master tried to move towards Margie, but an invisible force turned the air like treacle in front of him. 'Rubbish,' he scoffed. 'The girl's demented. These are fantasies!'

'Quiet, Mr Domini,' insisted Wainwright.

Margie's babble was unabated. 'And then there was this big light in the sky, like a shooting star. And it flew in and exploded all around us . . .'

Wainwright rounded on the Master. He felt her rage hit him like a wave. 'You were lying! You foolish, ignorant man, you've unleashed the Godhead's elemental energy, but without the Thought Core it'll run wild. Out of control. It'll cause untold devastation!'

The Master pulled his gun. 'Then give me the Core, you self-righteous old besom.'

'Never!' she cried. 'Never to such as you!'

'Only I can tame your rogue god now! Give it to me!'

Wainwright faced him defiantly and he flinched before her. 'This is the Core's work,' she accused. 'It never relents in its attempts to break free. It's seen you here often enough, Mr Domini. And the girl.'

'The girl?' he said, staring at Margie.

'Didn't she tell you?' Wainwright went on. 'She was coming here long before you appeared. Once the Core knew you had the shards, it probably sent her to find you. It was just waiting. The Core's stolen your ship. And sooner or later it'll bring the rest of its power here.'

'My dear Minister . . .'

'No, don't try to tempt me, Mr Domini. Devils always come in the most persuasive of forms. Yet I must forgive you. We've all been used. But the Core will never be released while I live.'

The Master's lips tightened with anger. He pulled the trigger, but there was no shot. He gave a yelp as an invisible force snatched away the Colt and flung it across the room.

Wainwright released a deep breath. 'Now crawl away, Mr Domini. Go and wait for the doom you've brought on us all. And may Time have mercy on your soul.'

The familiar fizz of an isotronic weapon sang out. Wainwright was held in a purple glow. Her arms flung themselves wide. Her body and clothes shrank before the Master's eyes, as if she were fading into the distance while still standing on the spot. Her doll-like form crumpled on to the stone flags of the museum. The silver armilla clattered down, spinning like a hoop beside the shrunken body.

Margie held a tubular black gun in her hand. It was the Master's tissue-compression eliminator.

'Where did you get that?' he hissed.

'In your *garage*,' she said coldly, 'before it left.'

He shot a glance at the display cabinet. The Flagstaff Tektite sat there, so innocuous in appearance, mocking him. He waited for it to explode out.

'Wainwright was the key that held the Godhead in check,' said Margie. 'It'll take a while for the Time Brace to unravel. But thank you for showing the way.'

The Master made a sudden dive for the silver armilla. He collided with a kick to the face from Margie's shoe. As he rolled across the floor clutching his jaw, he heard the doors crash open and the sound of many footsteps.

A something prodded him in the back.

'Okay, palsy,' said a rough voice. 'Let's get moving.'

Several pairs of hands pulled him up, tearing the seams of his jacket. A squat face worthy of an accountant hove into view. The Master winced. 'Good afternoon, Mr Clementi,' he said, surrounded by enough hoods to make a jazz band.

Joe Clementi, pudgy in a cream suit and fedora, and sweating like a warm ham. 'Not good for you, Dook. You've been fouling my patch for too long.'

'*Your* patch? Forgive me, I thought you were obeying orders from higher up. But then Mr Capone is always away in Miami when there's dirty work to be done, isn't he? How very convenient.'

A fist struck him across the mouth. 'Finish him off outside,' muttered Clementi.

'Mr Clementi,' choked the Master through swelling lips, 'a discerning man like you would never throw away such a golden opportunity.'

'Don't trust him, Joe,' called Margie.

Clementi wiped his damp neck with his black handkerchief. 'I don't take no orders from dime-a-time dames either, sweetheart.'

'Suit yourself.' She was standing beside the tektite display cabinet, toying carelessly with the discarded armilla. 'It doesn't bother me what you do with him.'

'Be it on your own head then,' observed the Master, and fixed Clementi with his eyes. 'But just think what I could offer you.'

Joe Clementi didn't budge.

'A man like you is wasted as one of Capone's puppets.' The Master honeyed his voice, the way he'd done with a thousand victims before. But his eyes did the talking. 'Do you think Capone will last for long? I give him a couple of years at the most. But you're different, Joe. Listen to me and you'll find more power than you've ever dreamed of. The whole of America at your feet. Money, women . . . clothes. Just listen to me, Joe Clementi. Just listen . . . And do what I tell you . . . '

He faltered and turned to see Margie laughing quietly. When he looked at the tektite, he could feel pressure aching on the inside of his skull. His eyes were talking to themselves. It was going nowhere. His mesmeric power was dead.

'Take him outside and shoot him,' said Clementi.

The hoods grabbed at the Master's arms, but he yanked himself free. He threw himself at Clementi, barrelling him towards Margie. All three of them keeled over and the girl struck her head against the cabinet.

The Master was up immediately, overturning another display case in an explosion of splintering glass and wood. His pursuers were no match for his agility. He was half way down the stairs before they had even reached the gallery door.

The rain fell in a deluge outside, hiding the ground under knee-high spray. The Master stopped, leaning gratefully against the huge statue of Lincoln. Clementi was no fool; another of his hoods was sitting in the Master's Buick.

The Master ducked down the side steps and headed out through the downpour into a park. Water ran from the brim of his hat, trickling inside his collar. Hearts pounding, he stumbled blindly through the mud and the rain-bent bushes. Havuri-sss-Cazcim had cursed him – it didn't matter, he'd been cursed from birth. A Minister of Grace had forgiven him – that was worse, he didn't want anyone's prayers. As bad as enduring one of the

Doctor's sanctimonious lectures. He had no empire, no power and no TARDIS in which to escape. Soon (how soon?) his stolen ship would return, bringing Armageddon with it.

At last, he reached the far side of the park. He clung to the railings, gulping in the saturated air. His energy seemed to leech away. The rain fell like a torrent of needles. Drenched, he stumbled out of the park and along a deserted sidewalk. The pressure inside his head was merciless. Lines of accusing grey tenements loomed on either side of the street. Fire-escapes zig-zagged up the buildings like iron lightning. He had started to shiver. This would never have happened to the Doctor. The Doctor would have brought an umbrella.

He leaned against the line of railings in front of a large building. He still had money. Thirty dollars stolen from a crooked policeman. Somehow he would find a way out. He heard foot-steps splashing behind him. A sharp pain exploded on the back of his head, outdoing the continuous drumming on the inside. He was shoved against the railings as rough hands worked through his pockets. He felt the wallet go, and the watch. Then a black wave of nausea broke over him. As the thief ran off into the night, the Master sprawled across a set of steps and lay unconscious in the downpour, one hand still clutching the silver armilla like a dead man clutches a straw.

The candle would not light. Its blackened wick stayed obstinately cold, despite the Master's concentration. It was an old trick – thinking a candle alight: the sort of test that a Gallifreyan adept in the telegnostic disciplines tries out behind the skimmer sheds after lectures. For now, like every other discipline, it played tag with his aching head. Nothing was certain. He turned away from the altar, deciding to leave the candles alone for fear of upsetting Father Sherrin. He shivered and trudged out of the chapel, back to the dormitory and bed, where he lay brooding silently on his headache for another hour.

The other residents of the Mission Hall kept clear of him. He

flattered himself that they were frightened. Father Sherrin let him
stay, partly from curiosity but mainly because he made better
soup than anyone else who'd ever found his way into the place.
The miracle of the turnip and two carrots, the Father called it, and
turned a blind eye to, or just never noticed, the missing bottle of
communion wine.

'I've heard of babies left on doorsteps,' the priest had said, 'but
you're altogether a different sort of gift, my friend. I'm most
grateful nonetheless. Something tells me you must be a devout
man, though to what I'm not sure. A vow of silence needs great
certainty of faith to maintain.'

Certainty! The Master rolled over on his lumpy mattress and
pulled the blanket over his head. In the little tent of rough wool,
he turned the armilla over and over in his fingers. No words for
four days now. Just an emptying of the mind. That was the easy
part of the discipline.

*And the adept shall perform simple tasks of kindness for his
fellows.*

So he made soup and thought endless mantras as he stirred the
huge pot. But nothing came clear. No sign that he was hunted. No
sign of his stolen TARDIS or wallet or watch. No end to the
nagging pain in his head that came from a lump of rock that
thought it was God that lay in a dusty museum. No sense at all.

Turn the silver armilla. Stir the greasy pot. Too long. The more
he looked, the less he saw. Nothing was clear.

Maybe the soup was wrong. Maybe if he made consommé.

At seven o'clock, after vespers, Father Sherrin bustled in, big
as a quarter-back, and sat on the end of the Master's mattress. His
avuncular face was tired, and when he spread his huge hands they
were red and blistered. He wanted to talk, as if his silent guest was
some sort of confessor.

'I had to conduct the strangest funeral today. A baby's death
is always the hardest to swallow, but this was mightily strange as
well. The whole thing was arranged by some smart-talking
lawyer. No details; I was just told to be there. I didn't see the little

one myself, but she was laid in a coffin no bigger than a cigar box, and I'd dug a grave the usual size. It was enough to break your heart. She couldn't have been more than a few days old. Born too soon, I suppose. There was only one pall-bearer needed, which matched the family. Just the mother, you see. A pretty girl with blonde hair and a skirt that would have labelled her a Jezebel in less sombre circumstances. Probably in disgrace, I thought. But then there's dark and light in all of us. We all have shadows.

'So after the burial, up on a part of the cemetery reserved for the wealthiest of Chicago's fine citizens, I offered her my condolences. She stared at me. I've never seen such cold grey eyes – they chilled me right through. And then she said, "Who's crying? This is where the wedding party starts." Then she walked away through the gravestones as if she was off to some speakeasy.

'I filled in the cavernous grave, covered up that little body, and came home. The strange thing is, she reminded me of you. Now don't be insulted. She was just someone else with great determination. Do you think I should find out more? No, of course you can't answer, and I shouldn't tempt you. The child's name was Grace . . . Grace Wainwright, like the museum. Though there's no family of that name round here.'

His massive shoulders heaved with a sigh. 'Thank you for listening, my friend. And now I'm hungry. What's the soup today? Turnip and carrot again? Well, bless you for that.'

The Master managed to contort his mouth into a smile of gratitude. He pulled an apron over the threadbare clothes that the priest had given him. His own clothes, Dook Domini's wide-shouldered suit, had been so caked with mud that not even a pig would wallow in them. He got on with doling out soup to the line of half-starved bums, privately cursing any who dared to show an ounce of gratitude, convincing himself that he was helping others only to help himself. He realized he was scrutinizing every face. Just as long as no one he knew came along and witnessed his ignominy.

So Margery Stokes was still waiting. Too bad, Margie. She'd

got too close – he didn't like anyone that close. He would exact recompense for that. Soon the energy of the Godhead shards would arrive from Blue Profundis in his stolen TARDIS. He must control it before it reached the Flagstaff Tektite. But they could never unite – not without Wainwright's power source. For want of a ring, the wedding would be off.

The Master touched the silver armilla in his pocket – an elegant piece of technology he could not quite analyse.

The soup queue had gone, so he left the washing-up to lesser mortals. His headache had cooled a little and he felt some of his strength returning. He glanced in a cracked mirror and was startled by the reflection that stared back. It was a far more vigorous man than he had expected. The skin had a bloom and the hair a gloss. He was encouraged. Strange, because he hadn't felt like the younger man he saw. He'd felt hollow, burned out, with eyes heavy like lead shot. In the mirror, his eyes burned fierce and bright; penetrating his mind; telling him to get a grip. He felt his hunched shoulders broaden again and his tight breathing expand. He was positively satanic. The eyes spoke to him, filling him with certainty:

You can claim what is yours by right. Months of meticulous preparation must not be thrown away. You have worked for this; unlike that wretched Doctor, who can walk unprepared into any situation, cause havoc in five minutes flat, accuse you of being jealous and still find time to deliver a boring lecture on the importance of morality. Not this time. You can still snatch triumph from the jaws of disaster. You have the armilla already. So go and claim what is rightfully yours.

You are the Master.

He pulled on someone else's coat and slipped outside for the first time in four days. In the dark alley at the side of the Mission Hall he kicked a street urchin and felt even better. Then he stole a car and went to the garage. It was deserted and boarded up. Hamilton had either fled with his rusty still or made a one-way trip to Lake Michigan. Next he drove to the Imperial. Two of

Clementi's hoods were on the front door. When he tried the back entrance, an ugly-looking new chef, fingering a heavy cleaver, summoned the kitchen *ragazzi* and had the 'feelthy scrouncher' thrown out.

He was considering either visiting Police Chief Mulligan or burning down the Imperial out of spite, when he heard a familiar engine. His own Buick, headlamps like baleful eyes, had pulled up at the hotel front with a couple of Portsmouths behind. Sam Kulisa was driving. Moments later, Margie emerged from the brightly lit foyer in a new, powder-blue outfit and cloche hat. Joe Clementi and a phalanx of his heavies trotted after her like poodles. She stopped suddenly at the car and stared slowly along the length of the dark street. The Master ducked back behind an ash can. Then she climbed into his Buick and the cortege drove north towards the museum.

The Master climbed into his stolen car and followed. In the rear-view mirror, he caught his eyes again, bright with determination. He left the car a little way from the museum and approached the building through the moonlit park. He could feel the pressure growing in his head, a certainty that he was being searched for, even summoned. Clementi's two hoods, muscle-bound as Ogrons and not half as handsome, stood either side of the Lincoln statue. Both were touting machine guns. The Master skirted the building until he recognized the correct first-floor window. He shinned up a drainpipe and peered cautiously in.

There were no lights inside. He could just make out a cluster of shadowy people in the gloom, but his own moonlit reflection kept getting in the way. So bright and clear, he was a silver figure in a real world; through the glass, not on it; staring back out at himself with blazing, irresistible eyes. His own malevolence gave him a thrill of excitement.

The eyes said: *This is your right. Come in and take your power. You have the armilla. Come in. We are waiting. You are the Master.*

Behind the reflection, the figures inside were slowly emerging into the angular pool of moonlight. Margie and Kulisa and Clementi and his mob. All facing him, waiting to applaud.

Come on in, the eyes insisted. *Stop wasting time. Bring the armilla.*

'I will obey,' he intoned. He was vaguely aware of another light reflected in the glass. Like a fierce star approaching in the night sky.

But the eyes drew him back. *Now. Do it now, Dook Domini. Give me the armilla. Obey me. I am the Master!*

He could not break from the stare. 'I . . . will . . . obey,' he was repeating. The new star was casting light brighter than the moon. It crackled like frost in the sky overhead. Steadying himself with one hand, he reached into his pocket with the other. He fumbled with empty fingers. The armilla wasn't there.

Give me the armilla. I need it now. Obey me!

Hands on the inside were forcing open the window.

The drainpipe juddered and the Master lost his grip on the sill. He snatched at the walls to save himself, clinging to the bricks above the drop. The shock cleared his head. The reflection had vanished. Wainwright's words came back to him: *The Thought Core gets up to all sorts of tricks.*

Hands lit by the fierce new star, reached through the open window for him. Margie's face appeared. 'Oh no,' he warned. 'Not for you!'

He kicked at the wall, and the drainpipe tore away, swinging wildly. He went with it, dropping clear to the ground like a cat.

There were shouts of anger from the window. He ignored them, staring up at the new star. It hovered, swaying slightly in the sky. Waiting to swoop like a hawk. He cursed to himself. He was looking at his stolen, possessed TARDIS.

Margie was leaning out of the window. 'Get after him!' she yelled. Behind her, there was a blue flickering glow from the room.

The star TARDIS was starting to weave back and forth in the air. The Master turned and ran, forcing his way through the bushes. He heard a crack, and a bolt of lightning struck at the terrace close by. He turned and saw another bolt strike further off. A group of Clementi's men rounded the side of the museum.

'That way!' Margie yelled, pointing from the window. The Master ducked as machine gun fire raked the bushes. The hoods were heading towards him, but a fresh barrage of lightning played down amongst them. Two men exploded in their suits. The others froze, unable to move for fear of being fried.

The Master began to laugh. The energy that had invaded his ship was blazing away at random. A mass of instincts out of control. Thoughtless. A rogue god, unable to unite with the guidance of the Thought Core. But *he* would control it. It would answer to him, once he had retrieved Wainwright's armilla from inside the lumpy mattress where he had tucked it.

Fresh bolts of lightning from the star TARDIS exploded against the museum walls. The Master seized his moment and ran for the car.

He drove without headlights for the Mission Hall. Let devastation rule. He didn't care if it ran amok across every planet in the Sol 3 system. An example with which to ransom the rest of the complacent Universe. All he needed was the armilla. And to know how it worked.

Mercury! He yelled in triumph, wildly swerving the car onto the sidewalk. The armilla was made of a hard mercury compound, not silver at all. That was how Wainwright might control the shards. Mercury acted as the interface between the rival forces of thought and energy that made up the Godhead. The engines of his own TARDIS ran on the same principle.

When he reached the Mission Hall, he saw an orange glow rising over the buildings, competing with the distant lightning that flickered in the clear night sky. The Wainwright Museum must be blazing by now.

It was late. A few candles burned in front of a plaster icon of St Augustine, otherwise the chapel was empty and dark. The Master ran silently through and up the back stairs to the moonlit dormitory. He picked his way between the sleeping men until he reached his own mattress. There was a slit that he had cut near the top. He fumbled inside and pulled out the armilla. It was warm and curiously light in his hand. When he held it up, he saw little metallic beads glinting along its rim. The armilla was sweating mercury.

He wrapped the object carefully in a piece of rag and began to cast about for a container in which to catch the liquid metal. Close by, one of the dark figures sat up and snarled a warning. The Master left and went down to the chapel.

The forces controlled by the tektite core would be on his trail already. Margie or Clementi or Capone's thugs – thugs he had used himself – or maybe something much worse. He must be ready for that.

So let them come. Once when he'd been a student, when his character was formed on the playing fields of Gallifrey, he'd seen a wedding flight of scissor bugs. Clouds of winged males darkening the sky; thousands desperate to couple with the nest's single queen. The mating frenzy had lasted a whole day, the filthy things tangling in his hair and crawling into his nostrils, until all the failed lovers had died of exhaustion or frustration. And all the time, he was smug in the knowledge that the queen was trapped in a jelly jar in his pocket.

He still needed a container and began to hunt through the cold cavern of the chapel. At the foot of the icon of St Augustine was a small cupboard. He forced the door. Inside, placed reverently on a couch of decaying velvet, lay a glass phial. It was mounted on silver clasps with a silver chain running from either end. It was half filled with water. The collected tears of the holy saint.

The Master unwound one of the clasps and flicked the liquid across the stone flags. A massive bible rested on a lectern nearby. He tore out a page, folded it into a funnel shape and rested the tip on the open phial. Then he unwrapped the armilla and laid it across the top of the funnel. The object was disintegrating. He watched the mirror droplets of mercury run down the paper and collect in the base of the phial. A few spilt globules ran as if they had thoughts of their own, to rejoin the liquid mass. The armilla was trying to escape. 'So you're being summoned too,' he muttered aloud. 'Well, we'll see about that.'

He heard a cough behind him and turned to see Father Sherrin looming amongst the rows of pews.

'Well, it's a pity about your vow,' said the priest. 'You were doing so well with it. To tell the truth, I hadn't expected you back.'

The Master eyed him warily. 'I'm sorry about your phial, Father,' he said. 'And the book.'

'Don't apologize. St Augustine's tears were a fraud anyway. Just tap water. But people have to believe in something.' He made his way closer. 'I was just reading about Augustine here. He preached about predestination and the efficacy of grace. *Whom He did predestinate, them also He called.* Romans, Chapter 8, verse 30. It's the page you tore out.'

'I believe that the flow of time can be moulded,' the Master said, and he smiled. 'Your god is far too rigid and old-fashioned for me to believe in.'

Father Sherrin raised a quizzical eyebrow. 'And are you still as charming with a gun in your hand?' He dipped into his pocket and produced the Master's watch. 'I found this when I found you. I imagine it was discarded by the thief. I've had it in safe keeping.'

The Master moved nearer. 'Father, how can I thank you? I thought it was lost. What can I offer you in exchange? Money for the Mission Hall?'

'What money, my friend? You don't have two cents to your name, whatever that is . . . or was. From the cut of your clothes I reckoned you'd fallen a long way, but don't assume that I want anything from you. I don't want your money. I'd say this is fair exchange for what you've had already.'

The Master snatched at the watch, but it was pulled clear. His eyes burned with hate for an instant, then he said smoothly, 'Oh come now, Father. You must need something. Just have a little faith in me.'

Sherrin sat and leaned back in the rough-hewn pew. 'I never expected to be tempted in so literal a way.'

'By the Devil himself? Oh really, Father.'

'The Devil fell a long way when he fell from grace. He wanted to be God and, in his envy, he's always looking for ways to pull the world down with him.'

'I've been called that a lot lately. I should be flattered. But for all you know Father, the Devil may have repented.'

'Oh, dear. If that's the case, I could be out of business. Light and dark again, you see. But I won't worry just yet, *Mr Domini*. You see, two of the men in the dormitory recognized you.'

'What shall I do? Make a confession?'

'Dook Domini? What sort of name is that?'

'An amusing one, I thought. The Duke of Dominoes is the trump card in an old Wallarian game of chance. It beats all other suits. Winner takes all.'

'There's certainly a lot of blood on your hands, Dook.'

The Master began to laugh. 'My dear Father Sherrin, all that gnawing guilt. It's the spring and foundation of your whole belief.'

'Guilt has a twin brother,' answered the priest. 'And his name is Compassion.'

'Weakness,' condemned the Master.

Father Sherrin stood and held out the watch. 'Take it anyway. You still make the best soup I ever tasted. So bless you for that.' He smiled as he dabbed out the sign of the cross in the air over the Master. 'Light and dark. Good and bad in everything.'

Relieved of the timepiece, he turned and began to snuff out the candles with his fingers. '*In nomine Domini, et filii et spiritus sancti.*'

The Master pocketed the watch. Then he silently lifted the heavy bible from the lectern and brought it down on Father Sherrin's head.

He stepped over the body and peered in the golden candle

gloom at the armilla. It was like an emptied husk. All the mercury had drained down, spilling out over the top of the phial. In fact it was flowing out like a metallic amoeba, all in one living cell across the velvet, trying to answer its summons.

The Master scooped it back with his hands, dribbling as much of the living fluid as he could through his fingers and into the phial. He screwed the lid back on, trapping perhaps half the mercury in the holy relic. On the stone floor, isolated globules ran to and fro around the priest's body, searching to join with others and complete their journey.

The wail of a police siren echoed in the distance, followed by a loud crash of falling masonry from somewhere much closer.

The Master blew out the other candles and moved to the window. He saw several figures run past. They ran blindly – in terror. Further up the street, something was moving. Something huge.

The moonlight sharpened its features white and black as it passed between the buildings. He could feel the tremors of its footfall. Fifteen foot high, loping slowly along as it searched, folds rippling in its stone clothes, the statue of Abraham Lincoln.

'What nonsense,' the Master complained aloud. 'It doesn't look a bit like me!'

The statue had cast aside the stone child it had carried, but on its raised arm sat a figure. Margie clung to her perch with one hand, apparently unperturbed. Something flickered blue in her other hand. The Master guessed it was the tektite.

An entourage of limousines brought up the rear. A slow cortege looking for a funeral. Clementi and his thugs were plainly under new management.

Suddenly a blaze of light soared in over the buildings. The star TARDIS was following too, waiting its chance like day follows night or alligators follow boats.

The Master moved quickly. With the silver phial in his pocket, he headed up the back stairs. He avoided the dormitory and slipped into the darkened kitchen. He hid the phial in a metal coffee pot and went back down to the chapel.

The cold light from car headlamps and a rogue god in the sky glared in through the tall windows. The Master straightened his threadbare collar and heaved open the heavy door.

Margie stood in the street at the foot of the steps. Her face was illuminated by a match held by Joe Clementi as he lit up a Lucky Strike for her. The hoods surrounded her in a shadowy wall. Behind them, the statue stared down with blank eyes and an immovable smile in its stone beard. The tektite flickered blue in its huge palm.

'Margie,' called the Master as he stepped into the glare. 'You took your time. I see you have new disciples.'

She blew a cloud of smoke. 'Didn't you read the news, Dook? Al Capone was booked for tax evasion. It's all over *The Investigator*.'

'So soon? Well, how are the mighty fallen?'

'I guess you'd know all about that.'

He eyed the weaving star overhead and the waiting colossus below. 'What do you want, Margie? I'm surprised the two halves of our errant Godhead haven't made a connection yet.'

She mounted a couple of steps. 'They're not complete, Dook.'

He raised a calculated laugh. 'Oh, really? You know I can't imagine why that should be.'

'The final shard is missing.'

'You mean the mercury bracelet?'

'No. That'll come when it's called.'

The Master tensed slightly. 'What then? There's nothing else. I gathered all the parts myself.'

Margie blew another self-satisfied cloud of smoke. 'The failsafe, sweetie.'

'What failsafe?'

'It needs someone's mind to hold the Thought Core and the Energy Focus in check. Like a kind of beef sandwich.'

'Ah. It's those over-zealous, Sunday School busybodies, the Ministers of Grace. They've added it to the system. They've imposed a morality, just in case. They're no better than the Alchemaitres.'

'Nuts to them. That's why the Core got you to gather the shards.'

'Me?' he said, incredulous. 'It wants *my* mind?'

'Sure it does. You're the smartest, Dook. I always knew that.'

'You'll give me that power? And I'll still be aware? In control? That'll make me a God.'

He paused. Her smile and the statue's implacable gaze worried him. It was too easy. 'No,' he said. 'On my terms, not yours.'

The lamplight caught her eyes. 'Dook, you're so goddam pig-headed. You're the only one round here with the brains. We're all real dummies next to you. So give it all you got!'

'Maybe,' he said. 'Yes. You're right, of course. Yes, when will I ever get another chance!'

A raucous shout broke their mutual stare. 'Stay where you are! Nobody move! You're surrounded!'

The Master knew the voice. He stared around wildly as Margie and the hoods ducked for cover behind the cars. Along the street, he made out the darting shapes of policemen. 'You Keystone Cop idiots,' he muttered, and then yelled, 'Chief Mulligan, call off your men. It's me. Remember? We had an agreement.' The street threw a cold silence back at him, so he continued, mellowing his raised voice. 'Back them off, Chief. Remember what I told you. It's all under control now. Obey me.'

He sensed the shape and colour of Mulligan's mind – tangled strings of blue-grey thought. He smiled at last, grasping the returned certainty in his own mind. *Come here, Mulligan*, he projected.

Footsteps stumbled in their own echo. He saw the dark shape of the Police Chief wandering into the centre of the street. Mulligan was muttering and shaking his head as if a crane fly was loose inside it. He stopped, looked straight ahead and called, 'Master?'

There was a crunching thud as the huge statue moved forward. Mulligan stumbled back in shock, raising the Colt at his side. It spat fire. Bullets pinged off the living stone. The statue grasped Mulligan in one huge fist and flung him the length of the street.

The Master ran for the safety of the Hall door. A spray of bullets zinged around him. From the street below, he heard the rattle of machine guns as Clementi's hoods took on the Chicago Police Department. As he heaved the door shut, he saw the statue swing slowly round towards him, its wide blank eyes filled with the same light that burned from the tektite in its hand.

The Master knew he was a marked man. In his head, he heard the voice, half Margie's, half Wainwright's, that said: *You took a vow of silence. Let that continue. You are needed.*

The Master choked as an invisible fist seized his throat. His tongue cracked dry. He could not speak. He saw the massive figure pick up a car in its path and toss it aside like a toy. Then he slammed the door and threw every bolt he could see. The chapel floor trembled with approaching footfalls.

He turned and ran as the door and most of the wall surrounding it smashed in. The statue forced its way through the gap, every movement flowing like a slow dancer, its head casting back and forth as it hunted.

The Master dodged into an alcove, unable to reach the back stairs without being seen. He groped in his pocket for the watch.

With a crash, the statue's hand lunged around the corner at him. It scraped against stone as the Master somersaulted away and ran between the pews, amazed at his own agility. The statue ignored the obstacles, crunching the pews to matchwood with its stone feet. The tektite burned fierce blue in its other hand.

The Master reached the pulpit and edged into the shadowy gap behind the steps. His fingers jabbed at the watch's task settings, activating a buzzing alarm.

That brought the statue straight to him.

He feverishly adjusted the settings, forcing the tone of the alarm into a higher and higher screech. Stone fingers grappled through the gap, unable to reach him. He covered his ears as the alarm shrieked even higher.

The chapel windows shattered in a glittering unified torrent of glass. Frustrated, the statue grasped the pulpit and wrenched the whole thing out of the floor. The Master was thrown down, trapped in a corner as the huge hand snatched him up.

He squirmed in its grasp, unable to yell or scream. With a final effort, he forced the screeching alarm against the stone sleeve. Dust began to plume from the statue. Its movement juddered and stopped. The head jerked forward as if it wanted to bite him, but the smiling mouth stayed shut. The Master kept pressing the watch against the arm.

Hairline cracks ran amok across the surface of the colossus. It froze. The giant cracked across and tumbled to the ground in a shower of stone splinters.

Dust was drizzling from the Hall walls. The Master fell to the floor, choking. So deaf, he could hardly hear the resonating alarm. He smacked it off and couldn't hear the gun battle outside either.

The tektite lay flickering in the dust. He reached for it, but an elegantly manicured hand snatched it up first. Margie stood over him. A blaze of light erupted through the hole where the door had been. The star TARDIS hovered into the Mission Hall.

The Master pulled back, turned and ran for the stairs. Only one thought drove him. Get the mercury link before they do. As he reached the top, he felt the fizz of a lightning bolt. As he entered the kitchen, it exploded behind him. The whole wall caved in and he was under it as it fell.

He was lying under wooden beams with a ceiling of plaster only inches above him. He pushed at it and started to force it up. Then he heard the sound. Or thought he heard it. A wheezing-grating sound – all too horribly familiar. And suddenly there was a great weight on top of the fallen wall which pinioned him down. He gagged on the dust that swirled around him, incapable of moving a muscle.

He felt footsteps clambering above him, but could see only a small section of the floor through a gap in the rubble. He tried to call out, but his voice had been stolen.

He strained to hear more, with half-deaf ears. 'Down here, Sarah Jane,' a deep voice was saying, but he did not recognize it.

A pair of scuffed brown brogues dropped into view accompanied by tweed turn-ups and the trailing ends of what looked like a long striped scarf. Then a woman's feet in lightweight canvas deck shoes joined the brogues.

'Where do we start then?' she was saying in a cultured English accent. 'You don't really imagine you're going to find any here, do you? It looks as if we're in the middle of a war zone.'

'We have to find some, Sarah. The TARDIS won't go anywhere without it.'

'Couldn't you have given them something else? I mean, I know you were rescuing me, but . . .'

'Pirates can be very fussy when it comes to swapsies. But those Grakinese Corsairs have a special affinity with mercury. They're insecure old space-dogs at heart and mercury reminds them of the mirrored swamps of their home planet. Anyway, it was either the fluid links or you.'

'Thank you, Doctor,' she said with sickening affection, and the Master's right heart missed several beats. His hearing was back with a crunch. *No*, he thought. *No*!

This was his worst nightmare: not just the Doctor, but a *new* Doctor. And he was interfering just like the old ones had always done. The feet moved away. There was no movement from the chapel below. What was happening down there? Why did no one come?

'What's that knocking?' said Sarah Jane. 'There's something inside this coffee pot.'

'Hot coffee should never be allowed to boil.'

'It's cold,' she said.

There was a clunk of metal, after which she added, 'Well?'

'Well, well,' observed the Doctor.

The Master heard the tinkling of a silver chain.

'I don't believe it,' the young woman exclaimed. 'I mean, it is, isn't it? I mean, mercury?'

'Yes.'

'But that's incredible. Like getting your wish come true.'

'Coincidence? Providence, Sarah?'

'Funny place to put it. Maybe someone up there has a sense of humour.'

He paused. 'Perhaps.' The plaster crunched above the Master, releasing another shower of dust. *Don't go*, he thought. *Don't leave me! Doctor!*

'Wait for me,' called Sarah. 'What about this place?'

'Just a quick test flight,' answered the disappearing voice. 'I can't stop and solve every problem I come across.'

A door slammed. The Master lay sweating for a few seconds. Then the grating of the TARDIS engines started, badly in need of a service, and faded into nothing.

The weight above relented. The Master angrily pushed against the plaster and forced a way out of his tomb.

Amid the chaos of the kitchen sat the empty coffee pot. The Master stood shaking, laughing aloud at his absurd defeat. 'Doctor! You ignorant, thieving buffoon!' He wanted to blast the whole planet to dust. And then he realized that the grip on his larynx had relaxed.

From downstairs, he heard the crackle of energy. He cleared the stairs in two leaps. The twin forces of the Godhead were still available. He would take them and unite them by force of his own will. None other.

He faltered at the doorway to the chapel. Margie stood in the central aisle holding aloft the blue blazing tektite. Opposite her hovered the burning star that was his own TARDIS. Shafts of light played in the dusty air. Father Sherrin's body was nowhere to be seen. The battle outside had stopped. The place swam in a reverential silence. Both the police and Clementi's outfit were filing in through the rent in the wall. The Hall's resident bums had already descended from the dormitory. They were all taking their places ranged along the surviving pews, congregating to witness the imminent epiphany. The Master stepped into the open chapel, ready to claim his rightful destiny.

He stopped. A heavily built figure was hauling itself up from the floor between the elemental forces.

Father Sherrin's countenance gleamed with silver. The left-over mercury from the floor had formed a mask across the priest's face. It carried him with it. The mask smiled when it saw the Master.

'Stop!' the Master shouted. 'That is my right! I should be God!' He ran towards the group, but a blaze of cold fire forced him back. 'No!'

Margie slowly, even reluctantly, let go of the tektite. It hovered in the air where she left it. A blue dwarf with a white giant. Tears were running down her face.

Streamers of light played between the tektite and the star TARDIS. Father Sherrin was rising gently in the effulgent web.

'Father!' shouted the Master again.

'He doesn't say a lot,' said Margie. 'It's a sort of vow of silence. Like before the talkies.'

'I'm the only one that's worthy! Not him! All of Creation should be mine!'

'You weren't here,' she said.

The lights were combining, becoming one huge radiant focus. A silver mirrored face, a new Godhead in which they all saw themselves.

'So there's light bits and there's dark bits,' said Joe Clementi. 'And then there's moonshine in a bottle.'

Sam Kulisa pushed back the brim of his hat and jiggled the eternal cigarette stub on his thin lips. 'What sort of card is this Dook of Dominoes? I never heard of that game. Sounds like a Jack of All Trades to me.'

'And Master of None,' said Chief Mulligan. His head nodded comically on its broken neck, and they all laughed out loud.

The Master ran across the chapel and scooped up an abandoned machine gun. He yanked back the bolt and pulled the trigger.

Nothing happened.

Faced with the staring congregation, he laughed again.

The Godhead began moving towards the gap in the wall.

'Looks like that's it for you then, Dookie,' said Margie.

'It's not a real God anyway!' ranted the Master. 'I could have given it *real* power! Not his sickening goodness!'

In an endless moment, he saw himself mirrored in mercury. Hatred twisted him. Cruelty gnawed at him. He was corrupt with malice. And old. Too old. Old beyond his centuries. The very engenderment of evil. And how he loved it. Revelling in its driving torture. And they were wrong anyway. The whole Universe was wrong in its self-righteous presumptions. It wouldn't end there.

'No light without shadows,' said Joe Clementi again. 'So maybe we need the dark.'

A tall grey box dissolved out of the air by the altar. The machine gun in the Master's hand became the short stubby barrel of his tissue-compression eliminator.

He nodded grimly to the Godhead, and it held his stare for long searching seconds. Then its shape roared with light. It passed through the gap in the wall and blazed away into the night sky and the Universe like a comet.

The Master drew his aching self up and walked proudly towards his restored TARDIS. The group parted to let him through.

He stopped in his ship's doorway, turned and aimed the eliminator at Margie. After a moment, he smiled coldly, the way she liked, and went inside. He had unfinished business.

Business, he might say, as usual.

Again the unearthly glow faded from Silverman's hands and the study was plunged into near-darkness. This time, I didn't bother to relight the candles.

'You know what, Silverman?' I said, as he returned the phial to the table. 'You ought to work in Hollywood. They never came up with a yarn as crazy as that one.'

My client was lost in thought. 'The Doctor, once more . . . ' he mused.

'Yes,' I agreed, 'but something doesn't add up here. His voice, Silverman: you described it as deep and booming; but that isn't what you said the first time.'

The psychic shrugged. 'The events in Chicago took place in the 1930s, obviously a number of years after those in England. A man can change a great deal in that interval of time.'

I grunted non-committally. 'And you can't say what he looked like?'

'I am sorry,' he replied, 'there is nothing more I can tell you. I have divined as much information as is possible from that particular object.'

'Well, it doesn't get us very much further,' I muttered. 'And then there's that word "TARDIS" again . . . '

We sat in silence for a few moments, then I nodded towards the table. 'We'd better try something else.'

'Very well.' Silverman flexed his bony fingers and reached down. In the dim firelight, I could just make out that he had picked up a crumpled pamphlet on which someone had sketched a strange, dwarf-like figure. He cupped it carefully in his hands, ready to start again.

The Straw that Broke the Camel's Back

Vanessa Bishop

'You . . . understand these things? I didn't know there were such organizations.' Maurice appeared dazed and uncertain, but was evidently trying hard to digest the information. Realizing this, the Doctor took one of the photocopied hymn pamphlets from the pew ledge, turned it over and, after fishing for a pen, sketched roughly on the back. He handed the finished drawing – of a slim figure with an oversized oval head and large dominating eyes – to Maurice. The old clergyman's expression told the Doctor that he was convinced. 'You'd better come through to the vicarage,' he said, his voice almost a whisper. 'We can talk properly there.'

In the dimly lit passageway outside the minister's study, a single figure peered through the crack in the door at those inside. Their conversation was clearly audible and the silent intruder began to listen intently, trying not to breathe too loudly . . .

'It's been two weeks now since it happened.' Maurice closed his eyes to visualize the scene. 'I was in the church at the time . . .'

'Our Father, who art in Heaven, hallowed be Thy name . . .' Hands gripped firmly in prayer, the Reverend Maurice Burridge began to speak the lines that had passed his lips a thousand times before. A neat, white-haired man in his late sixties, he sat, a lone hunched figure, his calming, saggy features barely visible in the darkness of the empty, silent church. 'Thy kingdom come, Thy will be done . . . ' His concentration was broken by the gunshot crack of a backfiring car. He closed his eyes again: ' . . . on Earth as it is in Heaven . . . ' There was a chill, fresh air that accentuated the church's natural stony aroma; Maurice felt it waft like a cold breath on the back of his neck. Pulling his thick woolly cardigan around him, he chastized himself for letting his mind wander. 'Give us this day our daily bread . . . ' The cardigan. Peggy had knitted it for him during her knitting fad, before she'd moved on to the pottery phase. Dear, funny Peggy. He really ought to ring her. Tomorrow . . . he would ring her tomorrow, arrange something for the weekend.

He returned to the prayer. It was the first one he had learned and, of all that he had read since, it was still the one of which he was most fond: ' . . . and forgive us our trespasses, as we forgive those who trespass against us . . . ' He squinted at the illuminated white face of his watch, which told him to his surprise that it was now morning. 'Lead us not into temptation, and deliver us from evil . . . ' His elbow caught the edge of a newly photocopied batch of pamphlets, sending three fluttering to the floor. Picking them up, he dusted off the black and white covers with the words 'Milton Bradbury Methodist Church – Favourite Hymns' Letrasetted unevenly above. Replacing the booklets on the pew ledge from which they had fallen, he reclasped his hands in a determined effort to finish his prayer.

Brightness. A sudden brightness. His eyes flashed upwards. Looking at the stained glass window, he gazed in astonishment, still mechanically mouthing the words of the prayer. A burst of light travelled across the deeply coloured glass panels, moving slowly from ruby red to emerald green to sapphire blue. 'For Thine is the kingdom, the power and the glory . . . ' The light illuminated the central crucifixion scene in a divine beauty from which Maurice could not take his eyes. Even after the light had tailed off downwards through the body of the Christ figure, he sat and gazed at the window as if in a trance. Was this it? The spiritual experience of which others had spoken, but which had always eluded him?

Suddenly he was shaken violently back to his senses; his heart leaped as the approaching car backfired again. Then there was the unmistakable sound of the wheels spinning through the rough gravel. It would not be the first time for a car to be found upon its side in such badly lit conditions. Lifting his body shakily from the pew where he sat, Maurice made his way out of the church. Peering through the darkness to the country lane that ran along the back of the church grounds, he spotted the blazing headlights. The driving was reckless, but no one hurt. His eyes followed the light until it disappeared.

Brigadier Alistair Lethbridge-Stewart sat silently in his office, elbows hunched upon the desk top and chin firmly rested against clenched knuckles, contemplating writing a report that he hoped he'd never have to file. Moments before, he had strode into the office, waiting impatiently for the phone call that would confirm his suspicions. The phone call had been received, suspicions confirmed. Now he felt confused; ideas, suggestions, accusations, all the considerations that had previously lain dormant within him, now flowed freely, prattling at him to take heed of what they had to say. Kicking back his chair, he stood up sharply. He recalled his military training: 'Rational thinking always helps you see things more clearly,' or so they'd taught him. But then he'd always been a straight thinker, right on top of everything, getting things moving. Somehow, though, he couldn't seem to apply that now.

He'd always had an understanding with the Doctor, a mutual respect. They didn't always see eye to eye, it was true, and much of the Doctor's reasoning was quite beyond him, but he had always publicly supported his eccentric scientific adviser, willingly and dutifully. So, in his eyes, he had every right to get upset at the Doctor's total reluctance to involve him in anything he did these days. He knew the Doctor liked to do things his own way, but he had never known him to behave so . . . the Brigadier tried to think of a kinder word, but only 'suspiciously' seemed to fit. It seemed that every time he wanted to speak to the Doctor, the man was rather conveniently on his way out. It was no wonder that, in a fit of pique, he had resorted to bringing in Sergeant Purvis to keep tabs on him.

To have the Doctor spied upon. It all sounded so sordid in retrospect, and he hadn't anticipated that Purvis would enjoy it so much. He would regret having to admit to that when it came to writing the report. But, at the same time, it had seemed like the only way to find out what was really going on. And now that he finally knew, he couldn't begin to take it in. His mind started to reel again. In any case, what did he actually know about the Doctor? What solid proof did he have that the scruffy little chap he'd first encountered in the London Underground was the same arrogant fellow causing him so much concern now?

The Doctor did not stand up to much examination. Things had become ridiculous and far-fetched; all this business about two hearts and coming from another planet. Fiction, total fiction, invented to add intrigue to the Doctor's character, making him an appropriately knowledgeable addition to the UNIT team. Indeed, there had been times whilst dealing with the Autons when he himself had been so busy that he hadn't had time to think rationally, and before he knew it, a complete stranger had been enrolled as a UNIT member. A complete stranger who demanded things left, right and centre, who was allowed to take liberties at every whim, and who was afforded all manner of equipment, half of which would never be seen again.

Hoax. Some elaborate hoax. Perhaps a major infiltration operation. Both of them in it together, the two Doctors, two separate people? He'd never been wholly sure about this regeneration business. There would have to be a whole ring of them to make it appear so credible and convincing: medical staff at Ashbridge Cottage Hospital, technicians, trusted members of UNIT even. An espionage plot of frightening proportions which he had, quite openly, been accommodating. He reminded himself how many times he had signed away important documents with the phrase 'With the help of Doctor John Smith,' and he felt a fool.

An agent. Working for someone else. It would explain a lot. Many of the Doctor's actions regarded by the Brigadier as 'misguided' could become clearer with a different motive. After all, he'd been perfectly willing to betray a UNIT mission to the Silurians for his own purposes. What if those purposes were power-motivated? He needed to succeed only once to impose a serious international threat. But who could his people be? He'd been heard to mumble of them. Exactly who was the Doctor working for?

The neatly printed version of Purvis's report lay taunting him from the desk. Again, he read the incriminating words:

> At first, as on previous occasions, the suspect's actions were those of a disappointed man. But his interest was drawn to an area about twenty yards from where he parked his vehicle. After five minutes of intense inspection, he returned to the car to collect a small box no bigger than a biscuit tin. This he took back to the area of interest, placed it on the grass and sat down beside it. After a further ten minutes, the suspect stood up and viewed the surrounding countryside, again failing to see me. Kneeling once more by the box, he extended an aerial of around seven feet in total. There he sat for a further hour, sometimes fiddling with the box but mostly staring at his feet, after which he dismantled the aerial, returned the box to the car and drove off. Inspection of the site has revealed nothing . . .'

The Brigadier turned the page face downwards, as if doing so would erase the words and their connotations. The Doctor was undoubtedly involved in something he wanted kept quiet and, as UNIT's scientific adviser, his conduct was no longer acceptable. Further action would have to be taken, but how to apply it? The Brigadier's thoughts tailed off as he heard his name being called. He turned abruptly to find that he and his troubles were no longer alone.

In the corner of the laboratory, Liz Shaw's frustration grew as she rattled the TARDIS door in a fervent attempt to get it open. This had become something of a habit. When alone in the lab, she would, without fail, try the doors on the off-chance that the Doctor had forgotten to lock them. She was aware that the police box acted as no ordinary cupboard – that had been made abundantly clear the day she had seen the Doctor awkwardly rolling out the machinery he referred to as 'the console'.

'What is he doing in there?' she muttered to herself, returning to the bench. She had caught the Brigadier off guard, she reflected.

'Don't you have the courtesy to knock, Miss Shaw?' he had barked at her. She had replied that she had knocked, twice, and asked if everythining was all right.

'No, Miss Shaw, everything is not all right. Please . . . sit down. I'd like to ask your opinion on a certain matter.'

Liz had been intrigued by this. The Brigadier rarely asked others' opinions, especially not a woman's. 'How has the Doctor seemed to you lately?' he had asked.

'His general wellbeing? Or . . .?'

'No, Miss Shaw, you misunderstand me,' he had interrupted brusquely. 'I'm talking about his behaviour. Would you say it's been odd . . . secretive even?'

Liz had begun to nod slowly. She was doing it now, even thinking about it. 'Yes . . . now that you come to mention it, he has been a bit secretive. No odder than usual, though; you know the Doctor.'

'I thought I did. He hasn't . . . told you anything at all that you think I should know?' He had rounded on Liz quite sharply. 'It's imperative that you tell me if he has.'

'Not a word. I'm as much in the dark as you are, Brigadier. Where he goes and what he does on these little trips of his is anyone's guess.'

'I need to know what he's up to. Try to find out, please, Miss Shaw. I'd be extremely grateful for your help. The Doctor trusts you more than anyone.' He had looked at her imploringly, trying desperately not to show his feelings and to retain the military stiff upper lip for which he was renowned. Liz felt she had left the Brigadier in the same contemplative mood as she had found him.

There was a cough.

'Can I help you?' The voice made Liz catch her breath, and she turned to see the Doctor standing in the TARDIS doorway. He could see by her expression that he had caught her by surprise, and he delighted in the awkwardness of her reaction.

'Oh . . . Doctor. You're back. I thought you were still out somewhere.'

'Evidently.' He strolled out of the TARDIS and, throwing her a deliberate glance, closed and locked the door with exaggerated movements, a performance which was to underline his awareness of her previous actions. He rounded it off with a cruel mimicry of her rattle at the TARDIS door. 'Was there something you wanted, Liz?' She had recovered her composure and now eyed him equally sharply, ignoring his question.

'Where have you been, Doctor?' He had pulled out his handkerchief and was polishing the lens of his eye-glass.

'Oh . . . out,' he replied, casually. She lowered her voice.

'The Brigadier's been asking questions.'

'Liz, the Brigadier's always asking questions.'

'No, I mean about . . . you.' The Doctor looked up sharply.

'What sort of questions? What did you tell him? I suppose he wants you to spy on me – is that it?'

Liz became exasperated. The Doctor could be exhausting sometimes, and infuriatingly accurate. 'You know me better than that, Doctor. He simply wants to know what you've been up to.' As the Doctor turned disinterestedly to walk away, she called after him, 'And, quite frankly, so do I. What are you hiding? I want to know, and I'm not budging from this spot until you tell me.'

The Doctor stopped, turned and looked at her. He looked slightly guilty, as if ashamed of saying she was doing the Brigadier's dirty work.

'All right, Liz. There is something. But I have my reasons for

not involving the Brigadier and I want you to respect them.' He
was as bad as the Brigadier – he was doing it again, putting her
in a spot. Piggy in the middle, as usual. But she'd go along with
him for the moment.

'You have my word, Doctor. So where exactly have you been
going on these little jaunts of yours?' The Doctor scratched the
back of his neck, as if contemplating where to begin.

'Well–' He was interrupted by the laboratory door swinging
open with some considerable gusto, and the Brigadier breezing
in. Liz raised her eyes to the ceiling in despair. The timing of the
man was beyond belief. He had just managed, rather successfully,
to thwart his own operation, an ideal opportunity having just
disappeared.

'I'd like a word with you, Doctor,' he began. But the Doctor
was already putting on his cloak, as though the Brigadier's arrival
were an instant trigger for his departure.

'Sorry, Brigadier. Just off out.'

'On another of your little trips, no doubt?'

The Doctor smiled sweetly. 'Little trips? Little trips? Oh
Brigadier, you have quite a talent for mind-reading. You really
ought to be in show business.'

Liz stood in the Doctor's path. 'What about our little chat?
Remember?' She tried to hint heavily at him by giving him a
variety of knowing looks, all to no avail.

'Sorry, Liz. Some other time perhaps.'

And then he was gone. Liz threw the Brigadier a look that
would have stopped many of his men in their tracks. The
Brigadier himself took it in with some bemused surprise.

'Something the matter, Miss Shaw?' he asked.

'Your timing!' she snapped, rudely. 'A few minutes more and
he would have told me everything. But oh no – you had to march
in and jeopardize the whole thing.'

The Brigadier's realization of what he had done only added to
his fury. 'I've warned you before about your tone, Miss Shaw,'
he reprimanded. 'May I remind you that I am your superior?

Regardless of your emotions, you will treat me with the respect that that position demands. Do I make myself clear?'

'Crystal!' retorted Liz, equally furious.

'Good! Then in fifteen minutes you will accompany me on a little trip of our own.'

'Really?'

'Yes, really.'

'And where, may I ask, are we going?'

'Milton Bradbury,' announced the Brigadier, 'along with the Doctor.'

The Doctor slammed his fist down on Bessie's steering wheel and never even apologized to her afterwards. He stared incredulously at the disused railway path, now littered with official UNIT signs and cordoned off with barriers of fluttering yellow tape. He directed his fury at a nearby soldier, positioned at the edge of the barrier.

'Corporal!' The young man turned to see who was addressing him and, on recognizing the Doctor, feared he was in for the worst.

'I demand to know what's going on here!'

'I'm sorry, sir, but you'll have to ask –'

'The Brigadier!' The Doctor completed the answer. 'Oh yes – no doubt he's behind all this. Of all the sneaky, under-handed . . . Is nothing sacred any more?' The sound of an engine behind the Doctor re-alerted his attention. He turned to see the Brigadier's car approaching. The UNIT soldier on whom he had vented his anger exchanged looks with another in anticipation of what was to come. The Doctor positioned himself upright, arms folded, a melodramatic stance that he used to great effect: a dramatic figure with black cape billowing as a crisp autumn breeze began to pick up. 'Very cosy,' he nodded scornfully, as both the Brigadier and Liz got out of the car. 'Very cosy indeed. I should have guessed that you wouldn't be able to keep your interfering nose out,' he accused, jabbing a finger in the Brigadier's direction. 'And Liz – I'm disappointed in you.'

'Now wait a minute –'

'I thought you were a friend – a loyal friend.'

'I will not stand here –'

'I expected more of you than this.'

'I will not stand here and be accused –'

'Let me deal with this, Miss Shaw.'

'Yes, Liz – let the Brigadier deal with this.'

'Doctor, as you are a member of –'

'Yes, we all know how the Brigadier prefers to deal with things. Your military tactics solve all the problems, don't they? Got the place wired up already, have you? No doubt the first rabbit or vole that raises its head will be blasted to kingdom come. There are no targets for you to shoot at here. In fact, there's nothing for you here, so may I suggest that you take your men and military bunting elsewhere.'

'On the contrary, Doctor, there seems to be more than enough here to interest you.'

'And, may I ask, how did you know where "here" was?'

'Miss Shaw told me.'

'That is a lie.'

'Too right it is!'

'I told her nothing. I did not think you would have lied to me.'

'All right. I . . .'

'Yes, Brigadier?'

'I had you followed. Three times.'

'Followed! Liz?'

'I knew nothing of this.'

'As I said, three times, and on each occasion you came within a thirty-mile radius of this area.'

'Followed? You mean you've been spying on me? Why? For what purpose?'

'Your actions are no longer accountable. You have become . . . suspicious. I feel I can no longer accommodate you.'

'You? Accommodate me? I am not tied to your apron strings. I do not need to justify my every action. When you have needed help, I have given it. I do not expect to be repaid by you and your jackbooted buffoons snooping around in my personal affairs.'

'You have stepped dangerously close to the mark, Doctor. I could have you charged for this. I simply will not tolerate such conduct from a member of UNIT. And, as a member of UNIT, no matter how eccentric and fanciful you may choose to be, you will operate on my terms and my terms alone.'

'I will operate on my own terms or not at all!' With that, the Doctor turned on his heel and marched off to the farthest corner of the UNIT barrage. The Brigadier slapped his baton heavily against his thigh in a fit of anger.

'Well, if that's what he wants,' he growled through gritted teeth.

Liz, uncharacteristically, placed a hand on his arm. 'Give me some time with him.'

The Brigadier, still flushed red with anger, looked highly dubious.

'Please,' she said, quietly.

He thought for a moment and, feeling quite drained, nodded. 'Very well. But one more chance is all he's having.'

Liz left his side and manoeuvred herself through the obstacle course of UNIT paraphernalia.

'Doctor?'

He stood with his back to her.

'What?' His grumpy response with its hard-done-by tones reminded Liz of a spoiled child. Despite his attitude, she felt sorry for him. He looked lost, as if he were fighting a losing battle all by himself.

'This isn't like you at all.'

Still he kept his back to her.

'Well, it's like me now.' There was a short silence, followed by an unintelligible mumble. 'I'm fed up.' The Doctor glanced sideways at her. 'I'm fed up. Fed up with all this. Fed up with military operations. Fed up with not being able to do things my own way. And fed up with him.' He gestured with his head towards the Brigadier.

'I know he can get your back up. God knows, there are times when I feel the same way. But he's only doing his job.' She looked him in the eye, questioningly. 'Haven't you got a job to do, Doctor?'

The Doctor rubbed his chin thoughtfully and, without a word, began to walk back along the path. After a few scuffed strides, he turned.

'Coming, Liz?'

'So this is where you've been coming for the past few weeks?' Liz turned to look at the Doctor, her loose blonde hair blowing in her eyes as Bessie picked up speed along the winding country lane.

'Not exactly, no,' he answered. 'I've been to a number of locations.'

'But all for the same purpose?' Liz was clearly working things through in her mind. He nodded.

'Yes. You see, Liz, for some months now I've been doing some research of my own.'

'Inside the TARDIS?'

'Yes, inside the TARDIS. Away from the Bri . . . ' He stopped himself. 'Away from people questioning and interfering when I'm trying to concentrate.'

'I might have been able to help.' She was put out at his exclusion of her, but now was not the time to show it.

'You had your own work to do.'

'You could have asked.'

The Doctor frowned at her in irritation. 'Look, do you want to hear this or not?' She didn't have the chance to answer. 'Good,' he continued. 'Well, shut up and listen then. You see, I was doing some research –'

'What, on the console?'

The Doctor let out a long, theatrical sigh and Liz bit her lip, promising herself that it would be the last interruption she would make.

'To assist my research, I managed to construct a rather nifty little monitoring device.'

Liz, before she realized it, broke her promise. 'Not another one! What does this one do?'

'It monitors!' retorted the Doctor sarcastically. 'It's not just any old monitor, though. What I've built with, may I say, some considerable skill, is a high-sensitivity, high-frequency SAI-modulating amplifier, capable of picking up signals that don't register even on the most advanced and cumbersome pieces of UNIT equipment.' Noting that she appeared quite impressed, he continued to bolster himself up. 'And that's quite an achievement, actually, Liz. UNIT equipment may be highly sensitive . . . ' And he continued to repeat the previous sentiment until Liz intervened.

'And I suppose you've managed to pick up one of these signals?' He beamed at her in self-satisfaction, answering her question. 'Doctor – you're a marvel!'

'Yes, I do believe I am!' Waving amicably at the driver of a trundling tractor which the yellow roadster had just overtaken, he added, 'So that's what I've been doing here.' With that, and unexpectedly to Liz, the Doctor fell silent again.

Was that it? Was that all he was going to give up? He had told her nothing but that he had built a device and that he was exceedingly clever. Neither of these statements were uncommon. After ten minutes of not a word spoken, Liz said:

'Can you elaborate on that, Doctor?' She hoped that he hadn't realized a tenuous link to a conversation he himself had closed.

The Doctor looked at her determined gaze and knew she wasn't going to give up. He began again in a familiar tone:

'All right. The accuracy of my equipment enabled me to pinpoint a thirty-mile radius within which to search for signs of

activity. It had to be a fairly insignificant area or UNIT's involve-
ment would have been called for straight away. So I was able to
establish a short-list of possible . . . ' The Doctor paused, knowing that the next words would cause some reaction: ' . . . possible
landing sites . . . ' Her reaction was as expected, but he managed
to silence her by continuing quickly: ' . . . and then eliminate
them, one by one, through visiting each in turn. I did this, so I
thought, alone.'

'And you've pinpointed it now, exactly?'

'Yes Liz. And I'm afraid soldiers are walking all over it back
at the rail path.' His voice went up a pitch, as if to cheer himself
up. 'I found some debris, though, which I examined carefully.
Although there should have been more. Much more.' They turned
into the main road and past Milton Bradbury Post Office. 'I
should have been quicker. I wanted to avoid all this.'

'So it's possibly a craft of some kind? That's what we're
looking for?'

'Not of some kind, Liz. I know precisely what kind of craft, and
of occupant. As I've said, I should have been quicker. Both are
gone, taken by someone, and I know it isn't UNIT.'

'Another professional body?' she suggested.

'No, certainly not. I found debris, remember? And the craft –
it would be easy to move, being no bigger than a . . . a motorcycle's sidecar. And it was quite obviously dragged, with great
lumps of turf being torn up. No, it was no professional job.'

'And they're in danger?'

'Yes.'

'From the occupant?'

'No. No – more themselves, really.'

In the bright sunlight which shone through the study window,
Maurice Burridge was reading intently, seated in his favourite
armchair and flicking through the pages of a large, leather-bound
book resting heavily on his lap. The fluttering of the thin pages

was the only sound to be heard in the house, continuing on and on until finally his hand came to rest on one page. Re-adjusting his spectacles which again had begun to rub the bridge of his nose, he read the words 'Faith, hope and charity', and sat in silent thought for a moment. He began turning pages once more. Phrases and words swam around his head, and he knew where to turn, which passages to read, which lines to look for; but even this ancient book couldn't give him the guidance he needed. Feeling confused, he closed it and returned it to the table. It wasn't wrong, he thought, just incomplete. He decided that, at this moment, he would find greater salvation within a pot of tea.

He made his way to the kitchen, but was stopped in his tracks by what he had come to term as 'the noise' – a hollow, whining sound which still affected his stomach more than his head and heart. He had qualms about going into the spare room, never really sure what he should do or how to react. The room gave him a strange feeling, as if he were detached in some way; as if his body, or perhaps his mind, was separating from itself. But he had to go, he had a duty to go. There was no one else, only him. Quietly he pushed open the bedroom door. The room was small. The window was small, and would let in little light; the blue curtain was almost unnecessary. Blue appeared to be the colour scheme that had been decided upon, although it had been unsuccessful, as the serenity was botched by the presence of a red wastepaper basket and a luminous green table lamp. Like the room, both of these items were small. The lamp was on a small cabinet, the cabinet by a small bed. And there it lay, huddled beneath an old crocheted blanket.

Maurice took in the reality of its presence for the hundredth time. Everything he had ever believed in denied this presence, told him that what he saw before him was an impossibility. He thought again. No, it was not wrong, just incomplete. He joked to himself about writing the next volume. Moving closer to the bed, he knelt by the side and looked sympathetically at his house guest, a figure of less than four foot in length; naked but for

Peggy's crochet work, its skin in some areas colourless, in others – particularly the chest – a milky yellow; its head balanced on the thinnest of necks and possessing all the shape and transient nature of a white party balloon. A small, lipless opening where the knot should be provided an area Maurice could call a mouth. He had no such luck when it came to a nose, nor ears. The creature had eyes – most definitely it had eyes – and when open they would surely fill a third of its blank face. But they weren't fully open, as Maurice had half-hoped they would be. As before, they were just long black slits. Perhaps, when they opened, he and the creature could have a better means of communication than sounds which meant nothing to the other.

Several minutes passed before the room was in silence again, the fragile form quiet, eyes now shut tight. Maurice took one last look before tiptoeing softly away.

The Doctor and Liz left the Forresters Inn and strode up the road.

'Not much luck there,' sighed Liz. 'I wonder if it's usually that quiet?' She glanced at the Doctor. 'Are we actually getting anywhere?'

'My dear Liz, short of knocking on every door in the vicinity, the pubs are our best option. There are two or three more to try yet,' he added, optimistically. They walked on in silence, the Doctor studying a foldaway map of the area and Liz thinking over what he had revealed to her about the mysterious missing craft. She concluded again that he had actually told her very little.

'Doctor?'

'Mmm?' He didn't look up from the map.

'Exactly what kind of . . .' She paused momentarily, checking herself not to make any assumptions with the next word: '. . . occupant are we looking for?'

'An intelligent humanoid. Little chap, about this high.' He gestured with his hand level to his waist, to show the height from the ground. 'To give it its proper name, an Eriscent.' He folded away the map, which he slid into his inside jacket pocket. 'What really frustrates me, Liz, is that it could be so simple: find the creature, repair the craft and send it back into space without a soul knowing. No fuss, no trouble, no anything – nobody else would have to be involved. And now UNIT have muscled in and messed everything up – just as they did with the Silurians; just as they do with everything, in fact. All they're doing is hampering a situation which could be resolved more quickly and simply without them. A typical Lethbridge-Stewart operation.'

'Talk of the devil . . .' The Brigadier and two of his men were striding heavily down the road towards them. Stopping only feet away, the three military men lined up across the pavement, a human barrage, daring anyone to cross it. The Brigadier stared stonily at the Doctor.

'So, this is where you've been hiding yourself? Too much trouble to come back and apologize, I suppose?'

'Hah! Me? Apologize to you? For what? Oh, I forgot to tell you – I found a lovely little site for you to hold shooting practice. Apologize indeed! That's rich, coming from you. Come on, Liz.' Immediately the two soldiers raised their rifles in warning. Liz could tell the Doctor was genuinely shocked by this, but despaired to see him keep up the pretence. 'Tell your monkeys to put their toys away, Brigadier,' demanded the Doctor.

'Oh no. This time you're not walking away. There's more at stake now than your blatant disregard of UNIT principles. You see, there's been a death, in suspicious circumstances, so you're going to tell me every single bit of information you know.'

'A death? Who?' asked Liz.

'A local. Pensioner by the name of George Palmer. He and his dog both died whilst out walking in the wood at the back of the church. His wife says they were all walking along quite normally when the dog suddenly turned on her and bit her, before collapsing in a fit. Her husband, she said, started screaming and ranting, holding his head as if he had gone quite mad, at which point it appears he slipped before she could stop him. He fell down the grass bank, his skull smashed open.'

Liz screwed up her face at the thought: 'Horrible.'

'Yes, not very pleasant,' agreed the Doctor, 'but I'm afraid I'm not prepared to help you.'

'I'm not giving you the choice, Doctor.'

'I'm sorry about the death of that old chap and his dog – very unfortunate – but the best thing you can do, as I've already suggested, is to pack up, take your men and go. Because I promise you, the longer you stay around here, interfering in things you could never understand, the more deaths there will be. And there will be more deaths, Brigadier, mark my words.'

'I see you evidently know all about it. I thought as much. You're down here being all scientific and there's a death, and the promise of more. And you want me to turn my back on it and go home? I have a duty to protect people. It's my job – can't you see that, man? No, I don't think you can. I don't think you can see beyond your own selfish purposes to consider what might be best for the majority.'

'Now wait a minute, Brigadier –'

'Be quiet, Miss Shaw! In fact, the more I learn about you, Doctor –' The Brigadier afforded himself a sarcastic laugh. 'That's a joke, I know nothing about you – all I realize is that you're an arrogant, self-centred –'

'Oh, arrogant, am I? Self-centred, am I? And how would you describe yourself, Brigadier? How would you describe someone who is quite prepared to let innocent people die because of his own bloody-mindedness?'

There was a long silence before the Brigadier spoke again. When he did, his voice was cold and unemotional: 'Your UNIT employment is at an end, Doctor. You're a disgrace, an encumbrance, your attitude despicable. Consider yourself relieved of your duties.'

Liz was the first to respond. She spoke urgently through gritted teeth: 'Brigadier! Think about what you're doing! UNIT needs –'

'Don't bother, Liz.' The Doctor pushed bitterly past the Brigadier and his men. 'I wouldn't have anything more to do with such a small-minded bunch of ignoramuses anyway. Let them blunder, see how far they get. I've got my own work to do.' And with that, he walked on up the road.

Liz stared in disbelief at her superior. 'I can't believe you just did that! I'd like to know what you propose to do without him.'

'We've managed without him before – we shall manage again. And as for your show of loyalty . . . '

'You're completely stuck without him and you know it!'

'You're trying my patience to the limit, Miss Shaw . . . '

'Of all the pig-headed . . . ' She was unable to find the words. Leaving the Brigadier in stunned silence, Liz followed the Doctor up the road.

It took several moments for the deep, cream-coloured lids to rise fully. When they did, a pair of complete black irises gazed wearily around the room, blinking several times to clear the misty film that clouded them. As to how it had come to be here it had nothing more than a vague memory of foggy images, but it remembered a great pain and a white-haired creature who had helped to take it away. Propping itself steadily on to two thin arms which looked as though the slightest pressure would snap them, it was able to assess the recovery process. The limbs were still weak, but the pain and cold numbness were gone, and the body structure appeared to be repairing successfully. Sliding its legs gently from the bed, it rested the flat, toeless feet upon the surprising softness of the floor, using a hand to steady itself as, slowly, it raised its slender form to its full height. Despite the trembling and wobbliness in its legs, the being felt an inner pride. The half-open door offered the next challenge; moments later, the soft feet began to shuffle ski-like across the room. The short journey ended at the top of a small staircase where, grasping the bannister with its paw-like hand, it descended, one stair at a time.

Val Jolley dumped her heavy shopping bag on to the front pew, puffing and sweating. Rotund, appearing physically older than her 34 years, she was a woman who easily filled her oversized clothes. Lugging a bag of canned food from the mini-market had exhausted her. Removing her navy-blue mac with its missing buttons, she caught her breath momentarily before unrolling several bunches of freshly cut, strongly scented chrysanthemums from their tissue wrapping. She took it in turns with Freda Richards to do the church flowers, every other Friday. Checking her wristwatch reassured her that she could take her time before picking the children up from her mother's. Scooping the flowers up in her chubby arms, she approached the connecting vicarage door in her mission to find some clean vases.

Through the noisy gushing of the water, Val heard a muffled sound. 'Evening, Reverend Burridge,' she called in response. 'Shan't be a mo. I'll just get these filled up and then I'll be with you. There are some nice snaps of the Sunday School trip in my bag, if you'd like to have a look.' No answer – perhaps it was the radio. Shrugging her broad shoulders, she lifted one of the pewter vases with both hands and carried the neat arrangement of pinks, purples and sunny yellows back into the church.

She spotted the telltale shadow almost immediately, thrown in a long, lean diagonal across the crimson carpet, and it made her turn sharply. As the cumbersome floral offering hit the ground with a deafening thump, Val Jolley found herself staring into two enormous black eyes which, in an instant, illuminated into myriad colours.

Minutes later, the Doctor almost collided with the frantic woman rushing blindly down the road towards him, her plump features an unhealthy red, her breathing a cacophony of gasps and wheezing.

'Of all the clumsy . . . ' he snapped, as she knocked his arm roughly. An irate glance at the building from which she had emerged, though, changed his expression. 'Of course! Why on earth didn't I think of that?'

'Think of what?' Liz was half listening, half staring back at the panic-stricken woman who had just ploughed into the Brigadier.

'The church. What marvellous powers of deduction! Yes, it all seems quite logical if you think about it.' Liz opened her mouth to deliver a sharp response, but was silenced by the Doctor placing a finger on her lips. 'Think about it, Liz. Come on.'

The chattering of the Forresters Inn was silenced as Val Jolley burst through the door, face dampened with sweat, her breathing now reduced to a coarse, wheezing rasp. She grasped a small, round pub table for support.

'You've got yourself into a bit of a state, haven't you?' calmed the landlady. 'Sit down and get your breath back.'

Val replied with 'Church' before a pain in her arm and chest silenced her. Her heart burst. She crumpled to the floor, pulling the pub table and two half-full pint glasses crashing down with her.

Maurice Burridge blinked sleepily as the study came back into view. He had been asleep for some time – although quite unintentionally, as the half-full mug of cold tea by his feet confirmed – and he had a stale, musty taste in his mouth. Exactly what had woken him he wasn't sure. He thought he'd heard a loud bump . . . probably in his subconscious, though. The distant wooden thump of a door closing brought him fully round. That would be Val, come to do the flowers. Placing the neglected mug upon the table, he wandered into the passage and through to the church, almost treading on the strewn mass of coloured chrysanthemums. As he peered around in bewilderment, a short cough pinpointed his gaze.

'Excuse me, Reverend.'

'Can I help you?'

'Yes, I believe you can.' Maurice watched the two approaching strangers sceptically – a man, rather theatrically dressed, whose towering height dwarfed the small churchman, and a blonde-haired young woman. The man spoke again: 'I've just passed a very distressed woman outside. She came out of the church, obviously in a state of shock. Perhaps you have some idea why that might have been?' Ashen-faced, Maurice tried to control the nervous tension in his voice.

'Did this woman say anything?'

'She didn't have time, she was running so fast,' explained the man, curtly. He looked Maurice straight in the eye, his expression deadly serious. 'I believe you know what she saw, Reverend. You must tell us everything. I can help you. There isn't much time.'

Maurice was baffled at the stranger's apparent knowledge – did this man really know what he was saying? 'How can you possibly help me?' he finally answered. 'I don't even know who you are.'

The other man sighed at the inconvenience of such a question – formalities bored him. Instead it was the girl who spoke:

'This is the Doctor and I'm Elizabeth Shaw. We're both representatives of . . . ' She glanced sideways at the Doctor: ' . . . UNIT.' Maurice frowned.

'Sorry . . . UNIT?'

'United Nations Intelligence Taskforce,' elaborated the Doctor in routine parrot fashion. 'Alien life forms, the paranormal . . . ' He watched the old man's face for a reaction; he was successful.

'You . . . understand these things? I didn't know there were such organizations.' Trying in his confusion to digest the information, Maurice watched as the Doctor took and sketched upon one of the photocopied hymn pamphlets. His throat went dry as he recognized the sketched image – the familiar oval-shaped head, large eyes and thin, wispy body. 'You'd better come through to the vicarage,' he whispered. 'We can talk properly there.'

'I was in the church at the time . . . ' And Maurice told his story. At times he seemed embarrassed by it, at others understandably confused. 'And that's when I saw it, through the trees, up on the old railway path. Well, I've always been a bit nosey, so I took a walk up to get a closer look.' He paused. 'I couldn't believe what I found. It frightened me, I'll admit that . . . I could see it . . . '

'The creature?' prompted the Doctor.

'Yes. I could see it lying inside the craft. I thought it was dead, but . . . so I managed to lift it out and, well, it was injured, you see . . . wrapped it in my cardigan and, yes, carried it back here . . . Was that right? Can you understand that?'

'Yes.' The Doctor nodded.

'Why didn't you call the police?' inquired Liz.

'I'm not sure. It didn't somehow seem appropriate.' Maurice continued in disconnected sentences. 'So I bathed its wounds with warm water . . . Was that right?' he repeated.

'What about the craft?' asked Liz.

'I went back for it straight away. I don't know how I managed to drag it back here. Not that it was heavy – just difficult to pull across the woodland.'

'And where is it now?' questioned the Doctor.

'Tool shed. I picked up a good many pieces that had broken off. I've got it all in fertilizer bags.'

'Good. That's safe for the moment, anyway. Tell me, Reverend – has the Eriscent tried to communicate with you in any way?' Maurice looked blank.

'Eriscent?' he repeated, questioningly. The Doctor, still holding the hymn pamphlet, held up the sketch again. 'Eriscent,' he reaffirmed, before folding the pamphlet in half and putting it into his jacket pocket. 'Has it tried to communicate with you in any way?' he repeated.

Maurice shook his head adamantly. 'Not at all. I have tried myself though –'

'Well, you mustn't!' interrupted the Doctor, urgently. Liz and Maurice waited for an explanation. 'And on no account must you attempt to try,' he continued, emphasizing each word dramatically. 'If you succeed, you're in great danger. You see, I not only know what this creature is, I know what it can do. We have been in communication for some time. It has been distressed, lost, in need of help. I guided it to Earth, to give it that help. In our communications, I have learned of its strange affliction. It warned me about it and was greatly troubled by the damage it could cause. You've been extremely lucky. If you had but looked into its fully open eyes, it would have tried to read your thought patterns and, Reverend, you would now be dead.' The Doctor delivered the words with a cold bluntness. 'A pity really,' he resumed. 'Quite an inventive method of communication. Works perfectly for the Eriscents, of course, but when attempted on other life forms, the brain becomes irreversibly scrambled, usually sending the person mad or into a fit similar to epilepsy.'

'So that's what happened to the woman outside?' Things began to make sense for Liz now.

'Yes – and to the gent and his dog, no doubt.'

Only feet away, the figure outside the study nodded grimly. The overheard revelations had provided the vital information he needed. Gun raised ahead of him, and without a sound, the Brigadier crept up the small staircase.

His hunting instincts took over. He chose the nearest door, slightly ajar and beckoning. Pushing it open with the tip of his revolver, he entered, looking cautiously downwards. Despite the reassuring feel of gunmetal against his palm, he was apprehensive. The uncertainty of the situation had made him so, and as he glimpsed the pale, phantom-like form on the bed in the corner, half-hidden under a blanket, he struggled to regain his military stance. Clenching the gun tighter, until it dug into his skin, he took a pace nearer the bed. The creature made no noise, but the Brigadier could feel its eyes upon him. He felt awkward, not being able to spout orders at the thing, but instead having to stalk it silently. He stood over the bed and, with his head turned deliberately away from the huddled mass, jabbed threateningly into the blanket with the revolver. The sudden, spasmodic reaction from beneath the crochet-work caught the Brigadier unawares as the faded cover was flung into his face. By the time the Brigadier had recovered his composure, the room was empty, the blanket in a heap at his feet.

The Doctor, Liz and Maurice heard the voices before they reached the top of the stairs. The open bedroom door revealed the back of a khaki, beret-clad figure speaking emphatically into a walkie-talkie radio.

'Brigadier!'

The military man turned sharply, anticipating the Doctor's question. 'It's gone. Escaped.' His voice was calm and steady. 'I had intended to capture it . . . ' He paused, returning the icy glare with an added air of pomposity: ' . . . for the good of us all . . . '

'But it gave you the slip,' taunted the Doctor. 'A weak, alien creature no bigger than a child of seven, and you let it walk past you . . . Oh, well done, Brigadier. You've done a marvellous job. You do realize what you've done?'

'It could be anywhere by now!' cried Maurice.

'Precisely. If it gets to the town, all hell could break loose! I assume you were listening to our conversation downstairs.'

Liz thought she detected a hint of embarrassment in the Brigadier's awkward reaction. 'I was.'

'Yes . . . sneaky tactics appear to be your forte. Ever heard of the camel and the straw that broke its back?'

'We wouldn't be in this situation now if –'

A distant crackly voice broke into the argument. 'Sir? Sir? Are you still there? It's in the woods, sir . . . ' The Doctor was already out of the door.

'Stay here, Reverend, in case the creature comes back,' he ordered. 'Liz.' He gestured at her with a commanding nod, an arrogance which, at any other time, would have caused an onslaught of rebukes. On this occasion, though, she simply obeyed.

Sergeant Mitchell scuffed his way around the old railway path.

He sniffed loudly, wiped his wet nose with the back of his hand
and checked his watch. It was dusk now, the breeze had evolved
into a gusty wind and soon he'd be off duty. Reaching deep into
his pocket, he hoped to find some stray Polo mints. His rummaging through bits of paper and the odd loose coin produced a
battered packet, only for it to slip through his cold fingers into the
deep, unkept grass.

'Sod it!' He began fumbling blindly through the damp clumps.
'Sod it!' He took a step backwards and heard the crunch of the
packet under his army boot. 'Oh, sod it!' Annoyed, he stamped
the remains into the earth. He heard someone approaching. 'Hey,
I would offer you a mint but . . . ' But Mitchell wasn't talking to
his replacement, as he had suspected. He lost his balance and,
clasping his head, writhed amongst the grass and mud. Then, with
what must have taken considerable control, he staggered to his
feet and, dragging his heavy boots through the grit, made a
disorientated route towards his confused UNIT colleagues. They
ran towards him, and Mitchell greeted them by collapsing at their
boots.

His home had become a watchtower. Maurice Burridge kept a
constant vigil at the small bedroom window, his own reflection
becoming clearer in the glass as it grew darker outside. Drumming his fingers impatiently on the sill, he looked at his watch for
the third time in as many minutes. Almost three-quarters of an
hour it had been gone now. Surely it would try to come back? But
all he could see from the window was the line of soldiers taking
up residence down below. Their stance mimicked the graves for
which they appeared to have so little respect. He leaned his head
wearily against the cold glass.

'What would Peggy say about all this?'

'I can't take my mind off those eyes.' The Doctor nodded, arms
resting on the inert steering wheel.

'Yes, poor fellow. It was very quick, according to that young soldier. But I should have been there, Liz. I should have been quicker. Now all we can do is wait, wait for another sighting, wait for another death. Unfortunate creature.' Liz followed suit as he climbed out of the car and headed across the church lawn towards the specified 'UNIT ONLY' area which a number of over-curious locals were currently attempting to penetrate.

'Doctor. For someone who doesn't want anything to do with us, it seems you can't stay away.' The Brigadier couldn't resist the gibe. With soldiers now firmly established in an official display of authority, the Brigadier felt, for the first time, firmly in control. His bombastic tones reflected his smug self-satisfaction.

Taking a deep breath, the Doctor looked his antagonist in the eyes. 'Despite your small-minded, stubborn attitude throughout this unnecessary affair,' he began, with an air of resignation, 'I'm prepared to make a deal with you.'

The Brigadier raised his eyebrows expectantly. Surely the Doctor wasn't about to grovel?

'I want the Eriscent captured and taken to a safe place where it can be cared for, counselled even, and for you to allow me to repair its craft and return it home.'

The Doctor's demands had begun to aggravate the Brigadier intensely. 'You want too much, Doctor. You always have. You ask too much. You never allow me the confidence that I have afforded you.'

'Brigadier,' the Doctor interrupted him, 'I know as well as you do that all this has been a sideshow which has been driven out of hand. You don't trust me do you, Brigadier? Nor I you. Hence this situation.' The Doctor paused, took one step closer to the Brigadier. 'You blew them up . . . didn't you?'

There followed a long silence. Inevitably it was interrupted:

'Round the back! Quick! Round the back!' It was Maurice, shouting, waving wildly from the vicarage window.

The cold stone felt rough against the Eriscent's skin, and its lack of fingers made gripping almost impossible, but still it climbed on upwards towards the open window.

'Why didn't it return the way it went?' Maurice's voice could still be heard, as could the Doctor's.

'Because there's a small army blocking its way.'

Unsettled by the shouting from the ground, the boyish figure clung on to the stonework as best it could. It struggled to get itself a holding on the narrowest of window sills of the second floor. The creature was obviously in trouble. Putting all its weight and strength on its hands, it managed to lift its waist above the sill, and like a gymnast, twisted itself to sit upon it. It sat facing outwards, head tucked into its chest, exhausted.

The Doctor recognized the danger instantly.

'Tell your men to stay put, Brigadier!' he shouted; and, to his surprise, the Brigadier bellowed the command. The majority stopped; four had already turned the corner of the vicarage. Liz followed in a desperate attempt to convey the command, the Doctor only yards behind her.

Liz turned the corner to see a UNIT soldier aim his rifle upwards. As quickly as it was raised, it was forced roughly downwards. 'Don't you dare!' she screamed. But neither of them were quick enough to stop the rifle being fiercely snatched by another. Liz, thrown to the ground, saw the other three soldiers crumple in on themselves, one still clutching his gun, the other two their heads. A single shot reverberated around the stone walls of the church, followed immediately by a piercing wail that sounded for all the world like a cry, and then the abrupt thud of the alien as its body hit the ground and buckled. Liz raised her head from the grass to see the Doctor, rifle still angled at the window sill, his face white and defeated. The Brigadier stood only feet away, his smugness no longer discernible.

'There,' said the Doctor, in a whisper audible only to himself. 'I'm sure that's made everything a lot tidier for you, Brigadier.' Liz was about to speak; she hadn't a clue what to say but she was going to do it anyway. But the Doctor silenced her by dropping the rifle to the ground with a clatter. 'The bullet didn't even touch it. It was frightened. The sound of the gunshot made it fall.' He said no more. He walked past Liz and stopped for a moment in front of the Brigadier. Strange. For the first time, he thought he saw a little part of himself in the Brigadier's face. A moment later, he had resumed the short journey from the vicarage back to his car.

'Hmm . . . I wonder what year that happened?' I looked at Silverman, but he said nothing, his skull-like face an impassive mask in the guttering firelight.

'And that Brigadier,' I persevered, 'he thought of the Doctor as two different people: a scruffy little guy – he could have been the one who got the clockwork bird – and a tall elegant guy in a cloak.' I scratched my head. 'You know, I've had some weird cases in my time, but this one beats them all.'

My client shifted position in his chair, clearly growing impatient. 'Physical appearance is unimportant!' he blurted out. I looked at him sharply, but decided to let that one go. 'I hired you to find out what's happened to me,' he continued, 'and retrace my steps since I came to this city. This is getting us nowhere!'

'Well, it's certainly thrown up more questions than answers,' I admitted, 'but I think we should carry on for a while.' I looked at Silverman. 'If that's okay with you, I mean.'

He gave one of his ghastly, rictus-like smiles. 'I am at your service, Mr Addison.'

'Good, that's settled then.' I quickly bent down to the table and, after a moment's consideration, picked up a little crystal which might once have been a piece of jewellery but which was now scratched and blackened as if it had been through a furnace. 'Try this,' I suggested, and lobbed it across to Silverman. He caught it one-handed and held it up to the light, regarding it appraisingly.

'An astute choice . . . ' he told me, nodding his head in approval. 'I feel this could add considerably to our understanding.'

Saying that, he cupped his hands around the crystal, held it out over the centre of the table and closed his eyes in concentration.

Scarab of Death

Mark Stammers

Edwin Carver ran. He ran as fast as his old, weakened and ungainly body would allow, although he knew with almost total certainty that there was nowhere on this stinking dust-ball of a planet where they wouldn't find him. Besides, the pain and dizziness constantly reminded him that his left shoulder had been hit by a blaster shot; and, judging by the growing red stain around the wound, he was losing a great deal of blood.

As he forced himself onwards into the heart of the desert, the winds began to whip the sand from the surface of the dunes and throw it into the air. Although he was a non-believer, Carver offered up a silent prayer to whichever of the gods had seen fit to take pity on him and provide the cover of a sandstorm. Within minutes, the visibility had become so poor that he could barely see his hand six inches from his face. Falling into the sand, he lay still, watching and listening for the approach of his pursuers through the blinding onslaught of the swirling grains and the deafening cacophony of the screeching winds.

A few minutes later he made out a group of five or six shapes heading towards him. He pressed his body harder into the dune as the gang of armed thugs came within feet of him. Blinded by the sands, they passed by and off out of sight, shouting to each other as they pushed on through the maelstrom.

Slowly, Carver rose to his feet. The effort to stand was almost beyond his remaining strength, but an inner force seemed to send him staggering onwards. As consciousness started to drift away, he felt the force take control of his shattered body. He thrust his left hand deep into the pocket of his jacket and stroked the smooth stone: the cause of all his misery, yet at the same time his only comfort. Simply by touching it, he felt a little stronger.

When he could no longer walk, he crawled, and when even

that was beyond him he dragged himself across the sand. Finally he could go no further. Carver rolled over on to his back and looked up into the swirling sands. He could just make out a giant black shadow. The pyramid. He began to sob, realizing that all his efforts had come to nothing. He had set out to carry the scarab as far away as he could and hide it where it would never be found, but in the confusion of the storm he had come full circle to his starting point. Now they would surely find him – and the scarab.

Realizing it would be only a matter of moments before he lost consciousness, Carver began to drag sand over his body, burying himself and the scarab which he still gripped tightly in his left hand. Soon only his face and right arm remained above the sand. He hoped that the storm would cover all remaining traces of him. He smiled at the thought that, although he may have dug his own grave, at least they wouldn't find the scarab. The universe and all its inhabitants owed him a debt of thanks, yet they would never know. He relaxed into the sand's embrace and, within a few short minutes, lost consciousness for the last time.

The transporter speeded across the baking hot sands of the desert on an anti-grav cushion which held it, and its incumbents, a metre or so above the dunes.

When the vehicle had first rolled off the assembly line, its sales brochure had boasted of the very latest innovations for the comfort of the discerning traveller: food and drink replicators programmed to provide luxury cuisine; air conditioning capable of providing the most comfortable climate whatever the passenger's species; virtual-reality computer-access terminals to while away those tedious periods of travel; and of course the very best inertial damping field drives for the ultimate in smooth rides.

After a decade of hard work, entropy had begun to eat away at the systems, leaving the transporter a little less comfortable. The food replicators had failed six years ago, the air conditioning had broken down soon after, the virtual-reality computers had never worked properly from day one and the failure of the dampers made for a fairly bumpy ride out to the pyramid site.

The transporter's passengers for this particular trip numbered only ten, including the two guides. At the front sat a young couple clearly more interested in each other than with the trip. Behind them were a group of four Antarean tourists, chattering inanely to each other whilst munching their way through a huge pile of packed lunches. The final two passengers – a man and a woman, both rather oddly dressed – sat at the back.

As the huge black pyramid came into view, one of the guides rose wearily to his feet and produced a tiny microphone which he held to his lips.

'Ladies and gentlemen,' he announced, 'behold the famous Black Pyramid of Beta Osiris, greatest surviving artefact of the lost Osiran civilization.'

He pressed a small button on the side of his microphone and a short fanfare punctuated his speech. The four Antareans briefly forgot about their food and rushed to the front, almost crushing the two guides and the young couple in their eagerness to take holo-pics of the giant structure. After a short period of flashing bulbs, the Antareans returned to their seats and the guide continued.

'For centuries, archaeologists had found evidence of the Osirans on planets throughout the known galaxies. Legends are told of the dark lord Sutekh's destruction of Phaester Osiris, and of his brother Horus's vow to pursue him to the ends of the universe and back, to exact retribution for the annihilation of their race. Yet it wasn't until the discovery of this lone moon and its mile-high Black Pyramid that myth could be separated from reality. Following that discovery, over twenty years ago now, visitors flocked here to see one of the great wonders of the galaxies.'

'Wealthy pleasure-seekers who despoiled the local culture with their hotels and casinos and transformed the indigenous population from a race of nomadic hunter-gatherers into a bunch of skivvies, hustlers and con-men.'

The guide looked up in astonishment and saw that the source of this acerbic observation was the tall man seated at the back of the transporter, his feet stretched out on the vacant bench in front of him. Seemingly oblivious of the oppressive heat of Beta Osiris's twin suns, he had a broad-brimmed felt hat pulled down over his face, a long multicoloured scarf draped around his neck and a heavy coat wrapped tightly around him. His companion, a dark-haired woman who wore a white cotton summer dress and a large cream-coloured straw hat with a red ribbon around the brim, leaned across and shushed him.

'Don't cause a scene, Doctor!'

'You know, Sarah,' the man replied, 'if there's one thing I detest it's guided tours.'

The guide cleared his throat in what he hoped was a suitably reproving manner, then continued with his scripted spiel.

'The pyramid has also been a site of unparalleled interest and importance for scientific research. After its discovery, a team of archaeologists carried out a complete survey, meticulously documenting its passageways and chambers and the many extraordinary relics found within.'

'Until they considered it picked dry of its secrets. Then they departed for new worlds, just like the pleasure-seekers who funded their work. Leaving the local economy to collapse into poverty and degradation.'

Again it was the tall man at the back who had interrupted. The guide shot him a venomous look. 'Please, sir, if you don't mind, people are trying to listen.' He glanced at the other passengers, hoping for a show of support, but found that they had all lost interest. The young couple were engaged in a passionate embrace and the Antareans were still devouring their sandwiches. He quickly concluded his announcement.

'We will be arriving at the pyramid in just a few short minutes now, so prepare yourselves to witness the marvel of the age and splendour of the ancients.' The guide sank happily back into his seat.

Sarah turned to the Doctor. 'Honestly, Doctor, I don't know why you dragged me with you on this trip when you obviously aren't enjoying it.'

'Because I've always wanted to see the pyramid, Sarah,' came the Doctor's reply, muffled by his hat which was still pulled down over his face. 'It's an extraordinary feat of architecture, and should give us a fascinating insight into the Osirans' culture.'

'I'm not so sure I want to find out any more about them if they were all like Sutekh.'

The Doctor raised his hat and placed it back on his head. Opening his eyes he turned to Sarah without sitting up. 'Oh no, none of them were as bad as Sutekh,' the Doctor grinned.

'Oh, good.' Sarah relaxed a little, pushing out of her thoughts the images of the hideous jackal-headed Osiran they had destroyed on Earth.

'Power mad, sadistic and evil to the last, but none as bad as Sutekh.'

Sarah shot the Doctor an icy look, but his face had disappeared back beneath the brim of his fedora hat. She got up and moved to the front of the transporter, deciding to use the last few minutes before they disembarked to take some more pictures of the pyramid with her trusty Nikon SLR, hanging from its strap around her neck.

When the transporter eventually ground to a halt within the vast shadow cast by the mountainous pyramid, it seemed as if night had suddenly fallen. The passengers clambered down from the open door of the vehicle, adjusting their eyes to the cold and the gloom as they did so. A large hole gaped in the northern face of the pyramid some thirty feet away. Its rough edges suggested to Sarah that it was not an original feature of the pyramid but a more recent addition.

'Looks like they blasted their way in,' she commented.

'Obviously couldn't find the real door,' the Doctor replied, his face now half-hidden by the guide book he was studying. 'On Earth, archaeologists in the 1920s often did great damage to the tombs in the Valley of the Kings in their fervour to discover their secrets. It seems some things never change.'

Glancing back, Sarah saw their fellow tourists heading off into the interior of the pyramid.

'Looks like the tour's starting, Doctor.' She began to walk towards the entrance, fitting a flash to her camera as she went, but before she had gone more than a few feet the Doctor called her back.

'I detest guided tours,' he reminded her. 'Besides which, I'd rather take a look at the outside.' He stuffed his guide book back into his jacket pocket and set off briskly towards the edge of the shadow and the eastern face of the tomb. Sarah fell in step behind him, jogging to keep up.

'What's so fascinating about the outside?' she asked indignantly.

'The hieroglyphics which cover the slopes, they've never been deciphered.' The Doctor stopped and turned to Sarah. She instantly recognized the look in his eyes; that special twinkle which meant that he had discovered a mystery to solve.

'But I suppose you might just be able to work them out?' The tone of Sarah's voice betrayed her amusement at the Doctor's schoolboyish compulsion to solve every puzzle the universe had to offer.

'Well . . . ' the Doctor replied, a sheepish grin creeping across his face, 'I did pick up a few clues from what I saw in the pyramid on Mars.'

'Then we'd better go and see what the Osirans have got to say for themselves.' Sarah overtook the Doctor and strode out purposefully towards the pyramid's marble-like slopes. 'You never know,' she shouted back over her shoulder, 'it might be the universe's oldest knock-knock joke.'

It was now the Doctor's turn to have to run to catch up with his companion.

After four hours of walking around the pyramid, watching the

Doctor copying down a mass of meaningless symbols from the carved faces, Sarah had reached her boredom threshold.

'So, have we reached any conclusions?' she asked, her voice brimming with sarcasm.

'Mmm?' The Doctor didn't even look up from his notepad.

'What does it say?'

'Well, I can decipher about seventy-five per cent of it. The usual sort of stuff. "The Osiran dynasty will outlast the galaxy and thrive for all eternity . . . blah blah blah." '

'Is that all?'

'No, there's more. This cartouche seems to have been carved at a later date.' The Doctor pointed to a section of symbols low on the wall. 'The characters are quite different.'

' . . . And you can't read it,' Sarah concluded.

'No . . . but given time I . . . '

'Doctor, the suns are setting and it'll be dark soon. The transporter will be heading back and I desperately need a bath and a long, cool drink.'

The Doctor looked at his companion. 'Yes, of course. I'm sorry, Sarah. I can finish this back at the TARDIS. Let's head back.'

As Sarah turned to follow the Doctor, her foot caught on something. Thrown off balance, she fell forward into the dune. The sand felt hard and uneven beneath her, and she realized that there was something solid buried just below the surface. Brushing away the top layer, she found herself staring into the lifeless eyes of a corpse.

Sarah's scream brought the Doctor racing back. His companion had crawled away from the still half-buried cadaver and was now pointing over to where it lay. After checking that she was all right, he crouched over the body, a grim expression on his face.

'He's been buried here for a couple of days, by the look of it. Covered over by a sandstorm probably.'

'How do you know?' Sarah had begun to regain her composure. Mentally she chastized herself for over-reacting. During her time in the TARDIS she had already seen a lot of death. She had hoped that she would have become hardened towards it, like all those journalists who managed to keep their heads through the worst carnage of Earth's bloodiest wars. Secretly, though, she knew that she never could be like that. Death always sickened her.

'The body's not deep enough to have been buried on purpose,' replied the Doctor. He began to uncover the dead man's chest, arms and legs. 'By the look of the blaster wound on his shoulder he died from loss of blood.'

Sarah picked herself up and forced her legs to take her back towards the corpse. The sickly smell of decay was being carried on the desert wind. Crouching beside the Doctor, she spotted something grasped tightly in the dead man's left hand, sending out shafts of silver light as it glinted in the evening sun. She pointed it out to the Doctor, being unable to bring herself to touch the dead man herself. Forcing apart the tightly clenched fist, set hard with rigor mortis, the Doctor retrieved the shining object. It was a small crystal stone of less than four centimetres in length, delicately carved into the shape of a scarab beetle.

'It's beautiful,' Sarah murmured.

'Look closer, Sarah,' urged the Doctor, whose face bore an expression of deep concern. 'Look into the centre of the stone. Can't you see those shapes at the heart of the crystal?'

Sarah looked hard, reaching out and tipping the stone towards her. When she looked up at the Doctor there was fear in her eyes.

'It's the Eye of Horus.'

'Yes. I wonder what this chap was doing with it out here?'

The Doctor began to search through the pockets of the man's tattered jacket. All were empty save for one, which contained a small electronic notebook with the label 'Property of Edwin Carver' stuck on the front.

'Well, Mr Carver, now we know your name, let's see if we can find out what you were up to.' The Doctor flicked through the electronic pages of the book, stopping now and again to read sections.

'It seems our friend was an archaeologist from Earth. He's made an extensive study of the hieroglyphics on the pyramid.' The Doctor took out his notepad and compared the dead man's work with his own.

'Has he deciphered everything?' Sarah asked apprehensively.

'If you mean the section I couldn't read, the answer is yes. He must have had a brilliant mind.'

'What does it say?'

'According to Mr Carver, it reads "Let the ancient one sleep for eternity, for all will end when he awakens." '

'What does it mean?' Sarah looked into the Doctor's face, searching for a little comfort. She found none.

'I don't know, Sarah, but I have a feeling it's not part of a knock-knock joke. More like a portent of armageddon.' The Doctor rose to his feet. 'You'd better get them to hold the transporter's departure. Tell them about the body, but don't mention the scarab. I'll stay here with Mr Carver while you fetch someone to help me carry him.'

'Okay. I'll be as quick as I can.' With that, Sarah ran back towards the main entrance to the pyramid, happy to be away from the corpse.

The Doctor watched until she disappeared around the side of the pyramid. He then pulled out a jeweller's eyeglass from his pocket and began to study the scarab in all its intricate detail.

After several hours of questioning, the Doctor and Sarah finally emerged from behind the thick wooden doors of the local police station and into the streets of the planet's only urban complex, called Azira in the holiday brochures but unaffectionately nick-named Hellhole by its inhabitants. It was late evening now, and the only illumination was provided by the multicoloured neon signs of the city's bars and brothels.

'Can't we go back to the TARDIS now?' Sarah's voice was hoarse from repeating her story of the body's discovery. She felt drained and longed for the luxury of a bath and a sleep in the safety of the ship.

The Doctor took the TARDIS key from his pocket and offered it to her. 'I have a few enquiries to make before I join you,' he whispered.

'Where are you off to?' she whispered back, not fully understanding why they were talking so furtively.

'I'm going to have a look around our late friend's hotel room. I believe it might afford some clues as to the nature of the scarab.' The Doctor held up Carver's notebook, which displayed the dead man's address.

'Well, be careful,' warned Sarah, taking the key. Normally she would have hated to be left behind when the Doctor was investigating, but for once she was too tired even to contemplate accompanying him.

'I'm always careful,' replied the Doctor sombrely.

The two travellers parted company and Sarah set off for the edge of town and the TARDIS. The Doctor watched until she was out of sight, then strode away into the shadows of the darkened alleyways. Unseen, two wraith-like figures broke from the cover of the shadows. The first followed Sarah, the second went after the Doctor.

The Hotel Splendide was anything but. It had taken the Doctor the best part of an hour to discover its location, deep in the least salubrious quarter of Azira's ramshackle suburbs. It was a three-storey construction and, like all those around it, a cheaply built pre-fab. The exterior was stained dark brown by years of pollution and, stepping through the front door, the Doctor could see that the interior walls had a matching patina. At the far end of the lobby was the check-in desk, separated from the main part of the room by a large metal grille. A notice informed guests that the grille had several thousand volts running through it and therefore any attempt to rob the clerk was unwise. Another sign warned that all weapons were to be handed in at the desk.

The Doctor considered by-passing the desk and going straight up the stairs to Carver's room, but he could see that his presence had been noted by a security drone which circled above his head. A door behind the desk opened and a small, dark-skinned man ame through. The stump of a long-departed arm hung at his left side and a deep scar ran from left to right across his pig-like nose.

'Single or double?' the clerk growled.

'Neither. I've come to visit a friend.'

'No visitors.' The man turned to retreat behind the door.

'Well, I'm not strictly a visitor, I'm just collecting a few things from Mr Carver's room. He asked me to fetch them for him. I won't be long.' The Doctor moved towards the stairs.

The clerk slammed his fist down on the counter. 'No one gets into that room until Carver pays me the two weeks' rent he owes.'

'Ah, yes, of course.' The Doctor began searching through his pockets, emptying out handfuls of miscellaneous junk. Finally he found a draw-string purse containing assorted coins from various different planets across the universe. After a great deal of searching, he located a thousand-credit piece.

'Will this cover it?' he asked, knowing full well that he could buy several days in the best hotel on the planet for half the face value.

'Yeah, just about,' the clerk lied, his eyes almost popping out of his head. He took a plastic code-key from a rack beside the desk and threw it through a slot in the grille. It landed at the Doctor's feet. Retrieving first the contents of his pockets and then the key, the Doctor made his way to the stairs and up to the second floor. The clerk was about to retire to his office when the street door opened again and a thin figure in black crept in. The clerk recognized the newcomer only too well, and fear began to sweep through his body. The man in black approached the counter and gestured towards the stairs that the Doctor had just climbed.

'He is not to leave until I return,' he ordered. The clerk saw a flash of steel blade in the man's hand.

'Of course, I will ensure that he remains,' replied the clerk,

putting on a fake smile. He watched as the figure retreated
into the night.

On opening the door to Carver's room, the Doctor quickly saw
that he was not the first to visit it. It had been ransacked. Every
possible place of concealment had been checked, leaving pillows,
mattresses and cupboards split and broken. Stepping through the
chaos, he began to sift through Carver's papers, which were
strewn about the floor. His attention was caught by the remains
of a scrapbook containing newspaper cuttings and interviews
spanning Carver's distinguished archaeological career. In his
younger days, it seemed, the man had been something of a
celebrity, frequently invited to the parties of the rich and famous
to amaze them with tales of his discoveries. The Doctor wondered
how he had ended up in this shabby little room, far from the glitz
and glamour of those earlier years. He soon had a possible answer
as, lying amongst the papers, he found a large number of betting
slips and IOUs, mostly from one of the city's larger casinos,
unoriginally named the Black Pyramid.

Finding no mention of the scarab, the Doctor turned his
attention to a computer terminal which had been knocked to the
floor and was now lying on its side. Picking the unit up, he noticed
that its casing had been damaged in the fall. He tried the start-up
switch, but nothing happened. Removing the broken cover, he
checked over the components and soon found a break in the
optical cabling. Dipping into his pockets, he located a clear glass
marble and jammed it into the gap between the broken fibres. The
terminal screeched and sprang into life.

The only data that had survived intact were a few of Carver's
personal electronic mail files. Letters he had sent out over the sub-
space communications network. The Doctor's fingers sped over
the antiquated keyboard until he found one that caught his
attention:

To Mr William Carver

Head Curator
British Museum
Earth

Dear William,
A stroke of good fortune has finally come my way and, if you
would oblige me with one small favour, I will no longer have
need to call on your generous financial support. Mr Nazir, the
owner of the Black Pyramid, turns out to be a collector of
Egyptian antiquities. He claims we have met before, although
I have no recollection of it. He has agreed to cancel all my
debts if I can acquire for him the small crystal scarab I
discovered on the last Cairo dig in '41.

I realize that the scarab is now the property of the museum,
but I implore you to send it to me. It is such a minor piece, and
I know for a fact that it has languished in a store room for
twenty years now. Is it too much to ask, considering all the
marvellous pieces that I have discovered and donated to the
museum over the years?

Mr Nazir has promised that he will pay my passage off this
god-forsaken dust-bowl, even get me out to the Epsilon
quadrant and the new archaeological sites on the rim worlds.

Brother, give me this last chance to redeem myself. My
future is in your hands.
Awaiting your reply.
Edwin

The Doctor switched off the terminal and opened Carver's
electronic notebook. Turning to the diary section, he scrolled
back as far as it would go. After a few minutes, he found what he
had been looking for:

Cairo, Earth, 24 July AD 2541.
This morning I found myself chasing a young pickpocket

through the streets of the city. He had taken from me a small
crystal scarab that I had found at the excavation site. I had been
so pleased with the piece that I had borrowed it to show my
friends and family. If I had allowed the little thief to disappear
with it into the maze of narrow backstreets, I would have had
to tell the chief archaeologist that I had not only removed the
artefact without his permission but also lost it!

The boy was quick and agile but, fortunately for me, poorly
nourished. After ten minutes he began to slow, and I was soon
within range to rugby-tackle him. As he fell, the scarab slipped
from his fingers on to the dusty street. One final mad scramble
left me holding the scarab in one hand and the boy's neck in
the other.

The boy twisted loose of my grip and aimed a kick at my
knee. I yelled, partly in pain but mostly in surprise, as he made
good his escape. Before he vanished, he turned back to me and
spoke.

'I curse you Edwin Carver,' he said. 'I curse you in the
name of the Cult of the Black Pyramid.'

I watched the strange young urchin slip away into the
throng of people before picking myself up and heading back
to meet my friends. How strange that the boy should have
known my name.

The Doctor closed the notebook. He knew now where the scarab
had come from and who wanted it here on Beta Osiris. The
answers to the rest of the puzzle no doubt lay in the hands of the
owner of the Black Pyramid, although he had already begun to
form some rather worrying conclusions. He decided he had better
get back to Sarah, just in case.

Closing the door behind him, he descended the stairs back to
the lobby, which now appeared deserted. As he turned to leave,
something heavy caught him on the back of the neck. The room
began to spin and he collapsed into unconsciousness.

Sarah had only a few more streets to pass before she reached the safety of the TARDIS, but the hairs at the back of her neck had begun to prickle and she had the unnerving feeling that she was being followed. She found herself continually looking back over her shoulder, yet each time she turned round she saw nothing but the empty darkened streets. She began to walk a little faster, listening all the time for the slightest sound. Without realizing it, she suddenly found herself running. Twisting her head round once again she finally saw her pursuer. He had abandoned stealth now and was chasing her openly.

Sarah wanted to race for the TARDIS but realized that she would be caught before she reached the familiar blue box. Seeing an open door in a nearby building, she flung herself through it, slamming it behind her.

The room in which she found herself was softly lit and decorated with plush red curtains and gaudily patterned wallpaper. Lounging on an array of heavily stuffed sofas and armchairs, which matched the decor of the room, were around twenty young females of various races, all scantily clad. Sarah suddenly realized that she had stumbled into a brothel.

None of the girls seemed particularly interested in Sarah's sudden appearance. They were all preoccupied with inhaling the smoke emanating from a strangely shaped jar in the centre of the room. From her position, Sarah could just catch a whiff of it, and it immediately triggered memories of student parties she'd attended during her years at college. She began to make her way across the room towards a door opposite the one through which she had just entered. Before she could weave her way past the giggling working girls, however, the door swung open and a heavily built man burst in. He carried a half-empty bottle and, from the way he was swaying about, Sarah judged that the rest of the contents were already inside him. His appearance was that of a bandit or a mercenary. Around his waist he carried a large blaster and across his chest he wore what appeared to be a string of grenades. Over the back of his heavily armoured shoulders was slung a large, sword-like weapon, its edges covered with serrated teeth.

'Hi girls, I'm back!' The man staggered further into the room whilst the girls clustered around him, shrieking like a group of teenagers surrounding their favourite pop star. Sarah realized that she would have to skirt around the throng if she was to make good her escape. Just as she thought she was home free, a huge hand reached out and dragged her into the mass of bodies. She found herself face to face with the drunken man while his hands clumsily groped her.

'Well, hello there. You must be new. Why don't you and I go and get to know each other better, hmm?'

Sarah's knee hit a bullseye. The oaf's eyes crossed and he collapsed to the floor on his knees. By the time he had managed to regain some of his breath, Sarah had broken free and fled from the room.

'I like her,' rasped the mercenary. 'She reminds me of my Taiyin.'

Sarah found herself back in the dark streets, a block away from where she had been chased. She looked around but could see no sign of her pursuer. She hesitated for a moment. Should she return to the TARDIS as she had originally intended, or should she try to find the Doctor? She knew that if she had been followed, the likelihood was that he had been trailed as well. Whilst she pondered her options, she pushed her hands deep into the pockets of her dress. The fingers of her right hand touched something smooth and round and, without having to look, she knew what it was: the scarab! She pulled it out and held it up to the light. The Doctor must have slipped it to her before they separated. So, he had intended to act as a decoy while she returned to the TARDIS with the scarab! Except that the plan hadn't worked. She made her decision: she would try to catch up with the Doctor. And when they were safely out of this mess, she would give him a piece of her mind.

Sarah had glanced only briefly at the address of the hotel when the Doctor had held up Carver's notebook and, although she could remember its name, she had no idea what street or district it was in. Luckily for her, the Hotel Splendide had something of a reputation. Having obtained directions from the revellers who spilled out of the city's many bars and nightclubs, she eventually found herself standing on the opposite side of the street from the building. She was about to cross over and make her way inside when she saw, emerging from the entrance, the man who had earlier followed her. He was accompanied by another man who, like him, was dressed from head to toe in black. Between them they carried the prone body of the Doctor. Sarah watched helplessly as they bundled her friend through the open doors of a goods transporter parked outside the hotel and drove off at high speed.

Sarah felt a wave of panic hit her. Was the Doctor still alive? Where were the men taking him? How could she find him again? However, her strength of character soon reasserted itself. She was an investigative journalist; she could find out what she needed to know. It was simply a matter of talking to people and asking the right questions. Someone was bound to know what was going on.

An hour of investigations had turned up precisely nothing. The desk clerk of the Hotel Splendide had ordered her out at gunpoint. Others who lived or worked on the street had shut their doors in her face. The sum of everything she had been told was that no one in Azira knew anything about anything. They were all plainly scared, and from that Sarah could only deduce that whoever was behind the Doctor's kidnapping was extremely powerful. There was just one person she hadn't yet approached: a beggar sprawled in the gutter at the far end of the row of buildings adjoining the hotel. He was little more than a bundle of rags, and the stench which emanated from them turned her stomach. Still, it was worth a try. After all, she had no other options left.

'So, you've finally got around to asking me, have you?' The

beggar's voice startled Sarah. She hadn't expected him to talk to her voluntarily.

'I suppose you didn't see anything either?' she asked him.

'Maybe I did, maybe I didn't.' Sarah looked into the man's eyes and saw to her surprise that they were deep and full of knowledge. 'Perhaps a small token may help me to decide.'

'I'm afraid I don't have any money or food.' She followed the beggar's gaze and saw that he was staring intently at her Nikon SLR, hanging by its strap at her side.

'An antique, that camera. Twentieth-century Earth, isn't it? Obviously still in working order. It could fetch quite a price at auction.'

Sarah considered the beggar's proposition. She'd had the camera ever since she started work. It had been a gift on her first day from her Aunt Lavinia, and she had treasured it like a good luck charm. Could she now give it away, even for the Doctor? She knew that in truth she had little choice. If she couldn't find her friend, she would probably never get off this planet. She lifted the strap over her head and passed the camera over to the beggar.

'Thank you, dear lady. I now remember clearly the events of which you have been asking. I believe you will find the answers you seek at the Black Pyramid casino, on the far side of town.' The man began to rummage through his rags. 'Please take this. It may help you.' He held out a small plastic card with the name of the Black Pyramid emblazoned upon it. Sarah took it and thanked him for his help.

As the young woman moved away, heading for the casino, the beggar sighed and scrambled to his feet. His shape began to blur and change and, within just a few moments, he had transformed into a tall, imposing figure bedecked in flowing scarlet robes.

'That's it, Miss Smith. Go and save the Doctor from his own foolishness. We cannot allow our most talented agent to get himself killed now, can we?'

A smile spread across the man's face as he operated the time ring on his wrist and dematerialised into the vortex.

Pain, blackness, a sensation of falling. Was this regeneration? No, but he had a splitting headache. Without moving a muscle, the Doctor began to assess his situation. He was lying on something soft and well padded. A bed. No, more like a sofa. Judging by the air circulation and the acoustics, he was in a large room. The sounds of breathing alerted him to the presence of another person no more than five feet away. At length, he opened his eyes.

The room was opulent in the extreme. The majority of the wall space was occupied by glass display cases, each of which contained some kind of precious antiquity. The owner obviously had a great affinity for ancient Egypt, as its relics were to be found in particular abundance. The Doctor's gaze eventually came to rest upon the source of the breathing sounds: a fat man seated in a high-backed wicker chair. He was dark-complexioned, wore a white suit and had a maroon fez perched precariously on his large head.

'Welcome, friend, to my humble establishment,' the man said, staring at him intently. 'I am Anwar Nazir, proprietor of the Black Pyramid.'

The Doctor sat up. On a low table between himself and Nazir he could see the contents of his pockets, which had been turned out for the second time that night.

'You are no doubt wondering why I brought you here, Doctor.'

'Yes, I had pondered on that. I also wonder how you happen to know my name.'

'Quite simple, my friend. My contacts at the police station told me about you and your companion Miss Smith when you brought in poor Mr Carver's body.'

'Friend of yours, was he?'

'Let's just say that we were partners in a business transaction.'

'And what kind of business would that be?'

'Mr Carver was acquiring a piece of Egyptian jewellery for me, in return for which I had generously offered to cancel his very considerable gambling debts. Unfortunately, he chose not to honour our agreement and disappeared before I received the piece in question. I was hoping that you might perhaps have found it when you discovered Mr Carver's body.'

The Doctor adopted an expression of goggle-eyed innocence. 'Me? No. All I found was an old notebook, which I attempted to return to Mr Carver's hotel room this evening.'

'Ah yes, Doctor, I heard about your unfortunate experience at the Hotel Splendide. Sadly, that area of our city is full of cut-throats and pickpockets. On behalf of the people of Azira, I apologize. When my men discovered you lying unconscious in the lobby I had them bring you straight here so that I might compensate you for your injury.' Nazir motioned to a large pile of credits which lay on the table beside the Doctor's possessions.

'I couldn't possibly take your money, Mr Nazir. And I'm very sorry, but I can't help you find your item of jewellery.'

Only Nazir's eyes betrayed his anger at the Doctor's refusal to co-operate. Well, if bribery wouldn't work, he still had one more trick up his sleeve.

'Never mind, Doctor. You rest here for a while. I'm sure your companion Miss Smith will be joining us soon. Perhaps she can help in the recovery of my trinket.'

Nazir rose from his chair and left the room without once looking back. Beyond the door, the Doctor could see several burly guards dressed in black, all heavily armed. Then the door was slammed shut behind Nazir and he heard the sound of a key operating the lock.

The Black Pyramid casino was an impressive building. A quarter-size replica of the genuine article in the desert, it was constructed from black glass and chrome and had elevators running up and down its four corners. On each of its expansive faces a giant neon sign announced its name.

Sarah stood in the forecourt under a canopy of imitation palm trees. She hadn't imagined such a massive building when she'd set off on her mission to rescue the Doctor. Where should she start? It could take days to hunt through the entire complex. She set off across the ground floor towards one of the lifts, weaving her way through a throng of eager gamblers from a wide variety of different races. Some of the games – roulette, blackjack and slot machines – were familiar, but most were completely new to her. At one point she had to skirt around a particularly large crowd which had gathered to bet on the outcome of a virtual-reality Russian Roulette contest, described by its neon hoarding as 'A Game Of Fun For All The Family'.

Eventually she reached the lift doors and pressed the call button. Above her, security drones were scanning the room, fixing the casino's patrons with their glassy stares, and she began to feel very edgy. Fortunately, the lift took only a few moment to arrive and she was the only person waiting for it. She stepped inside and the doors hissed shut behind her.

Studying the control panel, Sarah quickly concluded that there were two levels below ground and twenty above it. The lower levels were labelled as catering and transporter parking areas, the upper ones mainly as conference rooms and suites. The very top floor, however, was marked as private and its indicator light had only a narrow slot beside it in place of the usual push-button.

Sarah's instincts told her that this private area was where she was most likely to find the Doctor. But how could she get up there? Struck by a sudden impulse, she took out the plastic card that the beggar had given her and pushed it into the slot. Immediately, the indicator light came on and the lift began to rise. She quickly retrieved the card and the lift stopped again. Now that she knew she could get access to the top floor, she realized that like any good investigative reporter she would need some kind of a cover story. She hit the button for the kitchens.

Twenty minutes later, Sarah arrived at the top floor wearing a maid's outfit and dragging a cleaning cart behind her. The corridor outside the lift was empty, so she made her way to the nearest door and tried it.

Clustered around a table were five black-clad men, amongst them the one who had earlier pursued her through the streets of the city. He glanced up as she came in, but failed to recognize her. Sarah forced herself to start breathing again. She began to tidy the room around the men, emptying litter bins and dusting the ledges. The men were too engrossed in a card game to take much notice of her.

After fifteen minutes' frantic polishing, Sarah thought it safe to leave the room without arousing suspicion. She wheeled her cart along the corridor and round the next bend. At the far end was a large oak door, guarded by two more of the black-clad acolytes. Sarah wheeled her cart straight up to them, hoping her cover would get her inside. One of the guards waved her away.

'This room is not to be cleaned today. Mr Nazir's orders.'

Sarah turned and headed back in the direction she had come. Halting at the next door, she pushed her cart through and found herself in a room very similar to that in which she had encountered the huddle of guards. To her delight, she saw that it had a connecting door to the room from which she had just been barred. She tried the handle and, finding it locked, again took out the plastic pass card.

'You worked before, so don't fail me now,' she whispered, inserting the card into the slot below the handle. There was a tiny click, the door swung open and she crept through.

The Doctor was working his way around the room, examining the artifacts in the glass cases. He spotted Sarah from her reflection in one of the panes.

'If you could just make the beds, but leave the vacuuming till later.'

'Doctor!'

'Hello, Sarah Jane. Found ourselves a new profession, have we?'

'This is no time for jokes; we've got to get out of here. Come on!'

The Doctor shook his head. 'Not yet, I'm afraid. Have you still got the scarab?'

Sarah produced the crystal from the pocket of her apron and handed it to the Doctor.

'What are you going to do with it?'

'Give it to Mr Nazir.'

'What! But why?'

'Because he wants it very badly, and I need to know the reason.'

'But that could be terribly dangerous! This Nazir might have you killed the second you hand it over.'

The Doctor heard the lock of the door unlatch.

'No time to discuss it now. Wait in there and listen.'

He bundled Sarah out of the door through which she had just entered and threw himself back onto the couch. Moments later, Anwar Nazir came in.

Nazir was annoyed. None of his operatives had yet managed to track down the Doctor's companion. Either she had the scarab, in which case she must be found, or her capture and torture would make the Doctor reveal where he had hidden it. He decided to try a bluff.

'My dear friend. Your companion, Miss Smith, has now arrived, and is enjoying my . . . hospitality.'

The Doctor grinned. 'May I see her?'

'Of course, Doctor, once we have finished our little chat about my missing jewellery.'

'Well, maybe I can help you out there after all. What does this trinket look like?'

This is more like it, thought Nazir. I will have the scarab before the night is out! The scarab I first held as a small boy in the streets of Cairo. It will be mine again, and my destiny will be fulfilled.

'I search for a small crystal scarab no bigger than my thumb.'

'What, like this?'

The Doctor gestured behind Nazir's ear and produced the scarab out of thin air. The man grabbed it greedily from him.

'Where did you hide it! My men searched you thoroughly.'

'Not thoroughly enough, it would seem.'

Nazir was too enraptured to think logically about the crystal's sudden appearance. He stood in silence, gazing down at his prize.

'May I see Sarah now, please?' asked the Doctor, disturbing his reverie.

'Later, later. I have much to do. You will remain here until I return, at which time I will repay you fully for your help.'

Nazir's lips curled into a cruel smile. He strode from the room, carrying the scarab before him.

Once the door had swung closed behind him, Nazir turned to the two guards.

'Let him live – for the moment. I wish him to see what he has made possible. Then he shall die.'

The guards nodded and Nazir headed off to make his final arrangements.

Sarah burst back into room. 'What now?'

'Now we get out here and go after Nazir,' replied the Doctor.

'But how will we find him?'

'He'll be making for the pyramid, of course. Come on!'

The Doctor rushed into the adjoining room and began to ransack Sarah's cleaning cart, throwing buckets, cloths, bottles and other sundry items over his shoulder with wild abandon. He then removed the central shelf from the base of the unit and squeezed himself into the gap, motioning Sarah to cover the side with rubbish sacks so that he could not be seen.

With great difficulty, Sarah pushed the heavily laden cart out of the room and back into the corridor. The guards took little notice of her as she disappeared round the corner and made for the lift.

Minutes later, the Doctor and Sarah were heading out of the city and into the desert in a sporty Ferrari hover-car 'borrowed' from the casino's underground parking area. Such was the vehicle's turn of speed that they reached the pyramid site in less than a quarter of the time that it had taken on their earlier guided tour.

Parking the Ferrari a short distance away, they made the final approach on foot. The night was pitch black, providing excellent cover, but they kept low behind the sand dunes to avoid any possibility of detection. When they came within sight of the entrance, they discovered that four of the black-clad guards were patrolling outside.

'I think we must have got here ahead of Nazir,' commented the Doctor.

'But what good does that do us if we can't get past the guards?' hissed Sarah.

'We may not be able to get in this way, but remember that the true door of the pyramid is on the south face.'

With this, the Doctor set off at a run towards the opposite side of the pyramid, beckoning Sarah to follow him.

It took them a good ten minutes to circle round the giant edifice, all the time being careful to keep out of sight of any patrolling guards. When they reached the appropriate place, they crept up to the side of the pyramid and the Doctor began to read off the hieroglyphics, letting his hand run over the carved symbols as he went.

After what seemed an age, the Doctor gave a gasp of triumph and pressed against an oddly shaped cartouche. It sank a little way into the marble-like surface and, some four feet from where they stood, a small door grated open in the wall. The Doctor took Sarah's hand and led the way into the darkness beyond.

They found themselves moving through a maze of chambers and tunnels. Sarah's eyes took some time to adjust to the gloom and she repeatedly tripped and stumbled as the Doctor led her along the narrow passageways. To her relief, they eventually emerged into a large chamber lit by flaming torches. The chamber's ceiling – and, she presumed, the rest of the pyramid above it – was supported on a circle of eight gigantic columns. The Doctor crouched down behind one of them and bade his companion to do the same.

'What now?' asked Sarah. The Doctor just held a finger to his lips.

They had been waiting only a few minutes when a party of black-robed figures entered through a narrow doorway in the opposite wall. Their hoods were pulled down over their faces and they were chanting as they slowly moved to form a circle around a raised dais in the centre of the chamber. Their leader then stepped up onto the dais. It was Nazir.

'Brethren of the Cult of the Black Pyramid, I call you forth to hear me.'

'We hear you,' the other robed figures intoned back.

'Our vigil is near its end and soon our lord will rejoin us. Long millennia have passed since our god departed our world, but now we have found him again. We will call him back to us so that he may guide our destinies until the end of time.'

'So shall it be,' the brethren replied.

'We have survived the trickery of the false god Sutekh, now let his brother be amongst us. Rise Horus, pharaoh of all worlds!'

Nazir held the crystal scarab aloft and the brethren sank to their knees before it.

A rumbling noise rose from deep inside the pyramid, and the dais on which Nazir stood began to sink slowly into the floor. To Sarah's astonishment, the Doctor suddenly sprang from his hiding place and ran towards the rapidly disappearing dais. Without stopping to think, she raced after him. The brethren, deep in prayer, were taken completely by surprise. Before they could react, the Doctor and Sarah had leaped on to the dais, knocking Nazir to the ground. The dais sank below the floor and an iris-like cover closed behind it.

The Doctor was the first of the three to pick himself up. He helped the slightly dazed Sarah to her feet.

'How are you feeling, Sarah Jane?'

'Flattened, but otherwise unharmed. Next time, let me know in advance when you intend to throw yourself down a hole in the ground!'

'Sorry about that. Improvisation's always been my forte.'

They took stock of their surroundings and saw that they were in a small room, the walls of which glowed and swirled in bright colours, like a boxed rainbow. In the centre was a stone sarcophagus. Nazir, who had been knocked unconscious by the impact of their bodies, lay on the floor nearby. The Doctor prised the scarab from his hand. He then moved to inspect the sarcophagus. Its lid was shaped to depict the prone figure of the bull-headed god, Horus, and covered in a chrome-like finish which reflected the swirling patterns from the walls.

'Magnificent,' he muttered, awe-struck.

'Yes, isn't it,' replied Nazir.

The Doctor spun round to find the Egyptian with his arm across Sarah's throat and a small but dangerous-looking blaster in his hand.

'You will give me the scarab, or I will crush your friend's windpipe.'

The Doctor could see by the fire burning in the man's eyes that he meant to carry out his threat.

'Wait! Listen to me! If you intend to wake Horus, you should know that he was not the benign god of legend. He was a cruel and ruthless dictator who conquered and oppressed more than a hundred inhabited worlds.'

'No!' cried Nazir. 'He gave my people art and culture, he civilized us!'

'Yes. But to other worlds he brought plagues and famine, infertility and starvation. He would nurture beautiful societies of peace-loving people and then unleash a race of vicious killers on them, just to see what would happen. He played with the inhabitants of the galaxy like a child with a set of toy soldiers!'

'You're lying! Give me the scarab or I swear I'll kill the girl.'

Nazir tightened his grip on Sarah's neck and she began to choke.

'All right, all right. You win.'

The Doctor held out the scarab and Nazir grabbed it from him, releasing his grip on Sarah. Keeping his gun firmly trained on the two travellers, the Egyptian then backed across the room to the sarcophagus. He cast his eyes over the surface and quickly found what he was looking for: a hole the same size and shape as the scarab.

'What's he going to do?' asked Sarah.

'The scarab is a complex micro-circuit key,' replied the Doctor. 'Once it's in place, it will start the revivification process and Horus will return from the land of the dead.'

Sarah wished she hadn't asked.

With trembling fingers, Nazir lowered the scarab into place. A wave of energy immediately surged through his body. At first it felt wonderful. His pulse raced and his mind expanded with knowledge and power. But then he felt his consciousness being overwhelmed. His brain couldn't cope with the stream of energy being fed into it. He screamed in agony, and smoke began to rise from his chest and head. Eventually he fell backwards, breaking the contact with the scarab. His lifeless body hit the floor and disintegrated into millions of tiny fragments of crystallized carbon.

Sarah almost blacked out at the sight. The Doctor supported her until she had recovered, then moved across and leaned over Nazir's remains.

'The problem with crystal micro-circuits is that they can so easily short-circuit if they get heavily scratched.'

He held up an old pen-knife and folded the blade back into the handle.

'You . . . you knew that would happen?' asked Sarah.

' "Hoped" would be the right word. I couldn't tell if I'd done enough damage to the crystal. Fortunately, I had. The energy discharge was routed away from the sarcophagus and into Nazir. I couldn't let him unleash the evil of Horus upon the universe. The time for such gods is long past.'

He stared down at the crystal scarab, which had turned jet black. To Sarah's alarm, he then reached out and removed it from its slot. Nothing happened.

'Don't worry Sarah, the circuits are quite dead now. Help me to lift the lid off the sarcophagus, will you?'

'What!'

'I must know what's inside. If Horus is in suspended animation, he could still be dangerous in the future.'

Although she couldn't quite believe what she was doing, Sarah took hold of one end of the lid while the Doctor raised the other. Between them, they managed to roll it off and on to the floor. They then peered over the edge of the sarcophagus and saw the body within. It was shrunken and black, a pair of bull-like horns protruding from the leathery skin of its shrivelled head. Not for the first time in 24 hours, Sarah felt sick.

'Was it the short circuit?' she asked.

'No. He's been dead for, oh, perhaps a thousand years. Looks like the cryogenic systems failed on him. Never trust technology, I say.'

'Doctor!' Sarah interrupted the Doctor's musings. 'Look at the walls!'

Looking up, the Doctor saw that the swirling patterns had gone into overdrive and the walls were pulsing with energy.

'We'd better get out of here. All that stored-up energy with nowhere to go equals one very big bang.'

He motioned Sarah to join him on the dais and instructed her to touch a nearby wall panel bearing a set of hieroglyphics.

'What's it say?' asked Sarah as she pressed the carved figures.

'Up.'

The dais rose up through the floor and back into the chamber above, where the Doctor and Sarah found themselves surrounded by the angry brethren.

'Listen!' the Doctor announced. 'In a few minutes this whole pyramid will be showered in psionic energy. Anyone left inside will be reduced to a handful of carbon granules – just like your leader.'

As if to back up the Doctor's warning, a huge belch of black smoke suddenly billowed up from the room below. After a moment's indecision the brethren scattered, running for the exits. The Doctor and Sarah followed.

Once outside, the two travelling companions ran back to the Ferrari hover-car and sped away to what the Doctor deemed a safe distance. They looked back just in time to see the apex of the pyramid explode as a shaft of multi-coloured energy spewed forth, shooting high into the heavens like a gigantic roman candle.

Sarah gaped at the awe-inspiring sight, and even the Doctor was visibly impressed.

'That amount of energy will take a couple of centuries to drain off,' he reflected. 'Should bring in quite a few new tourists.'

A broad grin spread across his face. Sarah found it quite infectious.

As they strolled back to the TARDIS through the streets of Azira, now bathed in bright sunshine, Sarah puzzled over the questions that remained in her mind.

'Doctor, why did Horus go into suspended animation in the first place? And how did the scarab find its way to Earth?'

The Doctor seemed to mull these points over for a while before answering. 'I'm not a hundred per cent certain myself. Perhaps being master of the galaxy wasn't enough for him any more. With the rest of his species dead he may have become disillusioned with existence.'

'Or?' said Sarah.

'Or, it may have been yet another of his experiments. To see if any of the races he had ruled over would come in search of him if he left a few clues as to his whereabouts and some keys with which to wake him.'

'You mean there may be more of these scarabs floating round the universe?'

'Maybe. They do seem to cause nothing but trouble for those who own them, though.' The Doctor held the now black crystal in his hand.

'Do you think it's wise to hold on to this one, then?'

The Doctor gave a half-smile. 'I've never needed any kind of talisman to find trouble. It always finds me.'

The Doctor slipped the scarab back into his pocket as they walked in silence towards the familiar blue box that was their home.

I stared open-mouthed at Silverman as he replaced the scarab on the table and sat back in his chair. 'You thought that would add to our understanding?' I asked him, incredulously.

'Indeed,' he replied.

'Well,' I said, shaking my head in amazement, 'it's certainly given us a bit more to think about.'

'That is so,' he agreed. 'Another man referred to as "the Doctor". Perhaps it is an honorary title of some sort, which passes from one recipient to another?'

'Maybe,' I said, reflecting that the question of the Doctor's identity was actually one of the less perplexing aspects of the story we had heard. 'Or maybe he really can change his appearance.'

I got another match out of my pocket and went to relight the candles again, but Silverman stood up and put a restraining hand on my arm. 'I think I have a more permanent solution to the problem of illumination,' he told me. I half wondered if he was going to conjure a light out of thin air, but his solution turned out to be more mundane than that: he summoned Ramon with a tug on a bell-pull and instructed him to bring in an oil lamp. The Mexican returned a few minutes later, deposited the lamp on his master's desk, then hurried out again without a backward glance. The lamplight dispelled some of the gloom, but cast eerie flickering shadows across the study walls. I went over and turned up the wick, hoping to make it a little brighter.

My strange client, meanwhile, had risen from his chair and was pacing up and down the room, flapping his arms about in irritation. 'If only I could regain some of my memory,' he said, rapping his knuckles against his forehead. He cast me a sideways glance. 'I seem to recall that I was searching for something. A cylinder! Yes, I'm sure it was a cylinder. With the diameter of . . . of a large coin, and about this long.' He held his hands out about a yard apart.

'And I bet we should have seen the one that got away,' I muttered.

'What?'

'Sorry. Private joke.'

'Er, well . . . I think I must have left this cylinder some-where in the city, hidden it perhaps, and come back to find it. Yes, I'm sure I was searching for it; trying to retrieve it.'

'But you don't remember where you left it?' I asked.

'Of course I don't!' he exploded. 'That's why I want you to help me retrace my steps!'

I stood in silent contemplation for a few moments, then looked across at him with a smile. 'Well, I guess we'd better continue then, hadn't we?'

With some reluctance on my client's part, we all returned to our chairs around the table. Silverman sifted through the pile of objects and this time selected a small lump of yellow rock, which he held out in front of him as before. I pulled my jacket tighter around me as a blast of cold air whipped through the room and the weird glow started up again from Silverman's hands. Then the psychic began to speak . . .

The Book of Shadows

Jim Mortimore

For Paul, Alex, Toby and Robin i' the Who

331 BC

When his ship smashed a hole in time and vanished through it, Rhakotis knew he was going to die. But when the expected bodily dissolution did not come, he began to suspect he had been wrong to retreat from consciousness so quickly.

Nervously, Rhakotis allowed his awareness to emerge from his hind-brain. The pain overwhelmed him immediately. He was scared to perceive how badly his body had been damaged in the accident, even as he was surprised that it still lived. Rhakotis struggled to regain full bodily control. The pain from his shattered limbs made the task impossible. Eventually he was forced to isolate the part of his brain which dealt with such signals. This made working easier but did nothing to alleviate the dreadful grinding of shattered bones in his upper limbs as he struggled into an excursion suit.

When Rhakotis managed at last to fight his way clear of the dying ship, he was immediately overwhelmed by the environment in which he found himself. His surroundings drove all hurt from his fore-brain: of all the planets on which he could have crashed, a world containing water was surely the best.

Not only did the liquid provide for a slightly softer landing, but where there was water there was life; where there was life there could be intelligence; and where there was intelligence there would be *help*.

322 BC

'*Ian!*'

Barbara Wright scrambled to her feet. Pulling the Doctor

upright, she ran back along the still-collapsing mine gallery. But when she reached the place where Ian Chesterton and the TARDIS had been, there was only a loosely packed wall of glittering yellow-studded rock.

Beside her, the Doctor stopped to retrieve a small piece of the debris, which he examined in the light of one of his everlasting matches. 'Hmm, yes . . . good colour.' He tapped the rock with the handle of his cane and held it to his ear. 'Good density too, I should say . . . '

'How can you stand there blathering about gold?' exclaimed Barbara. 'Ian and the TARDIS are both buried under a ton of rubble!'

The Doctor slipped the rock into a pocket of his Edwardian jacket and stared at Barbara. 'If you hadn't been in such a hurry to explore –'

'If you hadn't insisted on collecting your own gold to make a wedding ring for Susan –'

'Yes. Well, this is all rather academic now, isn't it?'

Instead of replying, Barbara tore at the pile of rock.

'Do be careful!' said the Doctor urgently. 'If you disturb the equilibrium, the rest of the roof might come down and bury us too!' At Barbara's look he added, 'We must find help to free Ian. This is a mine after all. There must be miners somewhere.'

Shaking, Barbara stepped back from the rock face. 'You're right.' She glared at the wall of rubble, then turned and walked away.

After a while she realized she could hear the sound of murmuring voices somewhere up ahead. And the clinking of metal tools on rock. The gallery widened, then opened on to a large, dimly lit cavern, obviously one of the main seams. A large number of people were working at the rock face; so many they vanished into the candle-spattered darkness. Barbara saw men and women and children alike. As one they were pale through lack of sunlight, their skin chaffed and scarred from flying chips of rock, their lungs wheezing, choked with the dust they made as they worked.

The sound of their picks and hammers was a metallic din in the gloom.

Directly in front of her, the nearest man hacked wearily at the wall of rock with an iron hammer. The rags he wore had once obviously been fine clothes. Sensing Barbara's presence he turned. His eyes widened in recognition and he fell to his knees.

Barbara stared at the man, who lowered his eyes abjectly.

The sound of hammers gradually faded as the other slaves became aware of the strangers. In a few moments, Barbara and the Doctor were surrounded by a ring of hopeless, staring faces.

'They look so sad,' whispered Barbara. 'And why are they staring at me like that?'

'I don't know. Why don't you say something to them and find out?'

Trying not to let her nervousness show, Barbara took a step towards the slaves. At once another dozen knelt.

'Can you help?' she asked after a momentary pause. 'There's been a rockfall. Ian – a friend – is trapped.'

The kneeling man spoke. 'If your friend is trapped, why don't you have your guards free him?'

Barbara glanced at the Doctor. He waggled his eyebrows unhelpfully.

One of the kneeling men, a heavy-set Egyptian, raised his eyes. 'Has King Ptolemy decided to free us from the mines? Is there enough gold now to construct Alexander's coffin?'

Barbara's mind whirled. Did the Egyptian mean Alexander the Great? She needed more time to think this through. 'I can't discuss these questions now. There has been a rockfall. A man is trapped. You must help to free him.'

Now the Egyptian rose to his feet. 'You cannot free your friend because you have no guards . . . ' he mused quietly. In the silence, his voice carried to every corner of the gallery.

'My guards are . . . otherwise engaged,' Barbara improvized, still not sure where this conversation was leading but knowing she had to gain the initiative somehow.

'Indeed?' The Egyptian now approached with more confidence. He was still holding his hammer. He half-turned to the rest of the slaves. 'It's the Queen,' he said. 'And no guards with her, save this old relic.' He pointed at the Doctor. Barbara saw her companion's eyes narrow slightly in annoyance, though he did not speak.

The Egyptian's voice remained quite calm as he added, 'I, Susa, say that we can use her to escape the mines.'

An interested mutter ran through the crowd.

'Young man.' The Doctor edged in front of Barbara. 'If you will kindly furnish us with the help we need, we will trouble you no –'

Without warning, Susa leapt for the Doctor, hammer raised.

The Doctor skipped nimbly to one side. When his blow did not connect, Susa had no choice but to follow through or fall. He stepped forward and the old man's cane somehow tangled between his feet. He toppled, his head cracked against a stone and he lay quite still.

'Old relic, am I, indeed?' The Doctor smiled grimly.

Barbara knelt beside Susa and ran her hands across his skull. 'I think he'll be all right when he wakes up.'

The Doctor frowned, half-nodded, half-shook his head, as if his attacker's health was nothing more than a distraction.

Then all at once parts of the puzzle began to fall into place. Barbara straightened from her kneeling position. When she spoke, her voice rang clearly throughout the gallery. 'Slaves of Egypt, hear my words! Help us and I will guarantee your freedom.'

The Doctor looked sharply at Barbara but she shook her head: *not now*. She raised her voice so it would carry to the farthest corners of the cavern. 'No one was born to live in darkness,' she said. 'No one should kneel before another. Your bodies may be imprisoned, but not your minds. Don't you dream of the sun, of clouds, of fresh food for your children? I can give you these things. *Help us!* And as your Queen, I swear you will have them all.'

The man kneeling nearest her spoke. 'I have been so long in the dark that to feel the heat of the sun on my back would probably kill me.' He paused. Swallowed. Barbara became aware that the sound of metal on rock had died away completely, and the slaves were crowding forward. 'Better to die in the light,' the man went on, and in his voice there was a strength Barbara would not have believed he could possess. 'What do you want us to do?'

'For a start you can tell me your name.'

'I am an Israelite. My name is Aristea.'

'Well then, Aristea, the first thing you can do is get up off your knees.'

When Barbara had explained the situation, Aristea took some men with hammers and picks into the gallery in which Ian was trapped. Barbara began to follow them, but the Doctor held her back, guiding her to a gloomy corner of the cavern.

'My dear Barbara, you are taking the most appalling risk!'

Barbara frowned. 'You know how they treat women in this century, Doctor. If I'm not a queen, I'm a nobody! We'll never rescue Ian!'

'And what will you do when Aristea and the slaves find out you were lying, hmm?'

'Ah, but that's the beauty of it,' Barbara smiled thinly. 'With any luck they'll never know.'

The Doctor frowned. 'What do you mean?'

'Haven't you realized? Aristea mentioned the slaves here are digging for gold for the coffin of Alexander the Great. That means the date is around 323 or 322 BC.'

'Why?'

'Because that's when he died. And when one of his generals, Ptolemy Lagus, declared himself King in Alexander's place, *he freed all the Jews from slavery*. It's why he changed his name to Ptolemy Soter. Soter means saviour in Greek. Don't you see? The Jews are going to be freed anyway. They'll just think it was my doing, that's all. And this way we get the help we need to save Ian.'

The Doctor clasped his lapels and pursed his lips. 'Just because you have the knowledge to manipulate historical events to your advantage, it doesn't mean that you have the right to do so.'

'Don't be ridiculous, Doctor. You said yourself, you left your own people because they were content merely to watch, when you saw the need for intervention.'

'My dear Barbara, there is a world of difference between my perception of the Universe and your own.'

'Oh really, Doctor! When *you* see a wrong, you correct it! You've said yourself, the history of Earth is fixed. But the future is *not* fixed. Ian's future is not fixed and I want to change it! You see? Our goals are the same; whatever small differences there are in methods are of no consequence if Ian lives!'

'And what if he is already dead, hmm? Have you thought of that?'

'*He wouldn't dare die without my say so!*' Barbara started to cover her face with her hands, remembered it was a gesture she was trying to stop making, let them fall to her sides instead.

The Doctor's expression softened. 'I know you're upset. It is not unobvious, even to an old man, how much you care for Ian, but –'

'*Care for him!* I don't just care for him, I –' She hesitated.

The Doctor *hrrumph*ed gently. 'Perhaps you'd check on our friend with the hammer?' he suggested. 'We wouldn't want him to die either, would we? Especially since it was our fault he was injured.'

Barbara nodded. 'You're right.' She turned and walked slowly back to where they had left the unconscious Egyptian.

He was gone.

One of the slaves shuffled closer. 'I saw him get up,' he said. 'He went over near to you for a while, then went up there.' He pointed towards a passage leading steeply upwards from the gallery.

'So our violent friend was not as badly hurt as we had supposed,' said the Doctor. 'Tell me, what lies at the end of that passage?'

The slave said, 'The upper workings. Where the soldiers are.'
Barbara said grimly, 'If Susa overheard us . . . '

'You're quite right!' the Doctor exclaimed. 'If he realizes you're not the real Queen, the first thing he'll do is –'

There was the sound of running feet in the passage. Lights bobbed there, approaching rapidly.

'– fetch the guards,' finished Barbara bitterly.

There were twelve guards, all dressed in the leather armour and decorated sash of the Egyptian army, each brandishing a short sword. The soldiers poured down the steep passage from the surface, pushing their way through the slaves as if they didn't exist. But to Barbara's surprise, when the soldiers saw her, they too dropped to one knee and raised their swords in a salute. Perhaps the most amazed figure of all was Susa, who scuttled to one side with a hateful look.

Ignoring Susa, Barbara glanced at the Doctor and raised one eyebrow: *what do we do now?*

The Doctor shrugged.

The captain of the soldiers stood. He slipped his sword back into its scabbard. In a slightly reproving voice he said, 'Next time you choose to inspect the mines, my lady, perhaps you would consider taking some guards with you? It can be dangerous.'

Not knowing quite what to say, Barbara remained silent. She merely stared at the Captain, who added, 'If my lady would allow us to escort her to the caravan?'

'Er . . . ' Barbara shot the Doctor a quick look: *what about Ian?*

The Doctor gave a tiny shake of his head. Barbara realized she would only complicate matters if she mentioned Ian now. She would have to leave the matter of his rescue to Aristea.

'Thank you . . . ?'

The captain threw her a curious look. 'Arrhidaeus, my lady.' He gestured for them to precede him into the passage. The soldiers closed ranks around them. As they entered the tunnel, Arrhidaeus spoke briefly to one soldier, who ran back into the main cavern. A moment later there was an agonized scream. When the soldier rejoined the company, he was wiping blood from his sword.

'What happened?' Barbara demanded.

Arrhidaeus looked puzzled for a moment. 'Susa told us you were an imposter, yet it is plain you are indeed the Queen. The punishment for lying is death.' He smiled. 'And now I must see to the arrangement of the camels.' He marched away.

Barbara turned to the Doctor in mute outrage. He took her hand and patted it gently as they followed the soldiers from the mines, but the gesture brought no comfort whatsoever.

331 BC

She ran towards the light.

Before she had taken twenty steps, the streets of Alexandria were full of people. They were screaming, jostling, some standing quite still and pointing up at the sky, some kneeling in the gardens, others huddling together, frightened to open their eyes. She had to fight her way through the crowd. A man pushed his way past her, fear lighting his face – a younger but familiar face.

'Aristea!'

The man turned. His eyes met hers; but there was no recognition. Another group pushed their way through the crowd, chasing Aristea. The Israelite turned to run. A fist swung out of the crowd and clubbed him down. 'What are you doing! I know that man!' Hate-filled eyes turned on her.

'There's another one.'

'Another *Israelite*.'

'The King's *favourites*.'

'They'll bring the wrath of the gods down on us if we let them!'

She stopped. Perhaps getting involved wasn't such a –

Pain exploded across the back of her head. She fell, her forehead cracking against the road. A rock struck her back.

She was being *stoned*!

'Wait, I'm not –'

A second rock hit the ground nearby. A hail of tiny slivers cut her face and hands. Pain shivered along her right arm.

' –Jewish, I'm –'

Voices screamed all around her, punctuating the blows and kicks. Barbara fell and lay still, her cheek pressed against the ground, the gritty-smooth surface stingingly cold against her cheek.

'Please,' she whispered.

And jerked from another blow.

She curled into a foetal position.

Please.

After a long time the blows stopped, and there was the sound of running feet. The footsteps faded with distance. Then a new voice spoke quietly beside her. 'Where does it hurt? Can you stand? Can you walk?'

She moaned, a soft, hiccuping cry that bubbled out of her mouth with the blood.

'What's your name? Are you an Israelite? Your robes are purple, are you of royal blood? Have you come to see Alexander? Let me help.'

Pressure on her wrist, an arm around her waist. A hand covering her mouth to stifle her moans. The ground dropped away. Dizzying heights. She was standing. She opened her eyes. The night roared.

'The Egyptians! They're burning the Israelite quarter.'

'Wuh – where – going –'

'Somewhere quiet. The docks. We have to avoid the riots until we can get back to the palace.'

'Can't walk, can't *stand* –'

'There's no choice, I'm afraid.'

'What – name?'

'Ptolemy Lagus. Now *be quiet*. I have to get you away from here.'

' – *my* name – can't– '

'Shh!'
' –remember my– '
The darkness roared again with a voice of flame.
Daytime in the night.

322 BC

Outside the mines, the heat was a constant weight on her chest, only partly deflected by the robes Arrhidaeus had suggested she wear for the journey. The heat-sickness she felt was made worse by the lurching of her camel across the foothills. As they moved, Barbara gazed around at the harsh landscape. Shattered rock emerged from dunes of sand, a chiaroscuro of light and dark slashed across a featureless sky. She looked up at the rock, sculpted into fantastic shapes by wind-borne sand, and tried hard not to imagine what wind and sand like that could do to an unprotected human body.

She glanced at the Doctor, envied the way he swayed in time with his own camel, effortlessly in tune with the animal. As he rode, he gazed around himself with the air of one who expects to see the positive in every situation, one to whom no environment could ever be too harsh or alien, only fascinating.

'I hope we're doing the right thing.' Barbara's voice sounded thin and irritable. Fine sand ground between her teeth as she spoke.

The Doctor guided his camel closer to hers. 'What else can we do? As long as the soldiers believe you are the Queen they will defer to us. Otherwise . . . ' He shrugged. 'What do you know of Ptolemaic Egypt?'

'Well. Both the library and the Pharos lighthouse at Alexandria were listed in history books as being among the wonders of the ancient world. But I've always been more interested in the people of the time. History doesn't tell us much about them: there must have been huge quantities written, but only a fraction of it survived the Christian sacking of the city and burning of the library in AD 641.'

The Doctor shook his head sadly. 'And what of this . . . column?'

'It could be the column bringing Alexander's body back to his city to be interred. He died of a fever while planning a campaign against the Arabs. Ptolemy used possession of the ex-King's body to found his own dynasty.' She paused in thought. 'The Ptolemaic line threw up some of the world's most learned scholars, astronomers and mathematicians.' She paused. 'Ptolemy Soter was a special man.'

Arrhidaeus guided his camel alongside Barbara's. 'The caravan will soon be in sight. I hope the journey has been comfortable?'

Barbara attempted a graceful nod, but her camel chose that moment to stamp on a snake and the effect was ruined as her chin banged painfully against her collarbone.

With a perfectly straight face, Arrhidaeus acknowledged Barbara's gesture. 'I will send a rider ahead to announce your arrival,' he said. 'The King thought to meet you in the city, but I'm sure he'll be pleased to see you now.'

The Doctor frowned as Arrhidaeus left. 'We must be very careful when we reach the column. When we meet Ptolemy, he will surely realize that you are not the Queen.'

'I know. And what do we do then?'

The Doctor gave a thin smile. 'Extemporize?'

Barbara shook her head. 'Not funny.'

The first sign that they were nearing the caravan came when a single rider galloped out of the heat haze to meet them. The figure was small, clothed in white against the sun. As he drew nearer, Barbara could see the figure was a boy, no older than eight or nine years. He was slim, tanned, obviously fit. He could ride as if born to the saddle. He grinned enormously as he saw Barbara.

'Mother!' he cried as he reined in his horse alongside Barbara's camel. 'Why didn't you tell us you were coming to meet us?'

There were eight elephants in the caravan, perhaps a couple of dozen horses, and more camels than she could count. Soldiers marched alongside the animals. They wore leather armour, and their painted shields and scabbards gleamed in the sunlight. Crests of horsehair topped their helmets. They marched without speaking.

Arrhidaeus led Barbara and the Doctor towards the head of the caravan. The boy rode excitedly ahead. 'Race you!'

'Philadelphus will make a fine king one day.' Barbara glanced sideways. Was that the hard edge of jealousy in Arrhidaeus's voice?

Saying nothing, she followed him to the front of the column, where two pairs of elephants were separated by ranks of foot soldiers. On the backs of the two leading elephants were constructed tented litters. The trailing pair had been harnessed together and held between them a larger litter carrying a finely crafted wooden casket.

The Doctor peered at the casket. He leaned close to Barbara and whispered, 'If that box contains the body of Alexander, I would very much like to examine it.'

Barbara smiled thinly. 'Historians throughout the ages would have paid through the nose for the same privilege.'

'And you, my dear?'

'I just want to find out what happened to Ian.'

The Doctor sighed with annoyance. Without replying, he urged his camel in a wide arc around the elephants until he could get a clearer look at the casket.

Arrhidaeus looked quizzically at Barbara.

'My friend is a scholar from . . . er . . . Illyria.' Barbara struggled to keep both her anger at the Doctor and fear for Ian from her voice.

'His skin is very light for such a man.'

'He has a wasting sickness. You've seen how old and frail he is.'

'Indeed.'

'Yes. I have given him my permission to examine the casket. He is making a study of certain aspects of craftsmanship for a boo– for a scroll which he has been commissioned to write for the royal library.'

Arrhidaeus nodded thoughtfully. 'He would do better to study the craftsmanship of the Soma when it is built; I do not think Alexander would want to be remembered as resting in a wooden casket when half the slaves in Egypt are mining gold to build his tomb.'

Barbara nodded. By now they had reached the head of the column. A trumpet sounded in the still air. The soldiers reigned in their horses and sat at attention. The elephants lumbered to a halt. One of the leading pair dropped to its knees at the urgings of its rider, a slim, powerful man who looked to be in his mid-thirties.

Barbara realized this must be Ptolemy himself. He leaped to the ground, strode across to Barbara's camel and stared at her. Barbara waited nervously. The man's face was set; he obviously realized she was a fake. She tried to remember how they killed royal imposters in this time. Probably painfully.

Then, to her complete astonishment, the King swept her from the camel's back and took her in his arms. Barbara had roughly a second to register the hot smell of his armour and the rough texture of his skin, before finding herself in the most thorough embrace of her life.

331 BC

A full general although still in his mid-twenties, Ptolemy Lagus was old enough to appreciate the irony that left Alexander's own streets running with blood even as his armies swept across half the known world. Ptolemy increased his pace among the docks. What had begun as a pleasant, late evening stroll had turned into a bloodbath. And now here he was holding a half-dead barbarian dressed as Egyptian royalty while Eleusis burned and the gods fell from the sky into the open sea.

Ptolemy carried the woman through the crowds of people lining the docks and harbour causeway, all pointing out to sea and muttering nervously amongst themselves. He was about to instruct them to make way when the harbour erupted close by, showering him with water: something the size of a man, reptilian, partly clothed in reflective metallic armour, had broken the surface and clambered on to the causeway. The creature flopped to the ground. Ptolemy felt his stomach knot convulsively. His fear was instant and irrational. Here was something he was sure was unknown in all the world. Unknown – *alien*.

He stared down at the creature and tried to control his fear. Three of its four limbs quivered uselessly. It wheezed, openings in its head flapping to produce incomprehensible sounds. Other openings fluttered and he saw disturbingly human-looking eyes moving within. In its chest, the long, curved shapes of ribs distorted the shining armour in time with its ragged breathing.

The crowd began to point and make religious signs. One sailor stepped forward holding a fishing harpoon. 'That's no god! It's a monster!' He plunged the harpoon into a limb. The creature screamed.

As did the woman in Ptolemy's arms. 'Don't hurt him!' she gasped. 'Can't you understand? *He's asking for help!*'

322 BC

Alexandria was everything Barbara had ever expected and more. It glowed with colour in the early morning sunshine. The streets were full of robed people, all of whom had knelt as the caravan passed through a gate in the city walls and proceeded towards the palace. Musicians and poets honoured their presence with melody and verse. The buildings were little short of incredible: sweeping facades of white marble, endless rows of fluted columns, shallow steps leading to high, narrow entrances; beautifully coloured silks hanging from the walls, fluttering in the scented breeze from the ocean. The whole city shimmered in the sunlight so that her eyes ached.

In just moments, it seemed, they arrived at the royal gardens. These lay along an irregular crescent of land which protected the eastern side of the harbour from the open sea. To the north, the 300-foot-high octagonal tower of the Pharos lighthouse cast its shadow across the entrance to the harbour. Nearer, the sleek domes of the Temple of Isis glimmered through the trees. On the other side of the gardens, the palace rose into the sky, white on white, broken only by innumerable rows of windows and verdant terraces and hanging silks.

When they had dismounted and the animals had been led away to be watered and stabled, Ptolemy urged Barbara to explain who her companion was. Somewhat nervously, she repeated the story she'd concocted for Arrhidaeus.

'I see,' Ptolemy turned to acknowledge the Doctor. 'In deference to your age and health, I will not require that you kneel before me.'

Barbara winced but the Doctor merely nodded his thanks. 'Your words do justice to your wisdom,' he said, somewhat dryly.

Ptolemy said: 'I understand you are a scholar. You must stay with us. In my opinion, short of acquiring a new country for one's empire, there is nothing quite like acquiring a new scroll for one's library.'

Barbara interjected. 'Then we have much to discuss.' At Ptolemy's curious expression she went on, 'I was telling the Doctor how you have given the eastern quarter of the city to the Israelites.'

'And not just Eleusis but an enclave on the island of Pharos, where the Hebrew Law is to be translated into Greek. The scrolls shall be given pride of place in the royal library. Their position shall be symbolic of our interest in other cultures and systems of belief.'

'An excellent idea,' said the Doctor. 'I salute your wisdom.'

Barbara scowled suddenly. 'And I condemn it!'

The Doctor gave a frustrated sigh. 'I really must apologize for –'

Seeing Barbara's annoyed look, Ptolemy placed a restraining hand on the Doctor's arm. A faint smile played about the corners of his mouth, as if something about the whole conversation amused him greatly. 'Allow the Queen to speak,' he said. 'In the past she has shown great wit and character. Indeed, her intelligence almost equals my own.' He turned to Barbara. 'Speak, wife. I would hear your words.'

Barbara hesitated, then plunged ahead anyway. 'I was going to say, the translation of the Hebrew Law and its placement within the royal library can hardly be reconciled with the fact that thousands of Israelites are incarcerated in the mines and prisons.'

Ptolemy stopped walking. He beckoned to a hovering figure. Barbara was intently watching his face as the figure came silently forward. 'And how many slaves currently dwell in the mines and prisons?' Ptolemy asked the newcomer quietly.

A feminine voice Barbara thought strangely familiar said, 'Rather more than a hundred thousand, my husband. As you know.'

Ptolemy fixed Barbara with a steady gaze. 'So, it's only a small favour you ask.' He appeared to consider her words. 'And yet it amuses me to grant your wish,' he said with a lightly mocking smile.

But Barbara wasn't listening. The newcomer's words had finally sunk into her mind. *My husband?* She turned, eyes widening with shock.

The newcomer was an older version of herself.

'May I present my wife, Queen Barbara of Egypt,' Ptolemy said. 'Never has a more unusual face graced the royal line ... until now.'

Barbara was unable to tear her gaze from the woman. Looking at her was like looking into an invisible mirror framed by the blue waters of the Mediterranean.

The Queen glared contemptuously at Barbara – and she too realized she was face to face with herself. She blinked rapidly, her eyes rolled up and she toppled to the ground.

Ptolemy gazed down at the woman, her robes askew on the grass, and suddenly roared with laughter. 'I wondered which of you would be the first to faint.' He beckoned Arrhidaeus forward. The Captain deposited a fat purse in the King's outstretched hand.

'I think I'm going to have to sit down,' Barbara said.

Ptolemy smiled. 'You were a breath of air on such a long journey. Think of it as my little joke.' He knelt beside the Queen and began to arrange her robes more decorously.

Barbara seated herself on a marble bench beside a jade statue of Alexander's war horse Bucephalus and watched him. 'A joke? She's me! I mean, I'm her, that is –' Barbara shook her head, was unable to stifle a grin. 'When did you know I wasn't really . . . you know?'

'Oh, at once. The Queen rides as if born to the saddle.' He glanced at Barbara's bruised neck and chin. 'You obviously do not.'

Somewhat overwhelmed, Barbara glanced sideways at the Doctor for support. He frowned and said nothing.

Ptolemy turned to Arrhidaeus. 'Send soldiers to free the Israelites from the mines. Have the treasurer arrange to compensate their owners from the royal bank.'

The Captain studied Ptolemy closely for a moment, before nodding smartly. 'What would you have done with them when they are freed, sir?'

Ptolemy turned to Barbara with an interested look. 'The idea was yours. How would you implement its details?'

Barbara hesitated. Was Ptolemy playing some game with her? 'Make the slaves scholars or clerks. Let them work for the city that way.'

Ptolemy nodded. 'That for the older ones, certainly,' he agreed. 'But what of the others? Should we return them to family life also?'

Ptolemy was backing her into a corner. 'No, of course not.' Barbara searched her knowledge of history for the correct reply. 'The most able-bodied of them must join the royal army in case

Perdiccas continues to compete with you for the throne.'

Ptolemy nodded. 'A sound political judgment.' He indicated to Arrhidaeus that he should pick up the Queen and carry her back to the palace. 'I will join you in the war room to finalize the details.'

Arrhidaeus bowed, picked up the Queen and left.

Ptolemy nodded once in Barbara's direction. 'Consider yourselves my guests at the palace.' He turned to follow Arrhidaeus.

The Doctor waited until he'd walked around a turn of the path and then turned angrily to Barbara. 'Are you quite satisfied now?'

'Yes I am,' Barbara said angrily. 'Ptolemy's going to free the slaves from the mines – and Ian with them.'

'Yes, and now you have seen to it that he will be impressed into the royal army.' The Doctor grasped his lapel and sighed. 'More grist to the mill of catastrophe.'

'And what's that supposed to mean, exactly?'

'My dear, don't you see? Your interference could cause history to come completely unravelled.'

'Oh come now, Doctor. I see no evidence of –'

'Oh don't you indeed?' The Doctor pointed towards the harbour. 'What's that then?'

'The Pharos lighthouse. Ptolemy Philadelphus had it built in two-hundred-and–' Barbara broke off suddenly.

'Exactly! Ptolemy Philadelphus, whom we have seen only recently as a young boy!' He glanced at Barbara and went on. 'Nor is that all. When I examined Alexander's corpse I found out this: his entire cell structure was seriously damaged, I should say *ravaged*, and not by any Earthly fever. Whatever killed him was of extraterrestrial origin.'

Barbara put her head in her hands and tried to think. 'It's impossible. History tells us . . . ' she stopped. Stared at the Doctor.

'History,' he said quietly, 'is apparently being rewritten.'

'But how? You said we couldn't change it.'

The Doctor's head bowed in thought. 'Something else must be

responsible. We must find out what, before the scale of the problem increases beyond our ability to correct. You must talk to the Queen. Find out as much as you can about her life before she came here.'

'Yes . . . yes of course. But what about you? What will you do?'

'I will investigate the royal library. There may be a letter commissioning the Pharos there. With luck I will be able to learn how the knowledge of the future came to fruition here, in the past.'

'All right . . . Do you know how to get there? According to the history books, the library was a hard place to find.'

'I'll find it. I have a nose for a good book.'

Barbara watched as the Doctor left the gardens.

She would not see him again for eight years.

331 BC

With Ptolemy in the palace gardens was the man who had shaped the last decade of the civilized world. Alexander's face was ascetic, that of a scholar but, also, that of a leader. His conversation was old – but with a new twist. 'I must have more land.' He clapped a thin hand on Ptolemy's shoulder. 'I must annex Persia or have my military prowess be brought into disrepute. To do that I need soldiers, water, provisions, elephants, horses and camels.' He paused. 'Or Rhakotis.'

Ptolemy sighed. 'My friend, what you propose is highly dangerous –'

'*Dangerous*? Ptolemy, my mind is an engine whirling to collapse upon the thought that I *must have more power*! I wake at night drenched with sweat for fear of becoming diminished in the eyes of my people. I am a driven man. All Egypt knows my ambition, but only you know my fear.' He hesitated. 'That's why Rhakotis must become my ally in war.'

Ptolemy plucked a blossom from a bush, held it to his face and breathed deeply. 'I agree that Rhakotis probably has weapons capable of wiping out armies, even countries. But what other wonders might he have which would enable you to gain the power you seek *with no loss of life whatsoever*? Imagine the respect you would command if the King of Persia begged to be admitted to your empire peacefully.'

'How could this be accomplished except by the power of the gods?'

'By the power of *knowledge*. The whole world knows of your prowess as a fighter. Now show them you are an equally accomplished thinker.'

'You intrigue me, Ptolemy. Continue.'

'Using Barbara as an interpreter, I have spoken with Rhakotis. He requires refined gold to repair his vessel. In return for the gold, I have suggested he provide us with the knowledge of his people.'

'And what was Rhakotis's reply to the suggestion?'

Ptolemy hesitated. 'There I must confess to some ambiguity, for Rhakotis said this to me: "My knowledge cannot be yours, Ptolemy. But your own knowledge, both that which has been lost and that which is to come, that I *can* give you." '

'What do you suppose he meant?'

'I have told Barbara to bring him here to explain.'

Alexander's eyes focused on distant lands. 'With Rhakotis's help, Alexandria could become the cultural centre of the world!'

As if to confirm Alexander's words, Rhakotis and Barbara walked through the foliage to join them. Ptolemy glanced at the disturbing shape of the alien, so at odds with its demeanour. But his eyes were drawn to Barbara. She was dressed in a robe and sandals. Her hair was piled up and pinned with the gold clasp he had left for her.

She was quite simply the most exotic woman he had ever seen.

The alien spoke. The voice was soft, somehow *nervous*. None of the sounds made sense to Ptolemy, though Barbara seemed to have no difficulty understanding them. 'Rhakotis asks for your help constructing a diving bell which will carry him beneath the ocean to examine his ship.'

Alexander said eagerly, 'Beneath the ocean? He can do this?'

Barbara translated, listened to the reply, then said, 'Rhakotis can do many things. He suggests a meeting should be held as soon as possible to confirm the details of the operation. And how he can provide the knowledge you ask of him in return.'

'Excellent,' exclaimed the King. He clapped his hand on one pair of Rhakotis's shoulders and led the alien away through the bushes towards the palace. Barbara was left with Ptolemy.

'Have you recovered any of your memory?' he asked after a moment.

Barbara's face fell. There was an awkward silence. Ptolemy pursed his lips. 'I am . . . sorry. I understand how the lack of memory must –'

'No you don't, you don't understand at all! I don't know you, I don't know Rhakotis, I don't know where I come from, who I am or what I'm doing here!' Barbara stared wildly at him. 'I'm lost, don't you understand? I'm lost, and I'm going mad!' Abruptly she turned away from him and ran off into the bushes.

He called after her, but there was no reply.

322 BC

In the palace war room, Ptolemy stood with Arrhidaeus's sword at his throat. His dagger was sheathed at his side, but he knew that if he reached for it he would lose his life. '*I am the King!*' he hissed.

'I know, and I am sorry,' Arrhidaeus replied.

'I assume Perdiccas has paid you to assassinate me?'

'Perdiccas is the rightful contender for succession.'

'Only because of his guardianship of Alexander's son. Perdiccas would be a despot! A tyrant!'

'Your libertarian values are unpopular with the people. They need a strong leader.'

'I will *be* a strong leader.'

Arrhidaeus shifted uncomfortably, but his sword never left Ptolemy's throat. 'My loyalty is to the throne. Perdiccas is the legitimate heir, therefore my loyalty must be to him.'

Ptolemy remained motionless. There was a catch in his voice when he spoke. 'If this is about the bet we made . . . I am quite prepared to give you the money back.'

Arrhidaeus snorted, grinned, caught himself. 'Sir, I . . . ' He lowered his sword. He stared at Ptolemy.

Ptolemy gazed back silently.

Arrhidaeus whispered: 'My loyalty is to the throne. But you are my friend.' He swallowed hard. 'Will you go quietly from the city so I may spare your life?'

'And my wife? My son?'

'Yes, of course. Just say you will go! Please!'

Ptolemy held out his arm. 'You are indeed a friend.'

Arrhidaeus stepped closer, his arm rising to embrace Ptolemy. He barely registered the sensation of a light punch at his side. He blinked. Suddenly everything seemed so bright, as if the sun had come out inside the palace walls.

'My friend,' his voice was a whisper, all strength gone. Behind his eyes, a light began to fade.

Ptolemy held Arrhidaeus until he was dead, then lowered him gently to the stone floor. Drawing his dagger from the body, he wiped it clean and resheathed it.

When he stood, his face was shining with tears.

'Your presence here disturbs me,' said the Queen without turning from the morning room window.

Barbara stared fixedly out of the window at the storm clouds gathering over the ocean. 'Why won't you talk to me?'

No answer.

'The Doctor says –'

'Do not speak to me of the *Doctor*.'

'All right! Fine! Why don't we talk about your past then: where you grew up. What your life was like. Who your parents were. Who your first boyfriend was. Why you –'

'*I will not talk of such things*!' The Queen whirled angrily. She strode to the door with the plain intention of leaving Barbara alone, but Barbara moved swiftly to block her. She took the Queen by the shoulders, feeling an eerie vibration shiver along her own arms as she did so. 'Don't you walk away from me,' she hissed.

'How dare you! If you hurt me –'

'You idiot, I *am* you! Don't you understand? You must talk to me! Ptolemy says you've been married eight years. But you don't even know how old you are. You have no memory of a life before your life here. Try to remember, please. It's so important!' Barbara released the Queen, backed away, lifted her hands to her face. A minute passed and she became aware the Queen was staring at her, her own hands a mirror to Barbara's.

The same gesture. The same woman.

'Please.'

'I don't remember a life before this. Something happened to me! I *can't* remember!'

'But somehow you – I – went back in time eight years. Did the Doctor take you in the TARDIS? What happened there? I have to know!'

The Queen stared blankly at her. Barbara was suddenly aware that there *were* differences between them; character lines touching the corners of the mouth, subtle creases around eyes which were deeper, almost . . . haunted. A body which told the eternal story of childbirth.

'You know, it was a shock finding out I have a son – will have a son, I mean.' Barbara hesitated as the Queen sat down, then continued. 'It's not something I've considered before. I had my job and I'm still only young –' She bit off her words. 'Sorry, I didn't mean . . . '

The Queen shook her head. 'It doesn't matter. We should talk. It's just. . . Well, it was the shock of seeing you . . . and Ptolemy, with you, the way he used to be with me. It's all a joke to him, the two of us. He sees us as a challenge to his ability to provide love, you see. Sees us as the same woman even though . . . ' She hesitated. 'I'm not being fair to you. I'm scared and . . . jealous. Of you.'

Barbara stared at her in amazement. 'You're . . . ?'

'It's absurd, isn't it? How can I be jealous of myself?' The Queen smiled wryly. 'I've been panicking about it ever since you arrived.'

Barbara found herself shaking with laughter. 'Jealous? Of *me*?'

She looked at the Queen, who smiled. Barbara sat beside her, tried to gain control of her laughter. 'Philadelphus is a beautiful boy. You should be proud.'

'I know. I am.'

'It's amazing, you know, I could never –' She broke off. 'What am I talking about. I *did!*' Abruptly she dissolved into a fit of giggling. In moments the room rang with laughter.

The Queen regained her composure first. 'I do remember something. It was night. No: it was daytime. Daytime in the night . . . '

'You see,' Barbara cried. 'You *can* remember if you want to!'

'I . . . ' The Queen hesitated. 'I remember –'

The door to the morning room burst open and Ptolemy strode in with Philadelphus, the arm holding his son running with blood.

'We are betrayed!' he barked. 'Perdiccas has bought my army.'

'*No!*' Barbara cried as the Queen turned away.

Philadelphus ran to his mother and placed an arm about her waist.

'Lock yourselves in,' said Ptolemy. 'I am going to the library. Rhakotis *must* help us now!' The door crashed shut behind him.

Barbara paced the room, her mind a mad jamboree of thoughts. History hadn't happened like this: Perdiccas never reached the city. He was drowned along with half his army in the floods on the Nile Delta. This was all wrong! But the sounds of clashing steel and people screaming drifting through the open window told her that, whether it was right or wrong, it was happening. It was war.

And the Doctor was somewhere out there in it.

She turned to the Queen. 'I have to find the Doctor. We'll talk again soon.' Barbara ran from the morning room.

The first deaths came as the storm broke, as Barbara neared the library. A group of people ran from a narrow courtyard and tried to cross the Canopic Way, the main thoroughfare of the city. Soldiers were there first, swords drawn. The mob panicked, scattering back towards the library, where a middle-aged scholar was climbing slowly down the wide steps. His arms full of scrolls and papers, the scholar was unable to keep his balance as the mob ran past. He slipped on the wet marble, falling heavily. The scrolls and papers scattered across the paving stones. Automatically, Barbara ran forward to help. The man was dripping with rain and muttering angrily beneath his breath as she began to collect the fallen items. He heaved himself upright and began to do the same.

Their hands fell together on the book.

Barbara was aware, even as she lifted it from the ground, that something was wrong. The book was half bound in leather and cloth. There was no title. She had actually got half way to handing it back to the scholar when the significance of what she held struck her. A book. Not a scroll or a loose-leaf collection of papers, but a bound, printed *book*.

Their eyes locked. The silence stretched out between them. And Barbara understood without a shadow of doubt that he knew exactly what she held; what its significance was: an anomaly in this time.

The book was from the future.

Then more people ran past, yelling and swearing, closely followed by a group of soldiers. A man screamed as the soldiers caught up. He crashed to the ground; blood pooled around his head. He writhed briefly and then was still. Rain washed his blood from the pavement into the road.

And suddenly the streets were filled with screaming people,

their voices swamped by the sound of marching, the hiss of
swords through flesh. A group of yelling children ran past, got
mixed up in the fighting. The soldiers beat them aside.

She felt a sudden tugging sensation. The scholar was trying to
grab the book from her. Snatching it back, she lost her footing. By
the time she regained her balance, the man had vanished into the
library. She ran after him up the steps to the *promenoir*.

There were terrified people even here.

The scholar turned, skittered along a columned hallway,
vanished through a marbled arch. Barbara followed him outside
into darkness and silence. She gazed around herself in amazement.

There were no screams. No fighting. It wasn't raining.

It was *night*.

331 BC

Barbara stared around herself in amazement, now noticing other
details which added to the puzzle. The buildings, shining softly
in the moonlight, looked differently shaped: a dome here, a flat
roof where she remembered a broken pilaster. She noticed
particularly that one wing of the nearby Museum was entirely
missing. Every bit of paving and wall, every column, every
rooftop and statue she could see looked somehow newer. As
if . . . as if –

Barbara placed her hand against the nearest wall to keep her
balance.

– as if she had travelled back in time.

But how? The TARDIS was still buried under a pile of rock in
the mines as far as she knew. Were there other time travellers like
the Doctor in Alexandria? Had Susan somehow –

Light exploded across the sky.

Barbara stifled a shout of surprise. Had something blown up?
Was –

Then the sound came, battering her, smashing at the walls of
the buildings.

Sonic boom.

It was a spaceship – and it was out of control.

Shielding her eyes from the light, Barbara was able to make out the direction in which the thing was travelling: north. Towards the harbours. Towards the sea.

There were her answers.

The moonlit clouds bloomed with light as the ship smashed into the water.

Daytime in the night.

She ran towards the light.

322 BC

When the Doctor had left Barbara in the palace gardens he'd wandered for what seemed like hours along the streets of the city, before turning eventually into the Canopic Way. From there, a short walk brought him within sight of the library.

He slowly ascended the wide steps, passed through the *promenoir* and into the main reading room. Here columns supported a patterned ceiling. Statues flanked openings into other rooms. The floor was smoothly tiled marble. Shelves, filled with scrolls, lined every wall to the height of the second floor balcony.

The Doctor walked into the room. And into an argument.

'This scroll has no classification, Eratosthenes. It should not be on the shelves. How am I supposed to assign it a position in my reading schedule if it has no classification?' The speaker was a thin, fussy-looking man whose robes hung awkwardly from his bony shoulders. He leaned over a wide desk at a smaller, rounder man, appearing to point at him with his long nose. 'As director here it is your responsibility to ensure all scrolls are correctly indexed and shelved. Really this is quite intolerable.'

Eratosthenes moved out from behind the desk and stared up at his lanky aggressor with a languid smile. 'My dear Aristophanes, your *obsession* for reading and rereading the scrolls in the order in which they appear on the shelves is a pastime as familiar to me as it is mysterious. But as director here it is my responsibility to maintain the status of the library, not shelve the scrolls for your convenience.'

Aristophanes spluttered. The Doctor sniggered quietly to himself. It had been a long time since he had enjoyed a good snigger. Crossing to the row of shelves, he took down a scroll, stretched out on a reading couch and prepared to enjoy himself as the argument escalated.

'If you spent less time trying to prove the Earth was round and more time performing your duties –'

'If you had ever spent any quality time thinking about anything you'd know the word was *spherical*, not –'

'If you assigned as much money to the upkeep of an efficient indexing system as you do paying some Nubian slave to walk between here and Syria to measure the shadow of a *stick* –'

'If you had any idea of the knowledge I could add to the –'

'If you had half a brain in your head –'

'If you had any brain *at all* –'

The scholars stopped abruptly, aware they could hear the sound of someone *sniggering*. The noise seemed to be coming from a figure reclining with a scroll on one of the more distant reading couches. They looked at each other and then the figure.

When the Doctor realized the argument had stopped he lowered his scroll enough to peep discreetly over the top. The two scholars were staring intently at him from a distance of a few inches.

'Oh, er, yes. Ahem.' The Doctor cleared his throat, his grin fading quickly. 'That is to say, I was . . . er, wondering if you had any . . . er . . . religious works on hand.'

Eratosthenes said, 'This room contains volumes on chemistry, biology, botany, astronomy, astrology, my own works on mathematics and,' he glanced sideways at Aristophanes, 'geography.'

Aristophanes snorted. 'If you can ever find them.'

The Doctor glanced from one scholar to the other, unable to keep a grin from his face. 'Aristophanes,' he said. 'Eratosthenes.' He shook his head. 'I wonder, do you realize your lives were spent over three centuries apart?'

Aristophanes snorted again. It was an impressive snort, the Doctor had to admit.

Eratosthenes stared at the Doctor. 'If by that you mean I will not be born for another three hundred and fifty years, of course we know. How else do you think we are able to talk together except by use of the time-travel portals installed in the library by Rhakotis?' He glanced sideways at Aristophanes. 'How else do you think it is possible for the life of a library director and mathematician to be so swamped by the simple business of cataloguing scrolls *that it becomes impossible for him to finish his most important research*?'

'I suppose it's hardly worth pointing out that having time travel makes your *most important* research completely redundant.' Aristophanes held out the scroll. 'Here, you may as well take this. I certainly won't be able to read it until it's properly indexed.'

'Hah!' Eratosthenes snatched at the scroll, but the Doctor had already snagged it with a bony hand. As he looked at it, all amusement fled from his face. 'The Ancient and Worshipful Law of . . . ' He allowed the scroll to snap shut. 'This scroll must never be placed on the shelves,' he hissed. 'Never be read. Do you understand? *Never*.'

Eratosthenes blinked. Even Aristophanes was snortless at the tone of the Doctor's voice.

'It may already be too late . . . ' The Doctor waved the scroll. 'This is a copy made by your scholars. I must have the original.'

'It is on loan.' Eratosthenes thought for a moment. 'Aristotle has it.'

The Doctor stood. 'Where can I find Aristotle now?'

'I don't know. He could be in any time zone reached by the portals of the library. Anyway,' he added, 'you have a copy of it, so it can hardly be considered important; I thought you would want to meet Rhakotis. Discuss the temporal architecture of the library.'

'Yes, yes, indeed I do, but for the time being that will have to wait.' The Doctor stuffed the scroll into his jacket pocket. 'It's absolutely vital that I find the book from which this scroll was copied – history could depend on it!'

'That's all very well, but –' Eratosthenes was interrupted by the sound of shouting outside. Then the sound of running feet. Of swords clashing. A scream. They turned. Ptolemy stood in the doorway, sword clutched loosely in one hand, his arm running with blood.

'Where is Rhakotis?' he demanded. 'He must help repel Perdiccas's army, or we will all die and Egypt is lost!'

Aristophanes grabbed the Doctor by the shoulder and pulled him towards the nearest exit. 'If you've got any sense, you'll come with me!' he hissed. 'If anyone can find your book, I can – but not standing around here waiting for some soldier to chop us into bits!'

The Doctor hesitated. 'Barbara – my companion,' he agonized. 'I can't just leave her in the middle of a war.'

Aristophanes said, 'Which do you value most, Barbara or the book?'

With a frustrated sigh, the Doctor followed the scholar from the library – and into another time.

331 BC

She grasped the side of the wooden sailing vessel and gazed out across the sun-drenched Mediterranean. A north wind stole her breath and whipped her hair into her face. She pinned her hair back with the golden clasp Ptolemy had given her. He stood beside her at the railing, a man she had come to respect greatly for his intelligence, wit and compassion. She glanced sideways at him, but his gaze was fixed on the fleet of navy vessels transporting Rhakotis's diving bell out to the sunken starship.

Rhakotis was already inside the bell, as was Alexander, who had insisted on accompanying him despite the alien's protestations. A number of ships had been lashed together and used as a floating platform for an intricate device of brass and wood which Rhakotis had assured him would supply air to the diving bell while they descended to the sunken starship, and control its safe return to the surface. Other ships stood ready, some fitted with devices called *winches*, with which the starship could be towed into shallow water if it were salvageable.

Ptolemy pursed his lips at the sight of so many warships lashed into such an inelegant raft-like mass. 'Sea-going insanity. That's what it is,' he muttered.

'But it works,' Barbara said. 'You can't argue with that.'

'I can argue with anything,' said Ptolemy bad-temperedly.

She touched him lightly on the arm. 'What's the matter?'

Ptolemy frowned at the diving bell being swung into position between the ships. 'My friend who owns most of the civilized world is about to do something incredibly stupid to prove how clever he is.'

Barbara sighed. 'I thought that might be it.'

'Rhakotis indicated there could be danger – a temporal leak, he said – but Alexander is so *stubborn*. He's turned a salvage operation into a circus! Sometimes I think he doesn't deserve to –'

Barbara placed one finger to his lips. 'If you say it, you'll only regret it later,' she said softly. 'Walls have ears, you know.'

Ptolemy shot her a puzzled look. 'Maybe where you come from.'

Barbara smiled. 'A joke. That's better.'

Beyond the ship, the diving bell containing Rhakotis and Alexander was hoisted into position and released. With a great whoosh of spray, it sank into the ocean and vanished from sight.

Barbara turned away from the spray, taking Ptolemy's arm as the ship tilted with the wave.

Their eyes met.

She did not pull away.

322 BC

She was still in the morning room with her son when the gods came. Philadelphus was pointing out of the window to the ocean. She followed his gaze. Beyond the Pharos lighthouse, a circle of ocean a thousand yards across was gliding into the air.

'Mother.' Philadelphus tugged at her arm. 'Have the gods come? Are they going to save us?'

She continued staring out of the window. The water had humped into a dome. Now it was cascading back into the ocean with a sound to rival the storm whirling above.

A perfect globe of sky lifted clear of the ocean.

It began to expand.

She swayed dizzily. She placed one hand against the wall to steady herself, grasped a silk tapestry, wrenched it from its fastenings. One hand crushed the fabric while the other held her son so tightly against her that he cried out in pain.

A tiny image of the Pharos set in a storm-tossed ocean glimmered in the lower hemisphere of the globe. She realized she was looking not at the real sky but at a reflection of it, wrapped around an expanding sphere of perfectly reflective material.

The sight drove daggers of memory into her mind.

The image of the Pharos shifted, distorting as it slid beneath the lower hemisphere. The globe was moving. It passed silently across the Pharos and drifted closer, until the window was filled with a growing reflection of the palace, the window, her son, herself.

She sank to her knees, sobbing violently.

Philadelphus knelt beside her. 'Don't cry, mother. The gods have come. They will save us. They will protect father from Perdiccas.'

'*It's not the godsitsnotthegods*!' Philadelphus jerked back from the anger in his mother's voice. 'It's a ship! A starship! Oh dear lord . . . ' She raised her hands to her face, remembered for the first time in eight years it was a gesture she was trying to give up, let them fall to her sides.

She gazed up and out of the window at a curved silver void filled with an image of herself. The image was accelerating towards her, spanning time as well as space.

'Oh Philadelphus, don't you understand? I remember. I *remember*!'

Ptolemy. His love. The marriage.

A life together. A son.

And before that?

The riots. The rescue. Finding Rhakotis wounded on the harbour causeway. Translating between him and Ptolemy. Installing time travel architecture in the royal library. Providing books from the future in payment for gold to repair the starship's damaged engines.

Starship – timeship – *TARDIS* –

Barbara shuddered as doors opened in her mind, unlocking whole chains – years – of memory: from Coal Hill School to Totter's Lane to Skaro along the Silk Road to Cathay to the planet MarinustofifteenthcenturyMexicototheSenseSphereeighteenth centuryFrancetwentysecondcenturyLondon –

Another life as a teacher, a traveller.

Her companions. The Doctor. Susan.

Ian!

It had been eight years. What had happened to him? Would he remember her? Was he even still alive? Would he –

Wait. It wouldn't be eight years for him. Only she had gone back in time. He would be alive. He had to be alive!'

Barbara scrambled to her feet and, ignoring her son, wrenched open the morning room door and fled out of the palace into the storm.

The streets were filled with a deathly clamour as she ran. Thunder cracked overhead, driven aside by the globe looming over the palace. Lightning bounced from its polished surface. The sun shone briefly through a thin gap in the clouds. For a second the globe was encircled by a dazzling ring of light. Then, as it continued to move, the light was extinguished and a cold shadow crept across the city, drenching the streets in darkness. Barbara looked up to see a reflection of the city moving slowly above her, distorted by the rain.

A mob of terrified soldiers blocked the Canopic Way. Some had fallen to the ground, their eyes upturned, prayers spouting from their lips. The rest were fighting amongst themselves. Their screams and the clash of swords stabbed at her ears. Barbara jerked to a stop, then sidled along the wet pavement, her back to the wall of the nearest building. Just as she had almost cleared the mob, they turned to stare at her. Barbara glimpsed hooded eyes filled with dark intent as the soldiers moved towards her.

Barbara turned and ran; past other running people, fallen bodies, screaming children. Then her sandals rattled on shallow steps, slapped wetly across marble tiles, and she slithered to a halt, drenched with rain and tears, in the main reading room of the library.

The room was full of people, all drenched like herself, huddled together for comfort. They turned to look at her. Some knelt.

'Help us,' said a woman clutching motionless twins.

'Save us,' said a man with a mess of blood-soaked rags where his left arm had once been.

You're the Queen.

Where's our King?

Where's our army?

Help us!

Save us!

Her mind twisting with guilt, Barbara pushed through the mass of clutching, begging people.

Let me go, please, I'm not the Queen, I'm just a schoolteacher –

Her mind registered a heavy door, a corridor flanked with rough columns. Her sandalled feet slapped, heavy on blank stone. The cries turned to jeers, faded behind her. Before her; a hanging silk, out of place in the crude decor. Behind it, a door.

She opened the door, stumbled through.

Into the annex.

Rhakotis's room.

Her mind spinning, she took in the rows of shelves stocked

with scrolls, the reading couches, desks.

And other shapes: tall brass frames, flowing metal forms, a whirling crystal orrery. Shapes for which she now had names.

Computers.

Silver-wire drives.

A remote-control system for a starship.

And before it, Ptolemy's dagger at his throat, the alien himself.

'I tell you, Rhakotis, you must make the systems work!' There was a desperate calmness in the King's voice.

Rhakotis trembled nervously. 'Our bargain did not include this. The repairs to my starship are not yet complete. You know that.'

'You managed to get it out of the ocean,' Ptolemy scowled. His voice grew one notch calmer. 'It must work. If you cannot use your technology to stop the fighting, the city will be overrun and the future – my future – will be destroyed!'

'If you force me to continue holding the ship above the city, the engines will undoubtedly fail. If that happens, Alexandria will be destroyed; the future for which you care so much will never be yours.'

'You are clever, Rhakotis. You will make it work. If we can only convince the people that the gods are on my side, Perdiccas must concede. Victory will be mine! *Victory must be mine!*'

Barbara leaned against the wall. She was so tired. In front of her, the alien blinked. Though his attention was split between Ptolemy's demands and the demands of the control systems, the set of eyes facing the doorway widened as they registered her presence.

And seeing the alien react, Ptolemy turned also.

Barbara stumbled uncertainly into the room. 'Ptolemy – please stop – starship – over city – getting worse, not better – you're wrong, Ptolemy – wrong –'

Without taking his knife from Rhakotis's neck, Ptolemy spoke. 'What are you doing here? And where is our son?'

Barbara blinked stupidly. Son? She didn't have a –

Philadelphus! I've left him alone with the soldiers –

'Why did you leave him, Barbara? Is he dead? Speak! I demand it!'

'Philadelphus – I – Ptolemy, *please* –' She took a pace towards the King. Stopped as two lives crashed together in her mind. '– head hurts – can't think – Ptolemy, I love you – help me –'

'I instructed you to stay with him! If you love me, *how could you leave him at the mercy of Perdiccas's men*?'

Ptolemy turned away, his face a cold mask of betrayal. 'Hear me, Rhakotis,' he said. 'I am betrayed. My son is dead. If you do not wish to see Egypt die with him, make your starship work. Stop the fighting. Make Alexandria mine again.' He pressed his dagger insistently against the alien's throat. 'Do it now, or by the gods I'll –' He stopped as the humming sound of the control systems reached a climactic peak and then dropped sharply to silence. The glimmering metal forms dulled to a pitted texture. The crystal orrery whirled to a stop.

Rhakotis slapped away the knife at his throat. 'The systems have failed. There is nothing more I can do.' Ptolemy stared at him. 'Your future is ended.'

'*I will not allow it!*' Ptolemy lunged at Rhakotis, arm held loosely but in perfect control, muscles bunched, dagger gripped firmly, blade uppermost.

Footsteps pounded outside, the hanging silk was ripped aside and the room was suddenly full of screaming people.

And soldiers.

Perdiccas's army.

With a mighty yell, Ptolemy changed the direction of his movement, swung towards the nearest soldier, who raised his sword in self-defence. Ptolemy grabbed him round the back of the head and pulled him forward onto his dagger. King and soldier crashed together, clasped each other like brothers, then toppled slowly to the ground.

'*No!*' Barbara forced her way through the mob. Her mind was numb. She reached Ptolemy as he crashed to the ground and lay still, eyes open. A thin line of blood slipped from between his open lips.

'The King,' said a voice behind her. '*The King is dead!*'

And then the only movement was the unravelling of the two warriors, the only sound the soft sigh of death as the bodies rolled apart. And Barbara raised her hands to block out the sight which drove her screaming to the edge of madness.

The soldier who had taken the life of her husband, even as his own life had ended, was Ian Chesterton.

Above the city, the shimmering globe of Rhakotis's starship re-formed into a torus-shaped event circling a pulsing heart of light. The event burst violently, showering the city with a rain of dimensions.

Soldiers, slaves, husbands, wives, children and animals screamed, their minds undone, their voices one tiny rivulet in a whirling storm of silver. The storm ripped through past and future history, a montage of insanity gathering temporal inertia before contracting, shrinking back to one single event, one single moment of spacetime.

The pulsing heart of light swelled, descended.

Touched the city.

Flesh and marble splashed across the streets.

Clutching the bodies of the two men most dear to her, she knelt amidst the shattered ruins of the library. All around her the city was a wasteland. Fires guttered in the shells of buildings. Bodies lay half-melted in the shattered streets. Smoke filled the air and stung her throat. She was beyond tears, beyond emotion; a numb thing shaped like a woman but lacking a voice to cry, a heart to feel. She was nothing. A hollow shell. Her mind teetered on the very edge of madness. Guilt racked her. Stretched her to breaking point.

– *my fault, it's all my* –

For a time that was at once no time at all and all the time that ever was, she knelt among the ruins. The bodies she held cooled slowly.

Then beside her there came a sound. Rhakotis.

She whirled, dropped the bodies, threw herself on the alien. Clutching desperately to life where she thought no life could exist.

Beyond words, the alien folded her in his arms.

After a moment, she heard the sound of footsteps, the tapping of a wooden cane among the rubble. 'I thought I might find you here.' The voice was familiar, old and young at the same time, at once invigorating and calming.

Barbara turned. 'Doctor,' she whispered. 'Ptolemy's dead. Ian's dead. It's my fault. I've changed history. I've changed the world.'

The Doctor pursed his lips. Leaned on his cane. Waited.

Rhakotis broke the silence.

'The fault is not entirely yours,' he said quietly. 'We must carry the blame together.'

Barbara gazed beseechingly at the Doctor. 'I've never asked you for anything,' she whispered.

The Doctor did not reply.

'Please.'

'I am forbidden to interfere. Forbidden!'

'We left Susan in the future,' Barbara said quietly. 'The future I have changed. What will happen to her if you don't interfere?'

The Doctor turned away, but not before Barbara saw the anger on his face. He began to speak. Stopped. He took a book from his pocket. A small book, nothing special, half bound in cloth and leather.

'That's the book I took from Aristotle,' she whispered softly. 'Eight years ago.'

'Aristophanes found it for me in the palace. This . . . book, as you call it, is not a book at all. It was brought here from the twentieth century of this planet. But it doesn't originate there either.'

'Then where . . . ?'

'It comes from a library on my own world. I do not know yet how it came to Earth, but that is not important. What is important is that Aristotle acquired it for the library, using the transtemporal architecture that Rhakotis placed there to travel into the future.' He paused. 'Whether or not you are guilty, everything that happened here today can be linked to this book and, by extension, my own people.' He took a deep breath. 'And because that is so, I am able to offer a solution. A partial solution, true, and one with a price . . . but a solution nonetheless.'

He paused for a longer time, and Barbara could hear the crackling of small fires burning in the rubble.

'Time is a dangerous thing,' he said quietly. 'And to be manipulated only at the cost of total responsibility.'

He opened the book.

Barbara trembled. 'What will you do?'

'I will do nothing. The task is yours and Rhakotis's.'

He handed her the book.

'You are faced with a choice. To live forward from this moment, to accept the deaths that have occurred, to learn to live in the new world you have created. Or . . . ' He hesitated. 'To use the book to undo the harm that has happened here.'

'I choose to use the book!'

'My dear, have the grace to let me finish. Even my people have limits to their wisdom. The solution will come at a price.'

'What do you mean?'

'I know only that the scales of time must remain balanced. As for the rest, the book will know. Now you must choose.' He turned away.

Still Barbara did not look at the book she held. Instead, she gazed at Rhakotis. The price was his to pay also.

If the book was used, Ptolemy would live, history would be corrected, the world she knew would be remade. But . . . she would lose a son, a husband, eight years of life and love. She would lose part of herself. And *what if she had to lose Ian too*?

What if his death in the mines was the price she had to pay for correcting her own mistakes?

She looked again at Rhakotis and saw he too had found an answer. Looking past the tiny fires reflected in his eyes, to the understanding shown there, Barbara found herself thinking that her own loss might not be so great after all.

Then Rhakotis reached out for the book. Together, they began to read from its pages. As they read, Barbara felt something shake loose within herself. She began to cry. The tears were not for herself, not for Ian. They were for her husband. And her son who would never be.

The tears fell from her cheeks towards the pages of the book.

They never landed.

Time unravelled first.

331 BC

When his ship smashed a hole in time and vanished through it, Rhakotis knew he was going to die. But when the expected bodily dissolution did not come, he began to suspect he had been wrong to retreat from consciousness so quickly.

Nervously, Rhakotis allowed his awareness to emerge from his hind-brain. The pain overwhelmed him immediately. He was scared to perceive how badly his body had been damaged in the accident, even as he was surprised that it still lived. Rhakotis struggled to regain full bodily control. The pain from his shattered limbs made the task impossible. He tried to isolate the part of his brain which dealt with such signals; the dreadful grinding of shattered bones in his upper limbs as he struggled into an excursion suit broke his concentration.

When Rhakotis managed at last to fight his way clear of the ship, he was already dying. The gulp of water as the timefield of his ship collapsed shook him violently, but he was beyond all pain, all hope.

His mind fled desperately for the sanctuary of his hind-brain, but was distracted by a thought:

– the ship – the temporal explosion – the energy has to go somewhere –

Without even knowing the completed thought, Rhakotis died.

And nearly a thousand years in the future a city burned, taking the knowledge and wisdom of a world with it into the shadows.

Not for the first time that night, I sat scratching my head in bewilderment. 'Is that it?' I asked. 'But what happened to the Doctor and his friends after that . . . that time reversal?'

Silverman shrugged. 'I am sorry, Mr Addison, I can tell you no more.'

'Again the Doctor looked completely different,' noted the stranger. 'So that *could* be who I am.'

'Well, your appearance doesn't seem to rule it out,' I admitted, 'but let's not jump to conclusions.' I leaned across to Silverman and took the lump of yellow rock from his hand. 'So this is gold, eh? Maybe I *will* get paid my fee after all.' I threw it back onto the table. 'Let's try something else.'

Silverman perused the remaining items in the pile and picked out one that had caught my eye back in my office: the rolled-up local newspaper with the UFO headline. He was about to work his usual magic on it when suddenly the stranger reached across and snatched it from his grasp.

'No,' said the little guy, 'I don't think that would prove very productive. I think you should try something different.' I regarded him curiously, but kept my thoughts to myself. It was Silverman who broke the silence:

'By all means, sir.' He picked up a small piece of chalk. 'Would this meet with your approval?' The stranger grunted in agreement.

'The chalk it is, then,' I said.

Fascination

David J. Howe

The sun was a demon.

Every morning for the past two hundred days it had cracked open its cyclopean eye and stared balefully down at the defenceless country below. Under its unwavering gaze moisture was banished from the earth, grass and trees withered and numerous small animals curled up and died.

The people were desperate. Crops failed, families went hungry, and rivers and streams dried up. Even the drawing of water from the deepest wells became harder to achieve. Each week that passed without rain meant that more rope had to be added to the length already attached to the wooden bucket and, before long, the bucket would start to return empty.

In the brown fields and dusty stone lanes, bees foraged ever further in search of pollen, stray breezes stirred the dust into tiny whirlpools and the horizon shimmered in the constant heat.

The hot and oppressive tranquillity was broken by the sound of footsteps, scrunching on the dust and gravel of the stone track, and voices. One female, one male.

'You were definitely right about the heat, Doctor.'

'Mmm.'

'It's hotter here than Lanzarote!'

'Mmm.'

The figures appeared around the curve of the lane. The woman walked in front, stepping backwards along the lane, facing her companion. She had short, straight, brown hair cut in an attractive bob which framed a tanned face from which blue eyes twinkled. Her lithe body was clad in a pair of multi-coloured cycle-shorts with a baggy white T-shirt on top, tied up above her waist. The ensemble was completed by a pair of battered and dusty once-white sneakers on her feet and an orange baseball cap perched askew on her head.

Her companion was dressed in a pair of pink-striped white trousers and a white shirt, the sleeves rolled up to leave his forearms bare. His head was covered by a battered straw hat with a red silk band around the crown, and a pair of patterned braces held up his trousers. He too was tanned, and his normally blond hair was streaked with lighter patches testifying to many days spent in the sun.

'It's even hotter than Sarn!' continued the girl, skipping around to walk forwards again. 'And that's saying something!'

Behind her, the Doctor lifted the bottle of water he was carrying to his mouth and took a sip.

'Don't knock the heat, Peri,' he admonished. 'It can be of great benefit as well as essential to the growth of most living creatures.'

Peri smiled. For the first time since she had started travelling with the Doctor, she felt at ease. After all, it had been her idea to stop off for a ramble through the countryside.

'It's a shame that everything is so parched,' she commented, looking across the withered fields. 'I didn't think that it could be so persistently dry on Earth.'

Something caught her eye. Peering, she stopped walking. 'Doctor? Look at that!'

The Doctor came up behind her and gazed across the fields. In the distance he could see some lush greenery, but the shimmering heat made everything indistinct.

'Interesting,' he mused. 'Could be a mirage. Do you want to take a look . . . ?'

Before he had finished the sentence, Peri was striding off down the lane, looking for a way to cross the fields.

'Come on, Doctor,' her voice carried back to him. 'If it's a village then there'll be a bar, and I could murder a can or two of Bud!'

'Humans!' muttered the Doctor under his breath with a smile. He looked around at the countryside. Withered, brown, and slowly dying under the impartial gaze of the sun. He peered to where Peri had seen the greenery and it was still there. Adjusting his hat thoughtfully, he walked on.

After about ten minutes Peri found herself walking alongside fields full of healthy and strong vines. The grass bordering the dusty lane was lush too and the trees no longer looked shrivelled. Ahead of her she could see a sign at the side of the lane. She picked up her pace and trotted towards it.

As he walked further, so the Doctor's puzzled frown deepened. He looked back to check that he wasn't imagining things, but behind him was the same barren wilderness that he remembered walking through. Despite this, suddenly the earth was alive again, and even the air seemed to contain more moisture.

'Doctor!' called Peri from up ahead. 'It's a village!'

The Doctor hurried to catch up with his friend. He found her standing by a sign set by the side of the road. 'Sair'. A hundred yards or so further on, there were a couple of rough brick cottages, and beyond them an old brick tower jutted above the tops of the trees.

As the Doctor and Peri walked into Sair, the heat dissipated slightly. The cottage gardens were in full bloom. A riot of colour and fragrance assailed them as they passed. One of the villagers, a wizened and sun-baked old man, was sitting in his porch, packing a clay pipe with a mixture pulled from a faded leather pouch in his lap.

The man's deep-set eyes followed Peri and the Doctor as they passed, while his hands continued their task of preparing the pipe. Placing the stem between yellowed teeth, he raised his hand to cup the bowl. The Doctor watched with interest as flame appeared as if from nowhere. With a couple of puffs, the pipe was gently smouldering to the man's satisfaction.

'Doctor, it's wonderful. A real country village!' Peri exclaimed from further ahead, distracting the Doctor from his thoughts.

The Doctor wandered down the lane. The narrow lane gave way into a cobbled square. In the centre stood a monument of some sort, while orange and lemon trees, heavy with ripening fruit, sprouted from the paving. Along the sides of the square clustered the rough, sun-bleached porticos of several houses, in front of which were tables laden with fresh goods for sale: fish on one, meat on another, and fruit and vegetables on another. A confusion of small children chased each other around the trees and the monument, and across the other side of the square were arranged a number of tables and benches in front of what appeared to be the local hostelry.

'It appears so,' agreed the Doctor, 'but appearances can be . . . '

He spotted two people approaching them purposefully from across the square.

' . . . Peri? Welcoming party. I hope. Now stay calm and let me do the talking.'

Peri was at that moment contemplating an Adonis, sitting on one of the benches outside the inn. He was aged about twenty – the same as her, well, give or take a year – with short, light brown hair, tanned face, and a tidy, fit body which made her mouth water. He appeared not to have noticed her, being preoccupied with looking into a pewter tankard perched on the table in front of him.

'Peri.' The Doctor's slightly breathless voice broke into her thoughts of what the stranger's legs might be like.

She looked round to see that they had been joined by two villagers. A tall man of about fifty whose face showed intelligence and compassion, and a woman who might have been older. Her hair was gathered in a loose pony tail and her lined face seemed to convey a feeling of peace and inner serenity. Both were dressed in loose, light-coloured robes and carried themselves with a certain air of authority.

'This is Papus,' explained the Doctor, gesturing to the man, who bowed in Peri's direction, 'and Rasphuia.'

The woman held out her hand and Peri marvelled at the collection of gemstone rings that adorned it.

'Delighted to meet you, my dear.' Rasphuia's voice was gentle and light and reminded Peri of her own mother's voice – but without the accent.

'I . . . I'm Peri,' she stammered, taking the proffered hand with a side glance at the Doctor. 'That's short for Perpugillium,' she added with a wry smile.

'Papus here has kindly agreed to show us around,' said the Doctor with what Peri recognized as his particular form of mock enthusiasm. 'Care to join us?'

Peri's eyes momentarily shot back to the taverna where the object of her gaze was still tantalizing her.

'Well . . . I . . . I'm feeling a bit tired, Doctor. After all that walking in the sun, I mean. I . . . I think I'll just sit around for a while.'

The Doctor followed Peri's gaze and saw the boy.

'All right, Peri,' he smiled. 'But don't go rushing off without me.'

'Thanks, Doctor,' grinned Peri and swung on her heel to saunter casually off across the square.

The Doctor watched her go. Humans found enjoyment in the simplest of things. 'This is a fascinating place, Papus.' He turned to his hosts. 'Where shall we start?'

As she approached the inn, Peri's mind was reeling. Not four feet in front of her was the most gorgeous guy she had seen in months. And he was human! She remembered the last fling she had had with that English chap in Lanzarote. He and his brother had been persistent as hell. It was only after too much cheap beer that she had agreed to return to their place for a nightcap. She wondered what they had thought when she had not turned up to meet them for their little trip to Morocco as she had promised.

But what should she do now? What was the best approach? Then she remembered something the Doctor had told her and smiled. The direct approach.

She walked up to the table and parked herself opposite the Adonis. 'Hi, I'm Peri.'

The boy looked up at her and Peri felt that she could drown in those eyes. Blue as an ocean.

'Hello.' He eyed her slightly suspiciously.

'D'you come here often?'

Damn, damn and blast. Peri mentally kicked herself several times. Why did she have to choose that corny old line from the several zillion witty and interesting ice-breakers from her dazzling repertoire? As she agonized, she forced her face into what she hoped looked like a warm and interested smile.

The boy didn't seem to have noticed, however, and smiled back. 'I live here actually, but I haven't seen you around before.'

Peri inwardly relaxed. 'No,' she admitted. 'I've just arrived. Sightseeing really.' She gestured vaguely around.

'Can I get you a drink?'

'Thanks. A beer'd be good.'

The boy smiled and stood up. 'If we're going to be drinking together, I'd better introduce myself. Tablibik.'

He executed a smart, sharp bow. 'There's no need for formalities,' Peri laughed. 'Just get the drinks.'

Tablibik turned and entered the bar. Peri stretched out her legs and smiled. This was turning into a near-perfect day.

The Doctor was also having a good day. Papus and Rasphuia had taken him on a tour around the village and they were now sitting in the village office, a small stone building beneath the brick tower that the Doctor had noticed earlier.

Papus had explained their village history, how everyone was happy and contented and had everything they wanted, and now that they were sitting comfortably in the book-lined room, he turned to the Doctor.

'So what brings you here?' he asked, a smile playing about his lips. 'Idle curiosity is not something that we necessarily condone . . .'

The Doctor pushed himself up out of the comfy armchair and strode across to the bookshelves. 'Oh . . . just passing through.'

His hungry eyes scanned the dusty spines in front of him. 'We travel, you see, and every so often we stop to look around. It's really very simple.'

The Doctor smiled disarmingly at Papus. 'Interesting selection of books you have.' He wandered towards the table upon which a larger, leather-bound tome rested.

Rasphuia appeared in front of him, blocking his way forward. The Doctor peered over her shoulder briefly before turning back to face Papus. 'So many books on witchcraft and devilment. Odd for a small village, wouldn't you say?'

'Oh I don't know, Doctor.' Papus gestured tiredly around the room. 'When one has lived for a long time, one tends to accumulate . . . But you must be hungry. Let us prepare a meal. Won't you join us Doctor – and your friend too, perhaps?'

'That's a kind offer, but one I must decline at the moment,' said the Doctor. 'My friend, like me, is a stranger in a strange land.' He paused briefly. 'You have been most kind, but I feel I should return to my companion and bid you a good evening.' He gestured outside. 'Perhaps we can talk again tomorrow, when I am rested from my journeys.'

'As you wish, Doctor.' Papus rose to his feet and held the door open. 'We shall speak tomorrow.'

Peri looked at the empty pitcher of beer on the table between herself and Tablibik. Tablibik saw her gaze and shook his head with amazement.

'More?' he exclaimed.

Peri shook her head. 'Any more and I won't be fit for anything!'

'What is there to be fit for?' asked Tablibik innocently, placing his hand on her arm. Peri gave him a pinched smile and deliberately moved her arm away. 'Walking,' she said. 'And exploring.'

Tablibik laughed coldly. 'There's nothing to "explore" here.' His eyes narrowed. 'Why not stay with me?'

The last hour had, for Peri, dragged interminably. Tablibik may have looked good enough to eat, but an hour of listening to him droning on about how he had done this, how he had made that, how all the girls he had been out with adored him, had given Peri a pain in the gut. He was vain, arrogant, cocksure and a total creep. She wished that she had gone with the Doctor after all and not let her hormones get the better of her. After this experience she would never again moan about the Doctor's more enigmatic moments.

Peri was suddenly feeling very guilty. The Doctor. While she had been getting drunk, he had been doing what he did best – finding out about things. The Doctor did a lot of that. Looking again at the empty pitcher, Peri felt that she ought to see how he was getting on. After all, he had looked after her, kind of, on Sarn, and when she had asked him to take her somewhere 'interesting' he had complied – even if that moon had been on its outer orbit at the time and the 'crystal blue lakes and diamond waterfalls' had all been frozen. At least he had tried.

'What is it?' asked Tablibik, his eyes roving for the hundredth time over her body.

'It . . . it's my friend,' she stammered, the familiar speech impediment resurfacing as the stress of the situation increased. 'I really ought to go and find him. See if he's all right.'

She smiled falsely at Tablibik.

'I'll come back,' she lied. 'We'll stop by before we leave.'

Tablibik cocked an eyebrow. 'Promise?'

'Promise.'

Peri pushed herself up from the table, and swayed slightly. Alcohol always did that. 'Watch that first step,' she heard her old drinking pals say, 'it's a doosie.'

As she moved off across the square, Tablibik watched her go. It wasn't fair. He liked her, and now she was rushing off to find her friend. Well, no one walked off on Tablibik. A sly look crossed his face, and he raised his hand in her direction. Folding his middle two fingers down, he muttered, 'Conjure Jazer.

Conjure Sisera.'

There was a slight ripple in the air by Tablibik's hand, as if the heat in its vicinity had increased. The ripple then moved, lightning swift, towards Peri's retreating back. For a fraction of a second, a red and yellow shape, curved and mottled and writhing like an eel, spun out of thin air immediately behind Peri. Then it plunged straight into the girl's back.

Peri abruptly stopped and shook her head. Goose walking over her grave. It passed and she smiled again. Definitely out of practice on the old falling down water. She resumed her pace across the square. Behind her Tablibik smiled.

The fierce heat of the day had mellowed into a perfect late afternoon. A cool breeze played over Peri's face and chased up and down her legs, and she found herself wishing that it was Tablibik's fingers that were tracing patterns rather than the breeze. She frowned. Where had that thought come from? She shuddered. The last thing she wanted was to see that creep again. The breeze blew across the back of her neck, and she shuddered as goose bumps sprang up over her arms. She caught herself thinking about his firm body. Perhaps she had read him wrong. Those strong hands, good legs, and the cutest butt that she had ever seen. I wonder how good he is at kissing, she thought, and licked her lips. He was definitely kissable. He had seemed to like her too. Perhaps she should go back. Claim that she couldn't find the Doctor or something; she could think up an excuse. She shook her head. No, the Doctor was her friend too, he could be in trouble. But she could, surely, have another drink with Tablibik, especially as he was paying?

Suddenly Peri found herself getting very cross with the Doctor. Why should she have to drop whatever *she* was doing and rush to his side like some devoted puppy? She was getting on fine where she was. Tablibik had been considerate and kind, but the Doctor just made her feel inadequate. Was she going to be at his beck and call forever? She shook her head again. No. This time he had gone just too far. Forcing her to leave Tablibik like that.

Tablibik. She found herself seeing again his face, his body, the way his leg muscles moved when he got up to buy the drinks. Tablibik. She licked her lips again. Tablibik. What a body.

'Ah, Peri!'

She looked up to see the Doctor approaching.

'Had a nice time? Where's your friend?'

Peri clenched her teeth together. The bastard! Not content with pulling her away from her Tablibik, now he was rubbing her nose in it too.

'I'm fine,' she snapped. 'Did you get what you wanted?'

'Almost, Peri. Almost.'

The Doctor gazed at her with concern. 'Are you okay? You look flushed.'

Flushed! Ha! Peri determined to get one up on the Doctor.

'Flushed? No . . . It . . . It's just the heat. Can we stay here tonight?'

The question caught the Doctor unawares. 'Here? But the TARDIS is just over that hill.' He gestured vaguely in the air.

'I . . . I know, but it's a long walk, and this village is so beautiful, and the people are really friendly, and I just know that there'll be some rooms if we ask . . . '

Peri looked at him with her extra-special pleading expression. It had never failed with her stepfather.

The Doctor hesitated a moment, weighing up in his own complex mind the pros and cons. 'All right, but up and away first thing.'

Peri smiled and there was a fleeting flash of orangey red in her eyes. Brilliant. Phase one complete. She'd soon be back with Tablibik.

'And as you can see, the people of Sair have developed their own techniques in farming and irrigation, meaning that they can farm the land all year round, and not be troubled by such natural problems as drought and flooding.'

The Doctor was in full flow as he and Peri wandered around

the village. Peri looked about, but with little interest. All her thoughts were now on Tablibik and how long it would be before she saw him again. She was all but counting the minutes as the Doctor droned on about agriculture and wildlife.

Suddenly she realized that he had stopped walking and was standing a few paces behind, watching a group of women move slowly across a humped and grassy field to their left. As the women walked their lips moved and their right hands were all extended, pointing at the ground in front of them. Peri's jaw dropped as she saw one of the women, a young redhead of about her own age, point at a large stone in her path. The redhead's lips moved and the boulder crumbled where it stood. No force of any sort had been exerted as far as Peri could see, but the stone was no more. The redhead moved on across the field, and Peri saw that the other women were dissolving rock with similar ease as they went. One woman passed quite close and Peri caught her voice on the wind as she passed. 'Conjure Suphlatus . . . Conjure Suphlatus,' she seemed to be saying, and with each incantation another rock crumbled.

'Doctor . . . Did you see that?' Peri was incredulous.

The Doctor glanced at her and nodded. 'I think there is more at work here than mere agronomy, Peri. Notice the way that the rocks flush pale yellow before they disintegrate . . . ' His eyes clouded over with that far-away look that Peri knew meant that the Doctor was on to something.

'Perhaps we should get back . . . before they run out of rooms?' Peri suggested, aware that things were rapidly getting serious and uncomfortable, something which tended to happen when the Doctor was about.

'You're right, as always, Peri,' exclaimed her companion with a sudden burst of decisiveness. 'We must get our rooms sorted out. Come on!'

The Doctor set off back down the lane at a furious pace and Peri had to jog to catch up with him, glad that at least they were heading in the right direction – back to Tablibik.

As they strode into the square, a flock of white doves burst from the ground filling the air with a cacophony of beating wings and startled cooing. A man emerged from the frantic mass and raised his arms to the sky. He scowled as the Time Lord strode past, and Peri stammered an apology as she trotted after him. The man looked up at the wheeling mass. 'Conjure Alphun,' he called. Immediately the sky quietened, and the doves returned *en masse* to the ground, perching on the now smiling man's arms and head.

Peri looked back to see this, but when she tried to draw the Doctor's attention, his back was vanishing into the taverna. Peri's heart leaped when she realized that Tablibik was nowhere to be seen. He wouldn't stand her up, would he? He couldn't!

She followed the Doctor past the empty tables and into the dim coolness of the taverna's interior. The Doctor was at the bar, passing a randomly selected handful of coinage from a drawstring purse to a short, balding man wearing a stained apron. The man, who was presumably the owner, eyed the multicoloured and multifaceted assortment with some doubt.

'I'm sure you'll find something there that you can use,' smiled the Doctor enthusiastically. 'My credit is good all over the Nine Galaxies,' he added hopefully.

The man's eyes widened and he withdrew a golden item from the pile. Inserting the piece between his teeth he bit down, his smile spreading perceptibly as he examined the bitten sovereign. He looked up at the Doctor, the golden coin and the rest of the collection vanishing magically into the depths of his clothing. The Doctor smiled, doffed his hat at the man and headed off into the gloom in search of the rooms. After excitedly rushing back into the room behind the bar and exclaiming loudly that they had a gentleman staying with them, the man re-emerged and trotted after the Doctor, gesturing expansively to the stairs.

Peri stared in exasperation at their retreating backs. It was far too early to turn in and, anyway, she wanted to wait for Tablibik.

'Does the Doctor's credit extend to drinks?' she asked the

barman, who had at that moment emerged from the back room to catch a glimpse of their honoured guest.

Several well-chosen words later, Peri was sitting in a position which favoured the door, armed with a pint of the local beer and a small bowlful of black olives. She hoped that Tablibik would not be too long.

Upstairs, the Doctor had found his room by the simple expedient of walking into the first one he came to. It seemed that, apart from themselves, the place had no other residential guests, so they effectively had the pick of the rooms. The owner hovered fawningly outside the door. He seemed to want the Doctor to take his own room – or at least one better than this – but the Doctor reassured him that all was fine. Promising that he would drink with the owner and his family as soon as he was able, he closed the door.

The Doctor cast his eyes over the tasteful but austere furniture, the faded rug beside the iron and brass bedstead which topped and tailed a comfortable-looking mattress and duvet arrangement.

He crossed to the window which looked out onto the lane at the side of the building. As he stepped across the rug, his foot rucked it up slightly, revealing scuffed chalk markings on the polished wooden floor beneath. The Doctor frowned slightly and bent to take a closer look. He ran his finger over the marks and rubbed the residue between his thumb and fingers: the chalk was fresh.

The Doctor stood at one side of the window and peered out into the lane. Below stood Tablibik. The Doctor watched as the boy raised his hand to point at the Doctor's room. There was a momentary flash of opal light from across the room by the door, as if someone had taken a flash photograph. The Doctor frowned and looked at the door. There was nothing unusual to see. He crossed the room and tried the handle. Although it did not appear to be locked, the door would not budge an inch. The Doctor was trapped.

In the bar, Peri was becoming increasingly agitated at Tablibik's non-arrival. All thoughts of the Doctor had been excised from her mind, as she nagged and pulled at the hope that she would see Tablibik again. His presence had filled her mind and her expectation to the exclusion of all else, and she would sit and wait for eternity if that was what it took.

Suddenly, the main door opened and Tablibik was there. Peri jumped up, her heart beating faster, her mouth drying up as he moved, as if in slow motion, through the bar towards her. She waved, bouncing excitedly on the balls of her feet as he got closer. Then he was there, standing in front of her. She felt dizzy, she felt elated, she could hear the blood rushing in her ears. He smiled and held out his hand.

'Yes! Yes! Yes!' her mind screamed, and her body switched on to autopilot. Peri watched as if from across the room as the pretty American girl in the baggy tied-up T-shirt took hold of the brown-haired blue-eyed boy's hand. He held her tight and pecked her lightly on the lips. Then he led her willingly across the room towards the stairs.

The Doctor gazed down at the markings on the floor of his room. Using a piece of white chalk he had found in one of the dresser drawers, he had re-chalked the lines, to discover that they formed a triangle inside a square inside a pentacle.

He walked around the shapes thoughtfully and then stood looking at the locked door. He popped the lump of chalk in his pocket and crouched to examine the lock once more. There seemed to be nothing preventing the door from opening, and yet every time he tugged at the handle, there was a brief flash of opal light around the lock and he might as well have been trying to pull a door that bore a sign clearly telling him to push – and he had tried both options.

Humans . . . Why must they always be so infuriatingly naive when it came to messing about with the higher sciences?

Outside, dusk was rapidly falling. Checking the window once more, the Doctor smiled to himself. Never underestimate your opponents. That was something he had learned a long time ago: the hard way. He pushed back the curtain, opened the window and climbed out. The vines covering the wall made an excellent ladder and he was soon standing looking back up at the side of the inn. The light in the room next to his was suddenly extinguished and he hoped that Peri was not going to get into too much trouble before he could find out what was going on here. Turning, he hurried off towards the office, its tower a black shadow against the darkening sky.

Luckily, the building was deserted and dark, and the Doctor had little trouble in flipping the latch on one of the windows and crawling in. Rummaging in his pockets, he withdrew a small penlight torch and swung the beam across the ranks of silent bookcases with their ancient and dusty tenants. As he had noticed before, many of the titles related to demonology, and included several volumes that he had thought lost forever. Then the torch hit upon the large leather-bound grimoire lying open on the main desk.

Wedging his flashlight between two books on a nearby bookcase, the Doctor removed a piece of string from one of his pockets and carefully laid it on the uppermost page of the volume on the desk. Then he gently turned the book back to its cover. The cracked and creaking black leather was embossed with a symbol familiar to the Doctor from the floor of his room. The first page inside gave the title, *Nuctemeron*, and the author: Apollonius of Tyana.

The Doctor's eyes narrowed. Apollonius of Tyana had been infamous for spreading demonic infestation and possession as fast as his rival and contemporary, Jesus of Nazareth, could clear up the mess he left behind. The Doctor recalled that he himself had seen Apollonius chased into the wilderness by a posse of men wielding sticks and large stones. Could this book be the result of his subsequent exile?

The version of the text on the table was written in Greek, but, as usual, this gave the Doctor little pause for concern. He flicked through the first few pages, stopping occasionally to pick up the context of the work. It apparently described the 'genius' of demons uncovered and researched by Apollonius. The demonic force was split into several 'circles' and within each 'circle' were the demons of a particular level of 'genius'. In the lowest circle were those benign entities which controlled natural forces: the Doctor noticed that Alphun was the genius of doves, and that the genius of rocks was Suphlatus. As one progressed through the circles, so the demons became more powerful, until one reached the seventh circle where the genii of fornication, deception and death resided, together with those of numerous other unsavoury weaknesses.

As the Doctor flicked further through, more unfamiliar names were revealed to him: Tablibik was the genius of fascination, Sisera controlled desire and Jazer compelled love. An interesting collection, thought the Doctor as he reached the point where his piece of string hung.

The Doctor looked up sharply as a noise and a light from the front passageway alerted him to the fact that people were entering the office. As the light grew stronger, he quickly and silently pocketed the string and the torch, then slipped like a greased monkey back out of the window, leaving it slightly ajar behind him. Crouching down outside, he could hear two voices as their owners entered the room. It was Papus and Rasphuia, the latter somewhat agitated.

'We must find out more about them, I tell you! Who knows why they have come and what harm they intend?'

'Calmly, Rasphuia, calmly,' Papus soothed. 'We cannot treat people as guilty until we have proof. These newcomers seem friendly enough, although I will agree that the Doctor knows more than he will readily admit. It is, however, wise to retain some advantage in a foreign place and we should not prejudge when there may be no crime committed.'

The Doctor heard a rustle as someone drew the curtains by the window beneath which he crouched.

'The Shades have been anxious, Papus,' breathed the woman. 'They know that something is coming to our village, something which could mean harm.' She turned back to Papus. 'It could be these strangers!'

'Then we shall find out. My instinct tells me that we should trust these people, not suspect them.'

The voices and the light faded away as the elderly couple moved to another part of the building. The Doctor pressed his lips together in a thin line. There was trouble here. And, as usual, he was in the thick of it. Carefully opening the window once more he slipped back into the room, edged through the curtains and made his way to the door. In the outer corridor he stopped and listened carefully. Sounds were coming from somewhere above him, and he slipped along the corridor until he came to a flight of stairs which curled upwards. At the top was another heavy wooden door, slightly ajar, with light flickering around it.

Praying that the hinges were oiled, the Doctor pushed the door gently until it was open wide enough for him to see into the room beyond. Papus and Rasphuia were there, as was the source of the light, an orange globe hovering some five feet above the floor. Papus stood by the globe watching as Rasphuia positioned herself in the centre of the room, which was, the Doctor noted, roughly circular, with windows set several feet apart round the wall.

On the wooden floor was carved a larger version of the symbol the Doctor had found on the floor of his bedroom and Rasphuia was standing to one side of it, facing Papus, the light from the flickering sphere illuminating her features. She was muttering to herself and held one hand up in front of herself, pointing towards the centre of the symbol on the floor. As the Doctor watched, dust eddied in from the dark corners of the room and started to chase itself around in circles. There was no breeze in the room as these smaller clouds then joined together into a whirling column of dust about two feet high. It spun faster and faster until it was just a blur.

A dry, whispering sound insinuated itself through the fabric of the room, as though a hundred thousand mice were scampering about the walls. Rasphuia smiled. 'They are here.'

'Tell us about the strangers,' demanded the woman.

The whispering grew momentarily louder and then abruptly dropped to a background rustling, like a bird moving furtively in its nest. A parched and ancient voice murmured over the faint noise. It seemed to come from everywhere and nowhere, and carried the weight of ages in its sound.

'They are two. They are here and elsewhere. One is not of this Earth. Neither is of this time.'

Rasphuia's brow creased. 'Not of this Earth? Explain!'

'We cannot. We cannot see. The thoughts are clouded. He is near.'

Papus looked alarmed but Rasphuia calmed him. 'They are staying at the inn. They *are* close.'

The dry, mummified voice continued. 'He is near. He has known many times. He has great wisdom. We might speak with him.'

'What wisdom does he have?'

'Great wisdom. Wisdom beyond his years. Beyond his time.'

'Is he a threat?'

'Not the man. Watch the woman. She is already with one of us. Corruption of us will be easy. The girl too.'

Papus looked at Rasphuia. 'Corruption?'

The woman concentrated. 'Find the one called Doctor. He must be warned.'

'He is near,' the sexless voice croaked. 'He is close. We feel he hears this.'

The Doctor shifted position slightly and his foot scraped against a piece of grit on the step. The sound, magnified by the stairwell behind him was like a rock slide in the silence. Seconds later, the door was flung fully open to reveal a frowning Papus.

'Ah . . . hello,' began the Doctor lamely, glancing in concern at the whirling cloud of debris. 'I know this looks odd – but I can explain . . . '

* * *

Fresh and chilled orange juice, the Doctor mused, had to be one of the best things about this planet. He raised the condensation-speckled glass to his lips and took another deep draught. Outside, the sun was already warming the cobbles on the square and the villagers were up and about their daily business. Birds filled the orange and lemon trees with the tuneless babble of their song.

The Doctor placed the empty glass on the table in front of him.

'Up with the larks, Doctor?'

Peri grinned as she sauntered across the bar and slid into the seat opposite him. The Doctor smiled back.

'Sleep well?'

Peri's smile widened. 'The best night I've had in ages!' She looked out of the window. 'What a glorious morning! Who's for a constitutional?'

She leaped out of her chair and grasped the Doctor's hand. 'Come on, Doctor, let's explore. I love exploring.'

The Doctor got to his feet and followed her out of the taverna. Something was wrong here, he reminded himself. Rasphuia's Shades had been non-specific, but they had been certain of two things: that it involved Peri, and that it spelt trouble. He resolved not to let Peri's enthusiasm dampen his instincts.

Behind him, a shadow detached itself from the stairwell and entered the bar. Tablibik smiled after the Doctor. The girl was his, but the poor fool didn't realize it. Well, he would. He would.

Peri skipped ahead of the Doctor across the square. She was on cloud nine. Tablibik had been so . . . good! That was the word for it – although several others had occurred to her during the night. Now the sun was shining, life was good, and she was in love. But Tab had warned her to keep an eye on the Doctor. He was likely to be jealous, Tab had said, and although Peri thought this unlikely, she was on her guard just in case. She was also eager to try some of the new skills that Tab had taught her sometime after midnight.

'Come on, slowcoach!' she shouted, and ran lightly down a winding lane which led to an open grassy area. She stopped and waited for the Doctor to catch up.

'Peri . . . we must talk.'

'I bet this whole village is, what . . . eighteenth century? Seventeenth? Am I close, Doctor?'

'It's fifteenth century. Peri . . . '

Peri turned and wandered onto the grassy area which turned out to be the remains of an ancient and crumbling graveyard. There were newer-looking plots over to the left, but near the entrance the graves were all but hidden under the foliage, crooked slabs of mottled and cracked stone marking their positions.

'These look really old.' Peri crouched down by one particularly illegible stone and ran her hand over the lichen-encrusted surface. 'Can you read this? I can't.' Peri held her tanned hand over the ancient mottled slab. 'Conjure Eistibus,' she muttered, and almost pulled her hand away when it suddenly started tingling. The feeling was hypnotic, however, and somehow alluring. The air around her splayed fingers rippled as though she had dipped her hand into a still pool of water, and then, to her complete amazement, the lichen darkened and receded, and the words on the stone sprang into view. 'It worked! It actually worked! I bet –'

'Peri!'

The Doctor's sharp tone stopped Peri in mid-gush. 'Peri?' he questioned gently. 'How did you do that?'

Peri looked up at him, sudden fear in her eyes like a small child who has been caught with her hand in the cookie jar.

'There's something going on,' said the Doctor. 'Something that could mean a lot of trouble for us.'

He looked about anxiously, not noticing that Peri's eyes had suddenly narrowed in defiance.

'I think it would be best if you return to the TARDIS and wait for me there. You have a key and you'll be safe. Can you do that?'

'You just want me out of the way, don't you?' spat Peri.

The Doctor's mouth gaped open as Peri verbally launched into him.

'You can't stand to take second place, can you? Your pride won't take it.' She stood up. 'Well, Tab was right. You don't own me! You can't tell me what to do and where to go, and right now I want to stay here.'

Peri whirled on her heel and made to return the way they had come, but the Doctor grabbed her arm as she passed him.

'Peri?' He gazed into her red- and orange-flecked eyes and saw that something was very wrong indeed. 'Who is Tab?' he asked gently.

'A friend!' snapped Peri. 'More than you'll ever be!'

She pulled her arm away and ran back up the lane, heading towards the square.

The Doctor watched her go, steely determination crossing his face. He had often been accused of interfering, and, by all accounts, it was something he was good at. Well, he was going to have to interfere again. With a final glance at Peri's retreating back, he turned and strode off towards the tower.

Standing outside the inn, Tablibik watched Peri running towards him. She was sobbing and tears ran down her face. One side of her mind was screaming at her to get a grip and to go back and apologise to the Doctor, but the other, stronger side was saying that she was right to assert herself and that Tab would make everything all right. Tab would always make everything all right. All she had to do was listen to him.

Peri flung herself at Tablibik and sobbed in confusion and relief. He hugged her with his strong arms and stroked her hair, crooning gently and rocking her as she slowly recovered her composure.

She dried her tears on her T-shirt, and looked up. 'I bet I look a wreck.'

'You look beautiful to me,' smiled Tablibik and pecked her on the lips.

Peri's mouth broke into a smile. 'Oh Tab,' she murmured and sought out his lips with hers. As they kissed she ran her hand around his neck and up the fine hairs on the back of his head. She was safe now. Tab would look after her. Her mysterious, fascinating and expert lover.

The kiss broke and Peri allowed Tablibik to lead her back into the taverna without a single thought in her mind as to what the Doctor might have thought of her behaviour, or how he might react. As long as she was with Tab, she was safe and happy.

Some time later, the door to the Doctor's room at the inn was pushed gently open, and the Time Lord slipped in, closing it quietly behind him.

He moved across to where the chalked pentacle still marked the wooden floor and sat cross-legged beside it.

He waited.

In the next room, Peri sat on her messed-up bed facing Tablibik. She could listen to him forever, and he had taught her more than she would ever have learnt otherwise. She gazed with love at her mentor and he smiled.

'Now you are ready.' He brushed a stray hair from her brow and tucked it behind her ear. 'Let's tell your friend.'

Sitting on the floor, the Doctor pulled from inside his hat a small cloth bag tied with a length of string. He opened the neck of the bag and, licking his finger, dipped it in. It emerged with a fine white coating which the Doctor licked off with a slight grimace. Salt. From his trouser pocket he removed a handful of bullets – live ammunition saved from a war somewhere – and an old-fashioned thermometer. These he laid in front of him, arranging them around the pentacle on the floor. He then pulled the rug over and covered up the markings and the objects.

At that moment the door to his room was opened, and the Doctor looked up to see Peri. She entered and stood to one side looking down at him. Tablibik remained in the hall, watching.

'Peri! Are you all right?' The Doctor's eyes flicked between his friend and her lover and read instantly what both had perhaps hoped to conceal from him.

'I want to stay, Doctor.'

'Let's talk.' The Doctor gestured to the floor in front of him.

Peri glanced at Tablibik and he nodded. Peri sank gracefully to the rug and held out her hands. After a moment's hesitation, the Doctor took hold of them.

'I . . . I'm happy here, Doctor. I'm so happy. Tab loves me, and I love Tab, and I . . . I want you to be happy too. Please be happy for me.'

The Doctor gazed levelly at her. His face, as always, betraying little of the emotional turmoil that lurked underneath. Then, with a glance at Tablibik, he lifted the corner of the rug to reveal part of the chalked markings and the small bag of salt.

'I have encountered many evils, and fought many foes,' he began, 'but to make use of bewitchment to obtain your own ends is neither fair nor condonable.'

Peri frowned in puzzlement.

'You have been bewitched, Peri. Your "friend" has bent your mind against your will.' The Doctor gestured at the ground. 'But as long as you have free will, I can help you break the spell.'

Peri shook her head uncertainly, 'No . . . I . . . I'm sure this time. I –'

'The salt encourages thinking, the sulphur in the gunpowder in the bullets is for willing, and the mercury in the thermometer is for feeling. These combined will help you find yourself again.'

Peri looked around herself in sudden confusion.

The Doctor suddenly freed his hand from Peri's and pointed at her chest. 'Conjure Tabris!'

Peri jolted back as if hit by a sudden punch, and in the doorway Tablibik cried out.

'Have free will, Peri,' said the Doctor.

Peri recovered herself and sat up. She still felt for Tablibik but she was now not sure what she wanted.

'How could you possibly know –' spluttered the boy in the doorway.

'Conjure Havan. That's dignity, Peri!' the Doctor shouted.

Peri's face clouded and then creased in horror. She had lost all her dignity last night with Tablibik. She realized that it had all been a trick. She had been used. The creep had used her!

'No . . . ' She looked at Tablibik who was shaking with fury, his face turning red as his temper reached breaking point. As Peri watched he slowly raised both his arms towards the Doctor.

'Conjure Hahabi,' he muttered. The air roiled between his hands, and a sickly brown coiled shape sprang into life in front of him. The thing suddenly leaped across the room and hit the Doctor in the chest, knocking him back. The Doctor lay on the floor, his face contorting as he struggled and fought with some unseen assailant.

Peri stepped to try and help the Doctor but, realizing that it was hopeless, turned on Tablibik. 'What did you do?' she asked bleakly.

'Fear,' he sneered. 'What does your Doctor friend fear?'

Panic stricken, Peri looked from Tablibik to the helplessly squirming figure of the Doctor. Her face set as she made her decision. She stood up.

'You take that . . . that thing off the Doctor now!'

Tablibik just smiled and shook his head.

Peri raised her hand towards him 'Conjure Hahabi,' she hissed, attempting to throw the same demon back on him. Nothing happened and Tablibik's laughter stung her ears.

'You silly girl! Did you believe that I would be without protection?'

Peri looked hatefully at him and then back at the Doctor. If she could just remember some of the names Tablibik had taught her. Then she smiled. 'Conjure Labezerin,' she said quietly, gesturing at the struggling form of the Doctor. She looked back at Tablibik. 'If I can't hurt you, I can help him. That's success.'

On the floor the Doctor slowly stopped cringing and painfully pushed himself up on to his knees.

'I don't want to hurt anyone,' he began breathlessly, 'but I do intend to protect Peri and myself.'

As he got to his feet, Tablibik shot a worried look around and backed away into the corridor. The Doctor stood and fixed Tablibik with a confident gaze. 'Perhaps I should conjure some of the nastier demons to sit on your back.' The Doctor's eyes narrowed. 'Perhaps those from the eighth circle?'

Tablibik's eyes widened in surprise. Eighth circle? What eighth circle? They never mentioned that at the school!

'Persecution, for example,' continued the Doctor, seeming to enjoy the worried look now present on his opponent's face. 'Or maybe destroyer of children. Or perhaps we'll just go straight to weakener of bones and impotence. I don't think anyone around here would help you.'

As the Doctor started to raise his right arm, Tablibik let out a squeal of panic and turned to run, only to find his way blocked by Papus and Rasphuia who had been watching this exchange with interest. They moved along the passage and herded Tablibik back into the Doctor's room. As they entered, the Doctor let his arm drop to his side.

'Thank you for alerting us, Doctor,' Papus looked sternly at Tablibik. 'Coercion is not our way, boy, as you well know.'

Rasphuia's voice filled the room. 'We believe in free choice and take care that the powers entrusted to us are not misused.'

The Doctor smiled briefly and glanced at Peri who was standing looking at the floor. She felt used and had betrayed the Doctor. How could he stand to even look at her? She had been abused and felt it was partly her own stupid fault. She felt the tears well up inside her once more. How could she have been so foolish?

'The boy will be punished,' said Papus firmly. 'We shall remove a measure of his, shall we say, potency with women.'

'Perhaps also some manual work – without the assistance of demons?'

Papus nodded at the Doctor's suggestion.

Peri was sobbing audibly now, her self-respect in tatters around her. Rasphuia went over to her and scooped the girl's hand up in her own bejewelled fingers.

'Peri? Peri?' her voice broke through Peri's grief and the girl raised her head. 'Listen, Peri, for you I conjure Papus. The physician, the healer. Not all of our demons are evil, Peri, and the healer can banish those tormented souls that our friend here placed upon you. You will be yourself again.'

With this, Rasphuia placed her other hand on Peri's brow. She's so cool, thought Peri, cool and –

Rasphuia muttered under her breath. Peri's eyes flickered shut and a shudder went through her, raising the skin on her arms into goose bumps. Then she opened her eyes again. She looked at Rasphuia who smiled gently, at the Doctor and at Papus, both of whom were watching her intently. Finally she looked at Tablibik. She hated him. Hated him for what he had done to her. For soiling her and making her feel used. With Papus's help she could live with the feelings of disgust and shame, but she could never, ever forgive him for what he had done.

Looking Tablibik in the eye she stepped towards him. He flinched under her glittering gaze.

'You pathetic bastard.'

Her hand moved swiftly and she slapped Tablibik hard across his face. She smiled. That felt good.

'Welcome back, Peri,' murmured the Doctor. 'And thank you.' He shook Papus's hand. 'Both,' he nodded respectfully to Rasphuia.

The sun was still a demon and Peri broke into a sweat as soon as they left the influence of the village, heading back towards the TARDIS.

Peri contemplated the dry, dusty ground in front of her. She hoped that this little escapade was not a portent of things to come, and that travelling with the Doctor would occasionally be enjoyable and restful. She glanced sideways at her companion, who was, as always, striding along, searching the distant horizon for something which seemed to elude him. He was so mysterious, and yet always kind and concerned for her. If he wasn't so paternal then she could almost fancy him. As it was he was like the big brother she had never had, the father who had run off leaving her to fend for herself. The Doctor would never willingly leave her to her fate.

Of one thing she was now certain. The Doctor was about the only true friend she had ever had.

'Doctor?'

'Mmm?'

'Thanks.'

The unnatural glow faded once more, and Silverman returned the piece of chalk to the table. At least the room wasn't thrown into complete darkness now: the oil lamp continued to burn on the psychic's desk, casting its ghostly, flickering shadows across the bookcase-lined walls.

I lit a cigarette – the first since leaving my office – and leaned back in my chair, trying to digest all that we had heard.

'That makes five, by my reckoning,' I said at length, exhaling a ring of smoke.

The stranger's owl-like face creased in puzzlement. 'Five? Five what?'

'Five Doctors,' I replied. 'There was the scruffy little one who got the clockwork bird; the one with the booming voice and the scarf; the tall, elegant guy who drew that sketch on the hymn pamphlet; the old geezer with the walking stick; and now this younger, blond-haired one.'

'Mmm. So maybe I'm the sixth . . . ' he mused.

'Or the seventh.'

'Eh?'

'Or the eighth, come to that. Who knows how many there are?'

Silverman had sat in silence throughout this exchange, but now interjected:

'Perhaps we will learn the answer if we try another object?'

I gave him a slightly sceptical look, but nodded my head in agreement. 'Okay. What have we got to lose?'

Reaching down to the table, he picked up what seemed at first glance to be an ordinary light bulb. When I looked closer, though, I could see that it was filled with coloured gases, and wasn't quite the right shape. Also, the connector on the end was different from any I had ever seen before.

My client shook his head emphatically. 'No, not that one.' He leaned forward to take it from the psychic's hand, as he had done earlier with the newspaper, but I pushed him back into his chair.

'Wait a minute!' I told him. 'Silverman's the expert here. Maybe we should just leave it to his judgement.' The little guy seemed taken aback – shocked, even – but made no objection. I nodded to Silverman and he held the globe out in front of us, ready to continue.

The Golden Door

David Auger

The high, cantilevered dome of the Bukolian space port was reminiscent of the interior of a planetarium, bearing dramatic three-dimensional representations of stars and planetary systems. Whilst waiting to complete the various customs checks, off-world visitors would often pass the time trying to identify their home systems amongst the galactic vista suspended above their heads. As far as that seasoned traveller, the Doctor, was concerned, he already knew far more about astronomy than to let a mere architectural feature distract him from the fact that he had been stuck in a queue for nearly an hour whilst the Bukolian customs officials zealously inspected every passing creature's credentials.

The old man sniffed contemptuously, glancing at the other queues, all of which seemed to be moving faster than the one in which he and his companions stood. If they had travelled directly to Bukol in the TARDIS, he brooded, they would not have had to endure these confounded checks. But his companions had insisted on a holiday, and a voyage about the star-liner *Illyria* had seemed just the ticket.

The Doctor studied some of the other passengers from the liner. He spotted a group of Hirazudi commercial travellers, whose translucent flesh was enough to make most Earthlings' skin crawl. In another queue he saw a family of Kefanjii, whose constantly slavering tongues excreted an unpleasant mucus, the sight of which caused most Earth people to vomit uncontrollably. And as for the Quamak cine-vid starlet standing directly in front of him, well, her romantic performances would woo a human audience into screams of utter terror! He noted with self-congratulatory satisfaction that neither of his two companions appeared in the least bit put out by the crowd around them: Steven's

skin was not crawling and, best of all, Dodo was not suffering a
screaming fit! Clearly their journeys aboard the TARDIS had at
last taught them to respect the infinite variety of life forms
encountered whilst space travelling. At the moment, however,
the Doctor himself had little respect for the Bukolians.

'All this waiting is intolerable. If I stand here much longer, I
shall take root!'

Dodo cast Steven an exasperated glance. 'We're nearly at the
front of the queue now, Doctor.'

'About time, my child, about time!'

Steven smiled at the Doctor. 'The Bukolians are rather fanatical when it comes to bureaucracy. They do say that they should
run the Galactic Civil Service.'

The Doctor turned to the ex-astronaut in surprise. 'You seem
remarkably conversant with these creatures, my boy.'

'He's had his nose in your library again. He should have told
you.'

'Nonsense, my dear. It's about time you gave some thought to
your education instead of making a clutter of my wardrobe!'

Before the Doctor could pursue this particular hobby horse,
Steven tugged at the sleeve of his frock coat to draw his attention
to the fact that they had at last reached the head of the queue. The
old man turned to face the Bukolian customs officer. The Bukolians
were pale-skinned bipeds who moved with a grace which totally
belied their large bulk. Their hairless head had three eyes which
moved independently of each other and, positioned either side of
the mouth, two tentacles which they used to scratch their fore-
heads whilst puzzling over the minutiae of officialdom.

The officer drew the Doctor's attention to a long list of
questions which appeared on a video screen beside him. The
Doctor read through them, muttering 'Yes' or 'No' as appropriate. Suddenly he came to a question which made him look up
sharply. 'Livestock! Do we look as if we're carrying livestock,
hmm? Perhaps you think I'm the proprietor of a travelling flea
circus!'

The officer fixed the Doctor with his central eye. 'Just give the answer to the question, please.'

'Then it is a definite and unequivocal "No".'

'Very well, sir. Now, may I see your visa, please?'

The Doctor fumbled in his pockets and produced an object roughly the size and shape of a domestic light bulb. The officer took it and plugged it into a socket on the panel beside him.

The coloured gases inside the globe immediately began to coalesce, forming themselves into the image of a man's face. Fixing one of his eyes on this, the officer turned the other two to study the Doctor.

'This *is* your visa, sir?'

'Of course it is. You can see that, surely?'

The Doctor followed the Bukolian's gaze as the creature focused all three of his eyes on the image within the visa. It was of a man considerably younger than the Doctor, with fair curly hair and a supercilious grin.

Dodo and Steven had also seen the image, and turned to look at the old man in amazement. Dodo opened her mouth to speak, but was momentarily dumbfounded. It was as if she had just woken from a dream. 'Steven, that's not the Doctor!'

The old man clucked with irritation. 'Well of course it's not . . . ' To his amazement, he then realized that his companion was pointing not at the image within the globe but at *him*. His confusion was compounded when Steven turned to address the customs officer.

'I don't understand what's happened,' muttered Steven, glaring accusingly at the old man, 'but whoever this is, it certainly is *not* the Doctor.'

Shaped like the interior of a toppled pyramid, the Bukolian interrogation room had walls composed of tiny, green-tinted mirrors which returned one's reflection in a most disconcerting way. Pacing impatiently about the room, the Doctor was tempted to think that the mirrored effect was probably deliberate. Even though he knew full well that any form of malice was quite beyond the Bukolian psyche, his current foul temper disinclined him to feel in any way charitable towards his captors.

He had just begun to tap on the mirrored panels with his walking stick when the door opened to admit a Bukolian official whom he had not previously met. The large creature elegantly took his place behind the table situated at the highest point of the room. The Doctor indignantly took a step towards him. 'How much longer am I expected to suffer this gross imposition, hmm?'

The Bukolian remained silent, his central eye regarding the Doctor whilst the outer two mulled over the documents which he extracted from a wallet and laid tidily on the desk before him. Enraged, the Doctor banged his cane on the desk, scattering the documents everywhere. 'Am I to be graced with an answer, sir?'

The Bukolian's outer eyes shot up from the desk and all three fixed on the Doctor. However, the official spoke calmly. 'Please be seated.' The Doctor glared at him as if he was about to explode. The Bukolian repeated his request. 'Standing at these interviews is obligatory only once the suspect has been charged. And, after all, this is only a preliminary investigation.'

The Doctor grunted, but sat down.

'Thank you,' the creature continued. 'My name is Yerma, and I am a senior investigator in the Bukolian police force. As you are now cognisant with my position, are you prepared to return the compliment by dispensing with this charade?'

The Doctor half rose from his chair in anger. 'Charade!'

'So, you still claim to be the Doctor . . . '

'I do not claim to be anyone other than who I happen to be!'

'Those whom you call your companions seem to think otherwise.'

The old man looked down, his eyes moistening slightly at the thought of Steven and Dodo.

'I'm sorry, I cannot explain that.' He looked up sharply. 'For the moment!'

'For the sake of due process, I am forced to humour you. I will address you as "Doctor" until such time as you feel able to concede the truth.'

'My dear sir, I am not in the habit of lying.'

'Pardon me, but that is for me to determine. And, quite frankly, I have seen no documentation to persuade me otherwise.'

'Passes, licences, certificates – official twaddlation!'

'Such as this passenger manifest from the star-liner *Illyria*? I've checked the details quite carefully and discovered that we have a missing person.'

The Doctor regarded his walking stick indifferently. 'Oh, and that is my problem, I suppose!'

'I believe it to be very much so. Aboard the liner was a travelling artiste, an impressionist called Mykloz. A master of deception and disguise.' Yerma looked pointedly at the old man.

If the Doctor had not risen to his feet he would have fallen from his chair, flabbergasted. 'Is that the kind of mountebank you take me for? An *entertainer*!' He studied his distorted reflection in the tinted mirrors. 'Charming. Absolutely charming!'

'How could he have done it, Steven?' Dodo leaned forward, staring intently at her hands, which she clasped and unclasped as if she could ring the truth out of the air. 'How was it possible?'

Steven returned her gaze, momentarily puzzled, then cast his eyes around the opulently decorated VIP suite in which they had been asked to wait. When he looked back at Dodo, he saw that she was still expecting an answer. 'I don't know, Dodo. Perhaps . . . '

Dodo leaned closer. 'Yes?'

Steven cast another glance at the Bukolian guard who sat nearby, apparently disinterested in their conversation but no doubt remembering every word to report back to his superiors. 'It must have been some mesmeric effect. We were both with the imposter for some time and neither of us suspected a thing.'

'But why, Steven? Why should anyone want to impersonate the Doctor?'

'Considering all the scrapes he gets into, it does make you

wonder!'

'This is no time to be funny, Steven. The Doctor is obviously a prisoner somewhere. Maybe even . . .'

Before Dodo could express the dreaded thought which had occurred to her, the pneumatic hiss of the door announced the arrival of the Bukolian called Yerma. Before moving to join Steven and Dodo, he spoke briefly to the Bukolian guard who promptly left to carry out his bidding. Having enquired whether the two friends were comfortable, Yerma proceeded to discuss the old man who still claimed to be their companion, the Doctor.

Steven shook his head in amazement. 'He looks nothing like the Doctor.'

Dodo chimed in. 'He must be twice the Doctor's age.'

'Yet still he insists that he is your friend.' Yerma looked at each of them carefully. 'You are absolutely certain that neither of you saw him on board the *Illyria*?'

Dodo and Steven exchanged glances. 'Yes, absolutely certain.'

Yerma pondered for a moment. Human facial expressions could often be deceptive, but the two young people seemed sincere. 'I don't yet know why the imposter needed to conceal his true identity, but his attempt to bluff his way through immigration was obviously an act of desperation.'

'It's a good thing he overlooked the visa.'

'Don't, Steven. Just to think that he'd convinced us he was the Doctor . . . It makes me feel ill.'

Yerma continued: 'We are arranging a search of the liner for your friend, but you must prepare yourselves for the worst. If this imposter is as desperate as his actions suggest . . .'

Dodo looked at Steven. 'No, Steven. Not the Doctor. He can't be . . .'

At that moment the door opened to admit the old man, accompanied by the Bukolian guard. The Doctor brightened as he saw his two friends. 'Ah, Steven, Dodo. Isn't it about time you put an end to this play-acting, hmm?'

Dodo leaped to her feet, flinging herself at the old man with an anguished cry. The Doctor reeled in shock as the young girl frenziedly pummelled her fists against his chest, screaming incoherently. The guard tried to pull her away, but she clung determinedly on to the lapels of the old man's frock coat.

'What have you done to the Doctor? Tell me! Tell me!'

With Yerma's help, the Bukolian guard finally managed to break the hysterical girl's grip. The old man collapsed into a chair as the guard carried Dodo, still kicking and screaming, away. Perplexed, he turned to look at Steven. 'Steven, my boy, you must know who I am!'

Yerma restrained Steven as he made a move towards the Doctor. The young man glanced angrily at Yerma, then back at the Doctor with a look of utter hatred. 'I don't know who you are, or how you managed to trick us, but I'll tell you this. If you've harmed the Doctor in any way – I'll kill you!'

The old man, for the first time in centuries, was totally lost for words.

To the passengers who had travelled to Bukol, the star-liner *Illyria* was a luxurious pleasure palace which wended its way through space. They were totally unaware of the maze of gloomily lit maintenance passages and service areas essential to the function of the vessel.

After much badgering, Yerma had agreed that Steven and Dodo could accompany him on the search for their missing friend. Their reaction towards the imposter had dispelled any doubts he might have had as to the truthfulness of their statements. However, he kept a careful eye on them as he led them through the murky infrastructure of the *Illyria*. Occasionally he spoke into his wrist communicator, directing his officers' efforts as section after section of the ship was meticulously searched. They paused briefly at an observation hatch overlooking the main cargo hold. Through the glass, they could see more Bukolian officers swiftly clambering over containers, opening panels, shifting bales by hand.

But of the Doctor there was still no sign.

Dodo clung close to Steven as the search continued, holding her breath each time a hatch was opened. So far, her anticipation had been met only with disappointment. She looked up at her friend, her face clearly showing the strain she was under. 'Steven, if he's not on the ship, that can only mean that he must have been thrown . . . overboard?'

'Don't worry, Dodo. We'll find him.'

Working their way down to the deepest part of the vessel, Yerma's party eventually came to a particularly grubby-looking hatchway. When it was opened, the stench forced Steven and Dodo to cover their nostrils.

'This must be where they dump the rubbish,' observed Steven.

Yerma pressed a switch and the stained lights slowly flickered into life. Rubbish was piled in huge mounds beneath traps through which it was obviously dumped into the hold. A small creature suddenly bolted across the floor, disappearing into a roughly bitten hole in the wall.

'Rats,' said Yerma, dourly. 'Planet Earth's contribution to the galaxy.'

As they were about to leave, Steven noticed that a particularly mountainous pile of rubbish was starting to shift and sway precariously. 'Look out!' he cried, pulling Dodo away.

With an agile leap, Yerma just avoided the avalanche of rubbish which crashed to the floor right where they had been standing. When the subsidence had settled, he pointed out that it had totally blocked the entrance way. 'I'll order my officers to start clearing it from the other side.'

As the Bukolian started issuing instructions into his wrist communicator, Dodo saw that part of the pile of rubbish was trembling slightly, as if something was moving underneath it. 'Steven!' she gasped, grabbing his arm.

'Probably more rats.'

Yerma joined them. 'I don't think so.' Cautiously, the Bukolian began brushing aside the rubbish with the barrel of his laser pistol. After a few moments, he turned and beckoned Steven to assist him. As they swept away the remaining items of refuse, they uncovered the form of a rather stout, curly-haired man wearing a multicoloured frock coat, a luminous green shirt, bright yellow trousers and a pair of purple shoes with orange spats. His hands and feet were bound together with some old electrical wiring. Yerma gently turned the man's head until it was fully in the light. 'Is this your friend, the Doctor?'

Steven and Dodo looked at each other and smiled with relief. 'Yes!'

Yerma unbound the Doctor and propped him up against the wall of the chamber. He then opened a small flask and sprinkled some of its contents on the Doctor's lips. The Doctor rolled his head from side to side, murmuring as the liquid began to take effect.

At length, the Doctor opened his eyes and tried to focus on the figures kneeling around him. He blinked, as if surprised by what he saw. '*Steven*? *Dodo*?'

Dodo leaned forward, almost in tears as she clasped the Doctor's hand. 'Yes, it's me, Dodo! I was terrified that we would never find you.'

The Doctor peered carefully at Dodo's face, then at Steven's. 'It is you. Both of you. Unharmed, I trust?'

'You acknowledge these two humans as your friends?' enquired Yerma.

'Of course I do!' The Doctor grimaced, rubbing the back of his head. 'Some rogue thwacked me over the back of the head. I didn't get a chance to see if it was . . . *who* it was.'

Yerma introduced himself, then explained: 'We already have a suspect in custody.'

'Do you now. That's Bukolian efficiency for you.'

'We pride ourselves in the expeditious prosecution of our duties,' Yerma solemnly replied.

The Doctor rubbed his head again. 'I'm just sorry you didn't apprehend the felon before he made a punch-bag of my cranium!'

When Yerma described how the suspect had tried to impersonate him, the Doctor was outraged. 'Impersonate me. Impersonate me!' He climbed unsteadily to his feet. 'The fellow must be unhinged if he believed that he could replicate *my* characteristic wit and charm.'

'Somehow he even managed to make us see him as you,' admitted Dodo.

'The perfidious hobgoblin! I demand to see this vile creature immediately. Such audacity cannot go unchallenged.'

Suddenly the Doctor clutched the side of his head and began to rock backwards and forwards on his feet. Dodo moved quickly to help him, lowering him back into a sitting position. 'Doctor, you need to take it easy.'

'Yes, you're right. My head's still spinning. There are some things here that I don't fully understand . . . '

Yerma crossed to the hatchway, where his officers had now managed to force a path through the rubbish. One of them marched up to him and reported in hushed tones. Gravely, Yerma turned to face the Doctor and his companions. 'I'm afraid I have to inform you that we will be unable to facilitate your confrontation with the imposter.' He paused, obviously embarrassed. 'He has somehow escaped from our detention centre. I can only promise that there will be a thorough investigation into the matter.'

The Doctor looked up weakly from where he was sitting. 'An investigation? An investigation! What good's that going to do? Somewhere out there is a fiend who has impersonated me once already, and now has the chance to do so again!'

Yerma's outer eyes looked to Dodo and Steven for support, while the central one turned away in shame.

As the Doctor had clearly not yet recovered from his ordeal, Yerma arranged for him to be admitted to the city hospital. Steven and Dodo were loath to have their group split up again so soon after being reunited, but the Bukolian was equally insistent that they leave their friend in the physicians' capable hands and accompany him on a tour of the city.

The best way to see the city, Yerma explained, was on foot, wandering through the bazaars where creatures from every corner of the cosmos bartered their wares. The place was a riot of colour and sound; it seemed as if every conceivable galactic tongue was being spoken at once. And the exquisite aromas! It was enough to make any being's stomach quake with gastronomic anticipation.

When they paused for a while to eat at one of Yerma's favourite side-street restaurants, the Bukolian was disappointed to see that Dodo and Steven were indulging rather less than enthusiastically in their meal of Wawalinan lobsters. They sat staring at the multitude of passers-by with an expression which Yerma took to be something akin to awe. As he finished his own lobster, he regarded the two humans thoughtfully.

'You find the populace of our city more fascinating than its culinary delights? The sauce is too rich, perhaps?'

Steven looked at his plate and realized that he had hardly touched it. 'Oh no,' he replied. 'Not at all.'

'We're just worried about the Doctor.'

'If our physicians could hear you,' Yerma chided, 'they would feel most insulted. Your friend is being cared for by some of the top specialists on this side of the galaxy.'

Steven was again watching the crowds which milled past their table. He was almost spellbound by the spectacle. 'It's amazing that so many different races can live so harmoniously together.'

'Bukol is a haven for the dispossessed of the galaxy,' said Yerma proudly. 'Our philosophy is quite simple:

> *'Give me your tired, your poor,*
> *Your huddled masses yearning to be free.'*

'That's beautiful,' murmured Dodo.

Yerma scratched his forehead with his left tentacle. 'It's a famous piece of poetry from Earth's history. Have you not heard it before?'

'Dodo was never any good at history,' Steven hurriedly explained. 'Anyway, if you're so keen for Bukol to be a haven, why do you make it so difficult for people to come here?'

'Our immigration rules? There must be due process, or where would we be? You must appreciate how important order and protocol are to the Bukolian mind.'

'Granted,' Steven sullenly replied, 'but you're not the ones who have to fill out the forms!'

A six-limbed, yellow-skinned Udimi waiter approached the table and addressed Yerma: 'We would be honoured if our most valued customer would personally select the fruits for dessert.'

Yerma excused himself and followed the waiter into the kitchens, leaving Dodo and Steven alone for the first time that day. Dodo pushed her dish away from her.

'I think we should leave while we can.'

Steven looked undecided. 'There is danger. At least we are protected if we stay with Yerma.'

'Amongst the crowd we will be safer. The Doctor will find us when he has recovered his strength.'

Steven suddenly grasped Dodo by the arm. She followed his gaze to the opposite side of the road. Watching them was a tall humanoid with sharp, angular features and intense eyes. The stranger smiled a malicious smile as he realized that they had recognized him. His expression was like that of a hunter who, after many days' tracking, has finally caught wind of his prey.

Dodo turned to Steven in alarm. 'We must leave. We cannot stay here. Not now!'

'No!' replied Steven. 'Yerma will be back in a moment . . .' His voice trailed away as he saw that the stranger had started to push his way through the crowd, heading towards them.

The table fell over with a crash as Dodo jumped abruptly to her feet. 'Come on!'

Steven hesitated for a moment, then set off after the girl.

The two companions pushed their way through the crowd in

a desperate attempt to lose their pursuer. The jostling multitudes made their progress painfully slow, but at the same time afforded them some valuable cover. Steven glanced back, only to see that the stranger was still coming after them with deliberate, measured steps. However quickly they pushed on through the crowd, the stranger, with his leisurely, almost ponderous gait, seemed to get steadily closer and closer.

Suddenly Steven and Dodo stopped dead, looking at each other in utter terror. They had reached a clearing in the crowd and were totally exposed.

The hunter's smile vanished, to be replaced with a frown of concentration. His quarry seemed frozen to the spot as he slowly pulled a small, multicoloured sphere from inside his jacket. He raised the weapon to take aim, and a smile returned to his face. This time, it was a smile of exhilaration.

Just as he was about to fire, the air reverberated with a cacophony of discordant sound and a band of local musicians marched down the street, a procession of happy revellers trailing behind them. The stranger snarled with disgust: his line of fire had been completely blocked! By the time the procession had passed, the two targets were nowhere to be seen . . .

Saved by the unexpected diversion, Steven and Dodo had lost themselves amongst the throng of spectators on the far side of the street. They ran on for several minutes before eventually pausing for breath in a narrow alleyway.

Steven leaned against the wall, panting heavily. 'How could he have found us so soon?'

Dodo was recovering more quickly than her companion. 'He's determined to kill us, whatever it takes. We must find the Doctor. Only he can help us.'

'Of that I am quite sure,' came a voice from a darkened alcove. 'And I might add that I deserve a full explanation for your extraordinary behaviour, hmm?'

Dodo and Steven spun round to discover the source of the voice, breathing a sigh of relief when they saw that it was the old man whom they had earlier denounced.

'It's only you,' sighed Dodo.

'So, you do recognize me then, young lady.'

Steven took a step towards him. 'Can't you just leave us alone, old man? Just go away!'

As Steven and Dodo turned to walk past, the Doctor whipped out his cane to block their path.

'Tut tut. Not so fast. You don't think you're going to get away with it as easily as that, do you? Now, I demand an explanation!'

Dodo moved towards the old man. 'I'm sorry if we hurt you, but we had no choice.'

'What do you mean, my dear Dodo? What has happened to you both?' The Doctor glanced over his shoulder to make sure that no one could overhear them. 'We're alone now. Just the three of us. You can tell me what this is all about. You know you can trust me. Whatever trouble you've got yourselves into, I can help you.'

There was genuine sorrow in Dodo's eyes. 'I wish you could.'

Steven was beginning to look anxious. 'We must go. *Now*. Before he finds us again.'

Dodo smiled at the old man. 'Please let us go. It's for the best. Believe me.'

All three froze as they heard Yerma calling for Dodo and Steven. The voice was coming closer.

'Doctor, you must go before Yerma gets here!' cried Dodo.

The Doctor perked up at the girl's acknowledgment of his name. 'No. You're coming with me, d'you hear? Both of you!'

Dodo stared at the ground, lost in thought. The Doctor brightened. He was sure that he had managed to reach his companion and overcome whatever influence she was under. She looked up at him, hesitating for a moment, as if on the point of explaining everything. Instead she screamed: 'Yerma! Come quickly! It's the imposter!'

The old man shook his head in bewilderment as the young girl glared sternly at him. 'Go!' she hissed.

The Doctor could hear Yerma's footsteps approaching closer and closer. He was torn by indecision. On the one hand he wanted to stay with his companions and face whatever had to be faced, but on the other he knew that he could get to the bottom of this distressing affair only if he remained at liberty.

He turned and ran as fast as his ancient legs would take him.

Moments later, Yerma appeared in the alleyway. Dodo was crying. 'It was the imposter again. He was still insisting that he was the Doctor.' She buried her face in Steven's chest. 'It was horrible. So horrible.'

'We tried to stop him,' explained Steven, 'but he threatened us with his cane.'

After being told the direction in which the old man had fled, Yerma instructed the two companions to remain where they were whilst he went in pursuit. Once he had gone, Dodo immediately dried her crocodile tears.

'We must get back to the hospital and find the Doctor.'

Steven muttered his agreement. Before they could move, however, they heard a quiet, malicious laugh emanating from the shadows. Standing only metres away was the stranger who had chased them from the bazaar.

Dodo screamed.

The old man tripped over a loose paving stone and fell amongst a collection of rubbish bins piled outside the entrance to one of the city's older tenement blocks. Exhausted and dejected, he decided to stay where he was for the time being. He had lost Yerma almost ten minutes earlier but only now felt it safe to rest.

It started to rain. Before long, the ancient guttering had begun to overflow and water was cascading down the side of the building, soaking the Doctor. The tenement was a little way off the main thoroughfare, but the Doctor could still see police patrolmen out on the street, guiding the traffic as the multitudes hurried for shelter, and he did not dare to move.

He was beginning to regain his breath now, but his thoughts were still muddled as he tried to grasp the realities behind the events which had occurred since his arrival on Bukol. He closed his eyes, hoping to improve his concentration.

It was then that he heard the voices. They were almost spectral in nature. He opened his eyes again and saw that several creatures were standing around him. He felt not so much alarmed as mystified, as the rain seemed to pass right through the figures as if they were not there. The creatures turned to each other and babbled incomprehensibly, obviously discussing him.

The Doctor had never cared for zoos and was determined that no one – whoever or whatever these apparitions might be – was going to treat him like some blessed exhibit! He propped himself against one of the bins and painfully levered himself to his feet. He was just about to give the crowd a piece of his mind when he realized that they were no longer there. The rain continued to pound the pavement where they had stood.

The Doctor rubbed his cheek thoughtfully. He was not in the habit of seeing things, but then perhaps all the recent inexplicable events had started to unhinge his mind . . .

He was distracted from his reverie by the arrival of a shabby transporter vehicle, which pulled up outside the building. A figure emerged, sheltering under a parasol as transparent as the phantoms that the Doctor had just seen. The figure locked his vehicle and strode towards the building. As he approached, the Doctor could see that he was wearing a strange piece of head gear, with visors positioned at angles around it. The old man suddenly realized that these were actually vid-monitors which allowed the wearer to watch television as he went about his day-to-day business.

The figure stopped as he reached the Doctor, opening the visors so as to get a clearer view of him. For the first time since his arrival on Bukol, the Doctor smiled. 'Anu-Ak!'

The humanoid with the balding head and the goatee beard smiled back. 'Doctor! Of all the people I least expected to see.' He gestured towards the front door of the building. 'Come on up. You must be drenched.'

Anu-Ak opened the door and the Doctor entered, grateful that he had at last met someone who knew him for who he truly was . . .

After drying himself in the turbo shower, the Doctor relaxed in an easy chair and surveyed his friend's apartment. Fixed to the balcony was a collection of satellite dishes from which ran a veritable cat's cradle of connector cables to the different-sized monitor units and video-disk recorders positioned around the room. The glow from the screens provided the only illumination, bathing the place in a dazzling kaleidoscope of colours as the images flickered and changed. Several of the monitors simply snowed with static, waiting for the moment when a signal from across the galaxy would hit one of the dishes outside and charge them into life.

The Doctor chuckled to himself. Even after all these years, his friend had not forsaken his obsessive hobby of accumulating television programmes, no matter what their content might be.

Anu-Ak entered the room, carrying a tray of refreshments. As they sat and drank, the Doctor recounted everything that had happened to him since his arrival at the space port. Even though Anu-Ak was listening intently, his gaze seldom left the fluctuating images on his television screens.

Suddenly the Doctor realized that Anu-Ak had been distracted from what he was saying and become engrossed in an item on the local rolling-news channel. The newsreader was telling viewers about a dangerous malefactor at large within the community. On the screen then appeared a multi-dimensional portrait of the Doctor, beneath which a police telephone number flashed on and off.

Anu-Ak picked up one of his many remote controls and extinguished the image. 'You'd better stay here for a few days, Doctor. You'd be recognized out on the streets.'

The Doctor nodded. 'You know, that must be the very first time I have ever appeared on television.' He sighed at the irony of it. 'Well, fancy that!'

Struck by a sudden inspiration, Anu-Ak dived on to the floor and began scrambling about through a hoard of video-disks and cassettes which had been piled up in the corner of the room. The Doctor looked on bemused. His friend was like a child rummaging through a toy box in a desperate search for a lost plaything.

'Dear me, what is the matter, Anu-Ak?'

'It's here somewhere, Doctor. It's here somewhere!'

The Doctor glanced around at the disks and tapes scattered across the room. Anu-Ak was never the tidiest of creatures, but now he was outdoing even Dodo with the clutter he was making! The old man sniffed with sadness as he remembered his companions, hoping that it would not be too long before Dodo was again making a mess of his wardrobe. He quickly blew his nose lest his friend see how upset he was.

With an exultant yelp, Anu-Ak turned to face the Doctor. 'I've found it!'

'Found *what* exactly, my friend?'

'*This*,' exclaimed Anu-Ak, holding up a video-disk and pushing it into a nearby player. 'You were wrong about that news report being your first television appearance. *This* was your first appearance!'

The monitor screen flickered into life. The image was flecked with static which occasionally obscured the image, but the Doctor could clearly be seen, standing in what appeared to be a space control centre.

'It's a transmission from late twentieth-century Earth,' explained Anu-Ak.

An American news anchor-man was talking about a mysterious twin planet which had suddenly appeared in the solar system, and about the creatures from that world who had tried to destroy the Earth. He also mentioned the crucial part played in the creatures' defeat by a man called the Doctor, who had unaccountably arrived at the Snowcap space tracking station and subsequently vanished without trace. A close-up of the Doctor then flashed on to the screen. Anu-Ak apologized for the poor quality of the recording. 'The signal had been travelling through space for centuries when I picked it up.'

'No matter, Anu-Ak, no matter. We'll see what that pompous bureaucrat Yerma has to say about this. Let him accuse me of being an imposter now, hmm?'

'But that transmission is thousands of years old. How are you going to explain it?'

The Doctor waved his hand dismissively. 'Oh, a trivial matter. Just a simple measure of time, which is of no consequence.'

Anu-Ak bowed to the Doctor's judgement. 'Time is your dimension, Doctor.'

As they left the apartment, the Doctor tapped the video-disk thoughtfully. Anu-Ak had afforded him a brief glimpse into his own future. Chuckling to himself, he vowed to remember what he had seen, so that he could surprise his companions with his fore-knowledge when that adventure actually happened . . .

Dodo sat huddled in a corner, whilst Steven paced about like a caged animal. Their cell was cold and dank, illuminated by a solitary wall-light which often flickered on and off, leaving them in complete darkness for minutes at a time.

Steven's futile circuits of the room were beginning to irritate Dodo. 'Unless you're going to do something, give it a rest!'

Steven slouched down next to her. 'How much longer are we going to be cooped up in this place?'

'How should I know? What I *do* know is that you're making the wait even more unbearable!'

Steven ignored this remark and began to let his gaze wander about the room with the same monotony as when his feet were doing the walking.

Dodo shook her head in exasperation.

The Doctor who had been rescued from the rubbish hold of the *Illyria* now lay on an advanced therapeutic bed in a private room of the city hospital. In place of his garish everyday clothes, which had been cleaned and hung up in an alcove at the far end of the room, he wore just a simple nightgown. He was sleeping fitfully, tossing and turning as if haunted by a nightmare.

'No! You must not harm them,' he muttered.

Suddenly he woke with a start, sitting bolt upright with his hands outstretched before him as if to grapple with some unseen assailant. Realizing that he had been dreaming again, he rubbed his brow and exhaled slowly. 'I really must see a psychoanalyst one of these centuries.'

It was then that he became aware that he was not alone in the room. There was a figure standing in the shadows. Before he could call out a challenge, the intruder stepped into the light. The Doctor sighed with relief. It was a Bukolian medical orderly.

The orderly crossed to the bed and felt the Doctor's pulse. 'You've been dreaming again?'

'Yes, a recurring dream. The grand-daddy of them all!'

'Would you like to talk about it?' enquired the orderly sympathetically.

'No, thank you. Not at the moment.'

'Very well.' The Bukolian lifted the Doctor's arm, rolling up the sleeve of his nightshirt. After applying some ointment, he pressed an injection pad against the skin. 'This will help you to sleep more peacefully.'

The orderly retreated a few paces and stood looking silently down at the bed. As the Doctor stared back, the Bukolian appeared to shimmer slightly. The Doctor squinted in case it was a trick of the light, then watched in astonishment as the figure transformed into what appeared to be a column of translucent crystals which rippled from red to green to blue. Suddenly, like sand escaping through an hourglass, the crystals began to cascade to the floor. Almost immediately, the effect reversed itself: the crystals propelled themselves up into the air and re-formed into the shape of a man. Where once had been the figure of a Bukolian orderly, there now stood the tall stranger who had so terrorized

Dodo and Steven at the bazaar.

The Doctor gripped the sides of his bed. 'Mykloz!'

'Yes, Doctor.'

Mykloz approached the bed, smiling maliciously. The Doctor shrank back, feeling at a distinct disadvantage. He tensed himself, shuffling as best he could into an upright position.

'I can't say that I care for your bedside manner.'

'You must forgive me.' Mykloz gestured airily about the room. 'We Maleans seldom have recourse to facilities such as these.'

'That's only because you destroy any of your kind who might have need of them.'

'The gene pool of Maleas must remain unsullied by imperfection. The impure we must destroy, the weak we cannot suffer to live. It is our creed, Doctor.'

'And one you take great delight in enforcing.'

'We must all do what we are best fitted to do,' Mykloz sardonically replied.

'I assume it was you who battered me about the head and threw me down a rubbish chute?'

'Don't sound so offended. The blow was meant to kill you, actually.'

'Don't tell me we're slipping, Mykloz?'

Mykloz smiled again, humouring the Doctor. 'A minor reversal, that's all.'

The Doctor continued the verbal fencing. 'Whilst I was on the liner, I caught sight of a poster. "Presenting the Great Mykloz, illusionist and impressionist extraordinaire!" Don't tell me you've been using your shape-shifting abilities for a little moonlighting?'

'It was a suitable cover whilst I awaited the arrival of your TARDIS. I'm glad you saw the poster. It pleases me when my victims know that I am close by.'

Mykloz laughed as he saw the fearful expression on the Doctor's face. 'Don't worry, Doctor, your mutant friends are not dead – yet. Twice I almost had them, but they just managed to elude me. Actually, they have proved themselves quite resourceful. But then they are Maleans, however tainted their genetic composition may be.'

Mykloz began to pace about the room as he spoke. 'When they realized that you were missing, they used their shape-shifting abilities to substitute themselves for a young couple in the company of some old man. No doubt they hoped that he would protect them as you had done, but I was easily able to thwart their plans. Using a little sleight of hand, I replaced the old man's visa with your own. Of course, they then had to denounce him to avoid coming under suspicion themselves. He's a wanted criminal now.'

'Very clever, but then you're used to being under-handed.'

Mykloz laughed once more. 'Insult me all you like, Doctor, but it will do you no good. Your mutant friends will not escape me again, and the Bukolians will find a suitable culprit for their murders in that doddery old man. This time, you will not be there to interfere.'

'And what is that supposed to mean?'

'You are looking a little unwell, Doctor. How are you feeling?'

'Feeling?' Now that he thought about it, the Doctor realized that his head was muzzy and he was starting to suffer palpitations. He flung himself across the bed covers towards Mykloz. 'What have you done?'

The Malean gestured towards the Doctor's arm. 'I've administered an hymerulion compound. I will have no more problems culling those mutants. Not now that their protector, that famous bleeding heart the Doctor, is dead!'

Mykloz shape-shifted back into the form of a Bukolian medical orderly and left the room. Breathing heavily and doubled up with stomach cramps, the Doctor began to experience convulsions. Despite the pain, he tried to prop himself back onto his knees. Everything seemed to be spinning wildly around him, so he clutched hold of the bed, clinging on for dear life. Suddenly the room seemed to heave violently to one side. The Doctor lost his balance and toppled to the floor, dragging the sheets after him . . .

Steven was banging furiously on the bulkhead door. 'Hello! Hello! Is anybody there?'

Dodo regarded him angrily. 'You're giving me a headache, Steven. I don't know why you're bothering. I bet no one ever comes down to this part of the liner.'

Steven kicked the door in frustration. 'Wait until I get my hands on those two!'

'It was your idea to follow them down here.'

'What!'

'Oh come on, Steven. She had only to flutter her eyelids and you came running!'

'Look,' replied Steven defensively, 'I believed them when they said that someone was in trouble down here.'

'Too right someone's in trouble. It's *us*!'

Steven looked for a new target on which to vent his frustration. He saw a sorry-looking packing case with 'Fragile' stamped on the side and began kicking it in. When he had demolished it, he was disapointed to see that it was actually empty.

'Does that make you feel any better?' admonished Dodo.

To Dodo's dismay, Steven ignored her and resumed his pounding on the hatchway.

'I wonder who they were?' Dodo shouted above the din.

Steven paused in his assault on the door. 'Does it really matter?'

'Steven, they didn't get us down here for nothing. They must have had a reason.'

'Perhaps it was a practical joke,' Steven suggested.

'I'm laughing. Hah ha!' Dodo decided to try another approach. 'Honestly, Steven, if you were half the man you pretended to be, you would have found a way out of here by now.'

'I'd like to see you do better,' retorted Steven.

Dodo sighed. It was no use trying to reason with Steven when he was being this stubborn. She started clambering over a pile of crates towards the other end of the room, trying to get as far away from him as possible.

Steven stood watching her. 'Sulking is really going to help us.'

Suddenly Dodo gave a cry as she toppled from view. Steven immediately leaped up and clambered over the crates to see what had happened. When he reached the top, he burst out laughing at the sight which greeted him. The crate on which Dodo had been standing had collapsed beneath her and she was now lying spreadeagled amongst the wreckage.

'It's not funny, Steven.'

'No, no, of course it isn't.' Steven tried to stifle his laughter, but without success.

Grumpily, Dodo tried to gyrate her body into a more comfortable position. As she did so, she noticed that the collapse of the crate had revealed part of the bulkhead which had previously been inaccessible. She moved closer and started to pull away the remaining planks, uncovering the dark metal of a hatchway.

'Steven! Come quickly!'

Steven clambered over to join her and used his destructive talents to shift the last remnants of the crate. The locking clamps on the hatch had obviously not been used for some considerable time, and it took all of the ex-astronaut's strength to make them budge. Eventually, though, he was able to swing the door open. It was much smaller than the main entrance to the storeroom, but just large enough for him to crawl through.

'You wait here,' he commanded, but Dodo was in no mood to be ordered around and slipped through after him. They found themselves in a narrow tunnel which opened out on to a small platform positioned high above the liner's main cargo hold. There was no obvious way down to the ground.

'This is just a maintenance platform,' concluded Steven. 'To enable engineers to work on those gears up there.' He gestured above their heads to a rusting piece of apparatus which appeared to be part of a conveyor system designed to ferry items of cargo across the hold.

Dodo sat down and put her head in her hands. 'So we're no better off, then?'

Steven was just about to agree with her when he was struck by a sudden flash of inspiration. 'Wait a minute! See that carrying hook up there?' He pointed to a huge metal hook suspended from a cable on the underside of the conveyor unit. 'If I could just climb up there and stand on that, my weight should be enough to set it moving and take it down the line to the loading platform on the other side of the hold.'

Dodo wasn't keen on the idea. 'Steven, if you should lose your grip . . . ' The thought of her friend falling the hundred feet or so to the bottom of the hold was too horrifying to contemplate.

Steven, however, was insistent. Assuring Dodo that nothing could go wrong, he set off up the wall, making use of some crude rungs which he guessed had been placed there for the engineers' convenience. On reaching the same level as the conveyor, he leaned across and placed his foot securely in the hook, then swung his whole body over and took hold of the cable above it. As he had predicted, the conveyor immediately ground into motion, sending the hook swinging out across the hold and down the shallow gradient towards the loading bay on the far side.

Steven's progress across the chasm was painfully slow, and the hold reverberated with the sound of the conveyor's ancient wheels as they toiled along their track. Several times, Dodo caught her breath as it looked as if her friend was about to lose his grip and plummet to his death.

The hook had travelled only about thirty metres when suddenly there was an alarming screech of gears and the conveyor ground to a juddering halt. Dodo's knuckles turned white as she grasped the hand rail around the maintenance platform. She watched as Steven swung from side to side on the hook, attempting to restore some momentum to it. 'Be careful, Steven!'

Steven's efforts proved completely ineffective, and he looked across at Dodo. 'I'm going to climb down and hang from the hook. That way I should be able to get more leverage into my swing.'

Dodo was horrified. 'Don't, Steven! It's far too dangerous!'

Ignoring her, Steven cautiously contorted his body and slid his hands down the cable until he could take a firm grip on the hook. He then slipped his foot out and let his body drop sharply. Dodo breathed a sigh of relief as she saw that he had managed to hang on. Steven called across to her. 'Well, here goes!'

He began to swing his legs back and forth like a precarious human pendulum, but still the conveyor remained motionless.

Eventually Dodo could stand no more. 'Hold on, Steven. I'm going to climb up and try to get across to you.'

'No!' A trace of panic was starting to enter Steven's voice now. 'You'll never make it!

Taking no notice, Dodo started up the wall.

With a flick of a switch, Yerma deactivated the screen at the far end of his office and ejected the video-disk from the player built into his desk. His central eye examined the disk and its label thoughtfully whilst the outer two scrutinized Anu-Ak, seated on the opposite side of the desk with the old man who claimed to be the Doctor.

'I trust you had a licence to record this video material?' enquired the Bukolian sternly.

Anu-Ak squirmed uncomfortably in his seat. 'Er, well . . . Not exactly.'

'It is of course an offence to record any visual signal without first obtaining the apposite licence,' warned Yerma.

The Doctor shifted his position irritably. 'I rather think we should be paying more attention to the actual contents of the recording than to the authority under which it was acquired!'

All three of Yerma's eyes turned to focus on the Doctor. 'If this material was acquired illegally, it is inadmissible in evidence.'

The Doctor decided to take a more conciliatory approach.

'Yes, my good sir, I accept you have a valid point. Nevertheless, you must surely have drawn some conclusions from what we have shown you, hmm?'

Yerma paused for a moment. 'The recording seems quite genuine, and I accept that your appearance is identical to that of the man identified as the Doctor. These points I do not dispute. What does cause me some concern is the obvious age of the transmission.'

Anu-Ak swirled round on his chair. 'Told you so, Doctor.'

The Doctor cast his friend a withering look before addressing Yerma's point. 'My dear Yerma, old age comes to us all. It is simply that mine has lasted rather longer than most!'

Yerma paused as he considered what the old man had said. 'I think you are humouring me, *Doctor*!'

The Doctor beamed at Yerma's acknowledgement of his true identity. He was just about to reply when suddenly a loud commotion erupted outside. He cocked an ear as he heard some familiar voices – including one with the appalling accent.

'Nobody pushes me about like that, mister!'

The door flew open and Yerma's deputy entered the office.

'What is the meaning of this intrusion?' demanded Yerma, shocked that the proper procedures had not been followed.

The deputy beckoned to the two guards waiting outside and they escorted a disgruntled Steven and Dodo into the office.

'These two were discovered performing acrobatics in the cargo hold of the space-liner, senior investigator,' explained the deputy.

'Steven! Dodo!' Yerma was delighted to see the two youngsters again, after their disappearance at the bazaar.

'I don't know who you are, but I don't much care for your mates,' whinged Dodo, gesturing to the guards. Steven caught sight of the Doctor seated on the other side of the room. 'Hey, look, Dodo. It's the Doctor!'

Confused, Yerma scratched his forehead with his tentacle. 'I don't understand. What were you doing back on board the liner?'

The Doctor rose from his seat and put a welcoming arm around each of his companions. 'I have a feeling that they never really left the liner, Yerma – until now.'

'Are you implying that there are *three* impostors on the loose?' Yerma asked incredulously.

'It's the only theory that holds water,' replied the Doctor. 'Let me introduce Mr Steven Taylor and Miss Dodo Chaplet, two very good friends of mine!'

'It seems that you really are the Doctor, after all,' admitted Yerma. 'But then, who is that man in our hospital?'

The Doctor moved to join the investigator, a twinkle in his eye. 'My dear Yerma, that is something I am longing to find out!'

Yerma turned to his deputy. 'Arrange transportation – immediately!'

Yerma's hover car took ten minutes to negotiate the often-congested streets on the way to the hospital. The Doctor, Steven and Dodo sat gazing out of the window, fascinated by the sights of the city. Anu-Ak, however, had declined to accompany them on the journey, admitting to the Doctor that he feared more awkward questions from Yerma about his video collection.

On arriving at the hospital they hurried to the private ward, accompanied by a Bukolian physician who demanded to know what all the fuss was about. The physician called them to a halt outside the room, protesting that his patient must not be disturbed. Yerma overruled him and abruptly pushed open the door.

The room was in complete disarray. The sheets were torn and the bedside cabinet lying on its side with its contents strewn across the floor. Of the man claiming to be the Doctor, there was no sign.

Yerma crossed to the alcove where the man's clothes had been put. They were no longer there . . .

Yerma had arranged for the old man and his two companions to stay at one of Bukol's smartest hotels. Dodo and Steven now stood on the balcony, enjoying the spectacular views of the city, whilst the Doctor and Yerma sat inside discussing the recent events.

It had stopped raining several hours ago and there was now a warm breeze blowing down from the mountains, ruffling Dodo's hair. She inhaled the evening air deeply, as if by doing so she could also absorb the rich ambience of the city.

'This is brilliant!' she exclaimed. 'Beats the lid off dreary old London.'

'It is impressive,' Steven agreed. 'Actually, it reminds me quite a bit of London – but long after your time, of course.'

'Is that supposed to make me feel old?'

Steven grinned mischievously. 'Well, you *were* born several hundred years before I was!'

Dodo noticed some coloured lights flashing and moving against the darkness of the evening sky, and pointed them out to Steven. Yerma and the Doctor chose that moment to join them on the balcony.

'That's the Carnival of Universal Harmony,' explained Yerma.

'A carnival!' shrieked Dodo. 'Can we go? Oh, you'll come, won't you, Steven?'

'Of course. Yerma? Doctor?'

'Such frivolities do not suit my temperament,' admitted Yerma, 'but I will arrange for some of my officers to escort you. I would not want to risk losing you again!'

'I think I'll stay and spend the evening with our host,' the Doctor told his companions. 'We've just discovered that we share a passion for Aquilian architecture – fifth dynasty, of course. But you two run along and enjoy yourselves!'

The Carnival of Universal Harmony was like every fair that Dodo had ever visited, all rolled into one – and much more besides! The ferris wheel surpassed her wildest imaginings. Not only was it far bigger than any she had seen before, but even more amazing was the fact that, instead of being carried round on swinging chairs, the passengers floated weightless inside transparent booths. The other rides were equally astounding, taking Dodo and Steven through holographic recreations of planets on the far reaches of the cosmos and giving them virtual-reality glimpses of historic events in which they were able actually to participate.

Later, with their Bukolian escorts trailing at a discreet distance behind them, the two friends wandered amongst the many stalls where all manner of wonderful and baffling things were on offer. Displayed in one of the larger booths they discovered some delicate shells through which could be heard not only the sea but also the sounds of rain forests, tropical lagoons and various other environments. They had just decided to indulge in the culinary delicacies available from a Pranganese food stall when one of the Bukolian officers caught up with them and addressed them urgently.

'I am sorry to spoil your enjoyment, but I have just received instructions to take you back to police headquarters. I'm afraid it is a matter of some importance.'

Concerned that something serious must have happened, Steven and Dodo immediately agreed to accompany the officer. As they departed, a nearby figure quickly finished what he was eating and set off after them.

The Bukolian led Steven and Dodo to a quiet area on the perimeter of the fair, where a multitude of futuristic caravans were parked. Steven looked around, but could see no sign of a police hover car.

'What have you brought us here for?' he demanded.

Before the officer could reply, the figure who had followed them from the food stall stepped out from behind one of the caravans. With his tasteless, multicoloured outfit he could almost have been one of the carnival folk, but he had an air of authority about him which belied his unconventional appearance.

'You know,' he stated, 'this is the first time I've ever witnessed a Bukolian police officer failing to follow the correct procedure when dealing with members of the public.'

Steven and Dodo looked on in amazement as the police officer began to shimmer and change. Moments later, a tall humanoid with sharp, angular features stood before them.

Mykloz regarded the Doctor icily. 'You are supposed to be dead.'

The Doctor started to approach the Malean. 'Fortunately, you overlooked my exceptional constitution, Mykloz.'

Mykloz quickly produced his spherical blaster from inside his jacket. 'Come no closer!'

'What's going on?' demanded Steven.

'Silence!' commanded Mykloz, waving the blaster in their direction. 'You can dispense with your deception now.'

Mykloz stepped backwards, so that he had a clear view of the Doctor as well as of Steven and Dodo. 'In one way I am glad that you are still alive, Time Lord. It means that you can witness the demise of these mutants you have so struggled to protect!'

The Malean aimed his blaster at Steven and Dodo.

'No, Mykloz!' The Doctor's face was filled with horror. 'These are not the mutants!'

'Do you think that I am so easily distracted, Time Lord?'

Dodo clung to Steven in fear and bewilderment.

'Listen to me, Mykloz,' insisted the Doctor, edging closer to the hunter. 'You're making a calamitous mistake. These are not the Malean mutants. They are the *real* Steven and Dodo!'

Mykloz hesitated for a moment, regarding Steven and Dodo coldly, but then raised his weapon again. 'No, you lie!' As he took aim, he proclaimed: 'By the Order of all that is Pure and without Imperfection, I hereby fulfil my duty with the taking of your lives!'

The Doctor suddenly lunged forward, felling the Malean with an expert rugby tackle. As Mykloz hit the ground, his finger squeezed the trigger of the blaster and a nearby caravan exploded in flames. Debris rained down as the Doctor and Mykloz struggled on the ground. Steven and Dodo looked on as their rescuer fought desperately to wrest the blaster from the other man's grasp. It soon became clear that Mykloz was the stronger of the two, as he brought the blaster closer and closer to his adversary's head.

Dodo suddenly spurred herself into action. Picking up a piece of the debris from the caravan, she ran forward and brought it down with telling force upon Mykloz's arm. The Malean yelled in pain, letting the blaster tumble from his fingers. The Doctor quickly rolled over and sprang to his feet, scooping up the weapon from where it had fallen. Steven now moved forward to tackle the Malean, but Mykloz saw him coming and tripped him up, sending him careering into the Doctor. As they fell to the ground, Mykloz fled into the night.

The Doctor disentangled himself from Steven and helped him to his feet.

'Look, I don't mean to be rude, but who are you?' asked Dodo.

'You could say I'm someone already known to you,' the Doctor replied, brushing himself down. 'Sorry, must dash. Got a Malean to catch.'

As he, like Mykloz, disappeared into the night, Dodo turned to Steven. 'That was the man that Yerma described. He was the one pretending to be the Doctor!'

Mykloz took cover behind the power plant of the ferris wheel, considering his options. He came to a decision. His body shimmered and glowed as he transformed himself into the image of the Doctor with whom he had just been struggling. Emerging from hiding, he strolled towards the group of Bukolian police officers who had been escorting Steven and Dodo and were now anxiously searching for them. He was confident that, as the Doctor, he would be welcomed with open arms.

The Doctor watched from a distance, chuckling to himself as the protesting Malean was dragged away into custody. His mirth was short-lived, however, as he suddenly realized that he had best make himself scarce if he wanted to avoid the same fate!

* * *

Yerma reflected that Mykloz was one of the most arrogant and despicable subjects it had ever been his misfortune to interrogate. The Malean was making no attempt to conceal his prejudices and freely admitted that he had travelled to Bukol with the sole intention of murdering two fleeing mutants from his own planet. The Bukolian tried to maintain his professional detachment as he completed his questioning, despite the revulsion that was welling up inside him.

When Yerma finally left Mykloz in the charge of his deputy, he found that he had a foul taste in his mouth. He made his way to the space port's VIP suite, where the old traveller and his two friends were relaxing after their ordeals. Joining them at their table, he told them of Mykloz's unrepentant attitude and of his contempt for Bukol's multiethnic culture.

'I can only hope,' he concluded, 'that those two wretched creatures he was hunting will make good their escape.' Seeing the Doctor's astonished expression, Yerma rolled his eyes madly in the Bukolian equivalent of a smile. 'I think this is one occasion when the immigration laws have been justly flouted!'

They all laughed.

'What does Mykloz look like at the moment?' enquired Dodo.

Yerma scratched his head with one of his tentacles, clearly bemused.

'Remember,' added Steven, 'we saw him completely transform his appearance.'

Yerma was appalled. 'Nobody mentioned that to me!'

'Come, sir,' interjected the Doctor. 'Surely you are aware of the Maleans' abilities?'

'I knew he was an impressionist, of course, but I had no idea he was a shape-shifter.'

The Bukolian became highly agitated and hurried from the room, heading back towards the detention centre. The Doctor, Steven and Dodo followed close behind.

When they arrived, they found Yerma's deputy lying dead on the floor in a pool of purple blood. Distraught, Yerma spoke into his wrist communicator.

'Reception? This whole area is to be sealed off immediately. No one is to be allowed in or out without my permission.'

'Certainly sir . . . ' came the reply. 'But your deputy has just left the building.'

It was early morning and the carnival was deserted. The crowds had long since departed and the weary creatures who ran the rides and stalls had retired to the comfort of their caravans.

The Doctor watched as the sun rose behind the ferris wheel, its bright rays slowly inching their way across the fairground. In the morning light, he noticed that his multicoloured coat needed a good clean after his scuffle with Mykloz. Such trivial thoughts were pushed from his mind, however, as two clowns approached him across the field and started to perform a routine. He laughed as one of them tripped the other up with her oversized boots, sending him tumbling acrobatically to the ground. Eventually their impromptu performance came to an end, and the Doctor cheered and clapped while they took a bow. He then watched with equal admiration as they shimmered and transmuted themselves into the natural forms of the two young Maleans he had brought to Bukol on the liner.

They were a beautiful couple, reflected the Doctor. Only the Maleans could be fanatical enough to want to hunt them down and destroy them simply because they had started to feel empathy for other beings, and affection for each other.

Alëza, the female, approached the Doctor, her head bowed.

'Doctor, we have done . . . questionable things since we last saw you. When you disappeared aboard the *Illyria*, we knew that Mykloz must have taken you prisoner, or even killed you.'

'Yes,' agreed the male, Orsa. 'And as we were all stowaways, we could hardly go to the authorities for help.'

'But then, by chance, we discovered that one of your earlier incarnations was also aboard the liner, and . . . '

'And?' prompted the Doctor, gently.

'And we locked his companions in a storeroom and took their places,' admitted Alëza.

'We were terrified, you see,' explained Orsa hurriedly. 'We thought that if we could just get through customs and make our way here, as you had told us to, everything would be all right. But Mykloz was too clever for us, and it all went horribly wrong.'

The Doctor regarded them thoughtfully. 'Yes, I guessed something like that must have happened. I certainly can't condone your treatment of poor Steven and Dodo, but I understand why you acted the way you did. It's not easy to live in fear. Fortunately, no real harm's been done.'

Alëza looked up at the Doctor, imploringly. 'Will you still take us to the Sanctuary, then?'

The Doctor grinned broadly. 'Never fear, my friends. Before long, you will be beyond the reach of Mykloz and his kind forever. The Gatekeeper will join us here shortly.'

'But how do you know?' asked Orsa.

The Doctor shrugged. 'The Sanctuary was set up by my own people, the Time Lords. That was millions of years ago, before they lost their taste for action and turned their backs on the affairs of other races. They had discovered that there was something special here on Bukol which impaired the function of their time machines; another dimension, a sort of mini-universe, which coexists with this one but does not directly interact with it.'

The Doctor rubbed his chin reflectively as he recalled how he had first learnt of the Sanctuary's existence during his brief foray into the Matrix, the repository of all Time Lord knowledge. The Bukolians might feel justly proud that their planet was a haven for the dispossessed of the galaxy, but little did they realize that it was also the ultimate Sanctuary for those whom others had labelled freaks or deviants. The inhabitants of that strange dimension could peer through into the everyday life of Bukol, but only the most perceptive of observers could catch the occasional glimpse back the other way – and they usually thought that they were seeing ghosts . . . The Doctor was snapped out of his reverie as

Orsa spoke to him.

'Someone's coming,' the Malean whispered.

Wandering across the fairground, as if he had not a care in the world, was a dwarf dressed in the colourful garb of a circus performer. For a moment it seemed as if he was going to amble on past the Doctor's group, but suddenly he turned and came right up to them. He stood with his hands in his pockets, regarding the Doctor coolly.

'You're a bit early, aren't you?' The dwarf spoke with a strange, sing-song squeak.

'I was never much good at time-keeping,' smiled the Doctor.

The dwarf smiled back. 'That's rather amusing, coming from a Time Lord.'

'I was never much good at being one of those, either,' the Doctor admitted unashamedly. 'Alëza, Orsa, meet the Gate-keeper of the Sanctuary.'

With a mischievous giggle, the Gatekeeper took the two Maleans by the hand and led them to an open space near the centre of the fairground. From his pocket he then produced a small, star-shaped crystal, which he suddenly threw into the air. The crystal began to glow as it fell, and when it hit the ground it created a huge dust cloud out of all proportion to its size. Pulsing with an inner light, the cloud gradually coalesced into a beautiful golden archway.

Alëza and Orsa looked at each other in wonder. Through the archway they saw a domain they knew to be paradise.

As the Gatekeeper rejoined the Doctor, the two Maleans waved goodbye and walked hand in hand towards their new lives, their faces lighting up with joy as they saw the multitude of creatures waiting for them beyond the archway, all displaying their own customary forms of greeting.

Like Yerma before him, the Doctor felt moved to quote the words of Emma Lazarus, inscribed on the Statue of Liberty on the far-distant planet Earth:

> *Give me your tired, your poor,*
> *Your huddled masses yearning to be free,*
> *The wretched refuse of your teeming shore,*
> *Send these, the homeless, tempest-tossed to me;*
> *I lift my lamp beside the golden door.*

'No!' Mykloz's voice suddenly reverberated around the fairground.

Alëza and Orsa turned in horror to see the hunter hurtling towards them, his spherical blaster in his hand. The Doctor moved to intervene, but the Gatekeeper restrained him.

'No, Doctor! Look. The Gate is closing.'

Slowly but surely, the archway was shrinking, its golden glow beginning to fade. Mykloz raised his blaster and took aim at the departing mutants. He fired just as the archway finally vanished.

The Doctor and the Gatekeeper were thrown to the ground as the blast from Mykloz's weapon reacted violently with the residual energy. Shielding his eyes against the glare, the Doctor saw Mykloz suspended in mid-air, a dark silhouette against a vortex of violent colour, as the fabric of space and time was momentarily disturbed.

The Malean's face was contorted in a travesty of terror. Like a man drowning in quicksand, he flung his arm out in a desperate attempt to pull himself clear. But there was nothing for him to grasp on to.

The calm which followed was sudden and absolute. Mykloz had disappeared without trace.

The Gatekeeper helped the Doctor to his feet. 'A temporary rupture in the continuum,' he explained. 'No permanent damage has been done.'

The Doctor walked over to the spot where the archway had formed and began gently stirring the scorched dust with his feet. 'And Mykloz?'

'He could be anywhere in space and time. If he survived, that is.'

As the Doctor knelt down to examine the molten remains of Mykloz's blaster, the dwarf slipped his hands back into his pockets and shambled blithely away . . .

Silverman gave the usual shuddering sigh as he came to the end of his account and allowed himself to relax. Again the unearthly radiance drained from his bony hands and the room returned to normal – or as normal as it would ever get.

My client seemed strangely unnerved by these latest revelations; he sat there in stony silence with a dark, brooding expression clouding his features. 'What did you make of all that?' I asked him. I might as well have been talking to the table for all the reaction I got. I turned to Silverman. 'How about you?'

'Well,' he replied, having given it a moment's thought, 'clearly the Doctor can indeed change his appearance; and we now know of a sixth different form he has taken.'

'Yeah, the guy in the carnival outfit.' I rubbed my chin reflectively. 'The same man, but in six different guises . . . ' I glanced again at the little stranger, but he remained motionless in his chair, apparently avoiding my gaze.

'Do you wish me to try another object?' enquired the psychic.

'Well, okay,' I told him. 'Let's go for just one more . . . '

Prisoners of the Sun

Tim Robins

The time wave swept through the Kasterberous system. In its
wake, a battle fleet entered the gravity well of Gallifrey. Plasma
bolts ripped through the transduction barriers, sending seismic
blasts deep into the planet's core. The High Council of the Time
Lords, huddled in the fleeting safety of a fall-out shelter, traced
the origins of the battle fleet to Earth and realized that they had
brought this destruction upon themselves.

It was the first case of spontaneous human combustion she had
ever seen.

Engineer Silo had been at his work station, running a systems
check on the computer. He had been puzzled by the read out and
had asked her for help. Then he had asked, 'Is it sunnier than usual
here, or have little green persons been playing with the air
conditioning?' She had thought he had been joking. It had not
been warm and the air conditioning had been working perfectly.
The instrumentation had to be kept at a temperature that made the
room one of the coldest places on the SunTrap.

Seconds later, Engineer Silo had burst into flames.

She had run for the airlock and reached it moments before
blasts of halon had driven all the oxygen out of the room.

Safely outside, she had looked at the monitor. It had showed
a pair of Doc Marten's work boots and a fan of black ash: all that
was left of Engineer Silo.

She had signalled a medical emergency: a team of paramedics
were on their way. But it was the Director who arrived first. As
he entered the room, she knew there was something terribly
wrong at the SunTrap.

Gentle waves lapped around the dome of St Paul's Cathedral. The

Doctor shielded his eyes from the glare of the noonday sun. From his vantage point atop the dome, he saw small boats blazoned in the black livery of London cabs. The boats bustled tourists and business people between the city's historic monuments and skyscrapers, now fern-planted archipelagos.

The Doctor eased himself down to the water's edge, scooped up a handful of water and tasted it. It was warm and salty with surprisingly few pollutants. He sat back and listened to the buzz of water-skiers and the comical belching of iguanas. A dragonfly rested on his knee, then hummed away to dance among some reeds.

The Doctor removed his velvet jacket, unbuttoned his shirt and kicked off his shoes. He couldn't remember a time when London was this hot. Any time. Past or future. That was the problem. When was this present?

He peeled off his socks and paddled his feet in the water. Resting his head on his jacket, he lay back to think. Panic was bad for his image.

Since being exiled to Earth, he had put a great deal of effort into cultivating just the right persona. His choice of clothes had been particularly important for, as a Time Lord, he had few other pegs on which to hang his identity. His current costume shaped him into a kind of suave, sophisticated gentleman of action. It was based on clothes he had borrowed from Ashbridge Cottage Hospital, where he had been detained after his ignominious arrival on Earth. Although, in retrospect, the fedora had proved a mistake and was now buried unmourned in a trunk in the TARDIS.

The costume had also helped him cultivate what he considered to be an appropriate personality: concerned and grandfatherly to young women; concerned and intense when dealing with scientific problems; concerned but arrogant to people in authority; and concerned and dynamic when confronting threats to Earth. Different people read him differently, of course. Young women found him patronizing, his colleagues found him wilfully obtuse, officials found him childishly pedantic, and monsters found him arrogant and absurd – until he defeated them, and then he was reconsidered to be incredibly dangerous and first in line to be exterminated when the next invasion came.

Lying on the dome, the Doctor wondered what reaction was appropriate to suddenly finding oneself hurled through the vortex and unceremoniously dumped in another time without even a TARDIS console to take you back.

Just then, he heard the drone of a nearby speedboat and knew rescue was at hand.

Then he heard the siren and saw the captain's Navy fatigues.

Then he noticed the United Nations Intelligence Taskforce emblem on the side of the boat, and began waving again.

For a moment the UNIT sailor seemed to duck out of sight. The boat puttered to a halt, its prow knocking against the dome. The Doctor reached out, caught a mooring rope, steadied the craft and leaped on board. It was then he noticed that the sailor had been shot. The Doctor examined the body and calculated the bullet's trajectory. The shot must have come from the roof of the cathedral. He turned around. The killer was standing behind him.

'Get out of the boat.' The killer, a commando of sorts, wore dark clothes and a black woollen balaclava. Black dubbing was smeared across his face. The night camouflage was weirdly incongruous against the Caribbean sky and the water-blasted white cathedral dome.

The Doctor squinted. The commando's voice sounded familiar, but he was unable to make out the man's features.

'I'm afraid my sea legs aren't what they used to be. Would you kindly lend me a hand?'

The commando responded by tightening his finger on the trigger. The Doctor tried a different approach.

'Can't we discuss this like rational sentient life forms? I abhor violence.'

As the Doctor approached, the commando lost concentration; startled, he loosened his grip on the gun. A second later, the ball of the Doctor's left foot made contact with the commando's head, sending him spinning into unconsciousness.

At that, three more assailants entered the fray, abseiling down the dome. A further three, commandos like the rest, followed behind. They manoeuvred between rusted tubes of scaffolding which clung to the roof. Ignoring the fallen gun, the Doctor sprang into a back-leaning stance, distributing most of his weight over his rear leg. There were six assailants now, their moves subtle, disciplined and confident. They had been trained in martial arts, but then the Doctor had taught Bruce Lee all he knew.

The Doctor leaped. With his body parallel to the ground, he kicked two adversaries, took out a third with his head, pirouetted over the falling body and delivered similar blows to the remaining three. A perfect double-sankaktobi.

The Doctor was a master of Venusian martial arts. His sensi had been a Zen hologram created by Toyota, who had bought out the leisure planet when its North American backers had been bankrupted. He had visited Venus in an earlier incarnation, his body prematurely aged by too many gravities, too many narrow escapes from death. Now, in a younger, more powerful form, he applied his training to devastating effect.

'Kai!'

The Doctor kicked in, delivered a blow, then stepped against the knee joint of an attacker. There was a sickening click as the joint dislocated. Suddenly, the Doctor felt a numbing punch to his own leg. He faltered. A second bullet thumped into his shoulder. Turning, he saw the killer aiming at his head, and finally recognized him. Sergeant Benton fired again.

From the observation deck of the Telecom Tower, Sebastian Edge, Chief Executive to the Minister of Tourism and Public Order, looked across London and smiled. It was a travel agent's dream. Beneath the Caribbean sunset, he could still see the glinting bathyscaphes of Drowned World Tours Incorporated, which took sightseers beneath the waves to discover the secrets of the Great Barbican Reef. Some scuba devotees plunged from glass-bottomed boats to drift among the tropical fish that had made their home within the concrete coral of West One.

In the distance, Edge observed a motorcade of UNIT outriders slewing toward the Tower from the direction of Westminster Abbey. The distinctive manta ray form of a Stealth stretch hydrofoil plunged in their wake. Edge nervously thumbed the Nehru collar of his jacket. Shortly, he would be playing host to Director Helios of the Power Elite. Arranging security had been a nightmare; as had compiling the guest list.

Edge remembered when his job had been fun, a time before public order issues had crowded his agenda. Public order had always been part of his Minister's brief. When the water levels had risen, large numbers of the city's population had had to be relocated; some to the hinterland, most to the mountains of Wales. But now, policing, counter-intelligence and military concerns dominated his time.

It was all the terrorists' fault. Edge couldn't see why they had to be such spoilsports. Everyone agreed that the only future for London was as a leisure centre. Particularly now that the stock exchange had been floated into geostationary orbit.

As the sunset bled into night, Edge watched the water-borne motorcade cut across submerged streets, squares and courts which provided only the vaguest guidelines for the new waterways and shipping lanes that criss-crossed the city.

Inside the hydrofoil, Director Helios, from the Power Elite's Directorate of Energy, Speed and Information, projected his schedule for the next hour on to the bottom left corner of the left-hand lens of his mirror-shade Ray-Bans.

18.20: Dock with Telecom Tower.

18.23: Take accelerator to conference suite.

18.25: Formal welcome *en route* to auditorium.

18.27: Deliver presentation on the completion of the Virilio Net.

18.37: Dinner, share pleasantries and smorgasbord with the Minister for Tourism and Public Order.

18.45: Make apologies.

18.46: Depart from rooftop heliport.

18.47: Observe terrorist attack.

19.15: Arrive at the SunTrap.

20.20: Board Daedalus shuttle for space.

Director Helios thought briefly, then made a vital adjustment to the schedule. He cut the apologies at 18.45. This would bring his departure time forward by one minute. Jerusalem Rises, like all other terrorist groups, were inherently bad time-keepers, and he didn't want to be caught up in any unpleasantness. Besides, he wasn't sorry. For anything.

It was 18.25.

'Sim.'

'Sim be with you, director,' said Edge, arcing his hands in the customary gesture of diplomacy. Helios was dressed in a David Fielding original: a swept-back silver battlehat, half cycle helmet, half *Star Wars*, with a drop-down smoked visor and sloping cranial section that hugged a glistening asbestos polymer body armour. Edge thought the armour gave him a streamlined appearance, reminiscent of the heroes in fifties sci-fi films, although the only visible flesh revealed a skeletal jaw line, thin, tightly pressed lips and the nicotine pallor typical of all the Power Elite.

The Director strode into the auditorium. By the time Edge caught up with him, he was already taking his place at a sleekly sculptured resin podium. A crowd of delegates from the army, the government, industry and lifestyle magazines anxiously awaited the news.

'Sim,' said Director Helios. 'The Virilio Net is complete.'

A bilious coloured hologram revealed a web of computer systems ensnaring the Earth. Edge studied the schematic. He noted the absence of continents. The Virilio Net was a nervous system without a body, a non-terrestrial network whose electronic ganglia met at only five nodal points – satellites, orbiting just above the ionosphere.

Thwip, thwip, thwip, thwip, thwip.

The audience stood up and greeted the hologram with enthusiastic applause. Some even whistled. Swept up in the applause and the alcohol, Edge pressed closer to hear what Director Helios was saying. The Director was making a speech. Edge's eyes brimmed with tears of relief. He began clapping extravagantly.

'Delegates. My friends,' said Helios. 'At last, Sim in our time – the total uninterrupted, free flow of information is within our reach.'

More applause. Edge remembered he had duties to attend to. 'Our sphere of influence is complete,' the Director continued. 'Energy, military, transport and now information. A new age is here.'

Thwip, thwip, thwip, thwip.

Director Helios heard the helicopter slicing towards the Tower and realized the terrorists were going to be even earlier than he had anticipated. The human fools. He would have to skip dinner.

'It is time to forget. It is time to think new thoughts: new thoughts for a new world.'

It was time to leave. Director Helios finished his speech and surreptitiously signalled to his own helicopter. He would have to rendezvous with it above the Tower.

Thwip, thwip, thwip.

Outside the auditorium, Edge checked that the reception buffet had arrived. A few UNIT types were already downing drinks at the bar. Through the plexiglass window, Edge spotted something flying towards the Tower. It was dark now, but he could just make out the shape of a helicopter.

'Good Lord! That's a model 47G-3B-2! I haven't seen one of those for years.' It was General Munro who had spoken.

Edge remembered that the General had done something important during the battle with the Autons, although he didn't know exactly what.

'A great favourite with the Italians if I remember rightly,' continued Munro. 'UNIT bought about a dozen of them.'

'How manoeuvrable is it?' asked Edge. He was nervous. He could not recall seeing helicopters listed as part of the security arrangements. 'I mean, can it turn before it reaches us?'

'Not if it keeps up that speed.' The General was delighted at the opportunity to show off his knowledge to a civvy. Like many of the higher ranks of UNIT, he had gained promotion through loyalty to the Power Elite rather than competence in the job. 'Lycoming engines. Powerful, but their rate of climb is only three hundred and two metres per minute and . . . '

Thwip, thwip.

' . . . I say! You don't think the bally thing is out to get us?'

That is exactly what Edge did think. He made an executive decision. He decided to run. As he ran, he caught sight of the Director racing down the stairs to the open-air observation deck. Edge followed.

Thwip.

The helicopter hit.

The Telecom Tower had been a landmark since it was first constructed in the sixties. Back then it had been called the Post Office Tower and had briefly symbolized all that was modern about London in the sixties. For a short period it had been home of a computer called WOTAN, then the military had taken it over and added an extra thirty meters of Pave Paws tracking systems, intended to detect incoming ICBMs. This had long since fallen into disuse.

Now the Tower looked particularly impressive. From a distance, tourists imagined the mushrooming fire ball to be part of a magnificent *son et lumière* and wondered how they could get tickets for the next night's performance.

Inside the Tower, commandos, blacked-up like music hall minstrels, mowed down any remaining guests. Edge rushed to the observation deck and was greeted by the Director.

Smiling, Helios reached out, grabbed hold of Edge and hurled him over the balustrade. 'Watch the last step,' he said. 'It's a killer.'

By the time Sebastian Edge hit the water below, he was falling so fast he might as well have hit concrete. Just before his bones turned to jelly, he realized he was not going to receive that extra salary increment and so would never be able to afford that berth at the Knightsbridge marina he'd always wanted.

Above, two commandos burst on to the observation deck. Director Helios pulled a ripcord stitched into his belt. A helium balloon mushroomed above his head and he was jerked eight kilometres into the air. One of the commandos fired a round at him. 'Leave him, soldier,' counselled an officer. 'He'll have his day.'

Above the Tower, a helicopter extended Helios a welcoming umbilical cord and a safety harness. As the helicopter headed north towards the SunTrap, Helios imagined the Tower's final moments; its body snapping in half, Semtex detonating around the foundations of the broken stump, the stump folding in on itself and crumbling into the sea. The operation had been a success.

The lights were burning low on Detonation Boulevard. Women and children sat out the remaining minutes left until curfew, huddled together for warmth in the recesses of its Victorian brickwork walls.

Captain Mike Yates splashed purposefully through the ankle-deep slime which lined the thoroughfare. He stopped occasionally to acknowledge greetings from 'the Innocents', as he liked to call the people under his troops' protection.

Most of the tunnels of the nineteenth century sewer system were christened after the gallows humour of his troops: Napalm Street, Uzi Avenue, The Terrace of Fallen Hand Grenades. More important routes took the names of great ceremonies which had once marked the tempo of Britain's national life. Coronation Street, for instance, led directly beneath the British Library. It was along here that Yates was now heading, for his base of operations was located in one of the Library's great vaults.

Running the resistance from within the heart of the capital was not easy. The enemy was everywhere, even if, as Yates suspected, they had lost almost all interest in his war of attrition. He knew the attack on the Telecom Tower would change all that.

Yates arrived at a flight of rusting iron stairs and climbed into the Library. His office was crowded with objects gathered over the years from sorties into museums, art galleries and Toys U Need.

Sometimes Yates spent hours looking at the objects: a pair of soccer boots; a mug celebrating the marriage of Prince Charles and Lady Diana Spencer; an *Eagle* comic; a tin of boiled sweets; a photograph of his mother; a *Radio Times* cover dated 23 October 1993; an Action Man with eagle eyes and gripping hands; a ticket stub for the London Underground; a conker; a pound note; a jar of Marmite; a Hornby railway set. They reminded him of the Britain that would one day rise from beneath the waves. Yates believed that day was at hand.

The strike against Telecom Tower was merely a diversionary tactic, he thought. The real work was being done by his divisions in the North Sea. Under the water, a nuclear submarine had been restored to working order. It contained only two Trident missiles, but two were enough. One would be detonated in the atmosphere. Its magnetic pulse would disable all the northern hemisphere's computer system. The second would be exploded at ground zero. It would blanket the Earth in a nuclear winter, a 'natural' shield against the Power Elite's satellite-borne source of wealth and power.

True, the plan was not without its dangers. The Power Elite could use their solar power satellites as directed energy weapons. There was one such satellite in geostationary orbit above the North Sea, beaming solar energy down to the artificial island known as the SunTrap. It would be simple to realign and recalibrate the system to take out an ICBM. The Power Elite had done that in the past. Before the submarine launched its missiles, the SunTrap would have to be disabled.

Yates was also concerned that the Innocents might suffer reprisals for the attack on the Tower. But it was a dangerous world these days. That which didn't kill you, died first.

Yates sat back in a leather-upholstered chair. He needed to relax, so he aimed a remote and simultaneously activated a JVC television set and laserdisc player.

The disc ran Sarah Walker singing 'Rule Britannia' at the last night of the Proms. Union Jacks billowed beneath her outstretched arms. Yates shared the promenaders' joy. But the disc was part of a multimedia educational package, and soon the soundtrack turned from accounts of pride and patriotism to a nagging Greek chorus which spoke of 'imagined communities' and 'invented traditions'.

Yates selected the promenaders again, silencing everything except the music. But the mood had been broken. His left leg began to ache, even though it had been amputated nearly a year ago after an unsuccessful raid on the British Museum. The leg was now stuffed and mounted in a glass display case alongside the other commemorative objects in his room.

There was a knock at the door.

Captain Yates pulled a woollen mask over his face, leaving only his eyes and mouth visible. Sergeant Benton entered the room and greeted him with a salute. Yates acknowledged his fellow officer. Two commandos followed Benton in and bundled their prisoner on to a chair. They took off the prisoner's blindfold, removed the plugs in his ears and tightened the cables binding his arms behind his back.

Yates stepped up to the chair, grabbed the man's mane of blood-caked hair and pulled back his head. So the reports were true. It was the Doctor. The Great Traitor himself.

'You're lucky to be here, Doctor. My soldiers wanted to execute you without a trial.'

The Doctor tried to speak. His lips were bruised and swollen. 'If I am a prisoner of war, I trust you will observe the Geneva Convention.'

'The Geneva Convention?' Yates sneered. 'The Geneva Convention doesn't protect a traitor.'

'Traitor?' The Doctor seemed genuinely confused.

'A traitor to Earth and the British nation. You have caused the deaths of patriots. You have used your obscene alien science to enslave this planet. And you have disgraced the name of UNIT.'

Yates felt himself losing control as he remembered the time when the United Nations had first become the pawns of the Power Elite and he had set up a core of UNIT soldiers still loyal to the cause of democracy and the Crown. That had been twenty years before, and in the days that followed he'd seen many good soldiers put to death. Then he remembered the Brigadier and the part the Doctor had played in his 'execution'.

Yates pulled back his mask. He could no longer hide from his enemy. The Doctor didn't react. Yates became even more angry as it became clear the Doctor didn't remember him.

'May I ask why I have been brought here?'

A film of red mist passed over Yates's eyes. 'No, Doctor. You may not ask why. You may kneel down on the floor and you may die.'

Yates grabbed the Doctor's shirt, twisted him to the ground and shoved the barrel of his revolver into his mouth. The Doctor choked. Yates hesitated. A familiar, soothing voice was whispering to him in the back of his head. The mist began to clear. He signalled to Sergeant Benton to take the prisoner away. The Doctor was frog-marched out of the room.

Alone again, Captain Yates took several swigs from his hip flask, then lurched over to a reproduction nineteenth-century globe. He steadied himself, then pressed a thumb down on the British Isles. The globe's northern hemisphere pivoted open to reveal a bundle of electrodes. He selected a lead and jack plug and stuck them up his nose. A calming white light welcomed him to the Virilio Net.

The prisoner in the cell realized he was naked, but was grateful that he wasn't wearing an iron mask. Good. He could catch insects and eat them for nourishment, or he could save the insects and feed them to spiders then eat the spiders, or perhaps he could keep the spiders and feed them to birds and then eat the birds, or he could keep the birds and feed them to a cat and then eat the cat. Then again, it would probably be better to keep the birds for company. A lifetime in this prison could prove unbearably lonely, and birds were more cheerful company than cats.

Deep in meditation, the Doctor finally managed to pull himself together. Since being taken prisoner at St Paul's cathedral, he had learned a great deal about the world in which he now found himself. On the occasions he hadn't been blindfolded, he had picked up a lot of information from the commandos. They had mostly communicated to each other in a non-standard sign language, but that had proved no problem for the Doctor to decipher. Since his rooftop confrontation with Sergeant Benton he had also watched their body language to see if he could recognize any other former members of UNIT.

The officer who had so rudely shoved a gun in his mouth had seemed to know him. The Doctor did not recall the officer. Perhaps they had not yet met in the past? But the Doctor knew one thing just from looking into his eyes: the officer was completely insane. He had learned something else from looking up the officer's nose: there was a man-machine interfacing device lodged up his right nostril. This was interesting not only because of its intelligent use of the human body as camouflage, but also because the technology was far in advance of anything the Doctor had seen anywhere else in this time. Did the other soldiers know it was up there?

The officer's room had also proved an invaluable source of information. The clutter of bric-a-brac had reminded the Doctor of the fabled Memory Theatre of Giulio Camillo, in which a carefully planned arrangement of rampways, doors, objects and scribbled notes enabled whoever entered the theatre to recall everything that was then known about the Universe, from the divine supercelestial Sephiroth who had shaped the world, to the most mundane elements of existence.

Camillo's Memory Theatre had never been built, although he had explained its workings to the Doctor and the King of France during that long hot summer of 1530 and it had gone on to enjoy a more splendid existence as the subject of enthusiastic tavern conversation among the chattering classes of Padua than it could ever have had in real life.

The Memory Theatre that the Doctor had just seen was less splendid than Camillo's, but more revealing. He had spotted the cankerous form of a Time Lord message pod sandwiched between a framed one-pound note and a jar of Marmite. It was clear the message pod was intended for him, as it existed a chronon behind everything else in the room. This gap, the smallest time lag possible, ensured the pod was invisible to everyone except the Doctor, whose eyes were attuned to such tiny anomalies in the space-time continuum.

The fact that the pod was intended for him made him very angry indeed. The Time Lords had already interfered in his life when they exiled him to Earth. That had been just their first taste of power over him; now it seemed they wanted another bite. They were the Sephiroth responsible for his flight through the vortex. The Doctor scowled towards the heavens; the direction he always looked on those occasions he was forced to think of his home world.

Outside his cell, somewhere in the warren of drains, a radio played 'Scary Monsters' by David Bowie.

Rescue came for the Doctor in the form of a homicidal robot, which smashed down the door to his cell with a single blow just as two interrogators were about to cover his face with a wet towel.

The Doctor's regenerative abilities had already healed his bullet wounds, so he was feeling quite relaxed. He had heard the sound of gunfire outside his cell long before his interrogators had realized anything was wrong.

He was therefore fully prepared for the robot, immediately recognized it as some sort of Auton variant and knew just what he needed to do to defeat it.

The robot attacked, both wrists blazing. The two interrogators were flung across the room and consumed in columns of smoke.

By the time the robot had re-energized its weapon systems, the Doctor had freed himself using some classic moves that he'd picked up from Houdini. He grabbed his sonic screwdriver, which his interrogators had placed on a small desk, and began tumbling towards the robot along the ground, beneath the horizon of its sensors.

The robot attempted to refocus its aim, only to find that its target had sprung up in front of it and was now standing too close for it to use its arm weapons without injuring itself. The Doctor grinned, his nose pressed against the reflective surface of the robot's face-plate.

'Sorry about this, old chap,' he apologized, 'but I haven't the time to work out whose side you're on'. He blasted the robot with a chaotic amalgam of UHF waves. Sparks began cascading from its optical sensory array. Moments later, its head exploded, showering the room with a fine confetti of microcircuits.

The Doctor examined the body and found that his rescuer was an Auton in design only. There was no sign of the Nestene mind at work. The creature was part robot, part cyborg and part android.

The 'cybotoid', as the Doctor dubbed it, wore a sleek body-glove woven from Stealth material. The Doctor guessed the creature would be invisible to most surveillance equipment. Its clothes might even prove slippery to light waves, giving it a chameleon-like ability to reflect its surroundings.

The Doctor just managed to squeeze himself into the costume. It was about two sizes too small, but would provide some camouflage. He knew the cybotoid had companions, human and mechanical, so he slotted the gutted shell of its face over his own, wearing it like a mask. He could see through its featureless surface as if it were a one-way mirror.

Stepping out of the cell, the Doctor found himself in a scene from Dante's *Inferno* remade by Tim Burton as a sci-fi film. Down every tunnel he could see shadows, writhing in flames. He smelled burning flesh and heard the cries of innocents being put to the laser.

The Doctor began applying a ruthless logic to the situation at hand. The rebel base had been infiltrated. There was nothing he could do to save the rebels. The most logical option was to return to the Memory Theatre and retrieve the Time Lord message pod. He retraced the route, mechanically picking out sensory clues to the correct direction: a rusting 'street' sign swinging in the breeze; the sound of running water; a pothole; a blast of hot air; a rattle of a rusting iron staircase. He was there.

Cautiously he opened the door. Malfunctioning strip lighting bathed the room in a flickering blue fluorescent glow. An electrical buzz set his mind on edge. He ignored it and stepped over the corpse of a commando that was spreadeagled on the floor. He ignored that too. He had his orders. They must be obeyed. Flesh-things were weak, short-lived. They were of no consequence.

The Doctor wrenched off his robot mask and flung it from him. He looked back at Sergeant Benton. He was dead, poor chap. Probably killed in the defence of his superior officer, although typically there was no sign of the latter.

The Time Lord message pod remained untouched by the thick layer of debris which now decorated the room. The Doctor began to manipulate time. Allowing his mind to weave itself around the pod, he drew it slowly into the present. A chronon later, the pod fell into the Doctor's hands. But it failed to open. The message was not intended for him after all. Burned into one of the pod's slate surfaces was a name: Liz Shaw.

Outside, the fighting had reached the tunnel under the Library. The Doctor was suddenly confronted by Captain Yates lurching into the room. The officer fired two rounds towards the sewer's empty manhole. His uniform was dyed in blood.

'Take me to your leader,' said the Doctor.

Yates's eyes were glazed, as empty as his mind. He opened the globe in the centre of his office.

'I don't suppose you want to tell me which alien species gave you that equipment?' asked the Doctor.

He was right. Captain Yates did not want to tell him. After a brief communication with the Power Elite's computer network, he turned to his Hornby railway set and sent a model train chuffing along the tracks. When it entered a vacuum-moulded tunnel, a panel in the room swung open. Yates gestured the Doctor through it.

'This way, or you will die with the rest.'

Yates had also activated a self-destruct mechanism built into the sewer system. 'Ah yes, the ultimate sacrifice,' said the Doctor. 'Of course, other people are being sacrificed on your behalf.'

'This way, or you will die with the rest,' Captain Yates repeated. The Doctor walked through the passageway, which led up to an abandoned warehouse. He still carried the message pod. He had relocated it in time when the officer had first entered the room, so that it would remain invisible to everyone but him.

Their means of escape turned out to be a mini-sub, camouflaged in the colours of the Ballard Corporation. Soon they were under way, heading up the centre of England along a series of inland seas, across the Hadrian Canal and on to the sunken oil rigs which had once prospected the North Sea but were now Jerusalem Rises' submarine pen and the foundations of the power station known as the SunTrap.

Dr Elizabeth Shaw scrolled through the report on Silo's unexpected cremation. The death appeared to be unique, but she was certain it was part of a wider pattern of incidents at the SunTrap.

Staring out of her office window, she imagined she could see her reflection in each of the station's mirrored surfaces and that each reflection showed a different facet of her personality. The idea was fanciful. The SunTrap's reflective antennae covered an area the size of Manhattan Island.

Liz still remembered the day she had resigned from UNIT. The Brigadier had been angry – his least convincing emotion – but had accepted her resignation.

'He only wants someone to pass him his test tubes and tell him how brilliant he is.' How many times had she said that after becoming the Doctor's personal assistant?

Actually, the Doctor deserved credit for the SunTrap's existence. He had inspired her to create it and, of course, he was still helping her now. At a time when the Earth had been in desperate need of science to produce renewable sources of energy, the Doctor had opened her eyes to a world of alien technology. Then he had told her about a parallel Universe in which the Earth had been burned up in the search for a new gas. She had resigned the following month and gained a post as leader of the United Nations' Earthwatch Project. Once there, she had made sure that funds were directed only into viable research projects. The SunTrap and twenty similar stations around the globe had been the result.

Liz considered life had been good to her. She had even managed to avoid being married to a childhood friend who had become a Green. There was no way she was going to share her life with a man who believed science equalled pollution.

'There is no life on this planet which cannot be brightened by the light of science. So let us all bathe in a new Enlightenment for the Earth.'

She cringed as she recalled her acceptance speech for the 1987 Nobel Peace Prize. But it was just badly written rather than dishonest. She still believed science was a force for good. Even the side effects from the melting of the North Polar ice cap had had their benefits.

But the recent incidents at the SunTrap were of a different order. The computer had failed to locate the cause of the satellite malfunction that had set fire to Europe, and now it refused to explain Engineer Silo's death. Perhaps the computer itself was malfunctioning.

Liz stepped into her private accelerator and hurtled upwards towards the computer's core. The door opened to a vast amphitheatre of gangways, computers, flashing lights, workstations and foot-thick electrical cables. The room had its own solar gathering antenna which bloomed from the roof, greeting the sun with outstretched mirrored petals. Beneath it, in the centre of the amphitheatre, sat the distinctive pale green TARDIS console. Next to it, the Doctor lay entombed in a transparent sarcophagus.

Liz started to link the Doctor's mind to the computer. She disliked this task. Why hadn't the Doctor just cooperated? Men. He might be an alien but he was no different from Captain Yates and Sergeant Benton with their absurd group of freedom fighters. 'Jerusalem Rises' indeed!

Not for the first time, she felt pangs of doubt. Wasn't this the world she had always wanted? A global order based on science and on faith. Faith in the moral standards of Western civilization. That had been everyone's dream: NATO, UNCLE, NEMESIS, SHADO, all those great organizations that had inspired people in the late sixties. Where had it all gone wrong?

Then the door of the accelerator opened again.

'Hello, Liz,' said the Doctor. 'I have a present for you. Perhaps we could swap? I'll give you your message from the Time Lords if you give me back my body.'

Liz realized she had a lot of explaining to do.

'Doctor. What brings you here?'

'Time,' said the Doctor, deadpan.

'Really? Do you know what time this is?'

'Yes,' said the Doctor. 'It's time to tell the truth.'

So Liz explained about the Power Elite, the workings of the SunTrap and the recent problems with the computer. She even voiced her suspicions about the Director, noting how the disasters had started occurring when he had arrived.

'So you see, Doctor,' she concluded. 'After the last time you attempted to escape from Earth, the Power Elite wanted to execute you as a traitor to the human race. I persuaded them that we needed your help to guide our research. They allowed you to live, but kept you in suspended animation. Your brain functions were linked to the computer. But look . . . '

Liz picked a compact disc off her desk. 'I have developed a way of mapping the human mind on to a CD.' She turned the disc in the light. The Doctor saw Liz's own face captured in a hologram on its surface. 'This one contains all my thoughts and experiences,' she continued. 'I was going to map your mind too. Then set you free.'

The Doctor took note of every excuse, every appeal to science and progress, every gesture towards the 'glorious future of the human race' that Liz Shaw used to justify her actions. Then he brought the Time Lord message pod back into normal time and gave it to her. She took it. It didn't open.

'I think I'd better meet this Director of yours,' said the Doctor.

Dressed in the bright lemon overalls, white rubber boots and blast protective hood of a SunTrap technician, the Doctor was in workmanlike mood. He didn't bother to tell Liz how he'd escaped from Captain Yates. It had been easy enough to climb up from the rebels' foundation base into the SunTrap and locate her. But now time was running out. Jerusalem Rises would launch their attack soon, and after that their twin Trident missiles.

The accelerator bore the Doctor and Liz down into the depths of the SunTrap. Soon the Director's office was in reach. The Director's personal secretary greeted them with a welcoming smile and an Uzi laser rifle. The Doctor disabled her with a karate blow to the neck.

Director Helios was sitting behind his desk. He was grinning despite the fact that Captain Yates was standing next to him and apparently threatening him with a gun.

The Doctor noticed that the Director's desk was decorated

with merchandise from the London Science Museum: the Fluorescent Phone (£49.95); the Claw – chamber of living 'lightning' (£59.95); and a vegetable clock (£14.95), which ran off a couple of copper and zinc plates inserted into a potato.

There were also some toys which the Doctor did not recognize.

'I see you've brought a friend, Dr Shaw,' beamed the Director. 'You are admiring the merchandise, Doctor?' He picked up one of the toys. 'These are the new Power Elite model figures. My advisers tell me they will be big sellers next Christmas. Look Dr Shaw, this one is you.'

He held out the toy, but it snapped under the pressure of his grasp, its head flying off with a 'pop'.

'Christmas may be coming early this year,' said the Doctor, dryly.

'You refer to the Trident missiles,' said the Director. 'Captain Yates was quite excited about them. Do put that gun down, Captain.'

Yates obeyed.

'As you can see, Doctor, when the captain looked into the Virilio Net, the Virilio Net looked into him. It enslaved his mind. His troops have proved very useful for tidying up loose ends, disposing of unwanted reminders of the past.'

'Like the SunTrap?' asked the Doctor.

'When the Earth is shrouded in a nuclear winter, we, the Power Elite, will descend from our satellites,' continued the Director. 'We will be welcomed as angels.'

'Or monsters.'

'Doctor!' It was Liz who had intervened. Although she did not entirely understand what was going on, she did not want to be dragged into another of the Doctor's paranoid fantasies. If he wasn't brooding about misunderstood aliens he was scheming to fend off invasion forces.

'Yes, Liz, monsters. How else would you describe this omen of misfortune?'

'You are wrong, Doctor,' retorted the Director. 'I am good news for the Earth. My Power Elite have heralded a new age of progress. And when the planet is shown the folly of supporting extremists like the Captain here, we will also bring a new age political unity. No, Doctor, the only misfortune I portend is for you and all your Time Lord kind.'

Liz Shaw screamed as Director Helios's face melted on to the floor, his skin giving way to the glare of microwave radiation shaped into humanoid form. She saw the Doctor back away and remembered how shaken he had been when he had returned from the parallel world destroyed by the Stahlmann project. She realized he was scared.

'Who are you? What do you want with me?' asked the Doctor.

'I am Helios,' the creature obliged. 'Last of the Solarians.'

'I'm sorry,' said the Doctor, 'but that name means nothing to me. I meet a lot of species on my travels.'

'Your travels would have been impossible had it not been for the destruction of my people. Once we were a great civilization. Our children rode the solar flares, our explorers challenged the storms of sunspots twenty times the size of this planet. As pure energy, we spread across the face of our sun.'

'You lived on a sun?' asked the Doctor. He was even more puzzled.

'Until your kind exploded our star so that you could use its energy to become Lords of Time. Since then, my kind have existed as nothing more than background radiation to the Universe. That was until I was drawn to Earth by the solar collecting antennae of the first of the SunTraps. Since then, I have guided the human race to one end – to serve as my army in the conquest of time and the total destruction of the Time Lords.'

Captain Yates, forgotten by the Solarian, reached for his gun. The bullets exploded in the air before they reached the creature.

'True to yourself, to the bitter end,' sneered Helios.

Liz watched as Yates met the same fate as Engineer Silo.

The Doctor, realizing the Solarian was distracted, grabbed the vegetable clock and hurled it at the creature's head. The Solarian screamed and blinked out of existence in a shower of sparks.

'Just as I'd hoped,' the Doctor said, bending down to pick up a burned potato. 'The potato absorbed the vital microwave bands which were holding Helios together. His morphic resonances were irrevocably fragmented. Anyone for chips?'

Liz Shaw sagged back into a chair. 'But there was more microwave radiation than a potato could contain.'

'Yes. The rest of Helios has probably been gathered by the SunTrap.'

'You mean he's now part of the national grid?'

The Doctor was grim. He looked down at a prosthetic leg carved in ivory; all that remained of Captain Yates. He was feeling less than heroic. Helios's allegations had rung true. The Time Lords had used him to cover up one of their crimes. However, he realised the worst was still to come. At last he knew why the message pod would not open.

Back in the computer core, the Doctor inspected the TARDIS console. Under the Director's guidance, Liz Shaw's time travel experiments had progressed alarmingly well.

'Do what you have to do,' said Liz, nodding towards the console. 'You can go now. I'll pick up the pieces here. With the Director gone, the Power Elite will be in disarray. I can use that confusion. Together with New Jerusalem, I can build a new order.'

'No, Liz,' said the Doctor. 'There have been too many world orders. It isn't going to work. You see, when that message pod didn't open, I realized it wasn't meant for you. Or, more precisely, it wasn't meant for *this* you. I'm afraid this future isn't meant to exist. And it won't, once I return.'

'You can't do that!' yelled Liz. 'You can't deprive me of everything I've achieved.' She signalled security. The Doctor didn't bother with the pretence of operating the TARDIS. He simply sent a telepathic message to the Time Lords.

As the Doctor dematerialized into the vortex, he witnessed a final horror. In the light of Captain Yates's failure to return, his troops had assumed he was captured. Now, as a final gesture of defiance, they exploded their missiles. The SunTrap was vaporized in a mushrooming radioactive fireball.

The storm clouds. The thundercrack. The empty road.

She drives a gaily painted Volkswagen Beetle across Westminster Bridge, swerving away from the Houses of Parliament and into an underground car park. She is silhouetted against the mouth of an empty corridor. She marches down it. Her face is grim. Her shoes click against linoleum. Feet, face, feet, face. Thundercrack. She flings open the doors and confronts the Brigadier, hiding behind his desk. She slams the envelope on to the desk. She slams her fist on to the desk. A china cup and saucer leap with fright.

She drives the car back to her flat. Knightsbridge.

In the vaults of the Ministry a card is punched 'Resigned' and automatically filed away.

She flings a suitcase on to her bed. She bundles in her clothes. She checks the flight tickets. She looks at the photographs. Kenya. Palms, green; poinsettias, red.

Hiss.

The tower blocks outside the window wave in the breeze.

Hiss.

She falls to the bed.

Hiss.

Unconscious. Gassed. She wakens, feels her way towards the blind and opens it. She recognizes the village as Portmeirion, which she has visited on more than one occasion whilst holidaying in North Wales. But now the streets look narrower, darker, more menacing. Like the *judengassen* of Prague? She has been to Prague, teaching English as a foreign language. On the table a slice of pork speaks to her. 'What do you want?' it asks.

'Information. I want information.'

'You won't get it.'

She lunges at the slice of pork with a bayonet – British army issue. The monster is impaled. She looks at its features, sallow, rat-like, Kafkaesque.

'I'm not an adjective, I'm a free ham,' asserts the slice of pork.

She plunges the slice of pork into a bowl of cheese. She begins to spool up in strands of melted Camembert. The strands won't break. They get longer. They are coming from her navel. A cheesy umbilical cord. Camembert tentacles wrap around the pillars of the room. The cheese lurches to the top of the cathedral. She looks up. The cheese is growing exponentially. She remembers that the cheese must have absorbed the sliced piece of Kafka and appeals to its common humanity. 'You weren't to blame. It was your father's fault.'

In a moment of blind panic, the cheese fondue attacks.

Liz woke in a cold sweat, calling for Professor Quatermass to save them all. Another anxiety dream. Her points of reference were becoming confused. Her life was becoming less and less science and more and more fiction.

When the international intelligence community had learned of her appointment as personal assistant to UNIT's scientific adviser she had found herself head-hunted by a long line of increasingly strange covert operations.

The latest contact, furtively arranged through one of UNIT's many letter-drops, had been one John Ridge, a male chauvinist pig with a taste for garish cravats. One night, in a sleazy bistro, he had presented her with a top-secret portfolio containing implausible stories of killer rats and plastic eating mutant viruses. Then he had suggested they 'crash out at his pad'. She had declined, he had implied she was frigid, and she had emptied the remains of a bottle of red wine over his head. 'What next?' she had complained to a trusted friend over lunch at Frith's. 'Puppetmaster on Tracy Island?'

Liz began tidying up the detritus from the farewell party. She replaced the pair of liquid wax lamps and became momentarily entangled in the waving strands of a fibreoptic anemone. The apartment floor was carpeted in scatter cushions, bean bags and books: *The Trials of Oz*, *Zen and the Art of Motorcycle Maintenance*, *Bored of the Rings*, *The Day After Doomsday*.

A pile of reefer stubs marked the spot where James, Charles and 'Jools' had spent all night talking excitedly about repairing the hole in the ozone layer by replacing aerosol fluorocarbons with ozone-restorative gases and saving the Amazon jungle by reseeding it with genetically engineered fast-growing hardwoods.

Liz, as high as her Cambridge friends, had countered every suggestion with: 'The Doctor can do better than that.' The Doctor. What was she going to do about the Doctor? She opened her diary and scribbled 'Doctor – who?' under a page headed 'unfinished business'.

Her Zephyr Chime doorbell rang. She opened the door and found the Doctor standing on the step. He was wearing a bright lemon jump suit and had the large plastic 'L' she'd recently thrown out wrapped around his neck. His dress sense is improving, thought Liz.

The Time Lords had proved worthy of their name, although their sense of space had turned out to be as bad as ever. When the Doctor had materialized, he had found himself in a skip outside Liz's apartment.

'Hello, Liz. I couldn't let you go without giving you a present.' The Doctor held out the Time Lord message pod.

Liz blushed, floundered around for excuses. How had the Doctor found out she was leaving? She silently cursed the Brigadier. You would have thought a man in his position could keep a secret. She took the pod. It screwed open. Commenting on the unusual packaging, she reached inside and pulled out a palm-sized disc. Drifting on its surface was a shimmering three-dimensional portrait of herself.

'A hologram! It's beautiful, Doctor.' For a moment, Liz thought the image resembled a ghost trapped in a mirror. She said as much.

'I suppose it is a ghost,' replied the Doctor. He recognized the disc as the ROM mind-map that the other Liz had shown him in the computer core. Now it existed out of time; a memory of a time yet to be. 'You might think of it as a ghost of the future. Would you like to hear what it has to say?'

In the Doctor's laboratory, a necklace of dermatrodes linking her to the TARDIS console, Liz Shaw accessed the disc. Without the experiences and excuses that had eased her acceptance into the ways of the Power Elite, she confronted her future self in the cold light of the present.

'This future doesn't have to happen, does it, Doctor?'

'Of course not. That's why the Time Lords sent you the message. You see, Liz, it's all their fault. By exiling me to Earth, they broke the First Law of Time. They changed the future. You want to use what you've learned as my assistant to benefit life on Earth. But science doesn't work that way. Technology isn't morally neutral. It's given meaning by culture. And your culture won't be ready to deal with the power the TARDIS represents for many centuries.'

'But I can't unlearn what I know.'

'But you can choose not to use it, Liz. Or you can put your knowledge to different use. Few people get to know the outcome of their actions before they make them. You've had that chance. I know you'll use it well.'

So Liz Shaw returned to Cambridge and devoted her life to discovering the origins of the Universe. She wrote a book on the history of time which was so brilliant no one understood it. And, twenty years later, when she looked up from her rooms in Cambridge into a cloudless sky, she did not see a renewable energy source hanging there; she just saw a bright, sunny day.

A revolution of sorts swept through the Citadel of the Time Lords. Several cardinals had already been executed and the head of the Supreme Pontiff of Time, the hated 'Time Pope', was now being paraded around the Panopticon on a pikestaff. The Celestial Intervention Agency had managed to direct popular dissent against the clergy, leaving their secular power intact.

'The Doctor proved useful,' noted a Time Lord agent. 'We can use him again.'

'There is still some fine-tuning needed,' replied his colleague. 'We must ensure that the Doctor is kept busy on Earth. I have contacted the warders of Shada. They have allowed the one who calls himself the Master to escape.'

'The Master!' exclaimed the first. 'He's a homicidal maniac. And you know his relationship to the Doctor. The Master will destroy him.'

'As I said, some fine-tuning is needed.' The second Time Lord placed a bowler hat on his head. It matched his pinstriped suit. 'The Doctor will be warned.'

I took the disc from Silverman's hand. 'So, this is Liz Shaw,' I mused. The disc reflected the flickering lamplight like a mirror; a mirror from which an impossibly three-dimensional image of a young woman with long red hair was smiling up at me. With some reluctance, I returned it to the table.

'And that appeared to be the same Doctor who drew the alien figure on the hymn pamphlet,' noted Silverman, gesturing towards the crumpled piece of card with a long, bony finger.

'Yeah, that's right,' I agreed.

My client suddenly stood up, pushing his chair back abruptly. 'I don't believe this!' he muttered, pacing up and down. 'You two are sitting there discussing this as if it's . . . it's some sort of a game! Don't you *understand*?' He rounded on us with a look of manic intensity. 'I need to find that cylinder! You've got to *help* me!'

Silverman gave one of his ghastly, skull-like grins. 'My dear sir, that is precisely what we have been endeavouring to do.'

'Endeavouring!' The little guy shook his head in disbelief. 'But none of these stories has had anything to do with what's happened to me here in Los Angeles.'

'I have to say,' I chipped in, 'I think we may have learned all we can now.'

Silverman seemed to take this as an affront to his professional pride. 'I am sure you are mistaken, Mr Addison. If I am allowed to continue, I am confident that I will be able to reveal far more about our friend here.'

I threw him a sceptical look. 'Well, maybe, but I'm still not too sure what to make of all this. Weird planets, different time periods, alternative dimensions . . . I mean, it all seems pretty screwy to me.'

Disregarding this observation, Silverman started tapping his fingers on the table, apparently turning something over in his mind. 'There is perhaps something else I might try,' he admitted. 'So far, I have entered only a primary level trance-state. There is also a secondary, deeper level, involving a far more intense association with the dominant personalities imprinted on the artefacts. The technique is not without ... risk ... but it can often be particularly reveal-ing.' He turned to me, almost imploringly. 'Will you allow me to try once more?'

I took a deep breath. This was getting crazier by the minute. 'Well, okay, I guess so.'

I looked up at my client, who nodded and returned to his seat. 'Yes', he muttered, 'we must go on. I must find out where I went in the city!'

Silverman again perused the items on the table and, making a decision, picked up what appeared to be the mouthpiece to a brass instrument of some kind. He held it out in front of us, gripping it tightly between his fingers. 'Now, gentlemen,' he said. 'It is imperative that you give me your utmost concentration. Focus your attention on my hands. You may witness ... strange things, but you must allow nothing to distract you.'

Closing his eyes, Silverman began to mutter under his breath, like a magician casting a spell. The whirlwind whipped up again, more violent than before, sending the oil lamp crashing to the floor and books tumbling from the shelves around the walls. This time, the glow that emanated from Silverman's hands was so bright that I could barely keep my eyes on them. Despite his warning not to get dis-tracted, I recoiled in surprise as suddenly the psychic cried out, not in his own voice but in the clear, high tones of a young woman ...

Lackaday Express

Paul Cornell

I'm drunk. I throw a punch. James staggers, his nose erupting in a beautiful flower of blood. The blood billows. I can see the contours of the liquid in the air as I slow the scene. His cry becomes a pure note. I stop it. His cry is boundless, a hissing song of information.

So many details. The party was in Camden, when I was twenty. A messed-up old living-room, summer evening still bright through the net curtains. What is Bruce smiling about? And who is that person just out of vision in the kitchen? If I could crane my neck another inch, I could see who it is. Throughout the whole party, I obviously failed to take a good look at that person, or I could match him to a face, recall who he was.

But we don't look at everybody, we don't talk to everybody, we don't know everybody. If someone slams down a photo in front of you and asks Have You Seen This Person, the only honest answer you can give is I Don't Know.

The blood hovers. Freeze frame. Hah! If there were frames, if there were actually Moments, then I could slip between them and Out. I would be Free. But when I stop the motion, the image warbles with tiny changes. Things are moving through it faster than I can follow, like stopping the image just gives me the meanest glimpse of the next degree of time. Maybe that's why individual stopped sounds are complicated songs in languages that I don't understand. My freeze frame is a day in somebody else's life. Fast People are running through you as I speak.

As I Speak. Hah! Everything is happening As I Speak.

Okay. Let's try this again. Or try it Still.

Whip through to a later scene. The Revivalist Bar. Everything eighties, including dress codes. Alec puts down his glass and turns to talk. I appreciate him. I appreciate the music. I am an appreciator. This is the story of an appreciator in hell, and of what may become of her cat.

Pom Pom Phizishheoodhdie2hrfhfewjfcep;fdkpkdqwkrdjdl wqmjdwqhj.

I stop it, looking at Alec's eyes.

I let it go on.

'So . . . Catherine, you've thought about it.'

'Yes. I . . . I . . . have to say. No. I can't marry you. I'm sorry.'

I try to change it.

'Yes. I . . . I . . . have to say. No.'

'To say. No.'

'No.'

I can't change it.

He lowers his head and sighs. And sighs. And sighs.

Alec has such a wonderful sigh.

The TARDIS actualized itself into its familiar police-box shape in a metallic corridor. Typical corridor: all wires and plastic. An argument spilled out of the police box into the corridor.

'No! Don't you see, Tegan? I *can't* go back. Adric's dead. You have to learn to accept that.'

Tegan, near to tears, glared at him. Such an odd face. And it was an old argument, repeated many times before.

'I'm sorry,' the Doctor sighed. 'I didn't mean to shout.'

'You could break that law. It's only a rule, not a point of physics.'

'I can't. The First Law is –'

'Where are we?' Nyssa carefully interjected, causing the Doctor to look up from his shoes and Tegan to glower.

This is days before. James can't dance, but he tries. He's a floppy man. All over the place. There are revivalists all around us in the dark. As James turns I see something in his eye. He knows about Alec, even at this point. I now realize that. I wonder about letting this night go ahead. There are better nights. It is a week before departure for Hardy Base. I Don't Want To Be Alone. Hah hah hah hah.

'Interesting!' The Doctor tapped his knuckle on the locked door. 'This hasn't been opened for at least a year. I wonder why they abandoned the place?'

'Probably a lurking monster or a deadly virus,' muttered Tegan.

Nyssa ignored her. 'It's a scientific establishment, isn't it?'

'Very probably, Nyssa. From the gravity, I'd say we're not on Earth, but this does look like human technology. Ah . . . ' The door sprang open as the Doctor tried another six-figure combination on the lock. 'Just a matter of time, you see. No such thing as coincidence.' Ignoring the puzzled looks, he strode inside.

A mixture of destruction and science. Keyboards with indented gaps, shattered screens, upturned chairs. The centrepiece of the control room was a large upright cylinder, standing in the corner. It had an access lock, and seemed to be part of something larger, a segment of some vast pipe than ran through the ceiling and floor. It was made of perspex-like material. Tiny firefly gleams sparkled and died inside it, and it gave out silence like other machines gave out noise. A giant diagram occupied the wall next to it: a planetary globe encompassed by a circle, with a single light glowing at one point on the artificial circumference.

Nyssa beat the Doctor to it. 'A cyclotron!'

'What?' Tegan asked, mildly interested.

'What your people would call an atom smasher, Tegan.' The Doctor glanced around the room like an enthusiastic father at a school art contest, his hands buried in his pockets. 'A device for accelerating subatomic particles to tremendous velocities. An expensive toy, but rather fun.'

'Well, somebody broke this one,' Tegan muttered, blowing a sheet of dust from a tubular steel and plastic chair and flopping down in it.

'Oh, not entirely. The cyclotron itself is still functioning. It's just some of the measuring gear that's been damaged. That's odd. . .' A frown clouded the Doctor's face.

'What is?' Nyssa peered over his shoulder.

'An anomaly. Particle collision is still occurring, without any particle source being present . . . Help me think, Nyssa. Feynman diagrams . . . Negentropy prolonged indefinitely by random Higgs Fields. But the Yukawa Potential required . . . Is that permitted purely by quantum uncertainty?'

'Perhaps,' Nyssa nodded. 'But . . . '

'There's no such thing! I know! Bubble chamber, bubble chamber . . . '

'What the hell are you two on about?'

'Not now, Tegan!' The Doctor threw open an inspection cover and pounced like an intellectual puma. 'Here we are . . . '

Tegan sighed, and began to doodle in the dust. Random collisions of finger tracks. Whorls and spirals.

James is asleep. I go to the window and look out over the snow-covered ground. In the distance, off campus, stands the ship, the HMS *Cheshire*, silver against the dawn. I place the note on the desk and unlock the door. When I'm outside, I can hear him moving. The touch of cold air has woken him. He does not follow me as I walk down the frosty paths towards Hoyle Hall. I do not look back to see him at the window.

I am born. Very painful. Doing it again and again, you realize how much of it you actually remember. I hang in a nurse's grip and shout gibberish at the medics. My mother is beautiful. I love her in a powerful hormonal rush at that instant, a huge pleasure in that pain. Doing this enough will make a masochist of me. This is how they'll find me – hah! – they'll find me at mother's breast, age nothing. I want to say sorry to her in the suckling, sorry about that womb of yours, big mother. Sorry?

Sorry. I can't say it. I howl and scream. Sorry. It doesn't work. It's frustrating here, because at birth it's closest to the surface. It's just on the edge of working. That also keeps me coming back here, because one time maybe this baby will look up at Mum and say 'Sorry'. God, that'll scare them. Perhaps there is some truth in reincarnation after all, because a part of this baby me really wants to talk again. But it can't. It got infected with time as soon as it was conceived. Conceived. Hah! Like that's a moment, a frame, rather than a continuum. We're Conceived, I think, in that walk in the park, in holding hands, in glances across a crowded theatre.

I go back to that. I dive in on a Timer. I lose my mind.

The Timer brings me out at five years old. In the nursery. I can't tell if there's a wall down there in the wombtime or what. I lose my mind, all thought and even dreams, and I'm full of warmth and violent impulse. I'm fairly sure that I can't remember being Two Things. I think I just have fantasies about being egg and sperm both. Whenever the Timer brings me out – and I don't understand how I do the Timer, I just do it – I can just recollect the colours and the sounds. I don't have any real memories, because there's no thought in there. I'll get lost there, and that'll be like my version of Death. Maybe if I push it far enough one time I'll break through and become parts of Mum and Dad.

Pizza. Alec inspects an anchovy at close range. I taste pineapple, and take a careful sip of brandy.

'Good, is it?' he asks suspiciously.

'Mmm, very.' There is silence. He takes a box from his pocket, and produces a ring. Sometimes I think that the pride he shows here is condescending, like a magician pulling a rabbit from a hat. I swallow hard. My mouth is dry.

In Alaska, watching the total eclipse, I say to Alec: 'I want to see the Diamond Ring.'

Hah!

At the table, I can't talk. I can feel the chemicals in my blood: my own, the brandy, all sorts of stuff from food, changing my decision. But I can think and, in all my thoughts, I can't find any reason for my decision.

Why?

*   *   *

'Why?' Tegan had drawn a kangaroo, two Cybermen and a spiral.

'Because it might help you to understand,' the Doctor explained patiently. Shrugging, Tegan got up and peered into the viewport. It was dark. Then, suddenly, two tiny points of light appeared, sped apart, sped together again, and vanished. For a moment, the screen lit up with a galaxy of similar collisions. Then it was dark again.

'Yeah, right, I see.'

'Those are particles, appearing out of nothing and disappearing again.'

'I thought that was impossible.'

Nyssa smiled. 'That's a little like a horse rider dismissing evolution.' She nodded towards the TARDIS.

'Oh shut up.' Tegan sulked. 'There's a big difference between the TARDIS and these little things.'

'And what might that be?' The Doctor was looking down his nose at her.

'These little things aren't blue. Besides, you're surprised about them too, otherwise you wouldn't be acting like a couple of presenters on Romper Room.'

'Tegan, Tegan . . . ' the Doctor muttered testily. 'I'm trying to involve you in the world of science. Asking questions is often as important as getting answers. Now, as you say, for these particles to appear out of nothing is, technically speaking, impossible. But the Heisenberg Uncertainty Principle enables you to get away with it quite often provided either the mass of the particles or the time for which they exist is sufficiently small. It's a break in causality which gives a lot of undergraduates sleepless nights. The thing is, it's happening continually here, in a regular pattern. Matter appears from nowhere, travels in time on a particle level, and then vanishes, almost as if –'

'Wait a minute! Travels in time?'

'Yes. The very nature of the collisions means that some particles are being knocked backwards and forwards to us over a period of years. We're watching a slice of an amazingly complex pattern, extending all around the cyclotron and out into time.'

'No.' Nyssa was shaking her head in slow concentration.

'No?' The Doctor's face fell.

'Only forwards. The particles aren't travelling backwards to us from the future, but only forwards from the past!' she concluded with a bright little smile.

The Doctor took an inward breath, as if about to demolish her argument, then stopped. Finally, he frowned. 'Yes . . . How very odd.'

Tegan resumed her doodling as the two scientists dove back into their technicalities.

The globe of Hardy in the sky, cratered and rocky, no life. A line of blinding lights shines around its equator, the particle accelerator. The ship begins a slow turn towards the surface, and Hardy spins around the sky, swinging below the craft. The six of us, those at the forefront of particle physics, are on our way to look after the cyclotron. I'm excited. Forgetting everything I left on Earth, James's and Alec's meaningless little war. Forgetting. No. It's all still in here, but Hardy sweeps it away with promised excitement.

There's nobody out here but us. A year of lonely quantum mechanics. The baggage is odd: Frank Paxton brought his saxophone. Let's hope he's good at it.

He is good at it. Paxton wanders the corridors at night, playing with precision and depth. His notes sound like they echo right around the equatorial tunnel, out to the monitor labs at Tycho Point and Atlas. It's very sad. It gets to some of the others. I like it. It reminds me of mortality. Hah! It reminds me that after a year I'll have to go back and deal with what I left on Earth. Paxton is odd, though.

The bastard did us in! There he runs, past the end of the corridor, a plasma rifle under his arm. Where did they come from?

Wherever, he helps them get in, he helps them find and kill us.

Whimpering in the stores cabinet. Keep quiet, Madeleine, for god's sake! Paxton and another man step around the corner, and they don't see me under the boxes. They've heard bloody Maddy and her bloody sobbing. Paxton walks up to the closet door and opens it, exposing her.

'There she is.' The man, a Steppe Guerilla by the look of his rad armour, takes a step back and aims at Maddy.

'Frank, it's me, don't let him –'

The man fires. Small sound. Maddy's body jumps like a hiccup and falls still. I close my eyes. There's a tiny choking sound. What do the Steppe Guerillas want with us? There's no loot here for them. What has Paxton promised them?

I'll blow them all up. I feel fear inside. Experiencing the moment. The fear is real, real contractions in the stomach. I wait until they move on.

'I think it's a consciousness,' Nyssa mused.

The Doctor was pacing thoughtfully. 'Yes, I'd come to that conclusion myself. The question is, is it a natural creature that's somehow evolved from a string of particle events in the cyclotron . . . '

'Unlikely.'

'Or is it the result of an experiment? Beyond the technology, isn't it?'

'Yes, and beyond anything that the Traken Union ever tried. Not that we would have.'

Tegan had started to wander around the place, bored. The consciousness bit had intrigued her, but it had become so abstract as to be just another bit of technobabble. She stopped. 'Hey, look who's here!'

The Doctor turned and frowned. 'You, me, Nyssa. Who else?'

Tegan blinked. Why had she said that? 'I'm going nuts. It's like I was suddenly at a party, and I knew everyone really well, and –' She put a hand to her mouth. 'Wow. Sorry. Didn't mean to hit you that hard.'

The Doctor turned to Nyssa. 'Do you feel anything?'

'No. And I wouldn't expect Tegan to have a psychic experience.'

'Neither would I. Still. We learn something new every day. Tegan –' He strode forward and offered her his hand. 'I'm the Doctor. And you are –?'

Tegan slapped him. 'Pissed off.'

The Doctor put a hand to his face 'Well, now I think –'

Tegan put a hand to her mouth. 'Wow. Sorry. Didn't mean to hit you that hard.'

'Ah. I don't think we're getting anywhere, do you?'

Tegan was frowning again. The Doctor moved aside just in time to avoid the slap.

'Pissed off,' she told him.

'So I see. Well, before we get involved in something resembling Bavarian folk dancing, I think we'd better get you to a–'

'Pissed off.'

'Chair. Nyssa –' The Trakenite helped manoeuvre Tegan into a folding chair. 'This is very specific, not true telepathy at all.' He took Tegan's hand and looked into her eyes.

'I'm all alone,' she told him. 'I don't want to be alone.'

'You are not alone. You're with friends. Tell me how you feel.'

'Cold. Alone. Deserted. I know everything so well, like my head's become my neighbourhood. Every face, every taste and noise. I can tell you details about lime, saxophones, toasted cheese sandwiches. I know every word of every letter I read. I can read all the books I only even glanced at. I can hold myself quite still at moments of pleasure, and examine snowflakes on my thumb in every detail.'

'That isn't Tegan,' Nyssa frowned. 'Too eloquent.'

'Yes. We don't want to go too far. Tegan Jovanka, come back to us. Come back to your friends, Tegan.'

Tegan's fingers began to flutter in the Doctor's hands.

'Tegan . . . Tegan . . . Hey, what's going on?' She awoke, and Nyssa hugged her quickly.

The Doctor's mouth hung open. He'd just been struck by a conclusion. 'EPR . . . ' he breathed. 'The Einstein-Podolsky-Rosen effect. Action at a distance? It's terrible, but –' He seized a scrap of paper and a pen. 'Quickly, Nyssa, help me with these calculations.'

I'm typing on the main board, trying to activate some sort of self-destruct sequence in the fission reactor that powers the cyclotron and the base. I'm making it up as I go along and, looking at it carefully, what I'm doing is going completely in the wrong direction. There's shooting, far off. Paxton composed a lot of the codes for this thing and his password phrases are so ironic that they make you wonder about the internal contortions of the man. Here's one:

To be governed is to be watched over, inspected, spied on, directed, legislated, regimented, closed in, indoctrinated, preached at, controlled, assessed, evaluated, censored, commanded, all by creatures who have neither the right, nor wisdom, nor virtue.

I imagine him, sitting on some ledge with his saxophone, laughing down at us like a mad prince. Or in his lounge back on Earth, thinking that the instrument turns him into someone cool and eighties and stylish. All he does is annoy the neighbours, but he thinks he's this dude.

Worse, he thinks he's this dude with irony.

Damn irony.

There's shooting, far off. These noises are like the last movements of a piece of music. No, they're like a book, because I was always somebody who wanted to read the last page first. There's no entropy to the noises, no indication really that the end's in sight. It's just my own associations. I feel obliged to experience The End if I go this far.

I suppose that I'm alone now.

Alec and James will just have to keep on fighting with each

other. I'm not coming back. They'll blame each other. The Steppe Guerillas will have all the rich dataloads in their ship by now, and they'll be searching for me because I'm the last witness. I find what I think is the final destruction sequence. There's a noise behind me. It's Paxton, with his saxophone and a gun. He smiles. There's no way I can complete the sequence in time. Thank god that's not something I keep on trying to do.

I back towards the accelerator hatch, where we insert experimental packages. He turns, checking the settings on the gun. I'm going to be an experimental target. I put my hands on the handle of the chamber door, and throw back the locks, opening it.

Surprised that that's a door, he brings the gun quickly up to firing posture.

I jump in and

The End

I'm born. In an endless cycle, smeared out across my whole lifetime. All my life is my playground and I'm always alone, the sole inhabitant of a swarm of particles. I can remember every dream now, of every sleep I ever had, and there is one that tells me about this event in detail.

It's autumn, and I'm sleeping beside Alec, and I wake up, shouting that I'll never get out. The cat leaps off the end of the bed.

'I was trapped in my life. I *am* trapped in my life,' I bluster at Alec.

'You're not trapped. Who's trapping you?'

'I could see it all. The Guerillas and –'

'The Republicans? What you hear about this place isn't true. There's never been a terrorist alert inside the compound –'

'And all their other viewpoints and just the way the world's tugging itself apart. There's no future, Alec. I saw – Damn.'

And the dream is gone. Whatever chemicals stirred the future into my head that night . . . they stirred away into something else.

I wonder what that night means? Are we all in a cyclotron, and I'm just the only one in a cyclotron in a cyclotron? Are the voices, when I slow down to a shuddering stop, the dead? The greys, ready to leap out from the cracks? How can I die, too?

I have a pot of tea in a hotel in Bath.

The Doctor had finished calculating.

'Yes! There is a possible exit from the Moebius strip. Phase reversal at the initial node, of course. The entrance is the exit! Exactly here!'

Even Nyssa was lost now. 'Sorry, but what −?'

The Doctor was pacing, waving his glasses in front of him. 'Nyssa, you must take the TARDIS to these coordinates!' He grabbed a pen and the young Trakenite's hand and scrawled a string of numbers across her skin. 'Whatever you do, don't go outside. Just wait for me to . . . ah . . . arrive.' He jumped to the door of the cyclotron access chamber and grabbed the handle. He paused there for a moment. 'Now, there's no need to worry,' he told his companions. His face clouded a moment later. 'I hope.'

He pulled open the chamber door and leapt into nothingness. His body blazed silver and was whisked away into a burst of stardust. The door slammed shut.

'Doctor!' yelled Tegan.

The Doctor hit the top of his fourth incarnation and bounced off the reality gap between them.

He was aware of time, and yet timeless.

This was quite exhilarating.

He was in Bath, drinking tea.

A young woman stared at him, amazed.

'No!' She was screaming. She . . . *screamed*. The Doctor *stood up*. With an effort of will, he slammed the brakes on his progression through time.

He held out his hand. 'Hello. Please don't be alarmed. I jumped in the cyclotron after you.'

'Are you real?' She backed away. 'My god. How am I

talking to you? Talking! Hah! Are you real? Was that repeated? No, no –'

'I'm real. We're at a single moment in your life, rather a pleasant one by the look of it, with a bottomless pot of tea in front of us.' The Doctor reached down to the table and picked up a cup, taking a sip. 'Delicious!' he grinned. 'The qualities of English breakfast transcend all physics. Do you know, I always suspected that.'

The woman stared around the hotel dining room, turning her head with sudden jerks, amazed at being able to see in new directions. A maid was halfway to the table, frozen in a moment, her eyes unseeing.

'I dare say that you can relive any moment of your life, repeat it as much as you want,' the Doctor continued. 'But you can't change it. I know a way out. If you'll come with me, I can get us both out into real time.'

I'm doing a jigsaw with my brother, Andrew. How could that man I met believe in moments? No such things as moments, no such thing! But he made one happen, made everybody stand still. Maybe he's some sort of ghost . . .

Andrew sorts out the pieces in the box, trying to find ones with straight edges. Out of the corner of my eye, I see the man again. He's my imaginary friend. Andrew doesn't see him as much as I do now. He's growing up.

'Listen to me,' the man says. 'I know a way out. Please come with me.'

I'm on the dock, watching dead sharks being eaten by seagulls. James and Alec staged their own version of a confrontation last night, tried to stay up later than the other, wanted to see which one I loved more. Tore at me. I'm ready to go into the water because of them both. Ready to taste the salt and inhale the plankton. I don't. I *didn't*. I scream.

Ice cream. A great dollop of it floats on the surface of a Coke in the Revivalist Bar. Everybody's there. Marco and Antonia de Wolf and Lawson and Christopher Robin Bailey and many people whose names I never learnt. One of them dies later, bless him. Everybody else lives forever.

James is there too. 'I can't marry you,' I tell him. Everybody laughs. They think it's a joke.

The man in the cream suit is sitting beside me. The scene freezes.

'It is a joke,' I tell him. 'Why do I want to marry this saddo?'
He frowns. 'I've no idea.'

'I've been wanting to marry him all the time I've been in here. But he's too pretentious. Too melodramatic. I don't want to marry him now. How do you stop things still like this?'

'I just put my foot down and everything screeches to a halt. Easy, if you know how. Now, if you'll follow me to the exit –'

'If you want me to do that, you'd better ask me at a point where I'm likely to say yes.'

'Ah, I thought that this was one of those points.'

'Hah! Perhaps. Perhaps not.'

'What's your name?'

'Catherine. Call me Kate.'

'You know, Kate, I have had the opportunity to change the past, and I've always decided not to. I could go back, break the Laws of Time, but it's always seemed such an . . . unfair thing to do.'

'Unfair? Listen, I have had access to every little motion of human life and I don't really have much of a concept of fairness any more. Everything that happened to me happened like water flowing downhill. This way, that way, are we chemically inclined to murder today, are we using this part of our brain or that. People think that their body's a dictatorship and that somebody they call them is in charge. That's not true. We're all little democracies. And in the cyclotron I've watched the miniature parties of my head come and go. We are living in a chemical world, Doctor, and I am a chemical girl. Hah! I'm babbling, not used to saying new words –'

'Wait. You said Doctor?'

'That's what you're called when I'm eight. You're my imaginary friend. You know, your presence here may start to break up the structure of the Higgs Cloud.'

'Yes, I had thought of that, actually. It means that we've got only a short time before –'

'We have all the time in the world.'

Sunshine blasts down across the pub table. I'm walking slowly towards Alec and James, carrying a tray of drinks. There are lots of people around us at other tables. Some are friends, some I've never seen before. One boy I haven't seen since I was thirteen. I don't recognize him, and don't speak to him.

No sign of my imaginary friend. Good.

The pub's sound system is full of eighties compilations on chip. 'Domino Dancing' is echoing off pods as they slip by. Each one of them sends clusters of birds fluttering off the roads where they're nesting now.

'Who's the fourth drink for?' Alec asks.

'Quarter past three,' I answer. Then I realise. He doesn't say, he *hasn't said* what he said all that time ago.

I'm carrying a tray with four drinks and not three.

Why do both of them have to be here?

'Alec and James,' I say, still unused to having to invent and give voice to new words. 'I think you should both marry me. Say yes now.'

They look at each other, the bastards, and laugh.

'Why?' says James.

'Because if one of you marries me, then I won't go to Hardy, because the Hardy team all have to be single. Emotion will have triumphed over logic in my personality and I'll live on, on Earth, and die. Thank god.'

'What the hell?' Alec gets annoyed. 'Look, don't you mind which one of us marries you?'

'No, either one will do.'

They stare at each other, realizing something that I don't quite understand yet.

The crowd stand stock still, and the Doctor takes the extra glass off my tray. 'Orange juice.'

'No, the Pet Shop Boys, you bastard!' The soundtrack has frozen into a sustained 'Ayyyyyy!' from the speakers, and the voices are a 'burrrr'. No tangle of voices, no undreamed of things beyond time. 'What are you, anyway?'

'I'm a Time Lord.'

'Lords never know what's going on below stairs!' I snatch the glass back and head for the boy in the crowd I now recognize. He's looking up over my left shoulder, his eye in the act of dilating. 'Go on, let it go on, he fancied me when we were at school, maybe I can get him to marry me.'

The Doctor sighs. 'Why not just decide not to go?'

'I need an anchor. I need a physical, solid reason why that can't happen. You being here's disrupted the particle stream. I can do what I want now. I can change things so that when you go –'

'When I go I'm taking you with me.'

'No. No, I don't want to do that.'

He strides to the table, urgently. 'The fact that you remember me from your childhood proves that this isn't a rehearsal. This is real. If you try and change things, the universe will split down the middle. Time will compensate. I have bargained with Time before, and she always demands a terrible penalty. She has ways of healing rifts like this. Usually bloodthirsty ones.'

'So let me die. I'd love it.'

The Doctor looks down at his shoes quickly. 'It wouldn't be just you.'

'So what you're saying is that for the first time in . . . however long it's been . . . I can do exactly what I want, and that I shouldn't do it because of what might happen to a universe in which I'm no longer participating. That's a convincing argument.'

'You can't opt out of the universe. Responsibility isn't something which depends on space and time!'

'You're starting to shout like a vicar. Is that why everything weird quietens when you're around? Is magic afraid of you?'

'There's no such thing as magic. Now, I'd love to continue this discussion, but could we do so in the real world, because we really are running out of –'

I'm at a party and I turn my head to see who's just out of sight in the kitchen.

And it's him again. It's the man in cream. I don't want to tell him that I'm afraid, that I don't want to go, I don't want to leave this safe place.

He's opening the refrigerator and pouring himself another orange juice.

James lumbers towards me, a bottle of red wine dangling loosely from his hand like he's a drunken monkey. 'Bitch!' he shouts. 'You're just keeping me dangling, lying to me. You're just using me!'

I smile, and swing back my hand for the usual blow. But I can do anything this time. I'm not necessarily Pissed Off.

I drop my hand. 'James, I love you and I'd never do anything to hurt you. You have such beautiful eyes, and you talk so well. Let me stay with you forever.'

He grins sideways and shakes his head. 'Don't believe you. What are you –'

So I hit him anyway. 'Pissed off,' I tell him. Predictably.

While he's on the ground, clutching his teeth, I giggle down at him. 'Wow. Sorry. Didn't mean to hit you that hard.' Then I turn on my heel and march into the kitchen.

'You're here.' I nod to the man in cream.

'Kitchens and parties. The two are made for each other. Has history just repeated itself?'

'Yes, but for different reasons. Looks like James loses that tooth whatever happens.'

'Why do you keep trying to get married?'

'Because that'll get me out without ever having to –'

'Without ever having to know that you've been in. Without losing anything.'

'I don't know what you're talking about.'

'How will you take having to make a decision? What decision will you make, when these two boys are really stood in front of you in a real world where real things happen in real time?' His voice takes on a higher pitch, a pitch of exasperated anger. 'Not that such a reality will last for much longer under this sort of strain. Your refusal to come to terms with your private life may quite possibly mean the end of the entire cosmos!'

I put a finger to his nose. 'You sound just like James.'

'Eight-six-three!' Nyssa finished reading the back of her hand.

Tegan carefully tapped the last co-ordinates into the control pad on the TARDIS console. 'I don't understand this at all.'

'The Doctor has gone back in time using the cyclotron. We must follow and rescue him.'

'That's a bit of a role reversal. Let me get this straight. He's rescuing somebody who's trapped in there?'

'That's right.'

'So he dives in and grabs them. Why can't he just get right out again?'

'It's not like saving somebody from a swimming pool, Tegan. It's more like . . . like a river.'

'Oh, right! So he's gonna get washed downstream?'

'Exactly.'

'Right.' Tegan grinned. 'That's all I need to know.' She reached out and pressed the final button for take off. 'This stuff's not so –'

The TARDIS gave a sickening lurch, and a screeching noise filled the console room. The two women were thrown off their feet as a sickening parody of the usual take off noises ground the air around them.

'As you might say, Tegan . . . ' Nyssa muttered, grabbing the edge of the console, 'nice going.'

Around the corner strolled Alec, a sad smile on his face, looking like something out of advertising in his carefully retro T-shirt (Frankie Says I Am Nothing And I Should Be Everything). He sighed, in that way he had, and spotted the cat, lounging on the steps of Hoyle Hall.

'Hey, catpuss!' he called, and wandered over. 'She thought that you'd gone, moggie.' He stroked the cat behind the ears. 'I'm missing her so much. You too, eh?'

The cat was thinking that somebody was almost certainly going to feed it tonight. Tuna, perhaps.

'Come on then, I'll look after you.' Alec picked the cat up. 'Give me some good news to send to Hardy.'

The TARDIS plunged through the space-time vortex, butterfly shadows flashing off its exterior. It was being tossed this way and that. More awful still was the colour of the vortex.

What had been blue and blinding purple was now a bloody scarlet.

Nyssa was hitting controls frantically, trying to get the ship back on course.

'What's going on?' Tegan shouted 'What's wrong with the TARDIS?'

'Nothing!' yelled Nyssa. 'The problem is with the vortex itself! I think . . . ' She bit her lip, realizing the significance of her words. 'Tegan, I think that the universe is coming to an end!'

'All right.' The Doctor shouts. 'If you don't care about the universe outside your own world, perhaps you'll care about this!'

We're outside the pub. James and Alec stare up at the Doctor as he throws his glass to the ground. The orange juice splinters into the road, and the Doctor takes a deep breath. 'I'm going to hold myself to this moment!' he calls. 'If you want to do something positive, then all you have to do is take my hand!'

And he steps into the roadway. A pod is only metres away. James and Alec react, struggling to get to their feet.

He has his eyes closed. He's ready to be hit head on and die. Bastard.

I jump for him, grab his hand and –

Paxton spun in surprise. With a noise like a clap of thunder, a blue box had just appeared in the corner of the cyclotron control room. The floor rocked and groaned with the impact, and he staggered.

That shouldn't be there. He'd known that nothing was going to appear there. But that was ridiculous. How could he have? He'd been daydreaming and suddenly woken, or was this the dream and the waking – He remembered Kate throwing herself into the cyclotron, just seconds ago –

Kate threw herself out of the cyclotron, grabbed his saxophone and neatly swatted him over the head with it. She was followed by a very angry cricketer, who savagely wrenched the rifle from his amazed grasp and swung it to cover him.

'Be extremely glad that I have to play by the rules of the game!' he shouted in a quavering pitch.

And then he turned the gun on the room, emptying the full clip of the plasma rifle into the gleaming new surfaces and computer banks.

He hauled the female scientist after him into the blue box. Then he jumped inside himself, pausing only to toss the rifle back to Paxton.

The box vanished in a rumble of grinding gears.

A Steppe Guerilla entered the room.

'Hey,' he grinned. 'What happened to your saxophone?'

Paxton frowned. 'Complex . . . ' he muttered.

Behind them, on a barely functioning instrument panel, a pattern swirled for the first time: a pattern of particles forming and vanishing out of and into the structure of the universe itself.

The TARDIS sighed through the vortex, comfortingly normal again.

'Tea?' the Doctor asked, having frowned at what Nyssa and Tegan had done to his instruments. He found that he was holding a battered saxophone in his hand, and placed it carefully on the console.

'Please . . . ' Kate had been looking at her hands, aghast, and had barely noticed the greetings of the Doctor's companions. 'My God, what I was prepared to do . . . Is the universe safe?'

'Oh yes!' The Doctor tapped the TARDIS console affectionately and handed her a steaming cup of liquid. 'Universes are hardy old things.'

'But I nearly . . . Why did I do that?'

'Why do we do anything?' The Doctor met her gaze seriously. 'That's one thing I think physics will take some while to sort out, the science of moments. What we do and why. If it ever does. I think it'll be time for me to go home and start a bookshop. Speaking of which –' He picked up the TARDIS manual from the floor. 'There's a whole appendix on universal warping, which would have –' He stopped. The pages were torn out. 'Probably served as very effective kindling.' He frowned at his companions, somewhat abashed. 'Well done.'

Earth. The Doctor and Kate wandered along the campus walkways. He had his hands stuffed deep in his pockets, happily sniffing the spring air. She was more uncertain, gazing around herself like this would all vanish in a moment.

'I'm still getting used to the idea of living in sequence,' she told him. 'I can't relive all those memories now. They'll change and decay in my mind, be written over with all sorts of sentimental rubbish. I've lost my past . . . '

'Ah, but you've gained a future.'

The woman looked suspiciously at his boyish grin. 'I'm not sure if that's a good bargain. And I'm still worried about the consequences of you rescuing me. You took me out of that thing before you found me. Doesn't that break a law somewhere?'

'Oh, possibly. There will always be a creature that's you in the cyclotron. Whether or not it's the real you, or just a photocopy . . . Best not to ask, isn't it? Nobody will know unless they look, and since I'm the only one who's ever looked, I'm going to delude myself into being absolutely certain about it.' He grinned again. 'Do you know, I think I just said the most complete nonsense.'

Alec and James looked up from their game of pool and dropped their cues in shock.

Catherine, who'd been gone for only about two months, had marched back in through the door and struck a pose.

'How . . . How did you get home so early?' James goggled

'Hitched a lift,' she told them.

Alec glanced over his shoulder, quickly. 'I, ah, found your cat!' he grinned. 'He came back. I put down a litter tray for him in the lab. Tell you what, let's go and see him . . . '

Kate shook her head, smiling. 'In a minute.' She pointed to two women who were carrying drinks back from the bar. 'First I'd like you to introduce me to your girlfriends.'

From a corner table, the TARDIS crew watched the scene. Alec and James were frantically making gestures and trying to placate three women at once.

'Men,' Tegan opined.

'Indeed,' the Doctor nodded.

Nyssa raised a finger 'I've just worked it out. You *did* break the –'

'Hush, Nyssa. Besides, it looks like Kate doesn't have too many awkward decisions to make after all.'

'Kate?' Tegan looked at him suspiciously.

'Catherine,' the Doctor corrected himself. 'Time we were going, I think.'

'Yeah.' Tegan got up from her seat. 'So, what about Adric?'

'Tegan, Tegan, Tegan!' the Doctor sighed. 'Haven't you

learned anything?' The argument began again as the three friends made their way out of the building and headed back towards the TARDIS.

Later that evening, Kate finally got hold of a substitute key (neither of the boys were talking to her) and opened the door to the chemistry lab where her cat had been left. She coughed. There was an acrid smell in the air.

'Puss?' she called. The lab was dark. Switching on a light, she moved slowly through the jumble of equipment.

A nervous call answered her. On top of a lab table stood her cat. On the floor beneath it were the remains of a glass canister labelled Prussic Acid.

Kate ran to the window and opened it. Prussic acid was highly poisonous. Only a miracle could have saved her pet from being killed. Which was bad news for physicists everywhere.

But jolly good news for the cat.

Silverman sank back into his chair and closed his eyes, physically drained by his efforts. If it wasn't for the fact that he always looked like a corpse, I might have been worried. After a few moments he revived a little and, leaning forward, returned the saxophone mouthpiece to the table. To my astonishment, he then began to sift through the various bits and pieces still piled up there, apparently intending to try another one.

'Hey, hang on a minute!' I protested. 'I think this has definitely gone far enough now. We could sit here all week sorting through this pile of junk, and still be none the wiser.'

The psychic fixed me with a steely gaze. 'I assure you, Mr Addison, that I am devoting my utmost efforts to the task. Fantastic though they may be, the tales I have recounted are true descriptions of the history of these objects.'

'Look,' I replied, 'I'm not doubting your powers. If you say these things happened, then I guess I have to believe you. But there are still a lot of unanswered questions. Even if I accept that my client here is the Doctor, and that he flits about in time and space in a blue box called the TARDIS, I still don't know what brought him to LA, how he came to lose his memory or where he's put this cylinder thing he's after.'

'It's imperative I find that cylinder!' The stranger was becoming increasingly agitated, squirming in his seat and mopping his brow with a paisley-patterned handkerchief taken from the top pocket of his jacket. 'We must go on until we find something which relates to my experiences here in the city!'

I looked pointedly towards the newspaper that he had earlier prevented Silverman from examining, but said nothing.

'I am more than willing to go on, if you wish me to do so,' offered the psychic.

'No . . . ' I made a pretence of considering the matter. 'No, I'm grateful for all your efforts, Silverman, and I'd be glad to return the favour if you ever need my help again, but I think it's time I tried a different line of enquiry.'

'But this is ridiculous!' My client had risen from his seat and was literally hopping up and down now. 'You've just admitted we've learned absolutely nothing here!'

'No, that's not what I said at all! I may not have got all the answers yet, but I've picked up quite a few leads.'

The little man was baffled. 'But how can you have learned anything from what Silverman has told us? All these recollections have been totally irrelevant!'

I tapped the side of my nose with my forefinger.

'I'm the private eye, remember. Let's just say I've made a few deductions. You know, like Sherlock Holmes.'

Silverman had Ramon show us out, and we made our way back down the overgrown trail to the car. We'd spent longer with the psychic than I'd anticipated, and the first rays of the rising sun were already creeping over the horizon as we drove away.

My client's energy seemed undiminished after the bizarre all-night session, but I was feeling pretty done in and insisted that we stop off at a roadside diner for some breakfast. I demolished a plate of ham, eggs and hash browns, swilled it down with a mug of coffee, then visited the washroom to splash some water on my face and freshen up a bit. The little stranger, though, just sat there at the table, picking over his food and saying nothing.

We got back in the car and I drove out on to Highway 178, heading away from the city and towards Death Valley. Despite the time of year, the morning sun became uncomfortably hot as we moved further west and scrubland gradually gave way to desert. I slipped my coat off and threw it on to the back seat.

My client grew more and more uneasy as our journey progressed, constantly shifting his position and mopping his brow with his handkerchief. At first I thought it was just the heat that was bothering him, but then he started glancing nervously up at the sky, casting his eyes about like someone waiting for a bomb to drop. I followed his gaze, squinting up into the bright sunlight, but could see nothing out of the ordinary.

'Expecting rain?' I asked.

He quickly switched his attention back to the road, a slightly guilty expression on his face. 'Why have you brought us all the way out here?' he muttered, with obvious annoyance.

'Just following a hunch,' I told him.

His agitation intensified when, a few minutes later, I turned off the main highway and on to a side road leading to Ballarat, one of the old prospecting towns which sprang up during the gold rush.

'It's a mistake coming out here,' he grumbled. 'I've got no recollection of this place at all.'

'Maybe not,' I replied, 'but then you've lost your memory, haven't you?'

'I think we should turn back,' he insisted. 'I'm sure it was somewhere in the city that I left the cylinder –'

'Look,' I interrupted. 'you hired me to find out who you are and how you came to lose your memory, not to track down this cylinder thing. And when I'm on a case, I'm the one who decides how to go about it. I'm the private detective, remember.'

Although clearly unhappy, he settled back into his seat and we drove on in silence for a while. When the town came into view, I pulled off the road and brought the car to rest around the side of an old, disused gas station, out of sight of any other passers-by.

The little guy seemed relieved that we were going no further, but puzzled as to why we had stopped.

'What do you expect to discover here?' he asked, irritably.

'Well, why don't we get out and have a look around?' I suggested.

With an exasperated snort, he climbed out of the car and slammed the door behind him. I followed close on his heels.

The building was little more than a derelict wooden shack. The windows were all boarded up and the sign creaked back and forth on rusty hinges. Two broken-down gas pumps stood on the dusty forecourt, both registering empty.

'That place over there is Ballarat,' I said, pointing towards the town. 'Ring any bells with you?'

The stranger walked a few paces forward, peered into the distance, then shook his head emphatically. 'No. As I told you, I've no recollection of having been here before.'

'Are you sure? I thought perhaps you might have.'

'What's that supposed to mean?' he spluttered. 'I can't see how anything Silverman said could possibly connect me with this place.'

'No, that's true.'

'Then why in heaven's name have we come here?' he shouted.

'Well,' I replied, 'Ballarat is the place where they've been having all these UFO sightings – you know, the ones reported in that newspaper of yours – and I thought maybe we might find the Doctor somewhere out here.'

The little guy turned to face me, his mouth dropping open in astonishment as if I had just brayed like a mule. His expression showed even greater surprise when he saw that I had pulled a gun from my pocket and was now pointing it in his direction.

'But I *am* the Doctor!' he protested. 'If there's one thing we learned from Silverman, it's that.'

I smiled and shook my head. 'No you're not. You might look like him – although, seeing as how he changes his appearance about as often as I change my shirt, I don't know about that – but you're not the same man.'

For a moment I thought he was going to argue about it, but then he gave a resigned shrug of the shoulders, accepting that he had been caught out. His form began to shimmer and change, like heat haze rising from the desert sands, and then there was someone different standing in front of me. A tall man with sharp, angular features, he looked almost comical crammed into the same shapeless brown jacket, now several sizes too small for him. His other clothes, though, had transformed with him, and he now wore just a simple tunic cut from a shiny, jet black fabric.

I regarded him thoughtfully. 'Mr Mykloz, I presume?'

He inclined his head in acknowledgement. 'Very perceptive of you, alien. And how did you reach that conclusion?'

I grinned broadly. 'Well, to be honest, this whole business seemed pretty fishy right from the start. That cock-and-bull story about losing your memory, it just didn't ring true. And then, when we first got to Silverman's, you would have killed Ramon if I hadn't stopped you. That struck me as pretty odd in itself, but the more I learned about the Doctor, the more I got convinced that he would never have done that. He's not the sort of guy to kill someone in cold blood. I don't think he would even have stepped on a butterfly without at least saying he was sorry about it. And he certainly wouldn't have sat in silence while we drove half way across the state; from what Silverman told us, he couldn't keep his mouth shut for five minutes, whatever body he was using.'

'It seems I may have underestimated you.'

'Well, this shape-shifting business is pretty clever, I guess, as conjuring tricks go, but there's more to a man than his outward appearance: there's also his character, and that's not so easy to fake. Actually, you made things pretty simple for me. I mean, there was the newspaper, and then there was that visa thing. If you hadn't tried to stop Silverman looking at it, I'd never have guessed it was particularly significant.'

I regarded him thoughtfully. 'So, this is where you landed up

after Bukol, eh?'

'Indeed. And I have not been idle since my arrival.' He looked down at my gun, still pointed steadily in his direction. 'Now that you have discovered the truth of my identity, what do you propose to do about it?' He tried hard to sound casual, but there was an edge of desperation creeping into his voice.

'Well,' I replied, 'I propose to get you to answer a few questions for me. Like why you wanted me to trace the Doctor's movements in LA; what this cylinder is that you're after; and how you happen to be wearing the Doctor's jacket.'

He smiled slightly, but did not reply.

'Look,' I said, 'this is a gun I'm holding. When somebody points a gun at you, you're supposed to do what they tell you.'

He opened his mouth as if to say something, but suddenly recoiled in horror. 'Look out!' he shouted, pointing over my shoulder.

I laughed out loud. 'Now you really *are* underestimating me! That's the oldest trick in the –'

At that moment, I became aware of a high-pitched whine coming from somewhere above and behind me. I spun round and saw, hovering into view over the roof of the old gas station, one of the UFOs from the newspaper reports. A rapidly spinning silver disc with circular port-holes spaced at regular intervals around its outer edge, it looked like something out of a low-budget monster movie, except I couldn't see any strings holding it up. The air around it was rippling slightly, making it difficult to keep in focus, and I had trouble picking out the finer details. As I stood there squinting up at it like an idiot, Mykloz took the opportunity to jump me. He wrestled me to the ground, grinding my face into the dust, then shoved me roughly to one side. Scrambling back to my feet, I saw that he had somehow managed to get the gun away from me and was now aiming it straight at my head.

'I guess that wasn't very smart of me,' I said, ruefully. 'But then, it's not every day I get to see a flying saucer.'

With a grim smile, Mykloz tightened his finger on the trigger. I braced myself to make a desperate and probably futile leap to one side. Then, to my amazement, he seemed to change his mind, almost as if he couldn't bring himself to do it. Glancing up at the alien ship, which still hovered in mid-air somewhere out beyond the gas station, he motioned me towards the car with the barrel of the gun. 'Get in and drive!' he yelled. 'Quickly!'

I didn't stop to argue. Leaping into the car, I started it up and sent it shooting forward, barely giving Mykloz time to jump in beside me. The tyres squealed in protest, sending up a shower of gravel in our wake. Ignoring them, I swung the car back on to the road and headed full-speed towards Ballarat.

Mykloz kept me covered with the gun as we drove, but was more preoccupied with staring out of the back window at the UFO. Glancing in my rear-view mirror, I saw that it seemed to be following us.

'What do we do now?' I asked.

'Keep driving!' the Malean shouted back, sweat dripping from his forehead.

Just before we got to the outskirts of the town, he ordered me to turn off onto a dusty track running along the side of a low ridge. I looked back over my shoulder at the UFO, and for a moment I thought we had lost it. It hovered on towards the town, getting quite a reaction from a pair of young hitch-hikers on the road below. Suddenly, though, it changed course and came after us again.

I kept the gas pedal pressed firmly to the floor, and we were jolted about in our seats as the car lurched along over the uneven ground. After about ten minutes of this, an old wooden ranch house came into view. It looked about as run-down and deserted as the gas station we'd just left, and I would have driven on past it if Mykloz hadn't grabbed me by the arm and told me to stop.

Almost before the car had come to rest, the Malean had leaped out and was motioning me to follow. He shoved me inside the house through the battered front door, which hung half off its rusty hinges, then took me at gun point into a musty back room which had once served as a parlour. Through the broken glass of the window, I could see that the UFO had now caught up with us and was hovering just a short distance away. As I watched, a series of landing legs emerged from the underside of the hull and it dropped slowly down to settle on the ground, sending up a plume of dust as it did so.

Mykloz, meanwhile, had crossed to the wall and was fiddling with the lock on what looked to me to be nothing more than a walk-in cupboard. Flinging it open, he bundled me inside and slammed the door behind us. To my surprise, I saw that we were standing in a small, metal-walled chamber illuminated by a concealed light in the ceiling. Mykloz punched a button on the wall and I felt the unmistakable sinking feeling of descending in an elevator.

When we came to a stop, the Malean threw open the door and pushed me out. After everything I'd seen and heard in the last few hours, I guess I shouldn't have been too surprised by the sight that greeted me, but still it took my breath away. The room was about the same size as the parlour above, but that was where the similarity ended. In the centre of the floor was a large bank of instrument consoles, bristling with switches and levers, and around the walls were arrayed a multitude of screens and read-out panels. Suspended from the ceiling was a large black globe with a number of lens-like extensions protruding from it. Everywhere there was the glint of metal and glass.

In a state of near panic, Mykloz dashed aimlessly about the room, adjusting controls and peering at dials. He was making only a token effort to keep me covered with the gun and I thought about trying to get it off him, but before I could do anything about it there was a whirring sound from the wall behind me. The elevator was going back up again – no doubt summoned from above by the occupants of the flying saucer. Galvanized into action, Mykloz shoved me across the room to a door on the far side. Stabbing out a sequence of numbers on a small keyboard set into the wall beside it, he got the door open and pushed me through. Then he shrugged off the Doctor's jacket, threw it in after me and slammed the door shut again, locking me in.

My cell was a small white room, the only notable feature of which was a screen and accompanying control panel in the middle of the far wall. Seated on a low stool in one corner, with his mouth gagged and his hands bound behind his back, was a man I instantly recognized. I went over and got him untied.

'So here you are, Doctor,' I said. 'I guessed you must be somewhere about.'

The little guy stared up at me, perplexed. 'Er, I'm sorry Mr . . . ?'

'Addison.'

' . . . Mr Addison, but I don't recall . . . Have we met?'

'Well, only in a manner of speaking.' Grinning broadly, I picked up the jacket from where it had fallen on the floor and handed it over to him. 'This belongs to you, I think.'

'Er, yes, that's right . . . '

'Now,' I said, 'maybe you can tell me what the hell's going on around here. What's this Mykloz character up to, and why's he had you locked up like this?'

Leaping to his feet, the Doctor crossed to the screen and started adjusting controls on the panel beside it. 'Explanations will have to wait, I'm afraid. I need to find out what I've missed while I've been . . . out of action.'

I was about to protest, but the words stuck in my throat as suddenly the screen displayed a perfect colour picture of the outside of the ranch house, with the imposing form of the

UFO looming over it.

'I see Mykloz has company . . . ' mused the Doctor.

'Yeah,' I replied, still gazing in amazement at the crystal-clear picture on the screen. 'They just arrived.'

'Only just? Good, good . . . '

He adjusted the controls again, and the picture changed to show Mykloz's control room. The Malean had calmed himself down a bit since I had last seen him and was now standing by the door to the elevator, waiting for it to descend again. As the Doctor and I watched, the door swung open and two creatures emerged. I had half expected them to be hideous monstrosities, but in fact they looked pretty much like Mykloz: tall men with sharp, angular features, wearing identical jet black tunics. Mykloz gave them a strange kind of salute, tapping the clenched fist of his right hand against his left shoulder, and they returned the gesture.

'Harkoz, Syloz. Greetings in Conformity.'

The new arrivals exchanged a curious look. 'Greetings in Conformity, Mykloz,' replied the one he had identified as Harkoz. 'We have been attempting to rendezvous with you for some time.'

'We came in response to your signal,' rasped the one called Syloz, 'but were unable to locate you in this zone.'

'Yes, I . . . I . . . ' Mykloz seemed almost lost for words. 'I had . . . arrangements to make, in the city.'

Again the two newcomers exchanged a look.

'But when we finally located you,' continued Syloz, 'you drove off in one of the humans' primitive vehicles.'

'Well, I . . . I thought it would save time if I made my own way back here to the base.'

Syloz regarded him sceptically. 'Are you unwell, Mykloz?'

'No, no, of course not. Why do you ask?'

Harkoz stepped forward and addressed him in low, urgent tones. 'My friend, we have received word from the Grand Council. They are far from satisfied with the progress of operations on this planet.'

Mykloz was clearly shocked by this news. 'The . . . the failure of the racial-purity exercise in Europe was indeed unfortunate –'

'Unfortunate!' exploded Syloz. 'It was a shambles! We had spent years preparing the ground, substituting our own people for leading figures in the Nazi regime, only to have our efforts completely wasted! And the failure was not so much ours in Europe as *yours* here in America. Let me remind you that it was your responsibility to keep America out of the war.'

'There . . . there were unexpected difficulties.'

'Your agents, Mykloz, were totally unsuccessful in their efforts to infiltrate this country's power base. Do our shape-shifting abilities count for nothing here?'

'The Grand Council are growing impatient,' interjected Harkoz. 'They feel it might be better if we were to terminate our operations here and destroy this world.'

Mykloz was dismayed. 'No, that would be a mistake! There is enormous potential for us in this country. Racism is endemic. Under our influence, an organization like the Ku Klux Klan could easily become another Nazi Party. We could start again! And then, perhaps, a eugenics programme –'

Syloz brusquely interrupted Mykloz's babbling. 'We would not *have* to start again if you had not failed us in our mission! Perhaps you were better suited to the role of a hunter than to that of an organizer.'

'No, no, the failure was not mine. This planet must not be destroyed . . . ' Mykloz seemed on the point of breaking down. His two associates now exchanged a look of outright suspicion. Syloz stepped forward, fingering the spherical blaster holstered in a pouch at his side.

'You are behaving irrationally, Mykloz. Why be concerned for the fate of these humans? If I did not know better . . . '

Mykloz made a visible effort to compose himself. 'My concern is not for the humans, but for the valuable resources we would waste if we abandoned our operations here.'

Harkoz shook his head. 'I cannot accept your assessment, Mykloz. I feel the Grand Council have judged wisely in this matter.'

As the three Maleans continued to argue amongst themselves, the Doctor again adjusted the controls beside the screen. The picture disappeared, to be replaced by a diagram showing what appeared to be a series of electrical circuits.

'Just as I suspected,' he muttered, frantically punching buttons and turning switches. 'Time is very short. It's tempting to leave Mykloz to his fate, but when they realize he's going mutant they won't stop at killing him, they'll obliterate the whole planet. So I have no choice but to intervene.'

'Intervene?' I asked him. 'Isn't that going to be pretty tricky, cooped up in here?'

'Mykloz has grown careless,' he replied. 'Through this control panel, I now have access to his computer network, so it's a simple matter to hack into the control systems of his central power source and set up a positive-feedback loop.'

'Come again?'

'I can make this whole place blow up!' With a dramatic flourish, he completed his work on the panel. 'There!'

'Er, so how long do we have before this explosion happens?'

He scratched his head thoughtfully. 'Oh, about ten minutes, I should say.'

My jaw dropped. 'In that case, hadn't we'd better get out of here?'

'Ah, yes, that would be a good idea.' He went over to the door and started to examine the little keyboard set into the wall beside it. 'The trouble is, this operates on a combination lock . . . and it'll take me at least ten minutes to crack the combination.'

'Well, if that's our only problem ... ' I went over and nonchalantly tapped out a series of numbers on the keyboard. The door started to swing open, and the Doctor looked up at me in astonishment. 'I saw Mykloz type it in on the other side,' I admitted.

As we emerged into the control room, the Maleans reacted with varying degrees of surprise and alarm. 'What are these vermin doing here?' hissed Syloz, reaching for his blaster.

'You want to be careful who you insult,' I retorted, picking up a nearby chair and throwing it at him. The blow caught him on the side of the head and he tumbled backwards, cannoning into his compatriots. In the confusion, the blaster fell from his hand and rolled across the floor towards us. The Doctor gleefully scooped it up and held it out towards the three Maleans.

'Put your hands above your heads,' he shouted, 'or I'll ... I'll fry you like mincemeat!' His attempted threat sounded pretty feeble to me, but luckily it had the desired effect. The Maleans raised their hands, glaring at us with undisguised hatred. I went over and retrieved my gun from Mykloz, then followed the Doctor into the elevator. He hit the 'up' button and the door swung closed behind us.

A couple of minutes later, we were back on the surface. Holding Syloz's blaster at arm's length in front of him, the Doctor aimed it at the elevator controls and pushed the trigger. The whole wall collapsed in an eruption of smoke and flames.

'Pretty impressive,' I admitted.

'You'll see something a lot more impressive in a few minutes,' he told me. 'And if you don't want to be caught in the middle of it, I suggest we get out of here.' Dropping the blaster casually on the floor, he raced for the door. I didn't hang around to admire the decor.

Outside, we both jumped into my car and I sent it leaping

forward down the track, heading towards the main road.

After about five minutes, the Doctor decided we'd got far enough away and told me to pull over. We looked back just in time to see the ranch house engulfed in a massive explosion. The flying saucer caught the full force of it and toppled slowly over on to one side. Then it too went up, and a huge fireball blossomed over the desert sands.

A short while later, at the Doctor's insistence, we were driving back towards the site of the explosion. I took the opportunity to try to get some answers out of him.

'So, it was the newspaper report that tipped you off?'

'Yes. I saw it quite by chance, as it happens, but immediately recognized their so-called flying saucer as a Malean command ship.'

'And when you came out here, to the source of the reports, you ran into Mykloz?'

'Mykloz, yes . . . It's quite ironic, I suppose. After years of hunting down and slaughtering Malean mutants, he himself had started to mutate. He'd actually started to develop a concern for other creatures; something that's usually alien to the Malean psyche, at a basic genetic level. That's the thing about shapeshifters; their genetic make-up's just as changeable as their outward appearance.'

I scratched my head, trying to make sense of it all. 'So what's this cylinder thing that Mykloz was after?'

'Genetic stabilizer. It could never have been more than a temporary solution, mind you. But it would have bought him some time.'

'And you swiped it from him?'

'Er, yes.' He looked a little shamefaced for a moment, but then started to chuckle. 'He caught up with me in Los Angeles, eventually, and was convinced I'd hidden it somewhere in the city. He tried everything he could to get me to reveal where I'd put it, but of course I told him nothing.

Malean mind probes have never been exactly top of the range.'

'So *that's* why he came to me for help.'

'Yes, the act of a desperate man.'

'Thanks very much!' I laughed.

When we got to the area of the explosion, we found no trace of either the UFO or the ranch house. Where they had stood, there was now just a huge crater. We climbed out of the car and looked down into it. Lying on its side at the bottom was a tall blue box with a light on top.

'The TARDIS?' I asked.

'The TARDIS,' confirmed the Doctor. 'I left it in the ranch house kitchen. Fortunately, it's indestructible.'

He was about to set off down the side of the crater, but I caught hold of him by the arm. 'Hang on a minute. There's one thing I still don't get: where *did* you hide Mykloz's cylinder?'

Grinning, he rummaged in his pockets and pulled out one of the strange objects I'd noticed earlier: the little black cube covered with golden hieroglyphs. What he did next was even more amazing than all the other amazing things I'd seen over the past couple of days: flipping open one side of the cube, he reached in and pulled out a cylinder about an inch in diameter and at least a yard long, covered in flashing lights and buttons.

'Dimensional transcendentalism,' he said, as if that explained everything. 'A science the Maleans have never mastered.' He lowered the cylinder back into the cube, closed the lid and was just about to return it to his pocket when suddenly he changed his mind and handed it over to me. 'You have it,' he told me. 'Call it a souvenir. Something to amuse your friends with at parties.'

That said, he scrambled down the side of the crater and made his way over to the blue box. Producing a key from a chain around his neck, he unlocked the door and went in. I thought I heard him call out to someone – a guy by the name of Benny – but then the door clicked shut behind him and he was gone. A few moments later, a loud grating noise started up and, before my eyes, the box faded away to nothing.

I pocketed the little cube, got in my car and started the long journey back to my office.

Already published:

TIMEWYRM: GENESYS
John Peel
The Doctor and Ace are drawn to Ancient Mesopotamia in search of an evil sentience that has tumbled from the stars – the dreaded Timewyrm of ancient Gallifreyan legend.

ISBN 0 426 20355 0

TIMEWYRM: EXODUS
Terrance Dicks
Pursuit of the Timewyrm brings the Doctor and Ace to the Festival of Britain. But the London they find is strangely subdued, and patrolling the streets are the uniformed thugs of the Britischer Freikorps.

ISBN 0 426 20357 7

TIMEWYRM: APOCALYPSE
Nigel Robinson
Kirith seems an ideal planet – a world of peace and plenty, ruled by the kindly hand of the Great Matriarch. But it's here that the end of the universe – of everything – will be precipitated. Only the Doctor can stop the tragedy.

ISBN 0 426 20359 3

TIMEWYRM: REVELATION
Paul Cornell
Ace has died of oxygen starvation on the moon, having thought the place to be Norfolk. 'I do believe that's unique,' says the afterlife's receptionist.

ISBN 0 426 20360 7

CAT'S CRADLE: TIME'S CRUCIBLE
Marc Platt
The TARDIS is invaded by an alien presence and is then destroyed. The Doctor disappears. Ace, lost and alone, finds herself in a bizarre city where nothing is to be trusted – even time itself.

ISBN 0 426 20365 8

CAT'S CRADLE: WARHEAD
Andrew Cartmel
The place is Earth. The time is the near future – all too near. As environmental destruction reaches the point of no return, multinational corporations scheme to buy immortality in a poisoned world. If Earth is to survive, somebody has to stop them.

ISBN 0 426 20367 4

CAT'S CRADLE: WITCH MARK
Andrew Hunt
A small village in Wales is visited by creatures of myth. Nearby, a coach crashes on the M40, killing all its passengers. Police can find no record of their existence. The Doctor and Ace arrive, searching for a cure for the TARDIS, and uncover a gateway to another world.

ISBN 0 426 20368 2

NIGHTSHADE
Mark Gatiss
When the Doctor brings Ace to the village of Crook Marsham in 1968, he seems unwilling to recognize that something sinister is going on. But the villagers are being killed, one by one, and everyone's past is coming back to haunt them – including the Doctor's.

ISBN 0 426 20376 3

LOVE AND WAR
Paul Cornell
Heaven: a planet rich in history where the Doctor comes to meet a new friend, and betray an old one; a place where people come to die, but where the dead don't always rest in peace. On Heaven, the Doctor finally loses Ace, but finds archaeologist Bernice Summerfield, a new companion whose destiny is inextricably linked with his.

ISBN 0 426 20385 2

TRANSIT
Ben Aaronovitch
It's the ultimate mass transit system, binding the planets of the solar system together. But something is living in the network, chewing its way to the very heart of the system and leaving a trail of death and mutation behind. Once again, the Doctor is all that stands between humanity and its own mistakes.

ISBN 0 426 20384 4

THE HIGHEST SCIENCE
Gareth Roberts

The Highest Science – a technology so dangerous it destroyed its creators. Many people have searched for it, but now Sheldukher, the most wanted criminal in the galaxy, believes he has found it. The Doctor and Bernice must battle to stop him on a planet where chance and coincidence have become far too powerful.

ISBN 0 426 20377 1

THE PIT
Neil Penswick

One of the Seven Planets is a nameless giant, quarantined against all intruders. But when the TARDIS materializes, it becomes clear that the planet is far from empty – and the Doctor begins to realize that the planet hides a terrible secret from the Time Lords' past.

ISBN 0 426 20378 X

DECEIT
Peter Darvill-Evans

Ace – three years older, wiser and tougher – is back. She is part of a group of Irregular Auxiliaries on an expedition to the planet Arcadia. They think they are hunting Daleks, but the Doctor knows better. He knows that the paradise planet hides a being far more powerful than the Daleks – and much more dangerous.

ISBN 0 426 20362 3

LUCIFER RISING
Jim Mortimore & Andy Lane   •

Reunited, the Doctor, Ace and Bernice travel to Lucifer, the site of a scientific expedition that they know will shortly cease to exist. Discovering why involves them in sabotage, murder and the resurrection of eons-old alien powers. Are there Angels on Lucifer? And what does it all have to do with Ace?

ISBN 0 426 20338 7

WHITE DARKNESS
David McIntee

The TARDIS crew, hoping for a rest, come to Haiti in 1915. But they find that the island is far from peaceful: revolution is brewing in the city; the dead are walking from the cemeteries; and, far underground, the ancient rulers of the galaxy are stirring in their sleep.

ISBN 0 426 20395 X

SHADOWMIND
Christopher Bulis

On the colony world of Arden, something dangerous is growing stronger. Something that steals minds and memories. Something that can reach out to another planet, Tairgire, where the newest exhibit in the sculpture park is a blue box surmounted by a flashing light.

ISBN 0 426 20394 1

BIRTHRIGHT
Nigel Robinson

Stranded in Edwardian London with a dying TARDIS, Bernice investigates a series of grisly murders. In the far future, Ace leads a group of guerrillas against their insect-like, alien oppressors. Why has the Doctor left them, just when they need him most?

ISBN 0 426 20393 3

ICEBERG
David Banks

In 2006, an ecological disaster threatens the Earth; only the FLIPback team, working in an Antarctic base, can avert the catastrophe. But hidden beneath the ice, sinister forces have gathered to sabotage humanity's last hope. The Cybermen have returned and the Doctor must face them alone.

ISBN 0 426 20392 5

BLOOD HEAT
Jim Mortimore

The TARDIS is attacked by an alien force; Bernice is flung into the Vortex; and the Doctor and Ace crash-land on Earth. There they find dinosaurs roaming the derelict London streets, and Brigadier Lethbridge-Stewart leading the remnants of UNIT in a desperate fight against the Silurians who have taken over and changed his world.

ISBN 0 426 20399 2

THE DIMENSION RIDERS
Daniel Blythe

A holiday in Oxford is cut short when the Doctor is summoned to Space Station Q4, where ghostly soldiers from the future watch from the shadows among the dead. Soon, the Doctor is trapped in the past, Ace is accused of treason and Bernice is uncovering deceit among the college cloisters.

ISBN 0 426 20397 6

THE LEFT-HANDED HUMMINGBIRD
Kate Orman

Someone has been playing with time. The Doctor Ace and Bernice must travel to the Aztec Empire in 1487, to London in the Swinging Sixties and to the sinking of the *Titanic* as they attempt to rectify the temporal faults – and survive the attacks of the living god Huitzilin.

ISBN 0 426 20404 2

CONUNDRUM
Steve Lyons

A killer is stalking the streets of the village of Arandale. The victims are found each day, drained of blood. Someone has interfered with the Doctor's past again, and he's landed in a place he knows he once destroyed, from which it seems there can be no escape.

ISBN 0 426 20408 5

NO FUTURE
Paul Cornell

At last the Doctor comes face-to-face with the enemy who has been threatening him, leading him on a chase that has brought the TARDIS to London in 1976. There he finds that reality has been subtly changed and the country he once knew is rapidly descending into anarchy as an alien invasion force prepares to land . . .

ISBN 0 426 20409 3

TRAGEDY DAY
Gareth Roberts

When the TARDIS crew arrive on Olleril, they soon realise that all is not well. Assassins arrive to carry out a killing that may endanger the entire universe. A being known as the Supreme One tests horrific weapons. And a secret order of monks observes the growing chaos.

ISBN 0 426 20410 7

WHO ARE YOU?

Help us to find out what you want.
No stamp needed – free postage!

Name _____

Address _____

Town/County _____

Postcode _____

Home Tel No. _____

About Doctor Who Books

How did you acquire this book?
Buy ☐   Borrow ☐
Swap ☐

How often do you buy Doctor Who books?
1 or more every month ☐   3 months ☐
6 months ☐   12 months ☐

Roughly how many Doctor Who books have you read
in total?

_____

Would you like to receive a list of all past and
forthcoming Doctor Who titles?
Yes ☐   No ☐

Would you like to be able to order the Doctor Who
books you want by post?
Yes ☐   No ☐

Doctor Who Exclusives
We are intending to publish exclusive Doctor Who
editions which may not be available from booksellers and
available only by post.

Would you like to be mailed information about exclusive
books?
Yes ☐   No ☐

About You

What other books do you read?

Other character-led books (which characters?) _____

Science Fiction	☐	Thriller/Adventure	☐
Horror	☐		

Non-fiction subject areas (please specify) _____

Male	☐	Female	☐

Age:

Under 18	☐	18–24	☐
25–34	☐	35+	☐

Married	☐	Single	☐
Divorced/Separated	☐		

Occupation _____

Household income:

Under £12,000	☐	£13,000–£20,000	☐
£20,000+	☐		

Credit Cards held:

Yes	☐	No	☐

Bank Cheque guarantee card:

Yes	☐	No	☐

Is your home:

Owned	☐	Rented	☐

What are your leisure interests? _____

Thank you for completing this questionnaire. Please tear it out carefully and return to: **Doctor Who Books, FREEPOST, London, W10 5BR** (no stamp required)